BEHIND BLUE EYES

A Cyberpunk Noir Novel

Anna Mocikat

Behind Blue Eyes
Copyright © 2020 by Anna Mocikat

All rights reserved. Printed in the United States of America. No part of this book may be used or reproduced in any manner whatsoever without written permission except in the case of brief quotations em- bodied in critical articles or reviews.
This book is a work of fiction. Names, characters, businesses, organiza- tions, places, events and incidents either are the product of the author's imagination or are used fictitiously. Any resemblance to actual persons, living or dead, events, or locales is entirely coincidental.

http://www.annamocikat.com

Book Cover design by Ivano Lago
ISBN: 9798623054944

First Edition: May 2020

Chapter One

God's busy

Heavy turbulence shook the aircraft, yet it held course toward its destination. Its powerful engines barely produced any noise, and the black hull made it almost invisible against the darkness. Three more of the same type of aircraft followed it, traveling in formation, like silent birds of prey hiding in the shadows of the night.

The passengers inside weren't bothered by the shaky ride. Highly focused and ready for anything, they sat there in silence, secured with safety bars into long rows of seats facing each other. All wore the same tight black combat suits and gloves, firearms were strapped to their thighs, and everyone had a rucksack on their back. Matching, tight-fitting helmets covered their heads, cheeks, and upper necks. Only a small part of their faces was visible, and their eyes.

Behind Blue Eyes

All of them had identical neon-blue eyes.

Their stares were somewhat chilling and disturbing; the unnatural eyes and their unmoving faces made them look like an army of living dolls, waiting to spring into action.

"Approaching target area," they heard the pilot say, "Ninety klicks to go, drop-off in one minute thirty-five seconds."

However, there was nothing to be heard but the wind rattling against the plane traveling at high velocity across the stormy sky. The voice spoke directly into their heads.

"OK, people, get ready," another disembodied voice said. To everyone in each of the three stealth combat aircraft, this voice was almost as familiar as their own. It belonged to Metatron, the commander. "Our scouting drones report no movement whatsoever and minimal security measures. Everyone is sound asleep. They have no idea what's coming at them. Exactly how we like it," he paused for a moment before continuing, and the condescending tone in his voice indicated that he would enjoy the things to come, "Stick to the routine, and this will be a walk in the park. I won't tolerate any casualties today."

Nephilim prepared herself, running a final status check on her systems. Her neon-blue eyes were the shape of almonds. When she closed them for a moment, her delicate, pale face appeared to be that of a young woman in her early twenties. Anyone who assumed this, however, couldn't be more wrong.

A second later, she was content. All systems were operating within specified parameters. She was ready.

Opening her eyes again, she caught a look from Adriel sitting opposite to her. A slight grin flashed over his lips. His deep black skin contrasted with his unnaturally blue eyes, and they outright glowed in the half-dark. He, too, was prepared and agreed with the commander's words.

This shouldn't be much more than routine.

"Commencing descent," the pilot announced, "Drop-off in twenty-five seconds."

The aircraft lost speed tremendously, almost as if someone hit the brakes, then it started dropping. None of the passengers seemed to take notice as two Gs hit their bodies, and they were pressed into the safety bars, while outside the enormous rotor tubes of the vehicle turned ninety degrees and transformed the jet into a vertical take-off and land aircraft, otherwise known as a VTOL. It gave the aircraft the possibility to descend vertically from a great height like a gigantic elevator.

"Drop-off in ten seconds," the pilot's voice continued in everyone's head while all lights were turned off in the cabin, and the back hatch started to open. Strong, ice-cold wind made its way inside. "Five...Four...Three...Two...Drop-off at target position!"

The hatch was open now, the safety bars opened, and the men and women dressed in black quickly moved toward it.

The VTOL silently hovered in the air, sixty-five feet above the ground. Without hesitation, the soldiers jumped out from the rear, landing completely unharmed, immediately running off into the darkness and making room for the next to come.

Nephilim followed the others and leaped out of the plane without a second thought that a jump like this would most likely kill or at least gravely injure an average person. This was because she and her brothers-in-arms were not human. They were artificially enhanced state-of-the-art human-machine hybrids. Cyborgs in simple terms.

The impact was no challenge at all for the titanium bones and silicon-based artificial muscles of Nephilim's legs. Her internal sensors showed the impact had caused only sixty percent active system demands. If necessary, she could jump from a hundred feet without risking serious damage.

Without stopping for even one beat, she ran off into the darkness, spreading out from her teammates into a preassigned formation. They were a squad of twenty, moving silently toward the target location less than half a mile away, like a pack of dark predators approaching in the shadows of the night. Two more squads would be dropped off at other strategic locations and join the attack from flanking positions. That way, none of the targets would be able to escape the assault.

Although the night was tenebrous, Nephilim saw the target location they were advancing on as perfectly as if it were bright daylight. Her artificial eyes were much more than integrated night vision gear. Special software connected to her brain made it possible to see everything clearly with a minimum amount of light, similar to how a cat's eyes worked. Additionally, she activated a combat heads-up display, known as HUD that appeared directly in her line of sight, which would not only identify targets but prevent friendly fire.

"Hold position," she heard Metatron say, and the squad stopped. As usual, he was sitting in the command center, six-hundred miles away, controlling the operation. Surrounded by 3D holograms, he could not only overlook the whole situation captured by a drone from above but also link into the perception of any single unit on the field, see through their eyes, and hear through their ears.

"Prepare drones," Metatron commanded.

Nephilim grabbed her backpack and put it on the ground beside her feet. She opened it and revealed a black metallic cube. It made a soft click as it came to life. Within seconds it enfolded itself and turned into a flying drone—slightly resembling a black firefly—that was about the size of a small eagle. It hovered next to Nephilim's head, humming softly.

Each one of the soldiers had unique drones, directly linked to their neural system. Some drones had flying capabilities, others resembled ground predators in the form of insects or mammals. To be able to simultaneously, mentally control a drone during actual combat was difficult, required years of practice, and brought the term multi-tasking to a whole new level. However, once mastered, it was an incredibly effective combat tool.

Nephilim held still and waited for the commander to order the assault. She wasn't excited or scared that she was about to go into battle. Her artificially augmented heart didn't beat faster. Her lungs, securely sealed through a silicate membrane from any kind of poison or chemical warfare attack, didn't enhance their pace. Her mind was focused and clear. So were her ice-cold, artificially blue eyes, studying the target area. She came here to do her job, her duty. What she had been created for. The righteous thing. Furthermore, it was something she was very good at.

Adriel had stated, prior to leaving Olympias, that they should be back by breakfast.

The target area ahead was in shabby condition. Shacks and makeshift houses built in and around the ruins of old, overgrown industrial premises. The location was partly hidden by the remains of an old Highway bridge, its old asphalt cracked, with weeds growing everywhere, and some of its circling sidearms had collapsed. The ancient roads and self-made paths were covered with mud. It had been raining a lot, as it almost always did in this area. This was only one of the reasons why any sane person would never understand that people actually chose to live here.

The small settlement was surrounded by some archaic plantations and little fields, hidden in between old buildings. Everything here was designed to stay unnoticed, to not be found. And yet they had been discovered. Eventually, all of them were.

Metatron was right. These subjects here were completely oblivious of what was coming their way. Only a few guards were on duty, sitting on two of the old chimneys of the facility. They would have no chance to spot the attacking troops before sharpshooters took them out. After that, they would ambush those that remained in their sleep. Standard procedure, requiring a minimum of time, resources, and casualties.

Nephilim's scanner showed one hundred twenty-six human life forms in the settlement. There wouldn't be any left when the sun rose in less than an hour.

***

Jeff woke up from a bad dream. He couldn't remember what it was he had dreamt, but it had left him with this uneasy feeling that something wasn't right. A second later, he knew what had woken him. He felt Missy's wet nose on his cheek as she poked him with her muzzle, then ran to the door hectically.

Jeff sighed. "Is it that urgent, old girl?"

The big, shaggy shepherd dog usually slept through the night, but Jeff understood that she needed to go outside. Missy now whimpered and started scratching at the rusty door of his hut. The old bed creaked when Jeff got up, his neck hurt badly, as it did every morning. The scar, where the augmentation implants had been removed, would never really heal, and he knew that. They had fucked it up during the removing procedure. But he would still rather endure the pain for the rest of his life than have that thing remaining inside him.

Missy seemed to grow more nervous with every second that passed.

"OK, OK, I'm coming!"

Jeff quickly put on his boots and slipped into a jacket. What time was it? He had no idea, but it was still pitch dark outside and sure as hell freezing cold.

Missy let out a loud bark as if she wanted to tell him to hurry up. What was going on with her? She never behaved like that. Feeling increasingly uneasy with every second, Jeff grabbed his rifle and alarm device before he opened the door. Just in case.

When he left the small house that he shared with his dog, he at first couldn't see anything. The night was extremely dark, and a cold wind blew into his scarred face.

To Jeff's surprise, it wasn't a persistent bladder that made Missy beg him to follow her outside so urgently. Once out of the door, she stared into the darkness, growling. Jeff's home was on the periphery of the settlement. Beyond it, there were only fields. He had decided to live alone after his wife passed away. Binding himself to another being so closely had been a wonderful experience he never would have thought possible when he was growing up. The downside was that losing someone that close to the heart could cause more pain than removing all the implants simultaneously.

Missy started to growl louder, the hair on her neck standing up. She was staring into the darkness as if she could see something invisible to Jeff's human eyes. He licked his dry lips, becoming extremely nervous. Missy's behavior gave him the creeps. Something was wrong here. Very wrong.

A suspicion came to his mind, so horrible he didn't dare to finish the thought. No, it could not be. They were so far away. So small, so unimportant, so well hidden. They were safe.

Jeff looked up to the high chimney where the sentries stood on guard. He saw them moving. Everything had to be fine; otherwise, someone would have activated the alarm.

Missy bared her canines and moved forward, into the darkness.

"Missy! Stay!" Jeff commanded in a hushed voice.

BEHIND BLUE EYES

The dog did not listen. Jeff swore and followed her toward the highway bridge, trying to catch her. Then he suddenly froze in place.

For a second, he didn't believe what he was seeing, tried to convince himself that he was still sleeping, caught in a horrible nightmare.

The darkness was not empty. Eyes were lurking out there. Monstrous neon-blue eyes. Dozens of them.

Jeff turned around and started running faster than he ever had in his life. Missy noticed his panic and followed him barking loudly.

He opened the alarm device and pressed the emergency button. Suddenly a shrill alarm rose all across the settlement; white lights sprang on everywhere.

"They found us!" Jeff yelled into the device frantically, hoping that everyone having one could hear him now, "Ambush...Blue Death approaching from the south. God save us all!"

Those were his last words. Less than a second later, he felt a brutal force kick him off his feet and terrible pain. He landed in a puddle of his own blood, coming from a big hole in his chest. The last thing he saw before he died was a horrific mechanical creature, vaguely resembling a cat-sized scorpion, jumping Missy and ripping her head off with its claws.

***

"I'm afraid God's busy," Metatron said with blatant amusement in his voice as he watched how his people downright executed the man and his dog, "Can we help you?"

It was unfortunate that they had been spotted by coincidence and hadn't been able to take out the man before he alarmed the camp, but in the end, it wouldn't make any difference. The outcome would simply be delayed by a few minutes.

"Proceed as planned," he instructed his units on the ground, "Strike."

The command was what Nephilim had been waiting for. Her artificial muscles sprang into action, and she rushed forward. So did the rest of her squad. Coming from all sides, they raided the settlement like a pack of hungry wolves.

Within seconds the first houses were stormed and cleared without much effort. Most inhabitants were still half asleep and didn't give much of a fight when the blue-eyed killers invaded their homes, putting bullets through their heads. Screams of panic and agony could be heard everywhere, so loud that they almost drowned the shrill alarm. People tried to flee, ran helplessly in all directions, but there was no escape from an enemy that could move ten times faster. Others fell to their knees and begged for mercy, even though it was futile. The Angels knew no mercy.

But soon it turned out that the inhabitants of the settlement weren't as helpless as recon had initially indicated. After the first few minutes, which had indeed been like a walk in the park, Nephilim and her comrades encountered heavy resistance. As they approached the inner area of the former industrial facility, the enemy opened fire.

Through the eyes of her drone flying above her, Nephilim spotted shooters taking position on the roof of an old brick factory building. Two more stuck their rifles through rusty, corroded frames of glassless windows.

"Hostile shooters, roof, eleven o'clock," she warned Adriel, who walked close behind her. She leaped to cover behind an old truck from the pre-corporate era.

"Copy that," she heard Adriel directly through her commlink. He, too, took cover behind a corner, just in time when the shooters opened fire. "Enemies taking position at three o'clock as well."

High-caliber bullets riddled the metal of the old truck where Nephilim crouched. The enemy was much better prepared than they had anticipated. It was pointless to bring ordinary firearms in a battle against cyborgs. Only high-powered heavy caliber weapons could pose a threat to them. The bones of their arms and legs were made of titanium, and the close-fitting black combat suits they wore were fabricated from high-tech synthetic spider silk proteins; in this enriched form, this was an almost impenetrable material.

Nephilim turned her drone around and inspected the group of hostiles, who took position on the opposite building. Two men were about to mount a Heavy Machine Gun.

Through their comms, both Nephilim and Adriel heard that other units had encountered severe resistance as well. One particular structure in the center of the facility, which the hostiles were willing to defend by any cost.

"How about that. Who could have guessed this would be fun, after all?" Adriel asked.

"So much for being back by breakfast," she said.

Another salvo hit the antiquated vehicle she was crouching behind. Soon there wouldn't be anything left of it. She had to resolve the situation quickly, and she knew it.

"Cover me!" she told Adriel.

He did as she asked and started firing at the enemies on the roof to the left, forcing them into cover. Nephilim did not hesitate even one second. She rolled under the truck to the other side while she commanded her drone to dive toward her at high-speed. In the blink of an eye,

Nephilim was on her feet, sprinting and jumping in the air. The artificial insect legs of her drone transformed into handles. She grabbed them in midair and let the drone lift her up with neck-breaking speed.

Before the three men on the roof realized what was happening, she was hovering above them. One of them looked up and screamed in horror as he saw the black-clad woman with the angelic face and disturbing blue eyes drop down on them. Fifteen-inch-long titanium blades emerged directly out of her wrists. She stabbed the screaming man staring up at her through his eye into his skull while she slit the throats of the other two with her other hand. Then she turned her attention toward the two enemies with the Heavy Machine Gun on the opposite roof.

The HMG was activated now—and pointing at her. She threw herself to the side, hiding behind the roof wall, the blades disappearing back into her forearms. Then she lifted her guns over the ledge and connected her vision to the software inside. That way, she could see directly through her pistols, using them as a second set of eyes. Two shots and the men operating the HMG sank to the floor next to their splatted brains.

"You're such a poser," she heard Adriel comment.

Meanwhile, his own drone—a mechanical hybrid of a spider and a cat—scaled the wall and jumped into the face of one of the hostiles lurking at the windows. The man let out a scream of agony, then gargled as the creature cut through his face and neck. Terrified, his companion tried to help him, leaving his cover. That cost him his life as well as a precise bullet from Adriel's gun shattered his skull.

"Clear," Nephilim said, "Let's move on. I want to see what's in the building they are defending so fiercely. And I want us to be there first."

"Copy that," Adriel confirmed, "Will you still hang out with me once you're an Archangel?"

Nephilim ignored his mocking and moved over the roof toward the building in the center of the settlement. Adriel followed on the ground. His sensors noticed movement on his right. Turning his head, he saw a woman with greasy grey hair taking position in a window above him, an outdated machine gun in her hands. He did not bother to stop but shot the woman in the forehead on the run. Why did these people try to resist the inevitable? It was pathetic.

Adriel ran faster to catch up with Nephilim. He saw her jump the distance between two buildings and then engage two more hostiles, who got in her way. They were dead within seconds. She then jumped from the roof on the mud-covered road one-hundred fifty feet in front of him, cracking the old concrete by the force of her impact. Adriel spotted another hostile, who had been hiding on the street behind an old dumpster. He had something in his hand, ready to throw it at Nephilim. When Adriel's artificial eyes zoomed in on the object, his HUD highlighted it red instantly. This indicated a potential danger. The man swung his arm.

"Watch out, Neph!" Adriel said, "Four o'clock, EMP, incoming!"

He took aim and shot, but when his bullet hit the target, it was already too late. The man had thrown the EMP grenade toward Nephilim.

She reacted lightning fast. Without losing even one second, Nephilim threw herself down on her knees, stretched her arms, and clapped them together in front of her chest and face in a powerful, precise motion. It activated a shimmering energy shield, which emerged from her limbs and wrapped around her like a ball. The EMP grenade exploded right above her head with a blast of blueish lightning. The lightning bounced off the energy shield and disappeared in the ground. All of this lasted less than three seconds.

The shimmering shield around Nephilim vanished, and she jumped up again.

"Thanks," she said, running off as if nothing unusual had occurred, and someone hadn't just tried to deep fry her brain. Adriel shook his head, made sure there was no one else who might attack them from behind, then followed her.

A strong electromagnetic pulse blast, short EMP, was the most effective weapon against cyborgs. A direct hit by an EMP grenade not only instantly put a cyborg on ice for several minutes, by completely shutting down their systems, it also could cause tremendous damage to their hardware or programming. This was especially dangerous concerning the tech implanted in a state-of-the-art cyborg's brain. It had happened before, that strong blasts had outright fried cyborg brains and caused irreparable damage, leaving them behind as drooling vegetables, useless to anyone.

Every year new, more powerful EMP weapons were developed, but luckily for Nephilim and her brothers-in-arms, Olympias' own engineers weren't sitting on their hands either. The shield Nephilim had projected was nothing more than a portable energy version of a Faraday cage. Equipped with this countermeasure, she and her people were almost unstoppable.

The structure in the center was a mostly windowless, former production building, with a high chimney attached to it, of which the upper segment had collapsed over the years. Several smaller huts and self-made buildings had been constructed in front of it. Obviously, this was used as some kind of rudimentary town square with a primitive market. A fierce firefight was raging around it, and the building. The settlers were throwing everything they had at the attackers in a last desperate stand. They were nonetheless eliminated one by one by the blue-eyed troops in black, who advanced with the efficiency of machines.

"Pathetic," Adriel said as he and Nephilim arrived. Then he added, "And we are too late. There won't be anything left for us but twitching pulp."

"Not necessarily," Nephilim answered, "Look at the infrared scan.

BEHIND BLUE EYES

There are twenty-seven human life forms in a room at the eastern corner of the upper level. I bet, those are the ones they're trying to protect."

Adriel agreed, "Could be high-value assets of some sort."

Nephilim was already on the run. "Let's take a look."

She turned away from the fight and ran to the other side of the building instead.

"Hold position," she told Adriel, "I'll let my drone pick you up here."

"Copy that. I'll cover you."

Her drone came flying down, and once again, Nephilim grabbed it to use as a lift. This time, shooters appeared in the windows of a squat house opposite the center, and immediately took aim at her. She took evasive action and felt the projectiles flying by only inches away.

"Sons of bitches!" Adriel said, "I got this."

He stormed inside the smaller building, guns in his hands, his drone at his feet.

Nephilim let go of her drone and landed on the roof, rolling to cover.

"Roof is clear," she said, scanning her surroundings, "There's a hatch leading inside."

"I'm a bit busy here," she heard Adriel over the comm, "Multiple hostiles."

"Need backup?"

"Nah. They're as good as dead. Go ahead."

"Copy that."

As Nephilim moved to the hatch, the whole building was shaken by an explosion. Someone was throwing grenades.

"Careful now, people," Metatron spoke into everyone's head again, "Don't get carried away. I don't want to see casualties in the last few minutes of a flawless operation."

Nephilim arrived at the hatch and yanked it. It hadn't been opened for many decades and was rusted shut. But this wouldn't stop her. She focused her energy reserves into the artificial muscles of her arms and pulled. The hatch creaked then opened as if it was butter. Nephilim slipped inside.

The corridor below was completely dark. The noise of the battle raging outside was muffled here, but Nephilim heard over her comm that the attack was about to reach its end. It would probably take less than thirty seconds until her people stormed the inner building, eliminating the rest of the human defenders. She moved forward quickly, toward the room with the suspected high-value assets. Two heavily armed guards were positioned in front of it, yet they faced away from her and to the staircase, where they expected the attackers to approach from.

"They're coming," one of them said with desperation and a slight quiver in his voice, "Oh my God, they're coming. How did they even find us out here? Please, I don't want to die..."

"Shut up!" the other one snapped at him, "It doesn't matter now. Keep the EMPs ready. We're gonna take out as many of the blue-eyed bastards as we can. We need to hold them off until—"

He never got the chance to finish his sentence, as Nephilim rushed up behind them and stabbed both simultaneously through their throats with her integrated blades.

"Sorry to disappoint you guys, but there won't be any dead blue-eyed bastards for you today," she said, unmoved.

BEHIND BLUE EYES

One of the men died instantly, but the other briefly stared at her with wide eyes of horror and disbelief before he gargled and collapsed lifelessly like a ragdoll.

Nephilim turned to the door. She was really curious now about who or what was hiding behind it that was so valuable to all these people. Not willing to waste even one more second, she kicked in the door and rushed into the room, guns in her hands.

The room once probably used to be a spacious supervisor's office. It was semi-dark inside, the only light source was an antiquated floor lamp, its light flickering. The old drapes were closed. A ridiculous attempt at hiding from cyborgs with integrated infrared vision.

The room was filled with people. Children, to be precise. There were twenty-five of them, the oldest maybe twelve years old while the youngest was a baby, probably delivered only a few weeks ago. They all stared at Nephilim with pure horror in their eyes as she entered the room. Some of the younger ones started crying. Two women were with them. Obviously, this was the place the settlers brought their children to safety in case of an emergency.

"Stop! Don't move!" yelled one of the women, pointing an old double-barrel shotgun at Nephilim. She was middle-aged, probably younger since people living in conditions such as these usually aged faster than average. She had marks on her temple and scar tissue on the side of her head where augmentation implants had been removed, and no hair would ever grow again. The other one was younger and had an empty hole where her left eye once had been. She held a toddler in one arm and something in her other hand.

Nephilim stopped short. She had been prepared to fight and destroy whoever might have been hiding up here, but this was an entirely different situation. If possible, the Angels didn't kill children. Not because of ethical or humanitarian aspects but because they were valuable assets.

"Nephilim, stand down," she heard Metatron's voice command in her head. Obviously, he had been watching through her eyes and now directly took control due to the circumstances. "Try to resolve the situation."

"You're safe, I have no reason to harm you," Nephilim told the women with a friendly voice.

"Don't move! Don't come any closer! You fucking monster, you won't get them," the woman with the shotgun yelled.

"Please, lay down your weapons. I promise nothing will happen to the children. I'm here to help," Nephilim said with a smile, exactly the way she was trained to in such situations.

"Excellent," Metatron acknowledged, "Proceed."

"Shut up, you lying, evil bitch!" the other woman spat out, and the toddler in her arms started crying, "You're here to slaughter us like animals. And then take the little ones. Do you enjoy what you do?"

"You won't get them! Ever!" the woman with the shotgun repeated.

"I can bring them to safety. Offer them a better life. You know that," Nephilim said with a calm voice, "I understand you want to protect them, you only want the best for them. That's why they should come with me."

The shotgun woman laughed bitterly. "So they can become like you? Blue-eyed killers? Soulless abominations?"

"I'd rather kill them myself before I let that happen," the woman with the missing eye said.

Nephilim's scan showed what the woman held in her hand. It was a small aluminum canister.

"Possible life-threatening poisoning of valued assets," Nephilim said over the comm without the people in the room audibly hearing her.

BEHIND BLUE EYES

"I'm aware. Potential threat detected. Dispatching medical team to your position now. Resistance has been broken. ETA, two minutes," Metatron said, "Eliminate the threats, and procure the assets."

"I'm telling you one more time; lay down your weapons," Nephilim said calmly but with a definitive tone that left no room for discussion, "Step away from the children."

Nephilim saw the one-eyed woman letting go of the poison can and reaching for something behind her.

"See you in hell," the other woman said. Her finger moved to the trigger of her shotgun.

She never got the chance to pull it. Nephilim's reflexes were ten times faster than any human's. No human would ever win a direct stand-off with a cyborg. Before the woman could fire, a bullet from Nephilim's gun penetrated her forehead and turned her brain into pulp, killing her instantly. Simultaneously, Nephilim fired her other weapon striking down the second woman with a deadly, precise headshot. She jumped toward the collapsing corpse and caught the toddler before it could hit the ground.

For a second, the room was completely silent as all kids stared at her in shock. The ones who had stood closest to the two women were covered in blood and brain tissue. Suddenly Nephilim was confronted with more than two dozen pairs of terrified children's eyes, who saw her for what she was: a cold-blooded killer. The monster from their dark closets brought to life. And it had neon-blue eyes.

Then many of them started crying, screaming, shaking. Some tried to hide in the corners, others simply kept staring at her in shock.

"Threat eliminated," Nephilim said, carefully putting down the toddler, "Assets have been safely procured."

"Excellent work," she heard Metatron say, "Medics, they need universal antitoxins and tranquilizers on location. See to that asap."

***

Dawn arrived as the three black aircraft took off into the air. The early sun was hidden behind thick grey clouds, which indicated it would start raining soon, as it did almost every day in this region. The VTOLs were highly illuminated in reddish light as they quickly rose into the sky. The settlement below, which had been home to one hundred twenty-six souls only one hour earlier, was now ablaze. Soon there wouldn't be anything left but ashes and bones. Nothing ever remained when hit by Blue Death, everyone knew that truth.

Inside the aircraft, Nephilim and the others were sitting in their seats, calm and unmoved, as if nothing out of the ordinary had just occurred. None of them had been killed or even wounded. It had been a routine mission, a walk in the park, just as Metatron said it would be.

After reaching proper flight altitude, the black VTOLs transformed back into jets leaving the site with high velocity and minimal noise. Soon, the rural and industrial areas below changed into a vast, deserted city that was largely destroyed, showing indications of a horrible war long past. Wild vegetation was spreading, and there was mud everywhere, brought by the endless rain. In the center of the desolate city was a long strip of land which obviously had never succumbed to human development, even when the metropolis was still at its glory. It was now completely overgrown by vegetation, but in its center, a high obelisk still rose upward, reaching toward the skies above, miraculously undamaged by the catastrophe which had destroyed the city long ago. Only its pyramid-like tip had broken off. Not far away, the remains of a huge, formerly impressive manor still stood out among the blighted surroundings. It's color now left much to the imagination, but it once had been a brilliant white.

BEHIND BLUE EYES

The aircraft quickly passed over the once majestic city and political center of the world. There was nothing worthwhile here now. Instead, they took a course southward.

Chapter Two

Guardian Angels

"It was a flawless operation today," Metatron said with a thin, characteristic smile, "No casualties, no equipment loss on our side, a minimum of resources spent, and the target eradicated. One hundred percent efficiency; a perfect balance."

As always, the mission debriefing took place in the assembly hall of the HQ. It was a dimly lit room with black walls. The corps' logo was painted across the front; two huge wings in bright, neon-blue.

Metatron stood directly below on a small platform, facing and addressing all Angels who participated in the mission today. He was a slim man that appeared to be in his late thirties. In truth, he was much older, but age was irrelevant to a cyborg. Like everyone else, he was dressed in black. He had short, dark hair, pale skin, and slightly androgynous features. Combined with the piercing blue cyborg eyes, this gave his face an unearthly and predatory appearance. His speech and movement left no doubt that he was in command and truly enjoyed the position.

"Another terrorist cell has been successfully annihilated. I'm very pleased, and the Board will be too when they read my report. You have once again proven our value. You have shown we are invaluable. We are the Guardian Angels of Olympias. Custodio et mortifico!"[1]

Nephilim and the elite cyborg unit she belonged to, were known by many names. Blue Death, Blue Eyes, Blue Demons, Angels of Death or simply monsters, killers, bastards, sociopaths, and whatever else the humans came up with. However, these were unofficial names, since no one in their right mind would ever dare speak them aloud. Their official name was Guardian Angels of Olympias. Their sole purpose was to search and destroy anything that could threaten the Olympias Conglomerate, no matter if it came from outside or within. Any means were permitted.

"Custodio et mortifico!" they all repeated with one voice.

Metatron's smile widened. "Dismissed."

Everyone rushed to the door. Not only had this been a successful operation, but the short time in which it had been accomplished had given all of them the rest of the day off - provided nothing unforeseen happened that required their immediate intervention. This was something even a cyborg appreciated.

Adriel caught up to Nephilim and poked her with his elbow.

"Drink?"

"I would kill for one."

---

[1] Latin: Protect and Destroy

***

After WWIII shook the world in the 2030s, nothing was the way it used to be. The shape of the planet changed dramatically. In some places, the land was overcome by the rise of the oceans. In other areas, the Atlantic and Pacific retreated, creating new landmasses. Large parts of every continent became uninhabitable, the biggest metropolitan areas were destroyed, nations ceased to exist, and political systems crumbled.

But the destruction of one power gives rise to new ones. From the ashes of the old national, social, and power structures, new ones were born. These structures existed before the war, now taking profit from the downfall of the old world. New world orders filled the vacuum of a bygone era, creating a perpetually flawless system.

More than sixty years after their rise, everything that once had been important became irrelevant—nations, borders, cultural identities. The world was now divided between three mega-corporations. They shared territories, resources, and human capital between themselves, and had absolute power over everything. Production, consumption, population—anything that needed to be in balance, always.

The corporation in control of the American continents was Olympias Conglomerate. Their corporate headquarters, Olympias City I, was located on the East Coast of Northern America, stretching from the remains of what was formerly Atlanta, Georgia, southward almost to what had once been Orlando, Florida, and had a population of forty-five million people. It had been the best location available on the North American continent, since the Northern part of it was either destroyed or buried under thick ice layers. Meanwhile, the West was a radioactive wasteland. In contrast, the Gulf of Mexico was now dry land and fed a large amount of the population thanks to its excellent soil.

BEHIND BLUE EYES

Furthermore, the corporation had two more satellite branch locations. Olympias City II had been built over Panama, and Olympias City III covered everything between what was once Sao Paulo and Rio de Janeiro. Though, combined, both satellites had a smaller work and consumer force than Olympias City I.

Olympias Conglomerate had its own law enforcement and military troops to secure stability in the region and keep control over all aspects within. In return, every citizen of Olympias was granted an opportunity to live the perfect life. With stability and security, everyone could choose any occupation they desired. They consumed anything they wanted or craved. Nothing was impossible to achieve, no dream or goal was unattainable. There was no need to take care of anything or anyone but oneself. The corporation took care of everything. All that mattered was value. And everyone could continue to develop theirs further.

Of course, even the most perfect system would attract haters, and so there were people in Olympias, who tried to oppose it, damage it from within, or break out to live a life outside the society. This couldn't be tolerated.

Even worse, there were the other two corporations. Since the beginning of the new dawn, the three big players had been in constant conflict, corporate wars, espionage, or even full-on open war with each other.

That was why the unit Nephilim and Adriel belonged to had been created, the Guardian Angels of Olympias. To protect and destroy. A special force of state-of-the-art, high-tech cyborgs. Almost invincible warriors under total control, the perfect weapon. And a necessity, since the enemy wasn't sleeping either. The hostile corporations were continually developing new technologies, too, and didn't hesitate to set them into action. This was the reason why everyone in the squad had considered today's assignment an easy job. Humans were no match for them. The Angels had been created to fight other cyborgs.

***

"That was almost too easy," Adriel said, leaning back in the comfortable lounge seat, his drink in hand.

Nephilim shrugged. "Would you prefer to still be in the field?"

They were sitting in The Velvet, a bar they both liked to visit recently. The name was self-explanatory since the generous lounge furniture was all covered in dark-red velvet. Heavy candelabras and semi-opaque drapes separating the lounges and creating privacy gave the place a neo-gothic charm, which was quite fashionable lately. The décor there was much better than the omnipresent concrete, glass, and chrome outside.

The bar was on the eighty-seventh floor, and the huge windows allowed a good view of the northern part of the city. Not that there was much to be seen, since the district mostly consisted of other high-rise buildings, but sometimes, on one of the rare, clear days, it was possible to see the mountains from here. Nephilim didn't know why, but she liked that.

Today, however, the sky was cloudy and grey and gave the bar a gloomier atmosphere than it usually had, thanks to its interior design and dark tinted windows. It reflected Nephilim's mood perfectly. She knew that she should be content with what she accomplished during the mission, but somehow, she wasn't. And she even couldn't tell why.

She downed her whiskey and put the glass on the small table between them, then signaled the robo-waitress to bring another one.

"I see you're thirsty today," Adriel observed with a grin, then continued talking about the mission, "I will honestly never get how people can live like that. Or most of all, why? I mean, they leave a place where they have everything, rip out their implants, so they can live in the dirt? In shitholes like those? Why the hell would any sane person do that?"

"I can't understand it either," Nephilim said, "It doesn't make any sense."

"They are better off dead," Adriel stated, "In a way, we're releasing them from their suffering. And we prevent their ideas from spreading. They're dangerous and wrong."

Nephilim nodded. Adriel simply repeated in his own words what they were told. She knew that it was the only truth.

She studied his face as he finished his drink and ordered another one. Adriel was a handsome man. Like all Angels, he chose to wear black even when off duty, and he was in a fashionable suit now. Concealed under his jacket were two pistols and some spare ammo. Even in their free time, the Angels were always armed, since technically they were never really off duty. They were allowed—and meant to—take action any time it was necessary. Ordinary citizens were neither permitted to use or own firearms, and that was why the Angels wore them concealed; to blend in.

Nephilim, too, was wearing all black, although she preferred a more casual style. Tight pants, boots, a close-fitting top. She was hiding her own weapons under a leather jacket. Her matching, black, mid-length hair was cut in asymmetric layers, being much longer on the left than on the right side. It wasn't her real hair. Like all cyborgs, she was bald due to electrodes and other hardware planted under her skin and inside her skull. The hair was artificial, yet it was much more than a wig. It looked and behaved completely natural, even in the wind, or when it got wet. Attached by a magnetic system, it couldn't be blown or yanked off her head.

And, of course, she was wearing sunglasses to cover her treacherous and unique neon-blue eyes. All Angels had to hide them if they wanted to go unnoticed. Nevertheless, the eyes were always active. Automatically scanning and analyzing anything Nephilim looked at. Recording everything and sending it directly to the grid. In case she missed something, others would not.

Adriel's hair was snow-white, which was a nice contrast to his ebony skin. Contrary to Nephilim's, though, it didn't behave naturally at all. It stood straight up in the air—eight inches high—as if some invisible force were holding it. His cyborg eyes, too, were thoroughly hidden behind dark shades.

"I mean, those people are hard-ass fanatics," he said, "They preferred their own kids dead before sending them with us? How insane is that?"

"Yet it was me they called evil."

Adriel snorted contemptuously. "Are you kidding me? They break every rule and kill their own children, and *we're* evil? We're protecting what's right. We're the good guys."

"You should've seen the eyes of those kids. How they stared at me," Nephilim said.

She felt uneasy remembering it. Those little, accusing, terrified eyes. The horror inside them, seeing...her.

"You did great in there. As far as I heard, only two of the youngest died of poisoning. All others were saved. Thanks to you." He smiled at her, and it was a genuine, warm smile. "My guess is, at least ten percent of them are probably FUBAR[2], but the rest will turn out to be valuable. Maybe some of them will become Angels one day."

That had been what the two women in the room were horrified of most, Nephilim remembered. They would rather see their children dead than become like her.

---

[2] Tech slang: Fucked up beyond any repair

BEHIND BLUE EYES

Like all other Angels, she and Adriel had been recruited as children. Over the years, they had been educated, trained, genetically enhanced, augmented, and finally turned into what they were now. They didn't know anything else, and they couldn't remember anything of their lives before, not even their names. Everyone got an Angel name, once they became part of the corps. It was said that even Metatron didn't know who had come up with that idea in the first place. All they knew was that it had been someone from the Board. Someone with a very cynical sense of humor, since all Angel names came from the Bible, and that was one of the books banned in Olympias.

The drinks came, but instead of the robo-waitress, the human barkeeper personally brought them. He placed the glasses in front of them with a bright smile.

"On the house. For two of our most valued customers," he said bowing his head.

"Thanks, we appreciate it," Adriel answered while Nephilim gave the man a friendly nod, "We enjoy coming here."

"We're glad to hear that," the barkeeper replied, "enjoy your drinks."

***

When the barkeeper turned around, his warm smile faded as if it had never been there. His name was Marten, and he wasn't actually just a bartender, but the owner of The Velvet. Well, technically, he wasn't really the owner. The bar was his place, but he was only the leaseholder, for everything in Olympias was owned by the corporation. If not a direct associate, it was possible to have your own business as a leaseholder, contractor, or sub-contractor, though.

Marten went back to the bar and pretended to be busy there, but in truth, he kept an eye on the two black-clad figures sitting in the lounge at the windows.

They appeared to be just two good looking, young people from the upper-middle class, enjoying a few drinks in the afternoon. Maybe two people having casual sex and spending some time together afterward, such as many did these days. A substantial number of his customers fell into that category, and, gladly, the other patrons visiting his place today would most likely not notice anything suspicious. But Marten knew better. He had been running bars for more than twenty years and had an eye for people. It wasn't easy to fool him.

Marten knew exactly what these two were, and it made his hair stand on end to even look at them. The guy with the snow-white hair at least pretended to be human, smiled, and attempted to make small talk. Although his smile reminded Marten more of a hungry shark's than that of a human's. But the woman gave him the creeps. Her pale, Asian-Caucasian face was very beautiful, and the delicacy of her features gave her an innocent and youthful look. But there was also something cold and perilous about her. When she tilted her head and looked at him, he wasn't sure if he should feel aroused or run away screaming. She never smiled, stared out of the window most of the time when she wasn't drinking or talking to her companion. She didn't bother to pretend to be friendly or cheerful, as everyone else did.

Both had perfect, smooth skin without even a hint of irritations or wrinkles and no visible implants or augmentations whatsoever. This could either mean they weren't augmented at all, which was close to impossible nowadays, or that they had state-of-the-art implants. Only rich people had these, and the wealthy usually frequented other places than his.

No, they couldn't fool Marten. He had known exactly what they were, the very first day they came into his place, which almost caused him to have a heart attack. Literally. He had to visit his physician the next day

BEHIND BLUE EYES

and have him adjust his pacemaker. Marten had known the truth long before he witnessed the guy briefly lift his glasses to brush something off them and caught a glimpse of his eyes. Marten had been dreaming of those neon-blue eyes coming after him for an entire week and thought it would drive him insane.

Why, of all places, had they chosen his bar to drink at? After all, there were more than a hundred thousand bars in Olympias City. Why The Velvet, why?

The first time, Marten had hoped it only was a one-time visit, but they came back. Any second, they could draw their weapons and kill everyone inside the bar, including him, for no reason, and no one would stop them. No one would hold them accountable.

All Marten could do, was keep them content and do nothing to provoke them. After a while, they would hopefully get bored and find another place to haunt, or maybe they would get killed. That would be the best. If Marten was honest with himself, he had to confess that he would have loved to see both of them dead. Ripped into pieces. Those cursed blue eyes staring into nothing. Not able to hurt anyone ever again...

The woman lifted her head and looked at him, and it was just then that he realized he had been staring at her. Marten quickly turned toward his bottles and felt his heart pounding. He would need to revisit his physician tomorrow.

***

"I think that bartender knows who we are," Nephilim said, turning back to the window and sipping on her drink.

Adriel shrugged. "So what? We're allowed to be here, aren't we? And if that's the reason we get drinks on the house, even better." He chuckled.

"Well, his pants are so full of shit that he can hardly move," she replied.

He laughed. "What is this moron thinking? That we'll jump up and kill everyone? Pathetic."

"We should try not to scare him too much. My scan shows he has an outdated pacemaker. And I really like his drinks and this place."

Adriel lifted his hands in the air. "Hey! Don't look at me like that. I'm a lamb, and you know it."

That brought a smile to Nephilim's face. Adriel was the closest thing she had to a friend. She knew she could trust him as much as it was possible to trust anyone. She could always rely on him in combat, and it was pleasant to have him around in her spare time. They had been a team for four months now and had two more months to go. Angels were always teamed up in pairs, so everyone had each others' backs. One assignment lasted six months, then everyone got a new partner. This was so they weren't able to form deep, emotional bonds to each other; get attached. They weren't allowed to have a relationship of any kind, their family—their whole life—was the corps. Nothing else mattered.

Besides, everyone had to be willing to sacrifice their partner at any time, if necessary. A single unit was expendable, but the cause—often an important mission—was not. Of course, every Angel was an extremely valuable asset, since it took years to train them and the engineering and programming that made them what they were was worth a fortune. But in the end, sometimes even the most valuable resource needed to be sacrificed for the greater good. Emotional bonds could prove a hindrance in such cases.

"So," Adriel said as he leaned back, a grin on his face, "When are you gonna become an Archangel?"

Nephilim sighed, slightly irritated. "That again? Why the hell should I become an Archangel?"

Adriel's grin broadened. "That's easy, really. It's been two weeks now since Cassiel was KIA. Metatron will soon name a successor. And everyone knows that you are his favorite."

There were always five Archangels, who operated directly under Metatron. They controlled the regular Angels, and were Metatron's personal troop, working closely for and with him. They were entitled to bigger quarters, more C-Coins for personal use and many other privileges.

"Are you fucking him already?" Adriel kept digging.

Nephilim tilted her head. "Are you looking for an early retirement?"

Talking about retirement was an inside joke among the Angels. Sooner or later, they were either killed in action or were damaged so severely that they weren't able to fulfill their duties anymore. Sometimes they couldn't function, mentally, after doing the job for too long, or simply degraded in their performance. In all these cases, they were euthanized, and the hardware recycled. There was no *real* retirement for them.

Getting on Metatron's bad side wouldn't automatically lead to retirement, of course. He would never have achieved his position if he did not know how to manage resources without letting them go to waste. But it wasn't a wise thing to do either.

Adriel shrugged. "He never made a secret of it that he likes keeping his Archangels very close. So?"

It was true. Metatron expected the ultimate devotion of his Archangels, male and female. He not only chose the best among the corps, but he also wanted them to be ready to do anything for him, anytime.

"No," Nephilim said, "Happy now?"

"Not really. You seem upset and unbalanced. Ever since we arrived. What's going on?"

"Nothing...I'm probably just exhausted from today's mission."

"That thing with the kids got to you, huh?"

"No," she said quickly, "Of course not. Maybe I'm just irritated by your stupid questions?"

He smiled, but this time she could clearly feel that his smile wasn't genuine. "You know what you need? To get decently laid. It always helps. I would offer myself, but you know how it is..."

Nephilim knew. Adriel preferred men. Otherwise, it would not only have been acceptable but even expected for them to hook up. Promiscuity was an essential part of the Olympias' way of life, and Angels weren't excluded from that. As long as everything stayed casual, to be sure. Most common humans were scared or disgusted by them, so the Angels usually found their sex partners among each other—or in brothels.

"I heard there's this new place close to New World Plaza that's supposed to be quite good," Adriel continued, "I was about to check it out tonight. Wanna join? If we share some whores, we save C-Coins."

"I think I'll pass. Maybe next time," Nephilim said. She finished her drink and got up. "I'll go home and hit the sack early today."

When they went out the door, Marten was so relieved that he had to sit down for a minute and allow himself a double shot of Gin. His hand was shaking.

***

BEHIND BLUE EYES

"Be careful not to get a speeding ticket," Adriel joked.

That made Nephilim chuckle. Angels were permitted to drive as fast as they wanted, and if any regular police should ever stop her, all she needed to do was lift her sunglasses. No law enforcement member would ever dare to interfere with a Guardian Angel. They stood above the law and were only accountable to the Board directly.

Handling the AI police or security forces was even easier. Every Angel could override their programming within seconds.

They had arrived at the parking deck on the twenty-second floor, where they had left their motorcycles. They were identical, black, streamlined machines, built to go up to three-hundred MPH, and were impossible to operate without a neural link. Nephilim connected to hers, turned on the engine and jumped on.

"Take care, Adriel," she said.

"You, too, Neph. See you tomorrow."

She accelerated and drove off. The parking deck ramp led directly to the Speedway. As usual, there wasn't much traffic, and it shouldn't take her much longer than a few minutes to arrive home.

The Speedway was the fastest way to get around Olympias City. It had no speed limit and was located two-hundred feet in the air, bordered by ten-foot-high reinforced concrete walls on both sides. This was the reason why it had been given the nickname "Deathway." Its death toll was higher than on any other route. However, it was everyone's free choice to use it, so no one complained. And if people were ignorant enough to prefer driving themselves instead of leaving it to the AI, no one could help their poor choices. Besides, only a few people used it. About ten percent of the population owned a vehicle for themselves—mostly the privileged ones. Most of them frequented the Highway several stories below, which was slower and often crowded because it was also used by the countless autonomous taxis. The Deathway, however, required special access permission.

Below the Highway where several public transport lanes of various kinds, while on the lowest level, a whole road network for cyclists spread all across the city. Most citizens of Olympias did not need a private vehicle and were absolutely content living without one. The corporation provided transport to get anywhere, and profit could be made with other products.

Nephilim's motorcycle almost didn't generate any noise as she rushed down the Deathway at neck-breaking speed. Thanks to her lightning-fast reflexes and the fact that she connected the vehicle's software directly to her brain, she didn't need to worry about getting into an accident. All Angels not only had their own high-speed vehicles for private use, but they could travel on the Speedway as much as they wanted. The reason for that wasn't benevolence, but pragmatism. That way, they could all be called in quickly wherever they might be needed, even the ones off duty, who might be spread around the city. Plus, every one of them was trained to recognize critical situations on their own and be ready to intervene at any time. It was one of the reasons they were respected and feared so much; they could show up seemingly out of nowhere, at any time, at any place.

Nephilim passed by endless high-rise buildings of various shapes, like a forest of gigantic trees made of concrete and glass. The only color came from the oversized advertisements everywhere, projected on the walls as moving images or 3D holograms, advertising whatever was currently needed to achieve happiness.

The sky was still gloomy, and thick clouds hung deeply in-between the high-rises, creating a foggy atmosphere, and it was slowly getting dark when Nephilim saw the black pyramid rising up on the horizon. It was not only the center of the city but also the heart of the Olympias Conglomerate. She had almost reached her destination.

BEHIND BLUE EYES

***

She took a long, hot shower, in the hope that it would help her relax a bit. But it did not. Of course, she would never have admitted it, but Adriel was right. What had happened today had gotten to her. It confused her since she usually didn't give much thought to her actions. She did her job, her duty, what she had been created for. She followed orders. There was nothing wrong with that.

We are the good guys.

She heard the echo of Adriel's words in her mind. Were they really? Remembering the faces of the children today, she wasn't so sure about that. She was used to the fact that most people feared her. It made things easier sometimes. But when she looked into those children's eyes, for a second, she felt as if she could see what they were seeing: a monster.

The face of one girl in particular haunted her the most. She was maybe eight years old, had black hair and big brown eyes. It wasn't only fear she had seen in those eyes, it was deep desperation, all the pain of the world.

Nephilim turned off the water and stepped out of the shower, feeling confused and annoyed at the same time. What the hell was wrong with her? These thoughts, these feelings were unacceptable. They could lead to the early retirement she had been joking about only a few hours back. And she wasn't ready for that yet.

For a moment, she just stood there, water dripping down her body onto the floor. Then she stepped over to the mirror. At first, she could not see anything, the small bathroom was filled with steam. It disappeared through the vent, and she recognized her shape first, and then her face and body.

She looked into her own eyes. The neon-blue eyes everyone was afraid of, everyone hated. What was she behind these blue eyes? Was she really a monster? Was her conscience as empty as it was supposed to be? She had no answers to these questions.

All she knew was that this life and this body were the only ones she had.

Though, technically, they weren't hers.

All hardware inside her was the property of Olympias Conglomerate. She could not survive without it for even one minute. Which, in a way, made her property of Olympias, too.

She looked her naked body over in the mirror. It was perfect in every aspect. Proportions, skin, curves—nature only rarely came up with such flawlessness in a female body. And hidden below the beauty was an engineering marvel.

Although the majority of people had implants, augmentations, or prosthetics of some sort, they were almost always clearly recognizable as artificial. The sight of metal plates, maintenance ports, or wires sticking out of people's heads was common. Most synthetic limbs stood out from the rest of the body, if not when dressed, then when naked.

On Nephilim's body, there was nothing that indicated where the human part stopped, and the machine began. At least not at first glance, only when looking very closely. Sixty percent of her was artificial, while only forty percent remained biological.

Sixty/Forty had proven to be the magic number for perfect cyborg efficiency. In the beginning, the engineers had tried to implant human brains into fully synthetic bodies, for them to be most robust in combat. But they soon found that this concept wouldn't work. The human brain, needed a body it could relate to, it required basic human body functions, human needs, to be able to operate flawlessly. Brains implanted in fully synthetic bodies quickly developed some kind of "claustrophobia" and eventually went insane. The project had been a total disaster and waste of resources. Years and many volunteers later, the sixty/forty formula was finally introduced.

Nephilim went through the same procedure as every other Angel. Her limbs had been replaced by synthetic ones, which was only logical. The artificial silicate muscles made her run ten times faster than any human, jump from great heights, and over large distances. Her arms did not look much different than those of an athletic woman, who worked out on a regular basis, yet she could lift up a car or snap a neck with only two fingers.

The synthetic polymer on her artificial limbs not only looked real and matched the tone of her biological skin perfectly, but it also felt real. Additionally, her fingertips were equipped with sensors, which not only gave her the ability to feel what she touched, they also could scan and analyze surfaces, measure temperature, and detect unusual chemical components.

Besides that, her spine was improved for greater stability and flexibility, and almost all vital organs to be more efficient and robust. Finally, she had several neural implants, which not only enhanced her senses and mental performance but continuously connected her to the grid and made it possible for her to control external systems with her mind, such as her drone. And of course, there were the eyes. Both a blessing and a curse.

In return, her reproductive organs had been removed, since she would not need them anyway, but the parts necessary for sexual pleasure had naturally been left untouched.

To work at the highest level of efficiency, it was crucial that a cyborg was kept "happy," and its basic human needs were satisfied; the ability to sleep, eat, drink and fuck.

Still naked, Nephilim left the bathroom and walked through her apartment to the huge windows. It was a studio of moderate size, yet still bigger than most, situated on the ninety-eighth floor of a mid-class building. In the beginning, the Guardian Angel squad had been housed in barracks, but it was soon found that it increased their efficiency if they were allowed to have their own quarters. Zephon, one of Nephilim's former partners, always used to joke about it, that the reason for the change was to give them the illusion of free choice and being an actual person, but she had never given this statement much thought. It didn't matter now since Zephon had been sent into retirement two years ago.

The apartment was the property of the corporation and part of Nephilim's pay. It had come fully furnished and equipped with everything a human being needed to be content, including an entertainment console with an integrated VR port. The room was dominated by a big bed and had nothing personal inside whatsoever; no décor, pictures, stuffed animals, or whatever people liked to put up to make a standard place homey. The big holo-screen was on, as always. It could only be switched off when the apartment system went into night mode. Nephilim had turned the volume down to a minimum. She wasn't interested in the latest news; how great Olympias was doing compared to the other corporations or what the modern citizen needed to achieve happiness. She knew what most people out there weren't supposed to know; that Olympias was in constant danger and that it was her job to keep it safe. Plus, she was busy with other thoughts right now.

Outside her window, she saw the illuminated high-rise buildings of the Inner Circle of the city, and in their midst, the gigantic black pyramid. The Inner Circle was restricted area, only accessible by the people who lived or worked there; the Board, the management, and higher administration, but also movie stars, TV executives, or other VIPs. It was the most well protected district of the city. Directly at its rim was the Guardian Angels' HQ. Nephilim could not see it from here, but it was very close. All Angels lived only a few minutes away, but outside the Inner Circle, naturally.

BEHIND BLUE EYES

She stared at her own reflection in the window. With the darkness of the night beyond it, her eyes appeared not blue but like dark, glimmering holes. Again, she couldn't help but remember the horrified look in the eyes of those children. She wondered what would happen to them. Was it really such a horrible thing to become like her, that death seemed somehow preferable?

The reason why those kids had been valuable was that they weren't registered. They were like blank paper, they technically didn't even officially exist. The corporation could turn them into anything they wanted without anyone ever asking any questions.

Nephilim sighed. She needed to make her mind stop thinking right away, get to bed, and sleep if she wanted to be fit for the job the following day and perform her duties with efficiency. But she wouldn't manage to accomplish that on her own at the moment. She stepped away from the window and opened a drawer next to her bed. There she stored her drugs in several aluminum boxes. A huge variety of narcotics was purchasable legally in Olympias, as long as they came from official stores run by the corporation. Production and distribution of unauthorized drugs were highly illegal and punished with high penalties, including the death sentence. That was nothing that Nephilim and her kind had to worry about. It would be a severe waste of resources to send the Angels after puny drug dealers.

She chose one of the products, a purple gel she inhaled into her nose in tiny bubbles, then laid down on the bed. The high kicked in almost immediately, and she started feeling increasingly relaxed and content. Everything was good. Everything was as it should be.

She fell asleep with a smile on her face.

Chapter Three

Examination

She was woken by an alarm clock beeping directly in her skull, as well as a text message in her field of vision, saying:

NEPHILIM. REPORT FOR COGNITIVE EXAMINATION 8 AM SHARP.

She opened her eyes. It was 6:30 AM, and she knew that without consulting a watch, thanks to her internal chrono-system. It was still dark outside.

The integrated sensors in her apartment noticed that she was awake and switched into day mode. The lights and TV went on.

Nephilim sat up in the bed. Examination? Regular exams were never scheduled on such a short notice. What could this be about? No system showed any errors, and her biological parts were in excellent condition. She had performed flawlessly in yesterday's mission, even Metatron had acknowledged that. No one could assume that she had been feeling confused last night. Did she show too openly that she was unwell toward Adriel? Had someone listened to or watched their conversation in the bar? Or could it be...No, she couldn't believe Adriel reported her for suspicion of potential underperformance. He wouldn't do that, would he?

On the other hand, what was all that nudging about becoming an Archangel all about? Nephilim honestly had no idea why he believed she could be Metatron's choice, and she wasn't even sure if she wanted the job. Adriel, on the other hand, would like nothing more than to get such a promotion.

But it made no sense to be paranoid now. Most likely, Adriel had nothing to do with the examination, and she had to trust her partner, or she might end up dead during the next assignment. It would be necessary to find out if there was any truth in her suspicion, though.

Luckily, last night's confusion had passed completely. The Relax-X had been exactly what she had needed. The gloomy feelings she had experienced seemed like nothing more than a bad dream now. She yawned. Outside, the sky started to brighten up.

On TV, a colorful and cheery commercial was advertising a new dating platform, which automatically matched up participants for blind date one-night-stands and/or casual sex, using the data profiles stored on the Olympias citizen servers. It had one-hundred percent consumer satisfaction and advertised special deals for new members. Walking into the bathroom, Nephilim imagined how it would be to become a member. Seeing the faces of men matched up with her when they realized what was beneath the dark sunglasses would be priceless. It brought a smile on her face.

Thirty minutes later, she was as operational as she could be and ready to go. She grabbed a quick breakfast at the cafeteria in the parking deck level of her building, then rushed off on her motorcycle. It was common to eat on the run or in food parlors and restaurants. No one cooked anymore. Most apartments, like Nephilim's, didn't even provide a kitchen, for it would only be a waste of space. All it had was a coffee maker and a small fridge for drinks and ice.

It took her only five minutes to arrive at the Guardian Angels HQ. It was a black, cubic building, and, at first glance, windowless. In truth, the windows were tinted to match and were almost invisible against the smooth surface of the façade. The only contrast was the oversized logo printed on the front in neon-blue: two wings.

The bigger part of the HQ was located underground. In the center of the cube was a huge atrium, where a hatch opened. This was where the VTOLs typically launched and landed.

The sun was just rising when she drove inside the building, but its blackness seemed to swallow the early rays of sunlight.

***

Finwick, too, had a hard night. He had decided to give the new dating platform that everyone was talking about a try. Total disaster. How in the hell could it achieve one-hundred percent consumer satisfaction? Was he the only one for whom it hadn't worked out as hoped? No, he wasn't an idiot, but he knew his share about programming. As far as he was concerned, they had a crappy algorithm and hid it behind a deceitful advertisement, which made you believe it was your own fault if it didn work out.

The girl the system had hooked him up with was entirely not his type—obviously, she had never heard of plastic surgeries before. She had also been so boring in bed that he had almost fallen asleep while having sex with her. Vanilla sex was so not his taste, but she did not agree to anything else, so he took what he could get. Afterward, he decided that it was probably better to stick to VR next time. Cheaper and more satisfying. Apparently, she enjoyed it so much, however, that she asked him if they wanted to do it again casually. He paid for the room and quickly left without making any commitments.

It was common to take a room in places specialized for such occasions and not go to someone's home for a one-night-stand, though usually it only took a few hours and not a full night. No one wanted to get too personal and invite a stranger to their place. And the so-called *Funtels* existed in every imaginable design and price range. From the romantic fairy-tale-style bedroom, emphasizing popular movies, comics, or VR world décor, to the dungeons of pain—nothing was impossible.

However, this encounter and the fact that he had drowned his frustration in booze once home, had left Finwick grumpy, unsatisfied, and mildly hungover today. And it was only Wednesday.

Everyone was already busy in the lab when he arrived. Dr. Dinah Mendez, his boss, gave him a contemptuous look while her assistant Briana was rushing around like a busy little bee. Finwick couldn't stand her. She was too ambitious for his taste.

"You're late," Dr. Mendez said.

Finwick peered at the wall clock. He was late by one minute!

"I'm sorry," he murmured.

"We have a mental examination scheduled for 8 AM."

That surprised him. "What? I thought we only had routine checks today, the first starting at 11 AM..."

"It came in during the night. Special inquiry."

"The big man himself wants to have it done," Briana added.

Actually, she could have been cute if she wasn't such a pain in the ass. Originally from Olympias III, her skin tone always reminded him of freshly brewed cappuccino. She had hazel brown eyes and voluminous, curly hair, dyed fire-red.

Finwick's curiosity had awoken now. If Metatron himself wanted to have things done urgently, he usually had good reasons for that. He went to the console and looked at the holographic screen. "Who is it?"

More than five-hundred humans worked in the Guardian Angel HQ. Scientists, physicians, psychologists, engineers, technicians, and many more. Even after years, many of them still felt uneasy when dealing with the Angels; some were even scared, although no one would admit it. But not Finwick. He loved the Angels. Especially the female ones.

"Nephilim," Briana answered at the same moment Finwick read it in the file. The name alone sent shivers down his spine. His grumpiness and hangover were forgotten instantly.

"But wasn't she here just last month for her routine check-up?" he asked, raising his eyebrows, "Is something wrong with her?"

He dearly hoped not.

Briana shrugged, then moved closer toward him. "I have no clue. But it seems to be something out of the ordinary. Metatron even sent specific questions we are supposed to ask her."

She spoke Metatron's name as if he were God himself, and in a way, he was. At least inside these walls. Working for the HQ paid higher-than-average and provided several other unique benefits. Still, the nondisclosure agreement was hardcore, and if you broke it—or any other rule—being removed from the job took on a whole new meaning.

BEHIND BLUE EYES

"That's enough chit-chat," Dr. Mendez intervened, "And it's our job to question the subject, *not* our instructions."

If Finwick did not know better, he would assume she was a cyborg herself, or maybe even an android. She was wearing the same grey-blue suit all medical and scientific personnel had, and a white coat over it, which indicated that she was one of the lead scientists, however, she had never been seen without high heels. She had shiny black hair, green contact lenses, and several implants, on her temple, her neck, and of course, the one on her wrist that they all had, which was essential for doing their job. Mendez didn't look a day older than thirty, but Finwick knew that she had to be much older, since she had a son his age. And she was a bitch.

"Certainly," he said.

"Prepare everything, then bring in the subject. She's already waiting in the hall."

"I will see to that," Finwick said quickly.

"Of course, you will," a sarcastic smile appeared on Dr. Mendez's red lips as she sat down at her desk behind the window to check through her notes. The window faced a small room with blank walls and an examination chair in the middle.

Finwick finished his preparations, then stepped outside in the hall. She stood there, casually leaning against the wall, her arms folded, dressed in the plain, black uniform the Angels wore when not dispatched. Finwick's heart started pounding when he approached her, and she lifted her head, facing him. Most people considered the piercing, neon-blue eyes unsettling and frightening. Finwick considered them beautiful—and smoking hot.

"Hi Nephilim, it's nice to see you. How are you today?" he asked with a cheerful smile.

"Couldn't be better," she answered without returning his smile.

She tended to speak relatively slowly in a calm, smooth tone. It gave Fenwick the creeps and sent shivers up his spine at the same time. Her voice was extremely sexy, yet there was also always something cold and dangerous about it—which made it even more exciting.

"After you," he said, opening the door to the examination room.

Watching how she entered the room made his pulse rise. Sometimes he could not believe that she was more than half machine. She moved smoothly, like a cat. Not a kitten, but a panther.

Nephilim sat down in the chair, then briefly nodded toward the huge mirror facing her, of which she knew was an observation window on the opposite side, where people were watching her.

"You have a new haircut," Finwick observed, fixating her head in the designated part of the chair.

"My old hair was partially burned on a mission two weeks ago. I had to get something new."

"It suits you very well."

"Thank you."

He had to find the courage to ask her today. He had been considering it for months and yet always bailed out, and he could not understand why. It wasn't forbidden or anything; in fact, it happened from time to time that the Angels mingled with human associates, although not as often as it could. Most humans would rather stay away from the killer-cyborgs with their blue eyes.

Finwick obviously wasn't like the others. Nephilim's beauty, combined with the ever-present danger that followed her, attracted him. He admired almost all of the female Angels and found it difficult not to stare at them, but she was his favorite. If he was honest with himself, he had to admit that he even had a slight crush on her. On countless nights he had fantasized about having sex with her, her sitting atop of him while he was restrained, helpless. The fact of how dangerous she was and that she could kill him anytime with two fingers, or slit his throat with her blade, turned him on.

Finwick's hands shook slightly as he pulled her artificial hair back and opened the port on the left side of her skull, which led directly to her brain implants. She looked at him sideways but said nothing. He quickly got a grip on himself. This was not the time for daydream fantasies; he needed to focus. He would ask her later, after the examination, once back in the hall, if she would consider hooking up with him. The worst that could happen was her saying no, right? In that case, he would have to shift his interest toward another Angel. But if she said yes...he better stop thinking about it right now.

He stuck connectors inside the ports and linked them with the console attached to the chair, then checked the data stream using the implanted panel on his wrist.

"We're all set," he informed Nephilim, "You know the procedure. I'll pick you up in a few minutes."

She nodded but seemed deeply focused. He smiled at her, then left the room.

"You should be careful not to tip over," Briana said when he returned to the control room.

"I beg your pardon?"

"While licking her boots," she giggled.

Anger rose in Finwick. This chick was really stupid and annoying. Whereas the one behind the window was a goddess.

"It's wrong to treat them like humans," Dr. Mendez added, with an unmoved tone of voice, "They may look pretty, but they're nothing more than killing machines equipped with a minimum of humanity so they can be more efficient. You better remember that."

Then they started the examination.

As usual, it began with standard questions, asked by a neutral, artificial, feminine voice. Nephilim answered, and the team behind the mirror monitored her face, voice, and brain activity.

"What is your purpose?" was always the first question.

"Custodio et mortifico," she said without hesitation.

"What is it you are protecting?"

"The Olympias Conglomeration."

"Are you content with your purpose?"

"Yes."

"Do you agree with Olympias' philosophy?"

"One-hundred percent. It's not my place to have an opinion or make judgments pertaining to the philosophy."

"Are you ready to sacrifice your life to protect Olympias?"

"At any given time."

"Are you ready to sacrifice your life if a superior Guardian Angel commands you to do so?"

"It's my duty to always follow commands given by a superior Guardian Angel."

BEHIND BLUE EYES

Finwick looked up from the data running down the holo screen in front of him and into her face. It was his job to monitor her brain activity for anything out of the ordinary. If Nephilim should experience any kind of conflicting emotion, hesitate with her answers or try to lie, it would show in his data. So far, everything was perfect, as always.

He would never understand how she could be ready to sacrifice her life without a doubt. All Angels were indoctrinated to think this way since childhood. The test would instantly be considered a failure if any of them hesitated to answer this question, even for a millisecond. Finwick couldn't imagine that he would ever risk his life, not to mention sacrificing it. He would never do that, not for anyone or anything.

"Do you enjoy being a Guardian Angel?"

"Yes."

"Why?"

"I don't know anything else."

"Do you sometimes wish you could be something else?"

"I am what I am."

"Are you sometimes scared?"

"No."

"Would you ever hesitate to kill a person if commanded to?"

"Never."

"What do you feel when killing a person?"

"Nothing."

"Does it bother you to be feared and hated?"

"No."

Finwick frowned. What was that? The readings had shown a peak when she answered the last question. That had never happened before with her. She was always perfect. But this was no reason to be concerned, he knew. Many Angels showed anomalies from time to time, after all, their brains were still mostly human. As long as it stayed under five percent, everything was fine.

Next came a row of further questions concerning her daily routine, teamwork, and combat, followed by more inquiries about her thoughts of the core values of the Olympias society. After that, she was confronted with several images displayed directly in front of her vision. It was a mixture of gruesome footage of violence, blood, and death on the one hand and comforting ones on the other—such as a beautiful sunset, a puppy, or smiling people who were obviously having fun.

The pictures stimulated Nephilim's brain exactly in the parameters they were supposed to. It was impossible to fake these kinds of reactions since most of the activity took place on a subconscious level. The examinee behaved within specified parameters if neither the positive nor the negative images triggered an exceeding amount of emotions. Both types of visuals should leave the Angels without an emotional response.

Usually, this would have ended the examination, but not this time.

"I will ask you some more questions now," the AI interrogator said.

Nephilim's face stayed unmoved, yet Finwick clearly could read from the peak that she was surprised.

"Shoot," she said.

"What do you think of Metatron as your commander?" the voice asked.

"I can't imagine anyone better."

BEHIND BLUE EYES

Suddenly Finwick knew what this was all about. Metatron wanted Nephilim tested because he saw her in a more responsible position. He, too, knew she was special.

"Have you ever doubted any of Metatron's decisions?"

"Never."

"Would you do anything Metatron asks you to do?"

"Naturally."

"Would you kill a fellow Angel if Metatron asked you to?"

"Yes."

"Would you kill your partner if Metatron asked you to?"

"Of course."

Finwick almost jumped out of his chair in surprise. Holy shit, that was a blunt lie! Her face and voice did not show anything, neither did her pulse. She didn't hesitate; she wasn't unsure or battling with herself, as often might occur when they didn't answer the questions as they should. She simply had lied. It showed crystal clear on his screen.

"Do you feel the mission you participated in yesterday was justified?"

"It was."

"Why do you feel that way?

"These people were enemies of Olympias, terrorists. They posed a threat to everything we stand for. They deserved to die."

"What did you feel killing them?"

"Nothing."

"What did you feel when confronted with the terrified children you saved from the terrorists?"

"Nothing."

Finwick bit his lip. Another lie! And it had created an even bigger emotional peak than the first one.

"Do you believe you provided a better future for the children?"

"I do."

Another peak! This time it wasn't a lie but a strong emotional reaction of insecurity and doubt.

For a second, Finwick was stunned as he stared at the screen in disbelief. He knew the final results would be catastrophic. They would lead to a memory and personality wipe at best and death sentence at worst.

Unless he changed the result.

It would be no big deal for him. All he needed to do was change some figures, and the peaks would be gone. It would take him only a few seconds. No one would notice. He stole a glance at the two women conducting the procedure with him. Both were focused on their own consoles, and on Nephilim, behind the window. They wouldn't notice shit.

The examination was still running, and there were a few questions left, which were more about her intelligence than emotions. She shouldn't have any problems with these. Finwick felt his heart starting to race, his hands sweating. If he wanted to act, he needed to do it now.

It was madness! If he got caught, they would execute him. He had never done anything illegal before in his life. Hell, he had never even done anything out of line before. He was just a computer guy with a boring life and some kinky fantasies. What should he do?

BEHIND BLUE EYES

His hand was shaking. But then he glanced at Nephilim's angelic face and the unbelievable calmness she exhibited while going through all of this. Whatever she was hiding, she probably had good reasons to do so. And she lied because she wasn't ready to sacrifice a friend. Never before had he known anyone interested in anyone else besides themselves. She was unique. Could he stand by and let her die?

Suddenly everything went so quickly that only a minute later he wasn't sure if it really had happened or if it only was a dream. His hands moved across the holo-keyboard, beyond the screen, and his fingers—those of a programmer that knew how to do their job blindfolded—flew over it as fast as if they were artificial themselves. He deleted the peaks and changed the result into an almost perfect one, leaving just the first discrepancy to make everything look more plausible.

No one would ever notice the manipulation. He would delete the cache at the end of the day and pretend to stay overtime to run some system diagnostics, but would instead wipe everything that could ever lead back to him or what had just happened.

Nephilim was safe. And he needed to admit to himself that he had a crush—and was insane.

"Thank you, Nephilim," Dr. Mendez said through a speaker, so the cyborg could hear her inside the examination room, "That's it for today. Finwick will be with you shortly to unplug you and give you the results."

Briana yawned.

"Damn, it's always so boring with her. Does she even feel anything at all? Sometimes I think she's a robot," she said after Mendez had turned off the speaker.

"I told you, they're not human," their boss said with a shrug.

Finwick had to hold to himself together and not start laughing hysterically. The shirt under his suit was dripping with sweat.

***

Nephilim sat quietly in the chair, still plugged into the system, and waiting to be released. Nothing in her face or body language showed that she was concerned in any way. Yet her thoughts were racing.

She had no idea what this had been about, who had set it up, or why. But she hadn't been prepared for the questions asked and completely fucked up. She knew she had lied, but she had no other choice than to do so, since telling the truth would have been even worse. The truthful answers to the three questions which might break her neck, what she really thought—or even worse, felt—were contrary to anything she was supposed to be, and they might even indicate she doubted the system.

Every one of them knew since childhood that the system was the best that ever existed in the history of mankind. If a civilian openly doubted that, it could get them into severe trouble that even could result in a visit by Nephilim and her fellow Angels. But for an Angel, to doubt that what they did was righteous was heresy.

It was a death sentence.

She wasn't scared. Death she brought to others and the high risk to fall victim to it, herself, every day was such a constant part of her life that she was supposed to be desensitized to it. But the confusion she had felt the night before—and thought she had successfully overcome—was back. What was wrong with her?

Her only hope now was that maybe her feelings and doubts didn't show up on the scans too clearly. Sometimes it happened that the chart showed irritations and anomalies which were out of the norm, but not too severe. Then the result wouldn't be satisfying, and her chances to become an Archangel—if there ever were any—would be blown forever, but it wouldn't be a reason for greater consequences. At least not yet. She would have time to get a grip on herself until the follow-up in a week. She was sure that all her other monitored body functions did not show anything suspicious, for she had perfect control over those.

Now, there was nothing else for her to do but wait. She soon would know if she fucked up completely or not. Then instead of Finwick, fellow Angels would enter the room and escort her out.

But when the door opened, it was the IT specialist who came in. Nephilim had to control herself and not show how relieved she was. Never before had she been so happy seeing the little creep.

Finwick was a short guy, shorter than her, and a natural redhead with a freckled face and green eyes. He wasn't ugly, but there was something repulsive about him, mostly because of how he looked at her. Even a blind woman would have noticed that he was undressing her with his eyes, but a blue-eyed cyborg naturally saw a lot more. His pupils widened, his blood pressure rose, and his heart started pounding whenever they were in one room. In other words, he was horny as hell. Yet, he never behaved intrusive, but rather submissive in her presence. Nephilim knew exactly what these kind of men were attracted to and what they wanted. She had her share of them and was as uninterested as one could be.

Nephilim couldn't possibly have any idea that the "little creep" had just put his life on the line to save hers, but she was so relieved to see him instead of a death squad that she smiled when he entered the room. It meant that the result had been good enough to let her off the hook for now. She had time to work on herself and fix whatever was wrong with her.

Finwick stopped short for a moment seeing her smile, then beamed.

"Good news," he said, walking toward her, "Your results were excellent, as always."

Her smile faded. That was absolutely impossible. Even if she had managed to hide the lies, there must have been a peak showing that she was at least struggling with the answers. Otherwise, the system had to be flawed. Or something else was very wrong.

"I'm glad," she answered without any particular emotion in her voice.

She couldn't believe she would get away with it. That was almost too good to be true. On the other hand, beggars couldn't be choosers. Whatever had happened, it most likely saved her life.

Finwick started to unplug her from the system, and she noticed that something was wrong with the guy. Even more than usual. His hands were slightly shaking, but that was nothing new. They always did when he got to touch her, even if it was just to stick connectors into her implant ports. He was sweating, and that, too, was nothing out of the ordinary with him. But Nephilim noticed that he had lost a tremendous amount of body fluids in the form of sweat and that his body showed signs of a person who had just finished a one-hundred-meter dash. A person whose body wasn't trained for that at all. Besides, he seemed to be happy, euphoric even but tried as hard as he could not to show it.

"Thank you," she said when he was done, and she got up.

"It was a pleasure," he answered.

When Nephilim walked toward the door and opened it, for a second, she was sure there would be people standing there to take her away after all. But the hall was empty. It was incredible, really. She had never thought that anyone could cheat the system like that. After all, it was said that it was infallible.

She stepped outside, and Finwick followed her.

"Until next time," she said, hoping it wouldn't be too soon.

She turned around and wanted to take her leave, still hardly believing what had just happened when Finwick stopped her.

"Um, Nephilim..."

She turned back toward him. "Yes?"

"I...um...I was thinking...maybe—"

"Nephilim," a stern voice interrupted.

Nephilim's scan showed her who it was before she turned around to face the speaker. Gadreel approached at a resolute pace. She was no Archangel but worked directly for Metatron's office, which made her believe she was something better than the regular Angels. Nephilim faced her, curious what this was about now.

"Metatron wants to see you in his office. Delays won't be tolerated," Gadreel said.

Nephilim was surprised. This day couldn't get any stranger. Metatron had never before asked her into his office. He rarely did that with anyone.

She nodded. "I'm on my way. So long, Finwick."

She left the IT expert behind and followed Gadreel, who was already rushing back down the hall toward the elevators.

"See you later, Nephilim," Finwick called after her, and there was so much disappointment in his voice that it almost sounded like grief.

Nephilim dearly hoped that she wouldn't need to be examined for a while, so she wouldn't have to see him again anytime soon. Just before she reached the elevators, she was hit by a sudden insight that was simultaneously so absurd and plausible that it actually could be true.

Gadreel already stood in the elevator when she entered and gave her a scornful, sideways glance, but Nephilim ignored it. Instead, she looked back at the short guy, who was still standing there as if she would change her mind and come back. She knew exactly what he had been about to ask her, and her answer would have been rather unfriendly and maybe even humiliating for him. Now she was grateful it never came to that.

Was it really possible...?

If it was so, then this odd young man, to whom she had unmindfully referred as a creep, had just saved her life.

Nephilim's mind raced. Her inherited high intelligence was amplified by the software integrated into her brain. The Angels were designed to quickly make conclusions, especially when it came to humans and their behavior. Razor-sharp logic combined with enhanced intuition, a mixture every detective would gladly have sold his soul for.

One second later, when the elevator door had closed, Nephilim had done the math and knew exactly what had happened. The system was infallible indeed. However, the human who operated it wasn't.

She must have scored abysmally at the examination, just as she had feared. But for some reason, Finwick had changed the result. He could do that easily, he had the know-how, and the other two scientists most likely were monitoring different screens. The tension of the situation must have almost pushed him over the edge. The excitement and attempt to hide it had brought his unexercised body to its limits. He had lost more than thirty ounces of perspiration, and once it was over and he knew he had been successful, his body stopped producing adrenalin and pumped him with endorphins instead, which made him feel euphoric.

As long as no one suspected that she failed the test, no one would ever have any idea Finwick manipulated the result. And most likely, he was skilled enough to cover his tracks thoroughly. The only question that remained was, why?

Why would he take such an enormous risk? To get laid?

That was absurd. Few things were easier than sex in Olympias.

However, it was futile to speculate about that now. Besides, she had other things to focus on.

The elevator rushed at high-speed from the fifth underground floor to the sixth above ground floor.

"Did Metatron say why he's summoning me?" Nephilim asked the other cyborg woman.

Gadreel faced her and answered, sneering, "You like playing innocent, don't you? I was wondering what he sees in you. Maybe it's that. Maybe he simply wants to stick his dick into your innocent face."

Nephilim's answer came with a calm yet chilling voice, "I can carve the skin on your face off of your skull faster than you blink, then feed it to you. Maybe that's what he likes about me? How about we test it?"

Although all Angels went through the same basic training and augmentations, they still had different enhanced talents. Of course, Gadreel was equipped and trained for combat, but she spent most of her time inside the HQ. Nephilim, on the other hand, was one of the Angels who were sent to the front line of the most challenging and dangerous missions. She was one of the best. There was no doubt she could rip Gadreel into shreds if she wanted.

"You wouldn't dare touch me," Gadreel hissed, slight insecurity in her voice.

Nephilim shrugged without looking at her. "Watch me."

The elevator door opened, and both women stepped out as if nothing had happened. If it was true that Metatron wanted to make her an Archangel, it was now clear to Nephilim that Gadreel had badly desired the job. And she wasn't the only one; half the Angel squad wanted it.

Gadreel led her down a dimly lit hall toward a massive double-door. She knocked before opening it, then stepped inside. Nephilim followed her.

BEHIND BLUE EYES

Chapter Four

Archangel

It was a spacious office with large windows facing the black pyramid. However, it was impossible to say if it was sunny or cloudy outside, bright day or dusk, due to the windows' inky tinting. The dark furniture was expensive and showed either a sense of style or a skilled interior designer. Behind the huge desk, Nephilim spotted a console that could project up to six holo-screens simultaneously. It was switched off now but could only mean that Metatron liked to monitor events and people not only from the control room but from his office.

The commander of the Guardian Angels, the High-Archangel, was sitting behind his desk, leaning back in his chair, with his left hand under his chin, propping it up. Metatron's neon-blue eyes locked on Nephilim the instant she entered the room, yet the expression on his face was unreadable. He wasn't alone. Zephaniel stood by the windows leaning against a pillar. He was not just any Archangel, but he was known as Metatron's favorite for many years. He held the title of First Archangel. Zephaniel was his right hand, and second in command. Occasionally, he monitored and commanded smaller missions for him in the control room, and had his own office right next to Metatron's. In the field, he was famous for being extremely cold-blooded and gruesome.

"Nephilim," Metatron greeted her, "Good. Come and take a seat."

She did as asked, walked across the room, showing no emotion or insecurities, and sat down in the comfortable chair opposite of Metatron's desk. Whatever this was about, she knew that it was always best to stay cool and keep a poker face on. Gadreel respectfully stayed behind.

"I just got the results of your examination," Metatron said after inspecting her silently for a few seconds, "Not one-hundred percent but still very good. It seems the extra questions didn't catch you by surprise at all. You answered all of them perfectly, and that's all that matters. We already knew that you were flawless with the routine stuff, your records from the last few years speak for themselves. Besides, we've been watching you."

He fell silent for a moment, and that thin, trademark smile appeared on his lips while his fingers formed a pyramid in front of his chest.

"Your performance in the field is extraordinary. Your mind is sharp, and you're capable of making crucial decisions in seconds while still following orders to the letter. I like that."

He tilted his head toward Zephaniel, who had been silently watching every movement she made, like a coiled-up snake ready to strike at any time.

"I agree. How she handled yesterday's situation was remarkable. It could have gotten out of hand easily," the Archangel said with a cold smile, "And it's not the only thing I like."

Metatron nodded toward him, and it became clear that these two men were close and understood each other without using many words. He then addressed the other Angel in the room, "Thank you, Gadreel. You can leave us now."

After she closed the door behind her, Metatron turned his attention back to Nephilim. "Surely, you know why I have summoned you. Don't you, Nephilim?"

"I believe so," she answered as neutral as possible. Somehow, she had the impression that Metatron was playing a game that was highly amusing to him. And it was always better not to let your opponent see your cards when playing a game.

"It's not because you can rip someone's face off in the blink of an eye and make them swallow it. Although I have to admit, that the idea is intriguing," he said while his thin smile turned into a grin she had never seen on him before. It had a hint of sadism and genuine amusement. "Maybe you could demonstrate that sometime? I ask you to choose a subject other than Gadreel, however. She might be not the smartest in the corps, but we still have need of her, and I hate resources going to waste."

"I will remember that," Nephilim said, humbly.

She now knew that Metatron had meant it literally when he said he had been watching her. She couldn't help it, but it gave her the chills. Of course, every citizen of Olympias was accustomed to the fact that they could be monitored anytime. This applied to the Angels even more. Their brain implants were always connected to the grid. Everything they saw or heard was recorded in the implant itself and directly sent to the servers located deep down in the lowest level of the HQ. That way, no data could ever get lost; details which slipped an Angel's attention during an operation or investigation could be reviewed later on, and any of those actions could be monitored at any time. There was a whole team of investigators doing nothing else but randomly linking into Angel perceptions, controlling what they did, and monitoring if it was according to parameters. Metatron had the authority and tools to link into any of them whenever he wanted, from the control room, his office, and even his home. And he liked using this power.

Now, for whatever reason, Nephilim had woken his interest. She knew she should feel flattered, but it gave her an uneasy feeling instead.

"You know we need a new Archangel, and you are one of the prime candidates," Metatron continued.

"I'm honored."

"The decision hasn't been made yet. But so far, things are developing well for you."

He waved his hand toward Zephaniel. "You can leave us now. Continue on with what we were discussing before."

Zephaniel bowed his head. "Certainly."

He gave Nephilim a discreet wink, then left the room through a side door that led into his own office.

Once the Archangel was gone, Metatron kept silent for a moment, studying her with his cold eyes, his smooth, ageless face not revealing if he liked what he was seeing or not. No one really knew how old Metatron was or how many years he had been doing this job. None of the Angels remembered a time when he wasn't there. They came and went, but he always stayed. There were rumors that he had been there from the beginning and had actually founded the Guardian Angels, but no one could tell if that was true. One thing was certain; he reported directly to the Board of Olympias and lived in the Inner Circle. He was a very powerful man.

BEHIND BLUE EYES

"Tell me, Nephilim," he finally began, "Do you know why we exist? What our purpose is, really?"

"Custodio e—," she began to answer, but he interrupted her lifting his index finger and slowly shook his head.

"That's not what I mean, and I'm convinced you know that," he said with that thin smile again, "You're very smart, and you tend to question things and have your own thoughts. This can be a good or bad thing, depending on who you are. For a regular member of our society or an Angel, it can be a bad thing which could lead to serious trouble or even termination one day. You know that as well as I do. However, I want people close to me who are able to think more complexly than most. Who, in a way, resemble me. I want my Archangels to be the best in the corps, and the smartest. They need to understand the big picture. And at the same time, I expect unconditional loyalty and devotion. Do you think you could offer me all of that?"

"I do," she answered, looking him in the eye.

He smirked. "Of course, you say so. Every one of you does. It's up to me to decide who the best candidate really is. Sometimes I'm wrong, and I hate that. Few cases waste a greater amount of resources than sending an Archangel into early retirement. It hurts me every time. But with you, I have a good feeling."

Metatron rose from his chair and walked toward the windows. His slightly androgynous features and slim figure gave him almost an aristocratic air, while his smooth movements were somewhat predatory. Like any other Angel, he was wearing a black uniform, yet his had a different, more elegant cut.

"So, what is our purpose, really?" he asked again, staring at the pyramid, "Why does Olympias spend the effort and immense costs to have us? Research and development, engineering, maintenance; all of this is extremely costly. Not to mention the difficulties in finding suitable candidates, the years of training. A fortune is built into every one of us. You're wearing better hardware inside you than the residents of the Inner Circle, did you know that? Why make such an effort if AI is so much cheaper, easier to maintain. Most of the robotic police and troops' components come straight from the 3D printer, while every single part in us is custom made. Why do they go to such great extents?"

"Because they need us," Nephilim said, "We succeed where AI fails."

Metatron tilted his head toward her, and his eyes narrowed. "And why exactly would that be?"

"Only a human mind can fully understand human behavior, which tends to be irrational or against any logic at times. Only a human uses their mind, instincts, and empathy. AI fails in anticipating human behavior and is, therefore, easily outsmarted. It's a challenge AI developers haven't been able to master so far."

Metatron's lips curled into a grin. "Correct. And they never will. That's why we are indispensable, why Olympias can't function without us. The robotic army they are storing in the vaults below the city and at the rim of our territory is only good to fight other AI armies or keep an uprising under control, in the unlikely event one should ever happen." He paused for a moment to point out the importance of his next sentences, while his blue eyes seemed to glow at her. "They need us to hunt down humans. Only we can do that. No matter if they're terrorists or other subjects who have gone off the path, we will find and kill them. And we are the only ones who can face hostile cyborgs since neither human troops nor machines would stand a chance against them. That's why Olympias will always keep us up, no matter the cost."

He came closer and leaned his back at his desk, facing her. "We are superior. The perfect hybrid of human and machine, with the best of both, combined into one entity. We are the next step in the evolution of mankind. And the time will come when everyone learns that."

BEHIND BLUE EYES

"I understand," she answered, withstanding the urge to turn her eyes away from his gaze. It would have been a sign of weakness, and you never showed weakness to a predator. She knew that all too well because, in many situations, she played the part of the predator herself.

"We will see about that," Metatron said, "However, I have other obligations to attend now. We need to continue another time."

The High-Archangel walked behind her and stroked her neck with his finger in an undoubtedly intimate way, resting his fingertip on her jugular vein for a moment. She didn't flinch, nor would he find her pulse had risen, which could indicate she was excited or intimidated in any way.

"We'll continue tomorrow night at 9:00 PM. Gadreel will give you the address," he said, moving back behind his desk, "Wear something casual."

"As you wish."

"That's all for now. Dismissed."

She got up and walked toward the exit. Nothing about her outwardly showed how relieved she was.

"Oh, Nephilim, one more thing," he said just as she reached the door.

She turned back to him.

"Is this examination technician bothering you in any way? What was his name again..." he paused for a second before continuing, accessing the employee databank through his implant, "Finwick Connors. When I linked into your POV for the examination, I noticed his odd behavior toward you. I will have him removed if you wish."

Nephilim smiled. "Thank you, I appreciate your concern. But it won't be necessary. He's just a little, pathetic human who wishes to believe we play in the same league. If we start removing them for such trivialities, it would simply be an unnecessary waste of resources, wouldn't it?"

A cynical smile appeared on his face. "It certainly would. I'll see you tomorrow."

She left his office, and the examination was finally over. At least for now.

***

Nephilim downed her whiskey and looked out into the night, sunken in thoughts. Her face was reflected in the glass of the window and looked like a shadow floating in the darkness. Though, it never really got dark in Olympias. Myriads of lights shone in the skyscrapers around her, reflected by the endless surfaces of glass and chrome. Below, the multiple levels of streets and transportation lanes were flickering with lights and buzzing with life. And somewhere behind all of this, hidden in the night, were the mountains, Nephilim knew. Even her artificial, superior eyes could not spot them now, but simply knowing that they were there, gave her a feeling of security, and she couldn't say why.

She was sitting in The Velvet, having her third drink, alone. Usually, she liked coming here with Adriel, but not today. He was off to check out some new club, and she needed time for herself, to think and clear her mind. The bar was crowded at this time, and the buzz of voices combined with soft music somehow felt soothing.

Actually, the place had been full, and the robo-hostess was sending people away, but Nephilim came in anyway. The barkeeper flinched and turned pale as if he saw a ghost when he noticed her arriving, then welcomed her with such exaggerated excitement, that it was almost comical. The table at the window she and Adriel usually chose to sit at, had been occupied, but the bartender shooed the patrons away and gave it to his "most valued" guest. Nephilim knew that Adriel would have loved such a show, but for her, it was just a convenience she would acknowledge with a generous tip. Even though she was quite certain that the barkeeper would consider it enough of a tip if she did not kill him on the spot. Sometimes being a walking horror had its advantages.

She sighed inwardly. What a crazy day.

First, there was the examination that came out of the blue. Which she had fucked up infamously. Then this guy, whom she had classified as a total loser, had saved her ass, and she still couldn't figure out why he would do that. And not even one hour later, she had been in the position to return the favor—and she did so without even hesitating for a moment. Was she losing her mind? Lying to Metatron was more than playing with fire. After all, his question, if he should remove Finwick, could have been a trap as well. It was very unlikely that he had noticed the manipulation, but not impossible. The best decision would have been to let him eliminate Finwick; that way, any loose ends would have been tied up forever.

However, her answer had obviously not only saved the technician's life but also pleased Metatron, since she had chosen words from his own repertoire. He wouldn't waste resources for no reason. The strange, little freak with the shaky hands and goggle eyes was safe—at least for now.

That everyone was expendable in the end, and not much more than a resource was nothing new for her. It was one of the core philosophies of Olympias, and Metatron lived it to the letter. What had been interesting to learn, however, was how he saw humans, and that he believed cyborgs were superior; a higher, evolved species. Of course, he was right in a way, for Nephilim and her kind were superior in almost everything. They were feared, hated, viewed with disgust, a necessary evil—abominations. Yet, haven't they been created to protect humans and the society they lived in? Nephilim wondered if the Board knew what Metatron really thought about them and their kind, would they consider him dangerous and remove him?

It was probably the reason why he surrounded himself with Archangels he could trust, who shared his beliefs and were unconditionally devoted to him.

The question was, could Nephilim be one of them?

It was a job almost everyone in the corps wanted because it offered a promotion, more C-Coins, power, a better, more comfortable life. In truth, it was something very different, and Nephilim had learned that today.

She had no idea if she could become one of them. If she wanted to. Especially now, since she was so confused and unfocused. She did not know if she could share his beliefs and show the devotion he wanted to see—but it wasn't the sexual parts she was concerned about. Everyone knew that he had sex with his Archangels exclusively. And that his needs were rather special.

Sex between Angels tended to be rough, and even violent, simply because it was their nature, and they could do things humans couldn't. Yet Metatron's likings were extreme, even in their terms. He was a sadistic, control freak who satisfied his needs as he pleased, sometimes himself, sometimes by watching the Archangels doing it to each other—if only half the stories circulating could be believed to be true. When it came to gossip, Angels were as human as they could be. However, it was said that in time, if they got the chance to reach a certain age, every one of them became that way. It was what a lifetime of causing pain and violence made one become. Metatron was, in a way, the prototype for all of them.

Nephilim was not scared of that part of her potential new job. Sex was just sex. It meant nothing. Like everyone else in Olympias, she had had so much sex with so many different partners in her life, that it bored her most of the time. It was part of human life, like eating or sleeping.

BEHIND BLUE EYES

What concerned her more was that she might not show the necessary devotion in other aspects. What if he noticed that she was saying what he expected her to say? He was as intelligent as he was dangerous and ruthless. She might deceive him once or twice...but in the long term? He made it clear what he would do if he happened to make a mistake and chose the wrong person to be an Archangel.

She could still see the smirk on his face and hear his smug tone; *"Sometimes I'm wrong, and I hate that. Few cases waste a greater amount of resources than sending an Archangel into early retirement. It hurts me every time. But with you, I have a good feeling."*

It was as if someone presented her a poisoned dagger wrapped in silk. Nephilim had never heard a threat expressed more charmingly.

In any case, there was nothing she could do about it. She could not turn down the job, as it was his decision to make. For some reason, she had woken his interest enough that he seriously considered her.

Who would have thought that Adriel was right after all? And Nephilim believed he had just been mocking her. At least now, she could be certain that it wasn't him who set her up for the examination. After her talk with Metatron, it was obvious that it had been him who wanted her tested. It gave Nephilim a feeling of relief. She wanted to trust her partner.

Another drink was put on her table, but when Nephilim looked up, it wasn't the robo-waitress who had brought it, but a stranger.

"Hi," he said, "May I sit?"

He did not wait for an answer but took a seat opposite of her instead. Nephilim was so taken by surprise by his brazenness that she wasn't sure how to react for a moment. She felt irritated, all she wanted was to relax and think in peace.

The stranger was a young man in his early twenties with hair that was dyed purple and slicked back, with matching eyebrows. He was wearing amber colored contact lenses and black liner around his eyes. An expensive-looking implant stuck out of his left temple. Everything about him was outright screaming that he was extremely cocksure of himself. After a brief inspection, Nephilim decided to wait and see what this clown had to say before she sent him to hell. She did not need to wait long since he cut straight to the point.

"My name's Cev," he introduced himself.

Nephilim took a sip of her drink, leaned back, and said nothing.

"So, listen, I've seen you here before. You came here with that tall, white-haired guy. I guessed he was your casual, but since he isn't here now, did he dump you? Or maybe you dumped him?"

Nephilim nipped on her drink again, wondering how it was possible that some people could not read body language at all. Even an AI could guess that she was not interested but repulsed.

"Whatever. You seem lonely to me. And you're pretty, you look so innocent, you know? I think that's hot. So, I thought to myself, a pretty girl shouldn't feel lonely."

"Is that so?"

He moved closer and grinned. Nephilim's scan showed that he was highly intoxicated, alcohol, and three different synthetic substances, of which at least one was illegal. She did not care. She was off duty, and it wasn't her job to bunk in morons for illicit drug abuse. It was her job to kill people.

"How about, we go someplace, and I make you feel better. I can make you scream so loud that you'll forget about the other guy in an instant. I can do that for you."

"Can you?"

Behind Blue Eyes

He smiled slimily, slowly moving his hand toward her thigh. "Oh, baby, I can. And if you want, I can bring some friends. They think you're hot, too."

He nodded to a table not far away, where Nephilim could see some people sitting from the corner of her eye.

"I know just the perfect place, not far from here. It's called The Cave, it's new..."

"I think I know a better place," Nephilim interrupted with a soft voice.

"Whatever you want, baby."

"It's called the grave," she said.

"Oh? Never heard of that one..."

"It's yours, but your friends can come, too."

She grabbed his wandering hand and squeezed it sharply while she lifted her glasses with her other hand. Cev flinched back as if bitten by a tarantula, and suddenly seemed to shrink while he stared into Nephilim's eyes, all his cockiness gone.

She winked at him. "Rather not? Then I suggest you go back to your friends and rework your pick-up techniques. They're almost as pathetic as you are."

She let go of his hand, leaving clearly visible bruises where she had grabbed him. He ran off toward his friends as if all seven hells were after him.

Nephilim put her glasses back on and rolled her eyes. What an unbelievable idiot. Maybe Metatron was right about humans, after all.

She finished her drink and got up. It was time to go home, she had enough for one day. She briefly lifted her hand toward the barkeeper on the way out, whose pacemaker had a hard time keeping his heart going at a stable rate, left a generous tip, and exited The Velvet.

But, as it turned out, the day wasn't done with her yet. The parking deck was empty when she walked to her motorcycle, though not for long. Her scan showed them even before she heard their footsteps. It was almost impossible to sneak up on a cyborg, and these guys did a terrible job of it. She almost had reached her machine before she turned around to face them. It was Cev, who had followed her. And he had brought his five friends. They all seemed to be not much older than twenty, were drunk, high, and felt invincible.

"Seriously?" Nephilim said, irritated, seeing how they spread out toward her and tried to look threatening, "Are you fucking kidding me?"

Of course, a situation like this would have been indeed threatening for a normal woman—or man. But for an Angel, this was a mere joke.

"If you feel suicidal, go and jump off a roof. It will be quicker and less painful that way, I promise you that," she added.

"You think you're so special, huh?" Cev answered with blatant aggression in his voice, "With your blue eyes and fake limbs. You think you can do anything you like!"

She shrugged. "Actually, I can do anything I like with any you. I can kill you quickly or break every single bone in your bodies, and no one will care. But I'm willing to forget about what happened if you're good boys. So turn around, go home, and sober up."

That infuriated him even more. He pulled a gun out of his pocket and pointed it at her. Two of his friends followed his example. The other three produced telescopic batons and a knife. Nephilim sighed inwardly. These punks either had an unconscious death wish or had sent their brains into a frenzy with all the unauthorized drugs. However, possession of firearms was highly illegal in Olympias, and she had to inform the AI police about this incident, anyway. No matter how hard the penalty, there was always and would be a persistent black market for guns—and wannabe gangsters like these, who were willing to purchase and use them.

"Ha!" Cev laughed. "You didn't expect that, huh? Now don't move, or we riddle your sweet face with bullets. They say your heads are your weak points, it's where you can be killed like anyone else! Your head and your pussy are still human. We're gonna check out if that's true. We fuck you first, then splatter your brains all over the place!"

He laughed even more, obviously greatly pleased with himself. The others joined him while moving closer.

"I'm shaking in my boots now," Nephilim said, "This is your last chance. Drop your weapons, and I'll spare you."

Maybe. She wasn't really sure yet. This guy annoyed her—a lot. The others, however, just seemed to be stupid, drugged-up kids. But why was she even thinking about this? Usually, she would just have killed them all without even giving it a second thought. She had every right to do so. Metatron was right, humans were scum. So, what was there to even consider? She could draw her guns, which were hidden under her black leather jacket, and shoot all of them in the head quicker than any of them would even pull the trigger. End of story. Then she could go home and call it a day.

"No!" Cev yelled, "You drop yours, bitch! You're outnumbered six to one, what're you gonna do?"

"Kill you all, for a start?" she said while her brain did the math.

Cev opened his mouth for some more vulgarities, but never got the chance.

Like an attacking snake, Nephilim rushed forward. With inhuman speed, she grabbed the guy closest to her on the left, who was holding a gun. His arm shattered at the elbow and shoulder, making a horrible sound as she yanked and crushed it at the same time, simultaneously slamming her foot against his shin, which almost split in half due to the immense impact. The youth only had time to let out a brief shriek before his eyes rolled back and he passed out. Nephilim already had moved on to the one standing next to him. It all happened so incredibly fast in human terms that the guy barely had the chance to lift the telescopic baton he was holding. Nephilim grabbed his hand and rammed his own rod against his chin, smashing it into red pulp and bone fragments.

Her combat HUD, which had automatically sprang into action, indicated potential danger from the right. Cev pointed his gun at her, his finger on the trigger, his eyes wide with hate and fury. Nephilim reached out and pulled another attacker armed with baton and knife toward her with a sharp yank.

The move was so violent that she heard his fifth lumbar vertebra break, but that would be the least of his concerns. A shot was fired and hit the young man—whom she was now using as a human shield—directly in the chest. A fine spray of blood hit Cev and the other two in the faces as the victim, their friend, screamed in agony. Nephilim let the man fall to the cement like a wet sack and jumped the next, whose arms and legs she broke in less than a second.

A cold grin appeared on her face when she noticed that Cev and his last remaining friend were now running for their lives toward the exit. He fired one more shot in her direction without looking, but it went so far off target that she didn't even bother to give it any thought. One jump and she reached Cev's fleeing friend, who screamed in panic like a little girl. She kicked his legs, tripping him up. Once on the pavement, she stomped on his back and made sure he wouldn't get up again. Then she caught up with Cev, who had almost made it to the exit.

BEHIND BLUE EYES

She grabbed the hand holding the gun and squeezed it so hard that his bones broke, and he had to let go of it with a scream, while she simultaneously swirled him around toward her, almost like a dancer.

"Hi there, Cev," she said, putting her hand on his neck, clutching it until the point that he could still breathe, but barely.

"You know, it would take me zero-point-two percent of my muscular capacity to crush your trachea and watch you suffocate. Or," she moved her other hand toward his face and slowly produced the blade out of her wrist. His eyes widened so much that they almost appeared to fall out of their sockets as he watched the razor-sharp titanium blade coming closer. "I could pick out your eyes, open your skull and check if there's a brain inside. Because I'm not sure that you have one."

He tried to say something, but all that came out was a helpless rattle. Nephilim smelled urine and knew that he had pissed himself.

"But you know what, I'll let you live and learn the lesson to never bother a woman again in all your life. Because death is by far not the worst that can happen to you. And blue eyes see everything. However, AI police are inbound. You and your friends will get at least twenty, maybe twenty-five years of forced labor for possession of firearms, illegal substances and not to forget, attack on a public servant of Olympias. After that, hopefully, you'll learn how to properly walk up to a lady—if you're ever able to walk upright again."

Saying this, she moved her blade down his legs and cut through his calf muscles down to his Achilles. He tried to scream, or simply gasp for air, but couldn't due to her firm grasp on his neck, so he simply turned white as a sheet and passed out.

Nephilim saw the flashing lights of the AI police arriving, which she had called over the grid before the brawl had started.

"So long, Cev," she said, dropping the motionless body and turning around, then walked back toward her motorcycle. The AI would take care of everything else. There was nothing more for her to do, so it was finally time to go home. What a crazy day.

Chapter Five

Hunters

"You're shitting me, right?" Adriel laughed out loud. "I don't believe a word you're saying!"

Nephilim chuckled. "I swear, it's true. Everything happened exactly as I told you."

They both had some quick Protein Dogs for lunch and now walked along a spacious green area while Nephilim described yesterday's encounter to her partner. The park was on the ground level between a couple high-rises and adjoined to Prosperity Plaza—a vital hub for business and entertainment. It looked pretty with its flower beds and fountains. Some art installations were displayed at its center. The pieces had been chosen in a competition among art students from the most renowned art schools of

Olympias. The theme had been: *The Perfect Life*.

There was even a fake waterfall, dropping down from the cyclist transportation level directly over the park. Above that, soared the other three levels: for public transport, cabs and private vehicles, and finally, the Deathway. A slight buzz could be heard from there, and looking up from the ground, they almost appeared like overlapping veins connecting different parts of a gigantic organism. The waterfall was illuminated with indigo and emerald-colored beams. It was a bright, sunny day, yet sunlight rarely made it down to the lowest level through the maze of skyscrapers and multiple layers of transportation. So the urban planners had come up with other ideas to brighten up the otherwise dull street canyons.

Adriel shook his head. "Unfuckingbelievable. And I thought everyone had learned by now that messing with us is never a good idea. These guys must have been dumb as bread."

"Dumber, if you ask me."

"So, why didn't you just kill them?

An excellent question. One Nephilim had been asking herself for many hours last night.

She shrugged. "I wanted to teach them a lesson. Besides, I was in a playful mood."

That was what she had been telling herself. But was it really true?

"I'm sorry, I wasn't there to protect you from those savages," Adriel said with fake remorse.

It made Nephilim laugh. "Perhaps it's *you* who needs a lesson?"

"I would love that."

"I bet you would."

Behind Blue Eyes

Even though they were dressed in plain clothes, they weren't here for leisure, but on duty. If there wasn't anything big going on, the Angels were usually dispatched throughout the city; watching, observing, profiling, all while pretending to be normal citizens. While Nephilim and Adriel discussed their latest adventures, mocking each other and having fun, all their sensors were continuously on the lookout for unusual incidents or behavior. They scanned facial features of passersby, who otherwise went unnoticed by regular surveillance, the integrated software, giving them the ability to read from lips even when the target was at quite a distance, and probably felt safe. Their enhanced ears, making it possible to eavesdrop on conversations being whispered up to three-hundred feet away.

All this had proven extremely effective. Insubordination, and doubts in the system; these often began in typical, daily-life situations, in public places where people felt safe in the crowds, where it was easier to share thoughts that were usually well hidden. But this wasn't all. Sometimes the Angels helped to prevent crime or catch criminals, who otherwise slipped through the grid and moved in the shadows. If necessary, they could step into action anytime in ways beyond what was possible for regular law enforcement. However, the main focus for the Angels was, of course, the detection of hostile cyborg activity. The enemy, too, liked to blend in.

Ninety percent of the security and police work was done by AI police. It was the cheapest and most efficient way to provide safety and security for Olympias and its citizens. The AI police managed almost everything from traffic control to arrests, countless numbers patrolled the streets of Olympias to give the people a sense of security. It was one of the reasons why the crime rates were low for a metropolis of this size.

Besides the artificial officers, there were still some human police, but it was a relatively small force. They were mostly detectives who worked in homicide, narcotics, forensics, or detention of firearms. A well-staffed department was assigned to CCTV and prevention of unruly activities. Although the majority of citizens were convinced that Olympias provided the best living conditions in human history and believed themselves lucky to be part of it, there always remained a minority of subjects, who were dedicated to the destruction of it. A part of human nature, as Nephilim and all other Angels learned during their training, ugly and dangerous as cancer used to be before it was ultimately cured. And the same was the goal for unruly subjects—to cut out the disease they spread.

The majority of citizens did not mind that they were always being watched, and many didn't care. They were way too busy with themselves. When Nephilim and Adriel walked through the park, hardly anyone paid them any attention. Most people were hurrying somewhere. Life was keeping them occupied with jobs, endless possibilities of recreation, the need to perpetually improve oneself, becoming and staying beautiful, social activities, and obligations. It was a constant race against time—since it was always short—and there was so much to do, to explore, to be. Why would anyone want to pause even for one moment? There was no time to think.

Many people walking by seemed to be speaking with thin air, because the majority of them had implants in their ears, which made any other device obsolete. Another popular implant was often found on the temple. The standard models could provide grid access, or project virtual "glasses" in front of the wearer's eyes, which enabled access into the VR anytime anywhere—on a limited basis, of course, since the sophisticated environments needed special consoles and direct neural plug-ins. But it was enough for a quick social game, status update, or rush through the news. Plenty of people sat on benches using their mobile VR access during their lunch breaks. The pricier ones came with cognitive enhancements, as well as everything else.

Every implant manufactured by the Olympias Conglomerate or one of its specialized subsidiary companies was designed to also function as a tracking device. And since tech from one of the other two mega corporations was strictly banned and illegal, anyone who wanted implants—which was basically everyone—was traceable everywhere, at any time. Most people didn't know about this fact, however, and if they did, it didn't bother them. After all, there was nothing to worry about as long as one was a law-abiding citizen.

An AI police patrol passed by Nephilim and Adriel as they were about to leave the park and head toward Prosperity Plaza. Naturally, the robots could scan what they were and detect that they were armed, but they were programmed not to interfere with Angels, ever.

There were various AI police models for different jobs. Some were bipedal, while others had four legs and were reminiscent of centaurs. The ones used in traffic control mostly had wheels instead of legs. There were also artificial K9 units.

A large number of AI stayed invisible to most people: the drones. Thousands of them patrolled over Olympias in various shapes and sizes, and for all different purposes. The smallest was sparrow-sized and had been built to infiltrate and monitor. Almost noiseless, they could come very close to their target without being noticed. The most common ones were the size of a small eagle and circled at great heights, higher than the tallest buildings in Olympias. Yet their integrated cameras were so precise that they could take a picture of the fingernails of someone on the ground—down to the color of the nail polish they wore, as clear as if they were right next to the person. The biggest drones were almost like smaller, unmanned jets; fast and agile, and armed to the teeth.

The ground AI police were designed to look artificial and only slightly resembled humans or dogs. It had been a deliberate decision to make them look this way, specifically. Studies showed that humans preferred AI if they clearly resembled robots rather than being too humanlike. The phenomenon was known as the "uncanny valley"; the more natural and humanlike machines became, the scarier they appeared. And the leaders of Olympias wanted people to feel secure around their police. The same went for all kinds of robots used for primitive work such as cleaning, waste disposal, or housework. The only machines which were built as humanlike as possible were sexbots. Obviously, the uncanny valley wasn't a concern when it came to fucking. High-class sexbots could be purchased for private needs, yet were very expensive, everyone else who preferred synthetic flesh could visit one of the countless clubs offering it.

"So," Nephilim said after they walked in silence for a while, "How was your night?"

Adriel made a movement with his head that indicated he rolled his eyes, which remained unseen due to his dark shades. "Don't ask."

Nephilim grinned. "Now, you woke my interest. I'm all ears."

"OK, so I went to check out that new club they have been advertising so much lately. It's so hot that it took me one week on the waiting list until I finally got in, can you believe that? Anyways, it's called 'Game,' and that's basically what it's about. When you enter, you have to decide what you want to be for the night: hunter or game. There are men and women on both sides."

"Let me guess; you chose to be game," Nephilim added in.

Adriel stopped his report for a moment and gave her a sideways look, then continued, "You get a pin that projects a holo symbol above your head showing what you are, green for game and red for hunter. Then you enter a big maze, and they wish you happy hunting. Hunters have the choice of whoever they want to hunt; men or women. Game don't get options."

"What happens if you catch one?"

"You can do with them whatever you like."

"Sounds kinky. So, what happened?"

"It took me maybe twenty seconds to catch some guy...I would have caught any of them blindfolded and jumping on one leg."

"A hilarious sight, to be sure. What else did you expect?"

Adriel sighed. "No idea. Perhaps a slight hint of a challenge?"

"Did you show them who you are?"

He laughed. "Hell no. I didn't want them to run screaming in panic. But maybe I should have."

"What happened next?"

"I see, I won't get away without details. The guy looked at me with big eyes, and he said..." he mimicked a high-pitched voice, "*'Oh no, you caught me! Please, don't hurt me...I'll do whatever you want...*'" Nephilim chuckled while Adriel continued, "And one minute later he was all, *'oh yes, yes! Take me, have your way with me!*'"

Nephilim chuckled more.

"It was embarrassing," Adriel said, "At least I now know I'm not into role-playing games."

"Did you let him go then?"

"Of course not. He was kinda hot, and the entrance fee cost me a shitload of money. You can fuck your game right on the spot in the maze if you like or take them to one of the side rooms and chambers, which are equipped with all kinds of fancy torture stuff. So, I dragged him to one of these rooms and had my way with him there. Wasn't that bad, after all."

"But you won't go there again?"

He slowly shook his head. "That sort of place is not for us, Neph. It's for spoiled kids seeking excitement. We're real hunters."

"That's true. We don't rape people, though."

It was one of the core rules the Angels had. No matter how bloody their business got, rape was and has always been out of the question. Metatron showed zero tolerance for anyone who broke that rule, and punishment was severe. The reason for his severity was simple: they were the Guardian Angels of Olympias, not some barbarians. What they did was just and right, always.

Adriel laughed. "If that was rape, then I'm a virgin. This little deviant had the time of his life, you should've seen his face."

Nephilim grinned. "Humans always wonder how much stamina we have."

They had reached Prosperity Plaza. Right at its corner, flanking the park, was a massive Recreational Substances Store, or RSS. It was one of the two Olympias authorized chains for the manufacturing and distribution of recreational narcotics—natural grown, as well as a variety of synthetic ones. RSS's latest product was advertised and displayed everywhere. It was called Heaven, and it promised to offer you exactly what the name meant; to send you straight to heaven. Only for six hours, however, after that, the effect would fade away, and you would be ready to go back to work. Nephilim inspected the ad with curiosity. Maybe she should try the new product sometime. After all, wasn't heaven the place Angels belonged?

Directly next to the RSS, an enormous moving holograph advertised what was in the huge building next door to it; Olympias' best rehab clinic, specializing in detoxification of synthetic substances. "We bring you back to your feet, and to one-hundred percent effectivity within five days—without fail!" it said, "Come in and check out our special, seasonal offers now!"

Just because the use of a variety of drugs was legal in Olympias didn't mean one couldn't get addicted to them. Everyone was self-responsible. Besides, rehab was the second lucrative medical field after plastic surgery.

"So, you're the one getting laid tonight for a change, huh?" Adriel said after a moment had passed.

"Seems so."

Her examination and visit to Metatron's office were the first things she told Adriel about this morning. She had only briefly described what she and Metatron had talked about; that he was considering her to become his new Archangel. She was convinced that she wasn't supposed to reveal any details, although the High-Archangel never mentioned that anything he said was confidential. He made it clear that he wanted people he can trust, and if she told details to her partner, she would clearly prove that she was anything but trustworthy.

She also didn't tell Adriel any details about the examination. About the questions that had been asked and that she had fucked up and was only alive thanks to a guy she hardly knew. One of the reasons she had failed the test was that she wasn't willing to kill Adriel, no matter who gave her the command and why. It only could mean that she was much more emotionally attached to him than she had been aware of. She didn't just enjoy spending time with him and trusted him to have her back in battle—he was her friend, the only one she ever had.

The question was, did he feel the same? Or would he draw his gun and shoot her in the head without hesitation if Metatron told him to do so. She would never know.

Right now, however, he seemed to be excited for her and believed she would get the promotion. Even though it was something he was dreaming of, himself.

"Come on, Neph," he said with a grin, "He invited you to his home. Why would he do that? To discuss books with you? I say someone is going to get laid big time."

He paused for a moment, then continued in a serious tone, "I'm happy for you. In my opinion, they won't find a better Archangel than you, and I'm sure Metatron knows that as well. You are, by far, the best partner I've ever had."

Nephilim turned her head to face him. She saw honest cordiality in his face, admiration even. Adriel seemed to mean what he said, and it touched her. Maybe he, too, saw her as a friend. If he knew what she was really thinking, how she had been struggling with herself lately, how she had failed the examination miserably, would he still feel the same about her?

"Thanks, Adriel," she said, "I enjoy—"

They were interrupted as they both heard an alarm signal in their heads, followed by a voice.

"Field unit Beta forty-two, Adriel, Nephilim. Do you copy?"

"Copy," they both answered, non-vocally, through the comm.

"We have suspicious activity reported in the Oldtown district. You are the closest unit. Sending you the coordinates now. Investigate at once."

"Copy that," Adriel said, "We're on our way." Then he turned to Nephilim. "Sounds like fun. Let's go."

***

Less than fifteen minutes later, they left the Deathway and rode down to the ground level of the Oldtown district on their motorcycles. The region was nothing else but the former downtown area of Atlanta, which had become part of the Olympias City I megapolis after the beginning of the new era. Most of the city—and any other, since Olympias I spread over many former metropolitan areas—had been leveled and rebuilt over the years, to suit the changing needs of modern society. The transportation and road network had been completely redesigned, and new architecture was not only much taller than the high-rises of the old days to house a more substantial amount of people and businesses. They were also much more sophisticated in style, and produced their own energy, for every glass surface doubled as a solar panel.

Downtown Atlanta, however, had been considered sufficient back in the day and was left standing. Entering the district always felt like traveling back in time to a bygone era, buried in the fogs of oblivion. The high-rises here appeared small compared to the rest of the city, brittle even. Although the buildings had been modernized from the inside, the whole area had an antiquated feel about it. It was no wonder that over time, living here became less and less attractive. Meanwhile, the district had become the shabbiest of all in Olympias City I, and it was mostly inhabited by people on the lower scales of success. Oldtown wasn't really a slum—for true poverty did not exist in Olympias—but the people living here weren't willing or able to fully participate in society or benefit from it.

Many small businesses were run in this part of the city, some semi-legal, but as long as no one broke any major rule or tried to question the system as a whole, the administration did not see the need to demolish Oldtown. The Angels had been taught that it was human nature to always produce outcasts in their midst, no matter how perfect the conditions. It was something the Board was aware of, too. The best way to deal with this phenomenon was to give these people a place to exist in a controlled environment. Of course, surveillance in Oldtown was as thorough as everywhere else, even though the inhabitants believed otherwise. If they were considered dangerous in any way, or there was any hint they could become so, people tended to disappear, never to be seen again. Oldtown was a place Nephilim and her people visited quite often—and when they did, it was rarely just to investigate, but rather to eliminate.

"What a shithole," Adriel said as they rolled down the main street of the district. He always said so when they came here.

The ground level wasn't as organized as the rest of the city but had mostly been left as it was in the old times. The streets were poorly maintained and being used by pedestrians, cyclists, and vehicles; the latter, of course, a rare sight. Public transportation rushed by, high above the ground, with only a few stops in the district.

They reached the coordinates they had been given and stopped.

"I will never understand why people choose to live here," Adriel continued, looking around as they descended. They could leave their motorcycles behind without worrying. The machines were coded to their DNA and could not be operated by anyone else. If someone tried to mess with them, they would become acquainted with a shock of high voltage. "Don't they have any motivation in life, any pride?"

Nephilim shrugged. "It definitely would not be for me."

They took off their glasses and slowly walked toward their destination.

It wasn't necessary to blend in here. They came to investigate, and therefore could openly show who they were. Besides, it was more difficult to deceive the people here than in the rest of the city. Oldtown residents weren't as busy with themselves as most, and figures like Nephilim and Adriel stood out there, anyway. They were too well dressed, too smooth, too perfect to be living in this area. Many people who lived in Oldtown had had experiences with the Guardian Angels, had seen them in action, or heard stories about them. There wasn't a place in Olympias where they were more feared or hated than here.

It didn't take long before they were confronted with glances from those passing by that ranged from horrified to outright hostile. Yet no one dared to step in their way, talk to them, or look them straight in the eyes.

Although they did not show it, Nephilim and Adriel were highly focused, their minds concentrated, and all systems on alert. In their unit's internal terms, "suspicious activity" did not mean just anything. It meant that an AI patrol had scanned the traces of unauthorized tech. In such cases, the robot had the order to stand down and report to the Angels directly.

Unauthorized tech was defined as any hardware which had been manufactured by one of the other two corporations. It was highly illegal to trade or use it in Olympias, but of course, there was a black market for smaller parts, which were smuggled in and used by criminals. A trace of such intensity like the one recorded by the AI today, however, could only mean a large number of active implants.

It could still be nothing to be overly concerned about—a criminal who thought he could get away with illegal augmentations, a careless dealer hoarding too many parts, or even an incorrect reading by the AI police. But if not, there was only one other explanation: a hostile cyborg.

The precise position of the coordinates was inside an underground facility. The AI had patrolled up and down the street and caught the trace from deep below. Nephilim and Adriel entered the compound down the stairs which led into a large underground tube. The structure used to be a shopping center in the pre-corporation era and had an unbelievably antiquated ambiance since it had not changed much ever since. Walking down here almost felt like time-traveling a century and a half into the past. The dark red brick walls and brass pillars gave the place a gloomy, mysterious atmosphere, which was only disturbed by numerous neon signs and 3D posters advertising the businesses occupying the former clothing and souvenir stores. The Underground, which the slowly rotting place was still called, was Oldtown's tech hub. Countless dealers for used or flawed augmentations and spare parts had opened their businesses here; there were shops that specialized in repairing synthetic limbs, shops with augmentation software upgrades while also offering neural port implantation and maintenance, VR consoles, and software vendors, and a brothel with outdated sexbots.

Besides the huge main tunnel, the facility had a wing on either side, two lower levels, and a food court in its center, which served rather low-quality protein dishes and cheap booze. The place was crawling with people; everyone who could not afford the regular or high-quality stuff came here. A lot of the vendors were semi-legal or sold products of abysmal quality, yet Olympias let it flow. As long as the ongoings only hurt the people that chose to participate, and was no threat otherwise, authorities turned a blind eye.

People respectfully made room in the crowd when they saw the neon-blue eyes approaching in the subdued light of the tube. Some vendors gave horrified looks and sighed in relief when the two cyborgs passed by ignoring them. Nephilim and Adriel aimed straight toward a small store in the rear half of the tube. It was where the coordinates led them.

**

Bhanu's heart skipped a beat when he saw them coming. Their blue eyes were shimmering down the underground tunnel toward the glass front of his little shop, like a bad omen. Somehow, he had known this would happen. When he woke up that morning, there had been this itching in the back of his head, an indescribable fear, a premonition this was the last sunrise he would ever see. Of course, he had pushed this feeling aside. Stupid superstition, why would he believe in such things?

But now he felt he should have listened to his intuition.

Why, why in heaven's name did he take the job?

He knew why. A lot of money. More money than he would make in a year.

Of course, he had known it was wrong, illegal, dangerous. But he

BEHIND BLUE EYES

never thought they would catch him. After all, he was the best.

Karma. It had to be. Fucking Karma always got you; you could never hide from it. Karma was a bitch. His grandmother always said so. Well, not in those words, of course.

Why so quickly? Couldn't Karma at least give him a bit of time to actually spend the money he had earned? Instead, it hit him less than thirty minutes later. It wasn't fair.

His heart pounded like crazy as he watched them approach, a man and a woman. With their horrifying eyes, black clothes, and dull faces, they didn't look like humans, but demons. *Rakshasa*, from the depths of hell, coming for him.

For a moment, he almost thought they would pass him. Maybe they weren't there for him, after all. Maybe it was just a coincidence.

It seemed to him as if everything moved in slow motion as he watched them coming closer, holding his breath. Then they turned and walked straight toward his shop.

Panic grabbed his heart like an ice-cold claw. But then he forced himself to act. He only had a few seconds if he wanted a chance of survival. Quicker than ever in his life before, his hands flew over his keyboard, then pressed a button. He just needed to stall them for a few minutes, then all proof should be erased. And if everything went sideways he still had his little life insurance right in front of his counter. He wasn't utterly helpless; he had been preparing himself for something like this for a long time.

Bhanu's gaze fell on the little Ganesh statuette standing next to his computer. It had been his grandmother's, his lucky charm since childhood, and—like any religious symbol—illegal to own in Olympias. It stood in a position where his customers could not spot it, but these weren't ordinary customers. He quickly grabbed it and hid it in his pocket right before the two Angels of Death entered his business.

"Good afternoon," the man said with a smile that made Bhanu's skin cringe.

"Hi, how can I help you?" he answered as casually as possible.

The man locked his eerie blue eyes at his face, and Bhanu knew that he was scanning him, running his features through his database. The woman meanwhile didn't give him much attention but started inspecting his shop and his goods on display.

Bhanu ran a store for used limb augmentations. A variety of different models of arms and legs were spread around the shelves of his store. Some looked astonishingly real, others were basic metal models. He had arms and hands designed for various specialized functions that human hands couldn't do because they weren't strong or precise enough.

However, all of this was just a disguise. In truth, Bhanu made most of his money as a hacker, and he was an excellent one. In the back of his store stood a machine powerful enough to hack into high-security systems, and he also had a customized implant on his temple, which helped him to use the VR for his endeavors. Whatever data his clients required, he was able to deliver. Usually within twenty-four hours. He had been doing this for several years now and never got caught, never triggered an alarm system somewhere. It was unexplainable to him why the two demons had found him just now.

"Bhanu Chopra," the male cyborg said after a few seconds, "We are looking for the customer who visited you twenty-five minutes ago."

Bhanu's fingers cramped around the Ganesh statuette in his pocket. They were here for *them*. Not even because he had made a mistake. He would go down because of *them*!

He knew he shouldn't have taken the job! He knew there was something wrong about them the instant they had entered his store.

BEHIND BLUE EYES

It had been yesterday. They were two women. One was absolutely ordinary, a woman in her forties, from the look of her, a resident of the Oldtown district, yet without visible implants or augmentations. He had noticed that because people like her normally wore ugly implants of low quality. The other woman, however...

She was pretty, beautiful even. Her skin was brown, and her features indicated that she was of Indian origins, like himself. Her slim yet athletic body was dressed in clothes that looked ordinary at first glance, but consisted of fabrics of the highest quality when inspected closer. She moved with an elegance and agility Bhanu only had seen on gymnasts or acrobats before. She smiled but her face remained strangely cold, her eyes hidden behind dark sunglasses.

Bhanu was fascinated, but at the same time, his intuition warned him not to get involved with his visitors. Especially after they told him what the job was and what kind of information they wanted him to acquire.

But the money...it was so much money. Bhanu had a daughter he had to provide for. She was a natural child, not engineered or enhanced like almost all other children nowadays. Back then, he had been foolish enough not to want the perfect child but just her. Now her life was so much harder and more difficult than everyone else's. He needed the money to grant her a good future.

So, he had taken the job. Today, just twenty-five minutes ago, they had come back. Of course, he had the promised data, he never failed. As promised, they had brought the money.

"Twenty-five minutes ago?" he asked, scratching his head, "Phew, I'm not sure I remember. Today has been a busy day. I had many customers coming and going. Perhaps you can specify..."

"You're lying," the woman said, turning toward him, her artificial eyes piercing him, "Your voice pitch is unnatural, your heart rate has risen, pupils are widened, your palms are sweating. What are you hiding in your pocket?"

"N-nothing," he stammered, "Just a piece of carved wood."

"Carved wood," the man said with a grin, "Of course. I ask you again: Who was here twenty-five minutes ago? What did that person want from you?"

Bhanu felt panic overwhelming him. They would probably kill him if he didn't tell them. But they would for sure kill him if he told them. He only had one chance.

"My scan shows huge amounts of data are being deleted nearby," the woman said to her partner.

Now or never. Bhanu pushed the button. Two seconds was all he needed for the system to fire up. But he didn't anticipate that the blue-eyed killers were prepared for such types of attacks.

Everything happened so incredibly fast that it was difficult for Bhanu's eyes to follow.

The woman froze in her movement, yelling, "EMP!"

Then both cyborgs threw themselves to the floor, projecting an energy barrier around them that Bhanu had never seen before and thought technically impossible, until now. In the same instant, his own "life insurance" fired up and completely filled the front part of his store with heavy electromagnetic pulses—which should have fried his attackers, or at least immobilized them for a few minutes.

Nothing like that happened. With horror in his eyes, the hacker watched how the energy impulses were repelled by the shimmering shields, leaving the cyborgs hunkering inside, unharmed.

The EMP would only last for five seconds until its energy resources ran dry, so there was only one more thing he could do now: run for his life.

He turned around and fled to the back room, shutting the door behind him. It locked automatically, and although it was a reinforced security door, it would most likely not hold them off for long. His heart was racing when he crossed the small back area, which had been the center of his life for so long. High-capacity servers piled up in racks, three customized computers, two huge holo screens and an ordinary-sized one, state-of-the-art VR equipment, and cables and cords everywhere—seemingly endless lines of them. There was a 3D-photo of his little girl pinned up at his workspace. For a second, he considered stopping to grab it but kept running instead. Bhanu stumbled, and almost fell into his own rat's nest, then he was at the back door. He closed it after him. This door was made of reinforced steel, but he feared it would only slow them down for seconds, if at all. By now, the EMP probably had subsided, and they were after him.

Panic threatened to overwhelm him for a moment. Where should he go? How should he escape two killer cyborgs chasing him? They would hunt him down like an animal.

Then he heard them moving inside his store and started running as if Kali herself chased him.

Bhanu knew he could never outrun them, his only chance was to lose them in the crowd and maze-like structures of the many little shops and stalls. The hacker rushed down the narrow path leading behind the backsides of the stores, then turned into a small side alley that was used for deliveries. He heard them crashing through the door and picked up his pace. After one-hundred feet, he reached the main tunnel. Without daring to look back, he dove into the crowd of shoppers, which were numerous this time of day. Quickly, he pushed through them, ignoring the complaints and swears when he bumped into someone or stepped on someone's toes, his heart pounding.

He reached the food court. Delicious scents entered his nostrils and made his stomach rumble as he rushed through the tables, accidentally knocking someone's food to the floor. He barely noticed the owner of the plate jumping up and swearing to kick him in the balls, which was downright laughable compared to what the two *Rakshasa* would do if they caught him. However, there was hope; he had an idea. After all, he knew the place like the back of his hand.

Behind the food court was a small corridor leading toward stairs that led up to a former parking deck. At the end of the corridor, Bhanu dared to take a glimpse over his shoulder. He was sure that he would see neon-blue eyes directly behind him, cold hands grabbing for him. But there was no one to be seen.

Did he lose them? He did not dare to hope, not yet. They were famous for tracking people down. Maybe he had hit them with the electromagnetic pulse, at least a bit?

He raced up the stairs, all the way to the fifth floor, his sides burning and his heart pounding as if it might jump out of his chest at any second. It was a bright day, and the sun blinded him for a moment as he pushed open the door and entered the upper floor of the parking deck, which was now used for storage. Empty. No black-clad figures were waiting for him.

If he made it over the roof deck, he could slip into the adjacent building on the other side. From there, he would reach a ramp leading to the public transport area. If he could just board one of the sky trains heading to another district, they would lose track of him.

Bhanu concentrated all his remaining strength and ignored the horrible stitches in his side. He started running again, as fast as he could. He did not make it far.

A black figure jumped down in front of him, literally from the sky, cutting off his path. Bhanu stopped short. It was the female cyborg. She had used a drone to ambush him from the air.

BEHIND BLUE EYES

"Hi there," she said, her artificial eyes glowing.

Bhanu let out a shriek of despair, turned around, and tried running back to where he came from. But the door to the roof deck was kicked off its hinges, and the man stepped through, a sharkish grin on his face.

He didn't seem tired at all, while Bhanu felt like collapsing any second. His hunter was apparently having a good time.

"What do we have here?" the man said, "You left without even saying Goodbye. Not very polite if you ask me."

Bhanu sank to his knees, completely exhausted, close to fainting. His panic had turned into absolute despair. It was over.

"Please," he cried out, "Don't hurt me! I do whatever you want! I'll tell you everything."

"Relax," the woman said with a friendly tone, approaching him, "We won't hurt you. Tell us who visited your store."

"Two women," he said weakly, "I don't know them...I just did a job for them."

"You're a hacker," the man said, "Got some fancy stuff in your backroom. What exactly did they ask you to do?"

Bhanu cramped his hand around the statuette in his pocket again. Would they kill him on the spot if he told them? What should he do?

"I...I...didn't want to do it! They made me do it! I swear!"

The woman was very close now. "What was it?"

The man drew a gun that had been hidden under his coat. "You better start talking now, Bhanu..."

Bhanu opened his mouth but never got the chance to answer. His head exploded into a cloud of red mist, brain tissue, and bone shards.

***

"What the fuck?" Nephilim swore, watching Bhanu's lifeless body collapsing.

Someone had just sniped their only lead in a very suspicious case.

"Take cover!" Adriel yelled, and they both dove behind storage containers, which were set up on the roof deck. They made cover just in time as the shooter opened fire on them in a barrage salvo. High caliber ammunition riddled the old metal they were crouching behind. "We're sitting ducks up here. Do you see where the shooter is?"

"Negative." Nephilim quickly changed her position before her cover was destroyed by another salvo. "Opposite building several stories above us, I'd guess. Hold on!"

Her drone was still floating over the platform, far enough away that it had obviously stayed unnoticed by the attackers. Nephilim always had it stored below the seat of her motorcycle when she went on city patrol and had summoned it to chase down the hacker. It was a common tactic the Angels used when tracking a fugitive: one cyborg followed their prey directly, and the other tried to cut him off, preferably from the air.

She looked through the eyes of her drone, scanning the surroundings. Opposite of the deck they took cover at was an abandoned, old-fashioned high-rise. Only a few seconds later, the drone's HUD located an open window on the tenth floor a bit to the east of their position. A mounted, high-caliber HMG aimed at them from there. A little red light was blinking on the barrel.

Carefully, Nephilim moved her gun to the rim of her cover, and the HMG immediately started firing in their direction again.

"Got it," she told Adriel, "Seems to be motion activated."

"Son of a bitch," he said, "Can you take it out?"

"Do something to keep it busy and give me a sec."

"Copy that."

She grinned. "But keep your pretty head down. Would be a shame."

He answered by flipping her off.

She ignored it. "OK, go."

He threw a piece of debris in the direction of Bhanu's corpse, which was slowly being surrounded by a puddle of blood. The HMG started shooting. Adriel left his cover and jumped toward another container, rolling behind it, a storm of bullets following in his wake. The automated gun was so fast that an average human would never have stood a chance.

This was what Nephilim had been waiting for. With high speed, she maneuvered her drone to the window with the HMG. The weapon's sensors were busy chasing Adriel and didn't notice the silent flying predator closing in. An instant before Nephilim's drone arrived at the window, the sensors scanned the threat, and the barrel moved in its direction, but it was too late. While approaching, the drone shot a high-voltage charge at the machine, stunning it. Then it grabbed the barrel with its insect-like claws and twisted it with such force that it became deformed, effectively destroying the weapon.

"Neutralized," Nephilim said, getting up from her cover.

She let her drone scan through the room the HMG was in. It was deserted. Whoever had been there sniped out the hacker and then used the automated gun to prevent them from pursuit. "Room is clear."

"What a fucking mess," Adriel said, approaching Bhanu's lifeless body, " Someone was very keen on preventing this poor bastard from singing."

"Most likely a pro. I can't scan any trace of them in the room."

"We'll need to contact HQ for dispatch of forensic specialists up there. Our IT whiz can disassemble what's left of this guy's computer. For what it's worth, it seems he was a high-class hacker, and I'll be damned if his last job wasn't something very nasty."

"Nasty enough to get him executed before he could talk," Nephilim said, simultaneously flying her drone back.

"This stinks of Wasps, all over, if you ask me." Adriel frowned. "They've been suspiciously quiet lately."

Nephilim shrugged. "Could as well be Proms. The sneaky approach would fit their m.o."

She looked down on the dead man whose head was half missing, and who was still clutching something in his pocket. She remembered the look in his eyes right before his execution, pure horror in them. "What were you involved in, Bhanu? And with whom?"

Had he been more horrified of the people who killed him, or of her and Adriel?

Her partner poked her with his elbow. "Well, at least the hunt was good, don't you think? Nothing better than someone running for his life."

Chapter Six

The Incident

Nephilim arrived right on time at 9:00 PM, as requested. She did not want to be early since this could indicate excitement, and therefore, weakness. On the other hand, she knew that Metatron wasn't the type of man one should let wait, even not for one minute.

With a condescending expression on her face, Gadreel had given her an address within the Inner Circle of Olympias City I. Although ordinary Angels weren't allowed to live there, they had free access everywhere anytime. After all, threats could even turn up in what were, supposedly, the most secure places.

The leader of the Guardian Angels lived on the one-hundred eighty-fourth floor of a skyscraper which had been finished only two years ago but showed features of an antique Greek temple on its façade and interior. This had been a very fashionable architecture style in Olympias for many years now. Numerous buildings like this one rose in the midst of the glass and chrome monstrosities, especially in the Inner Circle. People here liked to consider themselves gods and deities compared to the rest, so it was only natural to live accordingly.

When Nephilim rang the doorbell, it was Zephaniel who answered it. She wasn't surprised to see him. Metatron kept his Archangels close, and Zephaniel enjoyed a privileged position among them.

"Nephilim," he greeted her, "9:00 PM sharp, right down to the second. But why would I expect anything else?"

The Archangel looked her over from head to toe, and a mischievous smirk curled his lips. "Sweet. I'm sure he'll like this."

Nephilim had decided to dress up for the occasion, well, as much as her sense of style allowed. She was wearing a black, loose, asymmetric dress, a leather jacket, and boots. Hiding the athletic features of her figure, the outfit gave her a youthful and vulnerable appearance.

Zephaniel stepped aside and let her in.

"Thank you," she said.

He would've been a handsome man—tall and muscular without being bulky, his face symmetric and slim, his whole appearance extraordinarily well-groomed. But there was something reptile-like about him. His narrow eyes, seemingly gleaming a colder blue than most, the thin lips, and the way he moved. Even a person with little evolved intuition would realize that this was a very dangerous and ruthless man—which was no surprise. After all, he had been learning from the best for many years.

Zephaniel closed the door and signaled her to follow him as he made his way down the hall. The first thing Nephilim noticed was that this place was huge, at least ten-thousand square feet, maybe more. Compared to ordinary living standards, this was a palace. Two other halls branched off the main one, leading to many doors and open spaces, and there was even an indoor pool behind glass walls. The lighting was dim, and the only sources in the hall were small lamps illuminating the various oil paintings displayed on dark grey walls.

When they reached the main living area, Nephilim could not help feeling impressed. It was a spacious open area, measuring at least three-thousand square feet, divided by columns and platforms of different height into sections, such as dining or leisure. In contrast to the architecture of the whole building, with its pseudo antique style, it had clearly been installed by a gifted interior designer. Everything was of simple elegance, dominated by dark colors with expensive-looking art displayed everywhere. The place radiated wealth and power, yet subtly and unobtrusively.

The living space was framed by huge windows, which offered a panoramic view of the Inner Circle and the black pyramid, which was very close. There was an extensive balcony outside the windows; a rare sight, since most buildings had smooth exteriors.

Zephaniel stopped at the entrance to the living room and pointed to the balcony. "Go ahead. He's expecting you."

She nodded and began to make her way to the panoramic windows, but he discreetly held her arm, whispering in her ear, "I can't wait to get to know you better, Nephilim. I hope you feel the same."

She turned her head and looked him in the eye. "Certainly."

Then she crossed the huge room to the balcony. She had never considered Zephaniel until now, thinking he was into men exclusively. She had been wrong. Apparently, he liked both men and women, like most people. Only a few were as strict about their preferences as Adriel was. Zephaniel wasn't really her type, but he was not too bad, and who could possibly know what game he was playing? It was better to stay on his good side, for sure.

Metatron was leaning against the glass railing at the corner of the balcony, facing both the spectacular view and his guest, his eyes glowing in the darkness of the night, a glass of wine in hand.

"Ah, Nephilim," he said, "It's good to see you."

"Thank you for inviting me. I feel very honored."

He smirked and kept silent for a moment, studying her. As always, he was dressed all in black, but it was the first time Nephilim saw him without his uniform or formal attire. His clothes were informal and plain, yet a closer look revealed that it was an expensive kind of casual.

"Would you like some wine?" he asked, reaching down toward a bottle and empty glass standing on the balcony table next to him. He started pouring the wine without waiting for an answer. Apparently, it had been a rhetorical question.

"Yes, thank you," she answered anyway, taking the glass he was offering her.

The dark red wine almost looked black in the night, and it smelled delicious. This was real wine and not the synthetic stuff most people drank. From what she had seen of Metatron's dwelling so far, she made the assumption that it was also expensive. Tasting it, she was astonished how good it actually was.

"A magnificent view up here, isn't it?" he said, taking a sip, "It makes you feel like you're standing on the top of the world, don't you think, Nephilim?"

She nodded. "It certainly does."

"And that's what we do. We stand on the top. On top of the food chain, on top of evolution," he continued, watching her closely.

BEHIND BLUE EYES

Nephilim realized that he was trying to figure out what she was thinking. While Zephaniel had looked over her body and styling, Metatron wanted to look into her mind and heart. For these were the only places that he had no true access to and had to rely on his own intuition and knowledge of human nature. He could see and control everything she did, saw, and heard. He could order her to do anything he wanted, and she would have to obey. Yet he couldn't control what she felt, and that was what he wanted when he said he expected complete devotion of his Archangels; to be in total control of their bodies, minds, and souls.

"That was excellent work today," he said, changing the subject, "As always."

"Thank you, I was just doing my duty. Unfortunately, our suspect got sniped right from under our noses."

He waved his hand. "That wasn't your fault. And in the end, it doesn't really matter. We would've neutralized the little piece of shit after interrogation anyway. I'm confident, our specialists will pull everything we need to know from his hardware in no time."

"Do you think it's one of the hostiles?"

"I'm certain about it. I believe it's something big. We should know by tomorrow."

He turned his head to the dining section of his apartment, where a housekeeping robot was preparing the table for two.

"Let's go inside," the High-Archangel said, turning to the door with a smooth, predatory manner, which was typical for him, "I hope you're hungry."

Actually, Nephilim wasn't. She didn't expect to be served dinner at Metatron's home. She didn't know what to expect at all. Her impression was that he was toying with her and that everything was simply a test.

Nephilim followed him inside and took a seat at the table he directed her to. The furniture was of exquisite, dark wood and slightly shimmered in the dim light. Metatron surrounded himself only with the finest quality, regardless of whether it was household property or people.

The atmosphere was quiet and peaceful. All she could hear was the crackling of the fireplace nearby and soft music playing, a style which she did not recognize. However, there was no TV screen to be seen or heard anywhere. Obviously, it wasn't standard in homes of the Inner Circle. And if they had them, they could switch them off anytime they chose. A true luxury.

"The music is beautiful," she said, "I've never heard anything like it."

"Glad you enjoy it. It's Chopin."

"Never heard of that band. Or is it a solo artist?"

Metatron smirked. "You could say that, yes."

The robot—which was, of course, the latest model—came back through a door that led to the kitchen, holding two plates. The delicious smell hit Nephilim's nose before she saw what was being served; steaks with a variety of fresh vegetables.

"It's real beef," Metatron explained, "I believe true hunters should consume meat. Enjoy!"

He started eating. She smiled and followed his example. It was clear to her what his last comment meant. He was referring to what she and Adriel had been talking about earlier that morning. Was he watching her all the time? Why? Didn't he have anything better to do with his time? She would need to discreetly warn Adriel to be more careful what he said and did when she was around. She didn't want him to get in trouble because of his loose lips.

Metatron kept observing her closely as she began eating, and she did everything she could to not let on that his last words made her feel uncomfortable. He knew that she understood their subtext, which was why she answered with a smile, to show that she wasn't bothered by his interest—and that, instead, she was flattered.

The steak was bloody when she cut into it, and it was an unfamiliar taste in her mouth. Like most people, she was only used to protein dishes; what constituted as fake meat. They were much cheaper to produce and more effective to feed masses of consumers. And people believed that this was the only way a modern, civilized society should be nourished. Fresh vegetables, like the ones Nephilim was served now, were scarce, too. Food supplements and flavor enhancers were much cheaper and more profitable. And most people hated vegetables anyway.

"Delicious," she said after swallowing the first few bites.

That characteristic, thin smile appeared on Metatron's face. "Nothing beats the taste of blood. The steaks are brought in from Olympias III. They still have stock farms there, though, of course, small in comparison to what they had in the pre-corporate times. It's not bad in Olympias III, but I like II better."

"I hear it's a nice place for a vacation."

Ordinary people did not travel, and most never even left Olympias I. It wasn't necessary to travel anywhere since Olympias City offered everything from leisure and entertainment a human being could possibly wish for. Besides, the VR made it possible to go anywhere, anytime, so why make an effort? Only members of the Inner Circle traveled to the other cities for vacation, as many had private aircraft, and the coastal regions of the satellite cities were covered with mansions.

Metatron chuckled, a noise Nephilim had never heard from him before.

"I never go on vacation," he said, amused, "Why should I? I'm not human. We have Guardian Angel branches in Olympias II and III. The look on your face tells me that this surprises you, my dear Nephilim."

He took a sip of his wine before continuing, his smile turning into a sneer, "Yes, I can read a lot from your face. Although, you're brilliant at hiding what you think and feel. It makes it even more interesting. You would be surprised how well I know you."

He paused for a moment, letting his words stand between them while looking her in the eyes, then continued, "Anyway, naturally, we have Guardian Angels in the satellites. II is especially infamous for its inhabitants being defiant from time to time. Hostiles also strike in the satellites, but less frequently. That's why our outposts there are smaller than the HQ, but nevertheless important. III specializes in training Angels for missions on enemy territory, which are usually one-way trips. The outposts are run by former Archangels who have proven to be extraordinarily loyal and effective, but I visit regularly. Maybe I'll take you along sometime."

Nephilim kept silent. Never in her life had she felt as naked and vulnerable as she did at this moment. The outposts in Olympias II and III weren't of much interest to her, but what he said before was. Was it really true, or was he just bluffing? If he really knew what she was thinking, wouldn't she be sitting in the euthanasia chamber instead of eating dinner with him?

He leaned back in his chair comfortably, seemingly enjoying the situation. "Let's cut straight to the point now, shall we? You know exactly why you're here, Nephilim. I want you. I've made my decision to make you an Archangel a long time ago and was just waiting for the best moment to do so. In fact, I was pleasantly surprised that Cassiel was KIA; otherwise, I would've had to get rid of one of my Archangels to promote you, and I dislike doing that. It probably would've been Cassiel anyway since she'd been underperforming lately, and I'd started to become weary of her. So, she did all of us a favor. A final, ultimate sacrifice for the cause, one might say. Perhaps the last assignment I gave her was simply too much for her capabilities. Who knows?"

His smile sent chills down Nephilim's spine.

"I'm deeply honored," she said, "But...why me?"

"Because you're special. In so many ways. You can't possibly know how special you are. It's not just that you're one of the best we have on the force, and how you manage to impress me every time I see you in action. And it's not only because your mind is sharper than most, and you question things everyone else follows blindly. It's much more than that."

"Why am I so special?" She did not bother to hide her feelings anymore. She was baffled and let him openly see this.

He smirked. "You will find that out in time, I promise. I have big plans for you. You can help me build the future. It all depends on you, however, if you are willing to fully commit yourself."

"I am," she said quickly, "I'm curious, though. What plans do you have for me?"

"You will learn about them when I decide the time is right. For now, I'm not one-hundred percent convinced of your dedication. I'll give you some time to think everything through before we speak again, and I make my final decision. Keep in mind what I'm offering you here."

"I will. I'm more than grateful for this opportunity."

"You should be. Now finish your steak, we don't want valuable resources going to waste, do we?"

Nephilim did as she was told, but the food had lost its flavor. She desperately tried not to think about the conversation they had just had, so the confusion wouldn't show on her face. The whole evening wasn't at all what she anticipated. She wasn't sure what exactly she had expected—

certainly not this. But right now, she needed to focus her attention on something more neutral.

After finishing her food, her gaze fell on the numerous shelves, which were positioned around a lounge of sofas and comfortable looking armchairs. They were filled with books. This section of the home was practically a library. She had noticed it before, right after entering the room, but only now realized how curious this sight was.

"You have a lot of books," she said to start a more neutral conversation. Somewhere in the back of her head, she remembered how Adriel had been mocking her about if she was going to discuss books tonight.

"Why wouldn't I?"

"It's a rare sight. Only a few people read books nowadays, and I've never seen so many in one place."

"And you didn't take me for a reader, I suppose," his voice sounded genuinely amused, "Well, to surprise you more, I've read most of them. They're not just decoration. Go ahead, take a closer look."

She got up from the table and walked to the bookshelves. Up close, they were even more intriguing than she had expected. There was a huge shelf full of books about history, art, architecture, science. Others contained works of fiction. Many of the books seemed to be very old and had names on them she had never heard: William Shakespeare, John Milton, Dante Alighieri, James Joyce, Aldous Huxley, Ray Bradbury...

"I must confess, I'm not much of a reader," she said, "I don't know any of these titles."

"That's because most of them are banned," Metatron said right behind her. Nephilim had been so fascinated by inspecting the antique books that she didn't hear him approach. She turned around to face him, utterly puzzled.

Banned? Everyone knew that certain books were banned for good reasons, and punishment for reading or owning them was harsh. It did not frequently happen, however, that people were arrested due to this felony since the majority weren't interested at all in reading anything except newsfeeds and status updates. Why would Metatron of all people have a collection of banned books in his home?

Metatron smirked. "The look on your face is priceless. You're asking yourself why I would collect illegal books and store them in plain sight. Because they fascinate me, and because I can."

He stroked over a line of books in an almost tender gesture. "You don't need to worry. Nothing you see or hear in my home is sent to the grid. I like to enjoy my privacy."

"What are the books about?" she asked, her curiosity woken, "Why are they banned?"

"For various reasons," he explained, "Some are religious texts, such as the Bible, the Talmud, or the Teachings of Buddha..." He pointed at a shelf to their left. "And we know that our society got rid of any religious systems since they are divisive, obstructive, and simply unnecessary for modern life. Other books contain historical events or scientific facts which don't correspond with our teachings or core values. Most are literary works that don't fit into our way of life and how we see the world. While some contain outright dangerous thoughts and need to be destroyed whenever a copy is found."

His fingers stopped at two books, then he turned toward her, watching her closely as he quoted, "'*All animals are equal, but some animals are more equal than others.*'"[3]

---

[3] From "Animal Farm" by George Orwell

Nephilim was stunned. This was a quote about animals, yet she clearly understood what it meant—and why this book was banned in Olympias. A place where everyone was equal, where all burdens of inequality of the past had been eradicated: race, religion, cultural identity. Yet, with a closer look, some people were still more equal than others—superior, even. She was unsure what Metatron wanted her to say, what he was thinking by quoting something like this. One wrong word could mean her end. Or was this what he really thought?

She turned away from his gaze and studied the book closer instead.

"George Orwell, *Animal Farm*," she read the author's name and book title aloud.

"One of my favorites," Metatron said and pointed at the second book from the same writer, with the cryptic title of *1984*. "This one is even better."

He paused for a second, then quoted, "'*Who controls the past controls the future. Who controls the present controls the past.*'"[4]

"I think I understand why these books are banned," Nephilim said slowly.

"Do you? I might let you read them sometime then. Only inside these walls, of course. You will understand I can't lend them to you. Since they aren't being printed anymore, I might never find another copy if they were lost."

"Of course."

Metatron looked her in the eye. "I have one more quote for you, one you might want to remember; '*If you want to hide a secret, you must also

---

[4] From "1984" by George Orwell

BEHIND BLUE EYES

hide it from yourself.'"[5]

He stepped closer and took her face in his hands, stroking it gently.

"I hope you enjoyed dinner, my sweet, intelligent Nephilim," he said softly, "Because now it's time for me to enjoy dessert. I'm sure you know that."

He came even closer, and for a moment, it seemed he would kiss her. Suddenly he grabbed her by the shoulders and smashed her against the wall between two bookshelves with such speed and force that the shelves shook, and the wall suffered deep marks from the impact of Nephilim's titanium bones.

Before she could react, he was on her, pressing her against the wall. Nephilim hardly believed what was happening here. She was strong and fast, superior to any human and most other Angels, but he was much stronger and faster. Whatever augmentations Metatron was wearing, they were much better than anything she had. She wouldn't stand a chance against him.

He saw that she understood the situation and grinned while he stroked her face again, tenderly. "That's right. Don't move, and do exactly as I tell you. I want to see how devoted you really are."

She nodded. "I'm all yours."

"Of course, you are."

His fingers stroked over her face gently, then his blade slid out of his right wrist. While pressing her against the wall with his other hand, he moved the sword toward her chest. With one sharp, precise movement, he cut through her dress and underwear from her neck down to her crotch, exposing her completely. The blade left a long red mark on her skin all the

---

[5] From "1984" by George Orwell

way down. He knew exactly what he was doing, cutting her just enough to make it slightly bleed yet without causing any serious damage to her biological flesh. After the first surprise due to his roughness and the sharp pain, Nephilim decided to keep her cool and go through with it, whatever he might want. She was certain he wouldn't really hurt her. That would be a waste of resources, and he hated that, more than anything. It was just sex, nothing more.

"Now I want you to keep your pretty eyes wide open and look at me," he said stroking her with his blade, "I will link into your eyes and watch through them when I'm fucking you. And I will fuck you many times. As you said yourself, we have a lot of stamina."

He let his hand wander over her naked body, but not cutting her this time, slowly sliding the blade back into his wrist. Then he started opening his pants while he pressed his other hand against her neck. "You can't possibly imagine how long I've been waiting for this."

Suddenly the door opened, and Zephaniel rushed in. Metatron turned his head toward the intruder, his eyes narrowing.

"Zephaniel, I told you not to disturb me," he said with a threatening undertone.

"I'm so sorry for interrupting, but I'm afraid this can't wait," Zephaniel said.

"What is it?" Metatron asked irritated, still stroking Nephilim's body.

"You might want to proceed to the control room asap, you'll be needed there, and I also believe you don't want to miss out on this one. And you, Nephilim," he said, letting his eyes inspect her in an impudent way, "Better get some new clothes and report to the HQ at once. We'll need you on the front line."

Metatron let go of her and was suddenly the focused commander again.

"What did they find?"

"They couldn't crack the hacker's data, he did too good of a job destroying it," Zephaniel answered, "However, they were able to trace back to his last hacking endeavor. I'm afraid you won't like this."

***

Less than an hour later, Nephilim was sitting in one of the high-speed stealth aircraft the Angels used when traveling to missions at further distances. The atmosphere inside was tense, very different than the relaxed mood they had been in on the way to their last assignment. While the last one was pure slaughter, mere routine, this would be a serious business. Not all of them would be sitting here on their way back but would return in body bags, this was a certainty. Wind shook the aircraft; a storm was building up, and it would hit them shortly after arrival at the drop point.

Adriel, however, did not seem to be bothered much by the tough mission lying ahead of them. Nephilim could tell that he was in good spirits as he sat next to her grinning. He loved challenging assignments and enjoyed the danger. It made him feel alive, he once had explained to Nephilim after they had gotten drunk together. Usually, Nephilim would share his excitement. She, too, enjoyed a challenge, and together they were unstoppable.

But not today. Today she was unfocused, confused, and agitated.

Adriel poked her with his elbow and whispered, "So, I guess your booty-call ended early?"

"Shut up," she hissed without looking at him.

She knew this was a very harsh reaction, and he did not deserve it, but there was no other way right now, no time to explain. Most likely, Metatron was busy in the control room and wasn't paying attention to her, but she could not be certain.

However, it wasn't in Adriel's nature to back down so easily. "Was it that bad? I thought-"

She grabbed his hand and squeezed it so hard that it had to be uncomfortable, even for his synthetic flesh. Then she faced him and formed one single word with her lips without saying it. "DON'T."

Adriel fell silent instantly. He knew her well enough to recognize that something was not right, and he better stop talking.

Nephilim turned away from him and stared down at the floor. She hoped that was enough, for now, to curb Adriel until she found a way to explain things to him. She would hate it if he got in trouble because of her. Obviously, she had to get used to the fact that Metatron was watching her—or through her—way more frequently than she would have ever imagined. Her life wasn't hers anymore.

She still couldn't wrap her mind around what had happened just an hour ago. It had been the most confusing, threatening, and overwhelming experience of her life—yet in some way also thrilling and intriguing. He was even more dangerous, ruthless, and cynical than she ever had suspected. On the other hand, he was also brilliant and sophisticated. He would quote long-forgotten books one moment, and assault her in the most sadistic and twisted way the next. He was unpredictable.

Joining him, submitting to him, would be the closest imaginable thing to a pact with the devil. He meant it when he said he had great plans for her, she was sure about that. He wasn't the type of man who made empty promises; he had no need for that. She would enjoy a life she would never have even dreamt of. But the price would be her soul. Not that she believed anything like a soul really existed, but metaphorically speaking. One day, she would become exactly like him. Was this what she wanted? Did she have any other choice? Or would he grow "weary" of her if she did not show the commitment he expected?

She wondered if Zephaniel had always been like this or if he changed under Metatron's influence. Into a faded image, a bleak copy, an imposter who would never become an original, no matter how hard he tried. She did not remember Zephaniel being any other way; however, he had been around much longer than she had. Who knew how he had been before? Maybe he and Nephilim weren't so different, and Metatron chose a particular type of person to mold them into something he desired? She asked herself if he treated Zephaniel better or in the same sadistic way he had treated her. After all, he *was* his favorite. Nephilim knew that there was no reason to feel relieved that her "booty call" had ended early. It had simply been postponed.

She was still amazed at what incredible strength and speed Metatron had shown when he had assaulted her. She had always thought that every Angel, more or less, had the same hardware implanted, depending on their field of specialization, but she had been wrong.

"Some animals are more equal than others."

Metatron's augmentations were so superior that he could have killed her within seconds, and she was positive that this was exactly what he wanted to demonstrate by assaulting her like that. To establish superiority, dominance. Total control.

What also had taken her by surprise was that he was able to link into her—and any other Angel's—vision directly. He did not need a console and holo-monitor to do that, he could establish a connection between their implants and watch the same way Nephilim did through the eyes of her drone. That meant his hardware and software was much more advanced than anyone else's. It also meant that he could be inside her head anytime; while sitting in a meeting with the Board, controlling an operation, or taking a shower. No doubt his multitasking abilities were likewise higher evolved than her own.

At the moment, the commander of the Guardian Angels seemed to be most interested in her, of all people, and she could not understand why. What did she do to wake his interest so much? What made her so special? She couldn't think of anything in particular.

The only things that made her special were the thoughts of doubt and confusion, which she should not have, and would get her in deep trouble if anyone found out. Her thoughts were hers, even if everything else wasn't anymore—at least for now. It scared her that Metatron could read her so well. It was as if she could not hide anything from him. Or was it as he said in their first meeting, that their minds were alike? Was this the reason for his interest in her? Was he fascinated by old books because deep inside, he had doubts himself? Or did he sneer reading them, because he lived precisely what they were denouncing?

"*If you want to hide a secret you must also hide it from yourself*," had been his advice for her, but how should she possibly do that? And what exactly did he mean by this?

Whatever she did, she needed to get a grip on herself, and she needed to please him if she wanted to stay alive. At any cost. And if she did well, next time when such a mission took place, she wouldn't be just sitting there among the others, waiting for orders; she would *give* them. An exciting thought, if she was honest with herself.

For now, however, she needed to focus on the mission ahead, to survive the next few hours. Everything else could wait until a later time. Every Angel knew that the easiest way to get killed in action was to have wandering, unfocused thoughts. Nephilim took a deep breath and pushed every disturbing thought from her mind.

"OK, people, listen up," an authoritative voice said.

Nephilim lifted her head. Dumah stood in the middle of the cabin, easily counter-balancing the heavy turbulence the aircraft was exposed to. She was an impressive figure, taller than most, and very athletic. Her high cheekbones, distinctive nose and slightly copper skin revealed unmistakably that she was of Native American descent. Her short hair was dyed neon-blue, matching the color of her eyes perfectly. Dumah was one of the Archangels, and the best when it came to field operations and close combat missions.

Three aircraft had been sent out, each containing an Angel squad of thirty. And every unit was led by an Archangel, which was unusual. They didn't get sent into the field often, but this mission was crucial. Metatron had deployed all of them except Zephaniel, who had stayed behind supporting him in the control room. Meanwhile, Metatron monitored and commanded the operation from afar, as always. Everyone knew what was at stake here.

"The target area is wide, but our intel indicates three possible regions where the enemy might strike. The weak points of the facility. A bomb placed in the right spot can cause a chain reaction that might destroy or severely damage the entire area," Dumah projected a big holo screen into the center of the cabin where everyone could see it. It showed a plan of the target area. She pointed at three different locations, then enlarged one section. "We're going to drop off at the northern point, defend it at any cost, and eliminate all hostiles if they show up near our perimeters. Clear?"

"Are we talking about Wasps or Proms?" someone asked.

"We don't know that," Dumah answered, "Our techs were only able to reconstruct the hacker's last target, not *who* he got them for. And he acquired detailed plans of *this* facility. We can only speculate who we are going to encounter, and, in my opinion, speculations are a waste of time. No matter who the enemy might be, we will destroy them. Any more questions?"

She looked around, her face stern and highly focused. No one said anything.

"Good. We proceed in standard formation for such deployments. Stick to your partners, and have your drones ready. I've made a wager with the other Archangels that my team will have the least casualties, so don't disappoint me. I don't like that."

Her smile was colder than a winterly wind gust.

"Drop off is in two minutes and thirty seconds. We lost contact with the AI running the facility about twenty minutes ago, but scans show that it's still standing and functional. That means we're not too late yet. We will stop them. It's what we do, what we were created for. Custodio et mortifico!"

"Custodio et mortifico!" they all repeated, as one.

Nephilim dearly hoped that they weren't too late. Dumah was right; for now, who had acquired the information was a secondary concern. No doubt, they would give them a deadly and challenging battle. The only thing that mattered was to stop them. What the hacker had stolen was so explosive that even Metatron lost his cool for a moment after Zephaniel had briefed him; the blueprints for Olympias' biggest algae-culture facility.

At first glance, this did not seem like horrible news; after all, they could've stolen higher classified data, such as the city's defense plans or the command codes for the robot army. However, that kind of information was so crucial that it was stored so well that even a high-class hacker could never find a way to steal it. Only an inside job would make that possible. What the hostiles had chosen instead was a so-called soft target. The data was still a challenge to acquire, which was why they had hired Bhanu, but it was possible. And it wasn't merely any data, it was the facility's blueprints. With this information at hand, the enemy could easily determine the weak spots and take out the whole plant with a small tactical team.

The algae-culture plant stretched across the expanse of the fifty-mile long coastal line. The algae harvested there made up sixty percent of the protein consumed in the Megacity. Its destruction might lead to a severe production shortage and even famine—which was unthinkable in a perfect society. Even the strongest system could be destabilized by something like that.

The enemy's plan was as clever as it was malicious. It had to be stopped at any cost.

The plant was a completely automated manufacturing program. No human workforce was necessary for agricultural production anymore, which was a good thing since no modern citizen would want to get their hands dirty doing this type of work, anyway. It also had an automated security system, consisting of sentry turrets and highly armed and armored combat robots. It was a bad sign that contact with the AI managing the facility had been lost. Hopefully the security system would at least stall the hostile advance a bit—but AI units were no match for cyborgs, which meant there was no doubt that the Angels would encounter at least a medium-sized enemy squad full of them.

The aircraft started vibrating, which indicated that it had converted into a VTOL, prior to its descent.

"Get ready," Dumah said. She took a seat for the last part of the flight.

When the vehicle reached its designated altitude, and the hatch opened, they jumped out into the night one after another, like silent shadows. They landed on a platform thirty feet above the water and immediately took cover, crouching and hiding in the semi-darkness.

***

"Beta squad positioned at drop point," Dumah reported over the comm, "All quiet here. Scans show no enemy movement so far."

"Alpha and Gamma in position as well," they heard Metatron's voice say, "Engage target coordinates. Proceed with caution."

"Roger that," Dumah said, "You heard the man, people. Proceed with extreme caution. We're on our own, the next squad is twenty klicks away, and we don't know what happened to the sentries. Hostiles are here somewhere, I can smell it. Now, move!"

They spread out in formations of six in various directions so they could come at the target coordinates from every angle. This way, their full force would remain invisible for a longer amount of time, and they could attack like a pack of wolves. The objective was about eight-hundred feet away at the joint connection, which had been identified as a weak point and one of the three most likely targets for a terrorist attack.

The facility was a great assembly of water tanks, reaching from one end of the horizon to the other, connected by iron catwalks, bridges, and platforms. From time to time, small maintenance towers rose up in the water. But that wasn't what made the plant special. The northern part had been built over the remains of a former port town that had flooded when the shape of the coastal lines changed. It was three-hundred miles away from Oldtown Olympias, and only ninety miles from the Megacity's suburbs. This must have been a very beautiful, historic town, as the remains of ancient buildings still sticking out of the water suggested. Right now, however, in the darkness of the night, with a storm moving in, and an enemy force lurking somewhere, an ominous foreboding hung in the air.

This was particularly true since the plant wasn't all wrapped in blackness. The main power had been cut off, and the lights weren't working, but there was sufficient illumination from the fluorescent algae in the tanks that even human eyes could have seen enough to move about unhindered.

BEHIND BLUE EYES

Not all, but some types, created a luminosity consisting of green and blue shades, giving the atmosphere a surreal ambiance. It appeared as if the Angels were sneaking through an underwater world as the strange colors slightly reflected off their black suits, which would have otherwise been invisible in the dark. Deep underwater, the remains of buildings were visible in the unearthly light, veiled by endless numbers of water plants, like ghosts whispers from times long gone. They became fewer the closer the cyborgs got to the target coordinates and further away from the shore.

"I don't like this," Adriel said over the comm that he and Nephilim shared, "It smells like a trap from miles away. And we're running right into it."

"I know," she answered, "But we don't have much choice. We need to protect that weak point."

"Yeah. Still, I have a bad feeling about this."

Suddenly bright lightning sparked across the black sky. And for an instant, the remains of a massive bridge became visible north of them. It featured two huge triangular towers of which one was severely tattered. The bridge loomed menacingly in the pitch-black night. The wind increased as the storm bared down upon them.

For another brief moment, the lightning also illuminated the remains of the sentry turrets on top of the maintenance tower closest to Nephilim and Adriel. They had recently been destroyed. Their group was very close to the target coordinates now—a middle-sized building standing above the water, slightly resembling an oil platform.

"You see that?" Adriel asked.

Instead of answering him, Nephilim switched to the channel the whole squad used. "Discovered neutralized turrets. Assuming hostiles within close proximity," she said.

"We've got blown-up security bots dumped into the pools here," someone else reported.

"Copy that," Dumah said, "Watch your sixes. Control, hostiles were definitely here. Contact highly probable. Any reports from Alpha and Gamma?"

"Alpha and Gamma report everything quiet so far. I'll let them check the pools," Metatron said.

Then hell broke loose around them.

Out of nowhere, two figures appeared right behind the two Angels who formed the rearguard of Nephilim's group. They attacked with long blades, slightly shimmering in the blueish light. One of the Angels was killed instantly. The stealthy attacker stabbed him in the back with his sword with such force that the blade pierced right through him, exiting through the left side of his chest. This would have been a grave injury but not necessarily the end, but the hostile finished him off, leaving no chance to live. With incredible speed and deadly elegance, he pulled his sword out and decapitated the trembling body.

The second Angel of the rearguard had better reflexes than his unfortunate comrade and dodged the blade of his attacker at the very last moment, rolling away.

Nephilim, Adriel, and the two others of their team jumped to cover, drawing their guns.

"We're under attack!" they heard over the comm from another team, "Wasps!"

They weren't the only ones who had been struck. Screams and shots could now be heard everywhere; muzzle flares flickering through the dark. A fierce battle had begun around the target structure.

Nephilim's sensors showed movement from her left. She turned her head and saw shadows running down the walls of the building—vertically.

"These bastards must've developed some kind of single unit stealth system. What the fucking hell?" Adriel swore.

"Nine o'clock, multiple hostiles!" Nephilim warned him.

"Regroup at target location!" they heard Dumah commanding.

Nephilim took aim and fired a round of bullets at the shadows running down the wall, following her intuition more than her eyes or sensors. The muffled scream indicated that she had hit at least one of them. A figure appeared dangling on an elastic rope, their cloaking device destroyed, and a smoking, bloody wound in their lower chest. Nephilim took aim again and finished the hostile off with a precise headshot.

Meanwhile, Adriel attacked the two Wasps who had assassinated their rearguards. One of his bullets hit one of them in the shoulder, then both disappeared again.

"Son of a bitch!" he shouted.

The other three figures running down the building took shape, reaching the ground. But they did not leave Nephilim and the others any time to shoot them. With swift movements incredible even for a cyborg, they dove into cover and instantly opened fire on the Angels. High-velocity bullets flew by them, destroying everything in their path; powerful enough to shatter cyborg artificial limbs, not to mention penetrating the synthetic spider-silk combat suits they wore.

Revealed now, without their cloaking devices, it was perfectly clear why the Angels called these enemies "Wasps." They wore tight black suits with yellow stripes on their shoulders and hips. Their black helmets covered their heads completely, hiding their faces, with a yellow visor over their eyes.

Wasps were the cyborg elite troops of TogbuaXiang, the corporate conglomerate which controlled Asia. They were one of the three corporations that had split the world up among themselves when the new order came into power. Its influence reached from China, and what was left of Japan, over Southeast Asia, to the remains of India in one direction, and to what was formerly Australia, New Zealand, and Oceania in the other direction. TogbuaXiang not only held the most significant amount of territory but had the biggest population, by far, of the three mega-corporations, at its disposal. And they always seemed to be one step ahead when it came to technical advancements.

The corporation split its capital between Hong Kong and Bangkok, same as it had been in the pre-corporate era when it had been nothing more than Asia's biggest telecommunications company. Unlike Olympias, which was run by a Board and administrated by CEOs, based on classically Western company principles, TogbuaXiang had always been an empire run by one family—and still was.

It was founded by a Thai-Chinese businessman, which was why the company HQ has always been split between Hong Kong and Thailand. The name was a mix of both languages as well and meant something similar to "well-scented Lotus."

However, the elite units, the "Wasps," had nothing in common with pretty flowers from Buddhist temples; they were the most deadly and dangerous squad the world had ever seen. Even the Angels feared them, for good reason.

Wasps weren't as heavily augmented and armored as Angels, but they were incredibly agile and fast. What they lacked in strength, they made up for in agility, which was spectacular. They preferred to attack from the shadows, and not only used highly evolved firearms, but also swords, which were an advanced, high-tech version of the classical Samurai sword. Swift as the original weapon, but sharp enough to cut through synthetic flesh and augmentations like butter. Their swords were the reason why Olympias' engineers had equipped Angels with their integrated titanium double blades a few years back—after too many of them had been sliced into shreds.

Not as robust as Angels, Wasps couldn't jump from great heights; however, they used elastic ropes to drop down on enemies, silently, like spiders descending on a fly.

And now they had apparently developed a cloaking device.

The Angels returned fire. As long as they kept them at a distance, chances were equal. But the three hostile cyborgs managed to advance, covering each other, leaping from cover to cover in a way which would have made any acrobat eat their heart out.

"We're suffering losses here," they heard Dumah report, "Hostile forces outnumber us, and they're equipped with unknown technology. Require backup!"

"Advance to target point at any cost," Metatron's voice was cold, "I repeat; any cost. Alpha and Gamma squads have secured sites without resistance, but they have found heavy explosive devices. We have to assume there's a bomb at your position, too. I'm leaving dismantling specialists at their locations and sending the rest of Alpha and Gamma to your position. Alpha is inbound, t-minus five minutes."

"Copy that," Dumah said, "Don't let them stall you, people. They are trying to keep us away from that bomb. We have to find it! Use the drones."

Adriel had already put his backpack down while Nephilim was covering him; now his drone emerged, ready for combat. They were the only notable advantage the Angels had over the Wasps. While he, Nephilim, and the other three remaining members of their team continued firing at the opponents, his scorpion-like drone crept toward them silently. Then it jumped the closest hostile, directly onto his face, stabbing its razor-sharp claws into the visor, which was their weak spot.

The Wasp screamed in agony as the claws pierced through his eyes into the brain. His comrade reacted instantly, drew his sword, and cut Adriel's drone in two, sparks flying in the darkness. But it was too late for his brother-in-arms who sank lifeless to the ground.

"Shit!" Adriel swore.

Nephilim let her backpack down from her shoulders as well, ready to deploy her own drone.

Just then, another massive lightning strike shot across the black sky. For less than a second, it revealed a dark shade creeping up toward Adriel's back. Nephilim reacted before even thinking. Expanding both her blades, she jumped behind him—just in the nick of time to counter a deadly blow of the assassin's sword to Adriel's neck. This time, the lightning was followed by thunder so intense that it made the metal of the bridge they were standing on vibrate. The Wasp staggered for an instant due to the force of Nephilim's counter, then attacked her with his sword at a frightening speed.

Nephilim held against him, parrying the devastating blows of the sword with her blades, her inhuman strength against his agility. Adriel turned around and saw what was happening, but before he could help her, he was attacked by the other assassin, who jumped him out of nowhere from the other side. Adriel dodged, then tried to shoot the attacker, which wasn't easy, as he kept jumping and pivoting, trying to stab him with his sword. The other three Angels continued their stand-off with the remaining two Wasps, who had descended from the building.

Nephilim's opponent attempted to jab her in the side, but she managed to spin sideways just in time, and the deadly blade cut the air only inches behind her back. She lunged out and elbowed the Wasp in the chest with all her might. The shorter and more delicate fighter was thrown back several feet and fell to the ground, yet jumped back into a crouching position in the blink of an eye. Nephilim aimed her guns at the enemy but had to jump in the air as the Wasp tried to cut off her feet.

Behind Blue Eyes

With a summersault, the assassin jumped up as well, trying to cut Nephilim in midair. She parried with her blades, then rushed into the opponent, hoping to destabilize and finally finish him off. Instead, they both crashed into the railing, losing balance and falling into the water below.

For a moment, Nephilim became disoriented in the water. Cyborgs, at least Angels, weren't designed for swimming, it was one of their few weak points. Their titanium limb bones were heavy and made them sink quickly. It took them a lot of effort to dive up or stay afloat. On the other side, they were able to hold their breath three times as long as the best human swimmers, since their bodies didn't need as much oxygen as humans.

Nephilim looked around and slowly started swimming up. Her enemy was nowhere to be seen, but she knew the Wasp had to be somewhere close. She was surrounded by algae and various water plants, which wrapped around her limbs, making movement more difficult than it already was. Underwater the illumination of the fluorescent algae gave everything an even more surreal atmosphere. It almost felt like floating through space.

Suddenly, she was grabbed by the leg and violently yanked downwards. The Wasp was right below her, sword in hand. He moved much more swiftly underwater than her. The assassin did not waste any time attacking with his blade. Nephilim dodged but was too slow. The sharp edge streaked her side, cutting right through her combat suit as if it were nothing but ordinary fabric, and into the flesh below. She felt a piercing pain, which she ignored. A gush of blood exited the wound and tinted the water red around her, contrasting eerily against the fluorescent plants.

She looked around. The Wasp was now in front of her, floating in the water, elegantly, like a dancer. Nephilim couldn't see her enemy's face, but she knew that he was looking her in the eye. Preparing to give her the final blow. Perhaps he was grinning behind his mask.

He lunged out. Instead of dodging or parrying, Nephilim grabbed his wrist and twisted it so sharply that it shattered. Wasps' limbs weren't made of titanium; their bones were infused with polyethylene to be more flexible—which also made them vulnerable. The sword fell out of his hand, and countless little air bubbles exited from under his mask, indicating that he was screaming in pain. Nephilim didn't give him the chance to recover. She wrapped her other arm around his neck, squeezed tightly, and twisted his head with one forceful move. The cracking noise of his bursting spine was so loud that she could even hear it under the water.

The body instantly slumped in her arms, and when she let it go, it floated lifelessly in the water, starting to sink. The helmet fell off, revealing that the assassin had actually been a woman, or rather, a young girl—younger than Nephilim, from the look of her. With her yellowish eyes wide open, the young Asian face, and the long black hair floating around her, she looked innocent and unearthly, as she slowly sank down into the green and blue illuminated depth. Like a creature from a fairy tale. A beautiful, deadly creature.

Nephilim looked at the woman who had tried to kill her only a few seconds ago and realized that they were alike. They had much more in common than she would ever have with any human...why were they fighting, killing each other? Where was the point in this? If they were superior, as Metatron said, why were they proxies for humans in their endless war? Because it was what they had been created for?

She realized that she was running out of oxygen and started swimming up toward the surface, leaving her nemesis to sink down into her wet grave.

Above the water, the battle was still raging, as screams and shots being fired indicated.

"Neph! Over here!" she heard Adriel call out.

BEHIND BLUE EYES

He stood at the railing to her left, waving, the relief in his face unmistakable. She swam toward his outstretched arm, and he pulled her out of the water as if she weighed less than a sack of feathers. The Wasp he had been battling with was lying on the ground, riddled with bullets. Their team members had finally managed to take out the other two attackers as well.

"Hell, you scared the shit out of me, Neph!" Adriel said, "When I saw the blood in the water, I feared the worst. Are you OK?"

He pointed to her side, which was still bleeding.

"Just a scratch," she said. It hurt, but she could clearly feel it was just a flesh wound.

He hit her shoulder warmly, smiling. "Thanks for saving my ass."

"My pleasure."

Adriel pointed at the oil-rig-like building. "We're not done yet, though. They backed up but still hold the target position. Alpha is inbound in t-minus three minutes."

"I guess it's time to get up there, then," Nephilim said, commanding her drone toward her, "Kushiel, join me. We'll attack them from above."

Kushiel was part of their team and also had a flying drone, similar to Nephilim's. He nodded and unpacked it.

"Dumah, while Kushiel and I try to get in from the air, it would help if you could launch an assault outside to distract them," Nephilim said over the comm.

"Negative," Dumah answered, irritated, "Join the others on the north side, we-"

"Positive," Metatron overruled, "Do it, Nephilim. Dumah, create a distraction."

"Copy that," Dumah said, and she didn't sound pleased.

"Alpha inbound in t-minus two minutes," Metatron added, "Gamma, in t-minus five minutes. Move!"

Nephilim grabbed the handles of her drone, ready to be pulled up in the air, but Adriel held her back. "Be careful up there. Our scans are blurry, we can't say for sure how many they are. Don't let them blow your pretty head off."

He quoted almost exactly what she had told him on the rooftop just twelve hours ago.

She grinned. "Are you flirting with me?"

He rolled his eyes. "Just go already. We'll create a diversion they've never seen before."

Using her drone, Nephilim flew up high in the air, keeping a distance and higher altitude than the target structure. Kushiel followed right behind her. He was still very young and had only become a full member of the Angels eighteen months ago, after finishing his final training and augmentations. Technically, he was still a rookie, though a promising one. He was good with air assaults, his specialization, and he followed Nephilim's lead blindly. Adriel was right, of course, this was a maneuver of high risk since they couldn't possibly know what was awaiting them inside. Maybe she was flying to certain death.

It would have been better to have someone more experienced at her side for such a stunt than a rookie, but this was how things were now, and she had to make the best of it. The wound on her side burned, and she tried to ignore the pain. However, the high-tech fabric of her suit had already almost completely dried after her involuntary swim.

"In position," she said over the comm.

BEHIND BLUE EYES

"Copy that," Dumah was all professional again, "All units, assault target coordinates now!"

"This is Alpha squad," Uriel, another Archangel—and squad leader—interjected. "Preparing drop off directly at target location roof in one minute thirty seconds. Hang in there!"

Nephilim waited a few seconds to give the others time to start their attack. Then she fell into a steep high-speed descent toward the building. She let go of her drone right before reaching the building and crashed through the glass of one of the huge windows on the main floor, drawing her guns. Two Wasps were inside, and she shot both in their heads before they could even turn toward her. She rolled off and took cover, while Kushiel followed behind her through the window. The spacious room was some kind of control center used by human engineers, who were still occasionally needed to maintain the otherwise automated plant.

A fierce fight was raging on the lower levels, and Nephilim heard movement on the roof above. Shots were fired. Nephilim quickly moved her drone out of range, so it wouldn't get shot down. She shouldn't need it inside here anyway. Unfortunately, Kushiel wasn't fast enough. His drone was hit and exploded in mid-air. Nephilim waved her hand, dismissively, to show him that it was not such a big deal. Every Angel lost a drone from time to time.

"Nephilim," Metatron's voice sounded unusually sharp, "We've dismantled the bombs at the other two locations, but they both had an integrated timer. You must find the bomb at your position. *Now!*"

Nephilim and Kushiel did as ordered, and both began to search and scan the room. It took only a moment until her sensors found a portable explosive device mounted at a control console.

"Got it," Nephilim said.

But when she moved closer and commenced a more in-depth scan, she froze.

"I'm afraid we have a problem," she said, trying to sound as calm as possible, "We only have forty-five seconds left until detonation."

It was indeed a grave problem. She was no expert in this field; in fact, her knowledge with explosives was limited to handling grenades or rocket launchers. She had no instruments with her that could help to dismantle the device, and it would be too late to get someone here who could handle the situation.

"Nephilim, take the explosive and remove it from the premises," Dumah commanded, "Take it away as far as possible before detonation."

It was a suicide order. Nephilim knew that she would die if she followed it, but she wasn't scared. Angels didn't die of old age. Only a few did the job longer than fifteen years. Sooner or later, this day would come for every one of them. It was the reason they existed; to fight, kill, and die. This bomb was most likely powerful enough to destroy a significant part of the algae plantation, especially if it created a chain reaction. But that wasn't all. It would bring down the whole building and its surroundings, wiping out the entire Beta squad and maybe even Alpha, which was still approaching their dropoff.

It was her duty to take one for the team.

"Copy that," she said and reached out for the device.

"No," Metatron interfered with such a sharp voice that she froze in her movement, "Nephilim, stay where you are. Kushiel, take the bomb and run. Now!"

When Nephilim looked up into Kushiel's face, she saw disbelief and pure shock. A silent plea was written all over it.

"*Move!*" Metatron's voice was threatening now.

BEHIND BLUE EYES

The rookie woke from his paralysis. He grabbed the bomb—of which the timer now showed only fifteen seconds left—and ran. Nephilim watched as he jumped out of the window, landed four stories below, and rushed away as fast as he could. Out into the night, far from the weak point, the ongoing battle, and his brothers-in-arms. Sacrificing himself for them all.

She, too, barely believed what had just occurred. Metatron had saved her life. He had jeopardized everything to do so, risking the loss of two squads and a facility—which was crucial for Olympias—by wasting precious seconds and assigning something so crucial to an inexperienced boy. He was not only watching her; he was watching out for her.

Seconds later, she saw a massive fireball, its flames reflected by the water pools around the explosion. The whole building trembled, and all the glass windows shattered as the shock wave hit them. Nephilim shielded her face with her arms, then looked at the mayhem of flames that the explosion had created. It had devastated at least a dozen algae pools, but the facility was safe—and so was everyone inside. Kushiel, however, had been vaporized.

"So long, rookie," Nephilim whispered, "Thank you."

She heard more noise on the roof. Alpha squad had finally arrived and was taking out the remaining Wasps still holding out there. It was over, their mission had failed.

Suddenly, she saw movement from the corner of her eye. A shadow was rushing across the room. Nephilim turned on her heels, drawing her guns. At the same moment, the enemy lost their cloaking. It was a woman with Indian features, who was wearing a slightly different uniform and equipment than the other Wasps, indicating that it was the squad leader or higher-ranking officer. The visor of her helmet was open, and the artificial eyes gleamed with hostility and confidence. She was running toward the shattered windows in an attempt to escape, but at the same time, pointed a weapon at Nephilim. It was an oversized pistol of a design unlike any the Angels used.

Before Nephilim could pull the triggers, the Wasp fired. A single, enormous, high-velocity projectile hit Nephilim. Luckily, the hostile was in such a rush, that instead of hitting her chest, the bullet only found its way into the synthetic flesh of Nephilim's upper arm, where it got stuck in the titanium skeleton, causing minimal damage.

Nephilim returned the fire, shooting the Wasp in her neck and face, yet not destroying the skull. If this was an officer, there certainly was useful information in that skull. The woman was thrown against the wall due to the impact of Nephilim's bullets, where she collapsed lifelessly, her face a bloody mass of biological tissue and riddled, metal augmentations.

Nephilim scanned the room for more attackers. She looked at her arm, where the strange projectile was sticking out and was about to holster her weapons when, suddenly, a spark appeared on her arm, followed by a bright blue flash.

Nephilim felt how her whole body first stiffened then cramped, as a horrible pain shot through every part of it. When it reached her head, it felt as if it would burst.

She collapsed. Flashes flew through her consciousness.

Mountains. A waterfall. Blue sky. Laughter. Lightning, blue lightning.

Mountains. Faces. Smiling. A man, a woman. Blue Lightning.

Mountains. Happy faces. Children. Sunshine. Blue Lightning.

Mountains. Screams. Fire. Blood. Blue Lightning.

Blue Eyes. Blue Lightning. Blue Eyes. Blue Lightning.

Lightning. Lightning. Lightning. Lightning. Pain.

Then everything turned black.

"Neph, Neph! Can you hear me?"

Slowly, she opened her eyes. Adriel leaned over her, as well as two Angels who she recognized as the squad medics. Everything was blurry, and her head felt as if it would explode at any moment.

"Adriel? What happened?"

He closed his eyes for a second, then smiled. "Thank goodness, she's back."

"You suffered a severe EMP shock," the medic said, "You're lucky to be alive."

"EMP?" She was confused. She could not remember anyone throwing a grenade at her. The last thing she remembered was the standoff with the Wasp officer. She moved her head and noticed that she was still in the control room, lying on the floor. Outside, it was raining heavily. A strong wind gusted thick drops of water through the broken windows onto the floor. The storm had finally arrived. "How long have I been out?"

"Almost ten minutes."

"What?"

She tried to sit up, but the medic held her down.

"You better not move. We don't know if you suffered brain damage."

"Don't worry, I'm sure you'll be fine," Adriel said. Briefly, it seemed as if he wanted to hold her hand but then decided otherwise. "Bad weeds grow tall."

She smiled.

Dumah entered the room. "She's still with us? Good, one less body bag, then. Get the stretcher and bring her to the VTOL. I want to wrap things up here quickly and get out. Forensics will handle the rest."

Nephilim tried to relax as she waited for the medics to transport her off. She hoped that she did not suffer any permanent damage. After all, she was awake, thinking, and speaking clearly. Her body functions appeared to be OK, and all systems reported going back to normal. Once she got rid of the terrible headache, she should be fine.

But then she realized that something was not OK at all. She had no access to the grid, and the grid had lost its connection to her. For the first time in her life, her head was quiet. She was alone.

Chapter Seven

Glitches

"It's something we've never seen before. Most likely a prototype," Dr. Emrich said, his pointy ears glowing red, as they usually did when he was excited.

Nephilim was lying on an examination bed, only wearing a thin, gray hospital gown. Her hair was pulled back, revealing her open implant access ports. The spacious room she was in was windowless since it was located deep in the underground section of the Guardian Angel HQ. Its walls were gray and bare with nothing inside besides the examination bed, a small table, several consoles—and a bunch of people. These people spoke about her as if she weren't there.

"It is amazing tech, to be sure," Dr. Mendez said, "The impact was incredible."

Since she was the chief neurologist, it was natural that she had been invited to the examination to offer her expertise. As always, she wore high heels, red lipstick, and a frosty attitude. Dr. Emrich pointed at the projectile, which was lying on the table. It had been removed from Nephilim's arm and was about the size of a quail's egg. A 3D hologram in front of the scientists displayed the details of the device.

"It's a genius concept, really," Dr. Emrich began. He was a thin, bald man in his early fifties who was one of the few people in Olympias who didn't give a damn about his looks. His always reddish ears were oddly small and pointy, which was why people called him "ugly elf" behind his back. However, this "ugly elf" had a beautiful mind and was the Guardian Angels' leading R&D scientist.

"The device is a high-velocity projectile, which means ordinary armor materials can't stop it. Once it gets stuck in natural *or* synthetic flesh, the projectile opens and reveals a miniature EMP bomb—with an astonishingly high electrical current."

Dr. Weinberg took over from there. A handsome man with brown skin, white coat, and the typical everything-will-be-fine smile people of his profession liked to wear, he was the institution's chief physician, surgeon, and implant specialist. "The reason why a small device is so effective against Angels like we've seen on Nephilim here is that the electromagnetic impulse is infused directly into the body from within. It would be dangerous for a human, but for a cyborg, this is a devastating weapon. The impulse travels unhindered through the whole body, using the metallic parts and augmentations, creating an overload in all systems. When it reaches the brain, anything is possible from a temporary shutdown and system failure to brain damage or even death."

"So, this is a cyborg killer," Zephaniel stated. Until now, he had been listening quietly with his arms crossed.

Dr. Weinberg nodded. "You could say that, yes."

Nephilim did not say anything. She had been told more than once how lucky she was to still be alive and functioning. There wasn't much she could contribute to the conversation, and no one was interested in what she had to say anyway.

She was glad that this thing had been removed from her arm, and the synthetic muscles were repaired. Even though she knew that the device had been harmless after firing its charge, it had still made her uneasy having it stuck in her body.

The cut on her side had been treated, too. It turned out to be much deeper than she had thought and felt when she was focused on battle. Doctors had "glued" it, and now she almost didn't feel it was there. "Glue" was colloquial for a high-tech paste consisting of enzymes, silicates, and protein-chains, which simulated natural coagulation and wound healing—on Speed. It is applied to a fresh injury, sealing it, so there are no stitches needed, then the chemical healing process starts. Nephilim's wound would be healed within a week, and after a month, not even a scar would remain to remind her that it had ever been there.

"Are there any counter-measures we can take against such a weapon?" Zephaniel asked.

Dr. Emrich shook his head. "I'm afraid not, but we will make it our highest priority."

"Until then, you better not get shot," Dr. Mendez said, laconically.

Zephaniel's eyes narrowed, and Nephilim noticed how much he resembled Metatron as he dealt with this situation. She wondered if it was intentional or subconsciously.

"Thank you, Doctor. Your advice is invaluable," he said icily, then turned back to the group, "What about the glitches?"

Now Nephilim was all ears. Finally, they had reached the topic which concerned her most.

All experts fell silent. Everyone seemed to hope one of the others would answer the question.

"I'm listening?" Zephaniel wasn't willing to let them off the hook.

"I have no explanation," Dr. Emrich finally said, "All implants appear to be working fine."

"Same here," Dr. Weinberg agreed, "All brain scans we did showed no anomalies. It doesn't seem she suffered any brain damage."

"Yet the glitches are there," Zephaniel said.

It was true. Although the incident was less than twenty-four hours ago, Nephilim felt fine again. Though headaches were gone, and internal systems indicated no malfunctions, what Zephaniel referred to as "glitches" were undeniable. Since the EMP attack, she had lost contact with the grid more than once. It usually lasted several hours, then she was back online without being able to influence it.

"Well, there's not much we can do at the moment other than wait and see how things develop," Dr. Emrich said, "Because of the duration of the contact, loss seems to get shorter every time, I would assume the problem will solve itself given enough time. If not, we might need to replace some neural implants, which is risky as we all know."

"We also could euthanize her, dissect the brain and find out," Dr. Mendez suggested, "After all, she's a defective unit, and therefore useless."

"No one is being euthanized here," a cold voice interrupted.

Metatron had been leaning at the wall a few feet away, listening and watching. Now, as he stepped closer, the expressions on Dr. Emrich's and Dr. Weinberg's faces clearly showed that they had almost forgotten he was there. Only Dr. Mendez stayed cool.

"If you geniuses need a guinea pig, find a pet shop. You will not conduct any experiments on an Angel, ever," Metatron said, "Are we clear?"

"Of course," Dr. Weinberg said, "We-"

"Furthermore, it's me who decides usefulness here," the High-Archangel interrupted him with a threatening undertone, "We will do as Dr. Emrich suggests, we wait and see if the problem resolves itself alone. Meanwhile, I want for you clowns to do what you are royally paid for: develop a countermeasure. What if Wasps attack with a full squad equipped with these weapons next time? Should our people simply 'try not to get shot?'"

He glanced at Dr. Mendez, and even her confidence seemingly shrank as she stared to the floor. "As you say."

A thin smile flashed across Zephaniel's lips.

"I also want this pistol and its projectile reverse engineered asap since we have been fortunate enough to get our hands on it. If they have it, we should have it, too. And a full team is going to develop countermeasures against that new cloaking system they have. I want us to be able to spot them *before* they decapitate our soldiers," Metatron continued with a calm yet chilling voice, "Besides, if TogbuaXiang can develop such a system, why can't we?"

"We...um...," Dr. Emrich's reddish ears had now grown pale, same as his face.

"Perhaps they have a better science team than we do, how about that?" Metatron wasn't finished with them yet. "Now, go and do your fucking jobs before I classify *you* as useless."

After the scientists were gone, he said, "Pathetic, all of them. Too bad we still need them."

He turned his head and looked at Nephilim, studying her for a moment.

"At least they managed to patch you up well. I'll see to it that they release you soon, the examination is over. Go home and get some rest, I want you fit for duty asap. A storm is coming."

"I'm ready," she answered.

The characteristic smile appeared on his face. He moved closer and caressed her cheek with the back of his hand.

"Don't worry," he said, "I won't lose you."

Then he left the room without saying another word, followed by Zephaniel.

***

It was early evening when Nephilim arrived at home. The sun was just going down. Its reddish rays were reflected from the glass facades of the skyscraper opposite of her building, making it seem as if it were on fire. But not as much as her mind, which was still trying to process everything that had happened within the last forty-eight hours.

First, her one-on-one with Metatron, which had been confusing and challenging enough in itself, then a battle with an enemy that had tremendously multiplied their strength since the last confrontation, finally an incident that had almost cost her life.

And now, "glitches."

She didn't really understand what was happening to her. Apparently, no one else did either. The effects of an EMP blast on a cyborg's brain were unpredictable and never the same from person to person. She was lucky that her neural structure hadn't been deep-fried. That was why Metatron took the new weapon the Wasps developed so seriously; it gave them an incredible advantage over the Angels. The only plausible reason why every Wasp unit had not been equipped with such a weapon was that it was still in a developmental state. However, next time things could be a very different situation.

Being hit by the EMP had been horrible, the worst thing Nephilim ever had to experience in her life. All other wounds and injuries she had taken so far were outright laughable compared to that.

Mountains.

Nephilim had not told anyone about the strange images she had seen shortly before passing out. She wasn't sure what they meant, if they were some kind of flashbacks, or merely fantasies she had before her brain overloaded and she blacked out. Somehow, she believed that what she had experienced was no one's business, and even more, an instinct was telling her that it could get her in trouble if someone did find out. So, she was better off keeping that confusing experience to herself. It most likely meant nothing anyway, and she would soon forget about it.

The glitches, however, were intriguing, she admitted to herself, and would never share that thought with anyone else. Since the incident at the algae farm, they had occurred three times, so far, lasting between three to five hours each time. In that time, she had been utterly cut off from the grid. She couldn't connect to it, and no one could connect to her; she couldn't use the internal comm, and no one could send her directions. She felt like an independent person, a separate entity—*free*.

For the first time in her life, she experienced how wonderful freedom could feel, even if it was only the liberation inside her head. No voices talking to her, no constant information flow, just enjoying the silence. No one listening to her or watching through her eyes.

How could something so simple be so delightful? And wouldn't it be amazing if it was always this way? These were outrageous thoughts, forbidden, and extremely dangerous, she knew. In fact, Dr. Mendez hadn't been so wrong when she said that Nephilim was a flawed unit, damaged, and useless. If Dr. Emrich was right and the glitches would pass eventually, the memory of them never would. The sweet taste of freedom.

Yet, Metatron would not hear any of it. He protected her.

She wondered how he felt about the glitches. He hadn't openly discussed it or shown any type of reaction, but she was certain that her connection losses bothered him more than anyone else. It meant that he had lost control, and he hated few things more than that, if anything. He had no choice but to accept it, at least for the time being. She smiled at this thought.

For now, everything was back to normal and functioning properly. Nephilim was connected to the grid, and her life wasn't hers. She needed to distract herself and stop thinking. It wasn't good for her.

She decided to take a long, hot shower first. It usually helped her to relax. She got rid of her clothes and walked into the bathroom. Here, she stood naked in front of the mirror and inspected the wound on her side. The cut was about twelve inches long, and still fire-red in color. Only a little bit deeper, and the assassin would have slashed right through her kidney, which could have turned out to be very unpleasant. The glue the cut was filled with had a flexibility that adjusted to every movement. Nephilim believed that she should be combat-ready in two or three days.

She was pleased with what she saw and was pretty sure that Metatron was pleased as well if he was spying behind her eyes—although for different reasons.

The shower was pleasant, yet did not really help in bringing her mind to rest. When she left it, her thoughts were still circling. She lay down on the bed and turned on the volume of her TV, to hopefully distract herself

BEHIND BLUE EYES

with some dull show.

The channel which was on aired the latest episode of "Amelia's World," and Nephilim was too lazy to search for something else among the hundreds of news, entertainment and movie channels available. In her mind they were basically all the same anyway, since they all were produced in Olympias Studios, their gigantic premises, adjoined to the Inner Circle in the Northwest, so the Stars and Executives didn't have to travel far for work. "Amelia's World" was the most popular and successful evening talk show; it had received every existing award, and was one of the most opinion-shaping shows modern TV had to offer.

The host, Amelia—an androgynous creature who had been doing the job for twenty years, yet never seemed to age even one day—had a special guest in her studio. It was located on the two-hundredth floor and offered a magnificent view over nocturnal Olympias City and the pyramid. And today, actress Jennifer Lennart had been invited to have a chat and promote her new movie.

"Why I Go" would have its premiere in a few days and was lauded as the most artistically valuable movie of the year. A hot candidate for the Icarus Award—the most prestigious award the entertainment industry had to offer. Lennart herself already had two golden Icarus statues at home and would probably bring home a third for her role in this masterpiece. Being only thirty-one years old, she was playing a fifty-five-year-old woman, who makes the decision to be put to sleep before age or disease could even start bothering her.

After showing the trailer and some scenes which demonstrated the actress' full potential, the two women started talking about the right age for the final step, which still was discussed controversially. Lennart stated that, actually, no age was too young, since it was everyone's free will and choice, and no one was entitled to tell people what they did with their bodies, or force them to live if they did not want to; it was inhumane. She could personally relate to the character quite well, as it was always better to leave the party as long as it was still fun and not when everyone was wasted and tired. The audience cheered and applauded.

Amelia agreed, saying that she couldn't imagine anything worse than discovering that she had grown old and undesirable.

Nephilim was bored. These kinds of issues did not concern her at all. Angels never got sick. And Angels never grew old.

She understood, however, that this topic was of high interest to ordinary citizens. It wasn't common anymore to leave death to natural causes. Everyone was entitled to choose their time of passing. Most people did it when they became gravely sick or grew old, the average age was between sixty-five and seventy-five. But no one would stop an individual who made the decision to end their life at twenty-one, for whatever reason. Even children were sent to sleep if they got seriously ill and suffered. Euthanasia was performed in a very humane and painless way. People simply went to sleep in a pleasant environment—to never wake up again.

No one was ever forced to go. Everything was free will. After all, who wanted to grow old, ugly, sick, and useless? Living in memories instead of participating in all the joy Olympias had to offer, a burden instead of a productive part of society? That was suffering, and who in their right mind wanted to experience that? Especially since there was no place for old people, no families who could take care of them? It was so much better to go with dignity.

Of course, sometimes people clung to life anyway against all reason. Then they needed persuasion from specialists, who made clear to them that it was in their best interest not to continue living. The Angels didn't do such jobs, they had more important duties. A special unit of social service workers was assigned to those cases.

Human remains were usually put to good use since everyone agreed that burying them would have been a waste of resources. Young and healthier bodies were harvested for organs or used for scientific and medical research, while old ones were cremated and used as fertilizer.

There were no elderly or sick people on the streets of Olympias, and that was exactly how people liked it. Except in the Inner Circle, of course. For some reason, the people there did not see much delight in dying with dignity, and clung to life as long as possible, using any and all means to prolong it.

"All animals..."

Nephilim turned down the volume since she couldn't switch off the screen. TV sucked. No wonder Metatron preferred reading books. And the antique, banned titles of his collection were probably much more interesting than today's bestsellers, which were generic, shallow, and told the reader exactly what they were supposed to hear.

She wished she could read some of the titles he had shown her. Let her mind escape from reality, if only for a short while.

Then again, she delighted in the idea of how wonderful it would be to be cut off the grid forever, or at least for a longer period of time. A sweet dream, a forbidden thought.

Suddenly she had an idea. It was utterly crazy, and yet, so exciting that it almost made her shiver. Maybe there was a possibility. And she knew exactly who could help her with that plan. All she needed to do was look for his address in the employee database and then wait for the next glitch.

She leaned back and tried to relax. It did not take long, and she experienced the strange tingling in the back of her head, which indicated the beginning of her next episode of freedom—at least for a short time.

***

Finwick was in high spirits. Today everything went as it should. His black stallion with fiery hooves and red glowing eyes rushed over the green plains at neck-breaking speed toward the sun, which was just sinking down beyond the horizon. He reached a forest with ancient, twisted trees, their leaves whispering in the wind, which was also blowing through his long hair, sticking out of his black, ornamented helmet.

He heard a howling close by, and the music rose to a dramatic crescendo as werewolves attacked him from the side. They were no match for his level sixty-two sorcerer. Without descending from his horse or even slowing down, he cast a devastating fire spell which turned his foes to ashes. He moved on and left the forest behind to find himself in a breathtakingly beautiful landscape of waterfalls and rivers. Sapphire blue water splashed all around him as he rode through a creek and to a waterfall. The drops of water and warm rays of the sinking sun felt real on his skin. He could smell the fresh flowers on the shore of the creek, and a distant thunder indicated an upcoming storm. Well hidden behind the waterfall was the Grotto of Nymphs, as he knew. Not only had he finally found it, but he had acquired the key to open it. It had cost him dozens of hours of questing, but now he was there...and it was said that it was more than worth it. He sighed in anticipation.

But suddenly, a red exclamation point appeared in his field of vision, combined with a signal that Finwick had learned to hate. It meant the game was telling the player that there was something in the real world that had to be taken care of. It could be anything ranging from a simple phone call to an apartment fire. Or it could mean that the player was in the VR for longer than ten hours and needed to get something to drink and some food. This security measure had been implemented after too many people had died of thirst, hunger, or exhaustion because they did not realize how much time had passed in the real world. It was easy to forget that you couldn't just respawn if your actual body died.

BEHIND BLUE EYES

"What the hell?" Finwick sighed in irritation.

What was this about? It couldn't have been more than three hours that he had been playing. First, he had cleared out a dungeon with some of his guildmates and killed an extremely nasty red dragon. Then, they went and defended one of their keeps against an enemy force. And now, to make a very enjoyable game session perfect, he had decided to finally check out the grotto, alone—he didn't want to share the nymphs with other players.

But the exclamation point did not go away. Finwick grumbled, then started the log off process. The handsome, tall sorcerer with his shiny armor and long hair disappeared, and Finwick was himself again. He opened his eyes and blinked. Everything was quiet, and his home wasn't on fire, so what was it that the damn system had been trying to tell him?

He spent almost every evening in the VR, like so many. There were thousands of different games to play or digital worlds to visit, something for every taste. From fantasy role-playing games where you could travel to distant places, times, or planets, to the weirdest sex fantasies; anything was possible, and there were no limits in the VR. A simple neural implant allowed one to enter, and the necessary hardware console could be installed into every apartment. But it was a costly way to spend time, for every virtual world cost a membership fee and there was no limit on how much players could spend in-game on equipment, clothes, houses, and whatever they wanted to acquire in the virtual world of their choice.

Finwick had memberships in several games and virtual worlds, including sex-based ones, where he could live all the fantasies he would never dare to fulfill in real life. His job paid well enough to make it easily affordable. However, his favorite VR place was the game he had just been interrupted from playing, "The Scrolls of the Ancients." It was an MMORPG in a gigantic, beautifully designed fantasy setting populated with every imaginable fantastic creature and monster, where thousands of players could go on heroic quests together or fight each other in epic battles.

In this world, Finwick was a hero; a badass who not only could face the most dangerous monsters but also hook up with the most beautiful women—even if many were guys in real life, he didn't care.

Finally, it became clear what had drawn him from the game at such an inconvenient moment; his doorbell had rung. Someone was at the door.

He unplugged the device from the implant port on his temple and sat up.

"What the hell?" he repeated, confused.

The clock showed it was 10:35 PM, and he was not expecting anyone. Not to mention that he usually didn't get any visitors at all. And the robo-deliveryman had brought his pizza more than two hours ago. So, who could it be?

A sudden insight made his blood freeze. It was *them*! *They* had found out what he had done and were now coming for him! It was exactly how they did it. They came in the middle of the night and made people disappear. Oh, no, no, no...

He was momentarily so paralyzed with fear, he could hardly breathe.

What should he do?

The doorbell rang again.

There was nothing he could do. There was no escape. Slowly he got up from the bed and walked to the door, like in a nightmare. Or a character in a bad horror movie, who knew without a doubt that the boogeyman was waiting for him in the basement, but still went down there.

His hand felt as if it belonged to someone else as it carefully activated the mechanism that unlocked the door.

When he saw who was standing there, his heart almost stopped, and his jaw dropped. It wasn't the boogeyman, and it wasn't a killer squad coming for him. It was *her*.

"Hi," Nephilim said, "I hope I didn't wake you."

It took him a while before he could answer. Was this a dream? "No. No, not at all. It's nice to see you."

She smiled, and he felt like melting away while his legs turned to jelly.

"May I come in?" she asked.

"Yes! Of course."

He stepped aside and let her pass. This had to be a dream. How often had he fantasized about this exact situation? Her arriving at his apartment and asking to come in. And once she was in, she would throw him on the bed and have her way with him violently...

He gasped for air as he closed the door while she inspected his place. It was only now that he realized what a mess it was. All kinds of stuff was scattered around the studio apartment, the bed was unmade, the sofa was covered with clothes, and a box with half-eaten lactose-free pizza was placed on the nightstand. Then he noticed what a mess *he* was, wearing only shorts, and an old t-shirt from the Olympias Tech College he had attended.

That definitely wasn't part of his fantasy; however, his body couldn't give a damn, and reacted with an erection.

"Nice place," she said.

He forced himself to stop staring at her and rushed to the sofa, shoving everything that was piling up there onto the floor. "Please, take a seat. Would you like something to drink?"

She sat down and crossed her legs, gracefully. "Sure."

Finwick hurried to the fridge, which was in the small corridor between the bathroom and the main living space. He opened it and stood as close to it as he could, pressing his loins into the cold in the hope it would eliminate his boner. It was embarrassing, and he didn't want her to notice. Although he was afraid she had, anyway. He worked with them daily and knew that they perceived things ordinary humans didn't.

"Beer?" he asked.

"Why not."

He waited for a few seconds, and his hardon started to shrink in the cold. When he brought her the beer a moment later, he was almost back to normal. But he was still so excited that it took him some effort not to drop the bottles.

"Thanks," she said.

He sat down on the edge of his bed, facing her. Somehow, he felt awkward and delighted at the same time. Could it really be that she was attracted to him after all? He glanced at her, how she sat on his sofa in the middle of his chaos, studying him with those neon-blue eyes people hated so much. Sublime, beautiful, and dressed in her tight, black clothes; extremely hot. He hoped she could not hear his heart pounding.

"How are you, Nephilim?" he finally asked to break the silence, "I heard you were wounded on the last mission."

He had been horrified to hear that.

"Just a scratch," she said.

"But, weren't you hit by that new EMP weapon everyone is freaking out about?"

"I was," she said calmly, "The EMP blast caused glitches in my implants. I'm losing connection with the grid temporarily. So, just so you know, no one can hear or see us now. My scan also did not show any larger data amounts leaving this place, so no one is surveilling you at the moment. We can be completely open with each other."

"I see..."

Not only were most people unaware of the fact that they could be under surveillance at any time through various tech everyone had in their apartment, but also someone could be hacking into anyone's higher evolved neural implants. Finwick, however, worked with the authorities and therefore knew this fact very well. He usually did not care since he didn't have anything to hide.

"I know what you did, Finwick."

Her words made him feel alternately cold and hot. His heart pounded harder. He opened his mouth to say something but then closed it and remained silent.

"It was very courageous, and I always will be grateful for that," she continued, "You saved my life."

He beamed. "I'm glad. And I would do it again."

Then all of a sudden, fear struck him like an ice-cold whip. If she knew, who else did? He was sure he had entirely covered his tracks.

"How did you find out?" he asked carefully.

She shrugged. "Deduction. I knew I screwed up the examination, and there was no chance in hell that I could've scored as well as I did. There could only be one explanation for that; someone manipulated the results, and that person could've only been you. But you don't need to worry. No one else knows and will never learn it from me. We alone will share this little secret."

For some reason, this caused a warmth to spread outward from his stomach.

She looked into his eyes. "Why did you do it, Finwick?"

The question hit him unprepared. He had no idea how to answer. Since he had no idea exactly why he had done it in the first place. To win her appreciation and affection? To get laid? Because he had feelings for her like never before in his life? Because he was insane?

"I...um...I," he stammered, hot blood rushing to his face, "Because I didn't want any harm to come to you."

He could have slapped himself the moment the words left his mouth. What was wrong with him? Why didn't he just tell her what he wanted, what he was craving for more than anything else?

She smiled, and for a moment, he had the crazy hope that she would acknowledge his heroism by taking off her clothes and jumping on him.

Instead, she said, "Now, I need to ask you for another favor."

Anything! Was the first answer that shot through his mind, but he forced himself to keep his mouth shut. After all, he wasn't a complete idiot.

"If you help me now, I'll offer you something priceless in return," she continued.

"What would that be?" he asked, trying not to show how excited he was.

She took a sip of her beer and locked her unhuman eyes on him.

BEHIND BLUE EYES

"Well, it's completely up to you."

He knew exactly what he wanted, and the thought alone made his arousal come back as if it had never been gone.

She said, "I could fuck your brains out right now if you'd like. It won't take me longer than three minutes..."

"Oh, yes, please!" he cried out and almost dropped his beer in excitement. This was too good to be true!

Nephilim smirked. "But that would be rather cheap, don't you think? You can get laid anywhere, it's no big deal."

"But not by you! You're not just anyone..."

Now it was out. But she had probably known all along what he wanted. Otherwise, she wouldn't have come forward so bluntly. He had to admit that he was really bad with women.

"I'm flattered," she said, "But you're right. I'm not just anyone. I'm part of the most feared unit in Olympias. And that's why you should consider thoroughly if my other offer isn't better than a few minutes of fun. If you do what I ask you, I'll be *your* Guardian Angel. I'll watch your back. If anyone messes with you, they mess with me—and won't survive. You can ping me directly anytime, and I'll be there. And if you want someone gone..." She lifted her hand and let her blade slide from her wrist, still looking at him. "They will be gone. No questions asked."

He stared at her with an open mouth. Somewhere in the back of his head, he was aware of how ridiculous he must appear, but he could not help himself. Suddenly he realized who he was dealing with. Looking at her, it was easy to only see a beautiful woman with delicate features and that body of a goddess. But in reality, she was not only one of the most feared but most dangerous people in Olympias. She was a cold-blooded killer. An angel of death. Taking lives was a daily business for her, like working on algorithms was for him. How many dead bodies had those blue eyes of hers seen? How much blood was on her hands? He shivered.

Yet he couldn't help but be helplessly attracted to her. Like a moth to the flame. A warning voice somewhere deep inside him was telling him that getting involved with her would eventually get him killed. But how could he say no to anything she wanted? And wasn't it already too late not to get involved?

She let her blade slowly disappear into her wrist again. "So, Finwick. What'll it be?"

Finwick bit his lip. He felt torn between his options. On the one hand, she was offering him the fulfillment of his desires, but on the other…he knew that he was weak. He had been bullied and tossed around in his life more than once. In the VR worlds, he could be the hero, but real life hadn't always been kind to him. With Nephilim at his side, he would be invincible. And perhaps, if they spent more time together, she would develop affection for him after all? For he realized that he had been wrong. A few minutes in heaven wasn't the fulfillment of his dreams. He wanted more than that. He wanted to be close to her as much as he could.

"OK," he finally said, "You're right. I'll take option two. But…don't take it the wrong way, OK? I would love to have sex with you! Maybe…we can have both?"

She chuckled. "No."

He shrugged. "Well, was worth a try, I guess. What's my end of the bargain? What would you have me do?"

"The glitches," she said, serious again, "I enjoy being cut off the grid more than I could've ever imagined. Yet Dr. Emrich is quite certain they are only temporary, and I believe he's right since every episode is shorter than the last one. Is there any other possibility to free me from the grid? At least for a longer period of time?"

BEHIND BLUE EYES

His eyes widened. "But...holy shit, Nephilim, do you know what you're asking? Why do you think we're conducting all these tests with you guys? They want to have total control over you at any time. In truth, they're scared of you; the Board as much as everyone else on the streets..."

"Certainly," she said calmly, "Because we're monsters, abominations, killers. What about you? Are you scared of me?"

He shook his head. "No, of course not. But, Nephilim, if they even suspect you're going rogue, they'll kill you."

"I know." She smiled. "You see, I was almost killed thrice last night. Death doesn't scare me. I want to feel alive, be myself, be free. Even if it's just for a short time. So, tell me, is it possible to get what I want? And can you help me?"

"It should be," he said slowly, "As far as I know, there's a device on the black market. A tiny piece of hardware that can be attached to a neural implant. It simulates to the grid that you are sleeping, which means you won't get any unnecessary signals, and there are likewise no visual or noise impulses. But in truth, you're awake and practically invisible. It's used by people who want to outsmart tracking devices, and is, as you can imagine, highly illegal. I could probably modify one for you, so it won't get detected as long as no one takes a deep scan of your implants."

Her smile widened, and she almost seemed like an excited little girl. "OK, let's do it then!"

He lifted his hands. "Wait, wait! I don't have such a device here, I need to acquire it first, which won't be so easy. Then I need to modify it–"

"Do you know where to get it?"

"The Underground in Oldtown would probably be the first place to look."

She jumped up. "OK, let's go. I should still have two hours off the grid, and that's more than enough time."

He squirmed. "But, but...Oldtown is more than an hour away from here, and it's the middle of the night."

Maybe he could convince her to stay and postpone the endeavor? Preferably in his bed.

She grinned. "Not if you ride with me. We'll be there in ten minutes. But you better get dressed, it might get too cold for you otherwise."

He stared at her, opened his mouth to say something, didn't know what, so he shut it.

What the hell was he doing? Had he totally lost his mind? Did he have a death wish? This was insane! Utterly insane!

***

Five minutes later, Finwick was convinced that not only was he a masochist but indeed had a deeply rooted death wish. Something must have gone terribly wrong in his childhood. But it did not matter now, because his life was going to end. He was *so* going to die.

He was sitting behind Nephilim on her motorcycle, riding down the Deathway at such neck-breaking speed that it made his stomach revolt, his limbs cramp, and his eyes almost fall out of their sockets. Yet he did not dare close them because he was scared he would tumble off the bike if he did.

There was a VR game called Deathway, and he had enjoyed playing it for a while before it got boring. It was a racing game that he had considered ultra-realistic and thought himself a good driver. Now he learned that no matter how realistic the VR was, it could never compete with reality since the player knew at any time that it was not real, that it was only a game he could stop and start again. The game and the real Deathway were entirely different, like comparing an apple to an apple pie.

Finwick knew exactly what Nephilim was capable of; he knew that she was an excellent driver because of her augmentations alone. She could probably race at this speed, have a chat with him, read the latest news on the grid and tie her boots at the same time. Yet he was still horrified watching how she maneuvered between other, slower vehicles and obstacles without decelerating even once. Luckily there wasn't much traffic on the Deathway at this time of the day, but still enough to be hazardous. He peeked over her shoulder and wished at the same moment he hadn't. The speedometer displayed one-hundred eighty MPH. Yes, it would take them less than ten minutes to Oldtown at that speed. If they survived.

The only good thing was how close he was to her. He had to outright cling to her body, holding tight onto her, feeling the curves of the natural flesh of her torso. She had told him herself to hold onto her firmly, and that was what he did. It would have, been exciting if he wasn't so scared. On the other hand, if he had to die, then at least pressed against the body of his Guardian Angel.

She turned her head toward him without decelerating even a bit. "Are you OK?"

He nodded. "Never felt better."

She could probably feel his heartbeat, blood pressure, and adrenaline, and knew he was lying, but, what the hell.

Nephilim smiled. "Hold on then!"

He did. Hugging her closer as she accelerated more and drove maneuvers he had thought impossible. At least for normal humans. She was such a badass!

And all of a sudden, he knew that he could and should trust her unconditionally. The fear disappeared as if it had never been there, and he started to enjoy his hellish ride on the Deathway. After all, no one he knew could say they had ever experienced anything like it.

Five minutes later, Nephilim took the ramp down toward Oldtown and continued with moderate speed on the streets below. Finwick felt a tingling in his face after the cold and merciless airstream had tortured his cheeks during the high-speed ride. He was excited and almost euphoric to still be alive. He exploited the opportunity to remain snuggled against Nephilim, even though there was no need for that now.

The Oldtown district buzzed with life at this time of day. Many people roamed the streets for business or recreational purposes. Flashy holograms and 3D ads were vying for attention and trying to lure potential customers into hot-spots, offering many kinds of entertainment—in various shades of shadiness. Finwick wasn't the type who enjoyed nightlife often, and if he did, it certainly wasn't in Oldtown, so he was fascinated to see a side of Olympias he hadn't known before.

A few minutes later, Nephilim drove into a small, dark side street behind a base building.

"Here we are," she said.

Finwick looked around. "Here?"

The whole place appeared rather untrustworthy and shabby.

She pointed at a door a few feet away. "That's a back door, but it will lead you right to the main stairs of the Underground's main tunnel. You'll hopefully find what we need there."

He stared at her. "Me? You're not coming?"

Nephilim shook her head. "I was in a raid here the other day and chances are high that someone might recognize me, which would be counterproductive. You're trying to acquire something illegal. I doubt anyone would be willing to sell you anything if you stroll the stalls with an Angel in tow."

Fear crept up his spine again, grasping his heart. He only was strong when she was around, how pathetic was that?

She smiled. "No worries, you're not alone. I'll monitor you from here at all times. If anything should happen, I'll be there within seconds. If someone messes with you, they mess with me, remember?"

He returned her smile, feeling the fear melt away like ice on a sunny day, and a warm sensation spread in his belly. "OK."

"One more thing," she said, pulled a card out of her pocket and handed it to him, "Use this for the purchase."

Finwick raised his eyebrows. It was a disposable C-Coin card. Almost no one used that kind of payment; it wasn't illegal, merely uncommon. The standard form of payment was by fingerprint, which was connected to everyone's individual bank account. It was the quickest and safest way of payment. And of course, there was a database storing records of every purchase or transaction anyone had ever made Since every bank was a sub-branch of the Olympias Conglomerate, the authorities had access to this data anytime. Most people didn't know that, and if they did, they didn't care. After all, there were many more important things to think about.

The only way to stay under the radar when purchasing something was by using a C-Coin card. Criminals liked to use them—and Guardian Angels. Not only because they didn't have fingerprints, but they stayed incognito when walking among humans. Otherwise, every vendor would see in their system what they really were, and people might run away in fear if they realized it was an Angel there in front of them, trying to buy a cone of ice-cream.

"Makes sense, doesn't it?" Nephilim continued, "Or would you prefer to buy illegal tech using your fingerprint? There should be more than enough on that card. Use as much as you want."

"OK," Finwick said, taking the card. Of course, it made sense. Why did he turn into a drooling moron when she was around? He had always been proud of his intelligence, he had been top of his class at tech college! He had to get a grip on himself, or she would never consider giving him a chance.

Finwick took a deep breath, then smiled, trying to show confidence. "I'll be right back. With everything we need."

***

Later, back at home, Nephilim could hardly hide how excited she was. She was back online and tried to behave as normal as possible, so as not to raise any suspicion. The glitch had ended when she had been on the Deathway, driving home. It always came with a soft plop and a feeling of pressure in her head. The episode had been less than three hours, and she knew she had to be careful not to run out of time during the next one.

Luckily, this time everything had been over when she got back online. All Metatron or anyone else monitoring her would find was her driving down the Deathway toward her home, as she often did, late at night. Like most other Angels, Nephilim enjoyed an extensive nightlife—though maybe not as excessive as Adriel. *Carpe Diem* and *Memento Mori* were important parts of an Angel's existence. When life was dedicated to being short and could end every minute, you had to enjoy every second of it.

It seemed as if she was driving home from having some fun; instead, she had just committed something that could only be described as treason.

BEHIND BLUE EYES

And it felt fantastic. It almost felt as if something slumbering deeply inside her had finally woken up. A part of her she didn't even know was inside. She couldn't remember ever feeling so euphoric in her entire life.

So far, everything had gone smoothly. It had taken Finwick not even twenty minutes to find what he needed. Obviously, he looked so unsuspicious that every dealer of illegal or stolen tech had considered him harmless, and he had no problem buying the hardware he had been talking about. He had no idea that he could be the perfect mole—and, clearly, neither had anyone else. Nephilim knew how difficult it was to find suitable people to uncover black market dealers. It wasn't the Angels' job, of course, they were just called to have a raid and "clean up" if things got too inconvenient, but Olympias police had a hard time dealing with them.

Finwick's cheeks were blushed in excitement, and he was beaming all over when he came back from the Underground, and proudly declared it was all taken care of.

Nephilim had been struggling with herself, wondering if it was fair to get him involved in the matter, but he was the only one she knew capable of helping her. Besides, after what he had done at the examination, she knew that she could trust him. The risk for him was minimal, nothing would trace back to him—and he was having the time of his life.

When she brought him back to his apartment and arranged to see him the following night—so he could integrate the hardware into her implant—his eyes sparkled with excitement and happiness.

He was so much into her that she could have easily taken advantage of it. She could have promised him sex, and he would've done anything she wanted. When he was done, she wouldn't need to hold up her end of the bargain, and there was nothing he could do about it. She could have dropped him or even disposed of him discreetly. But this would've have been lousy of her. Finwick had saved her life, and there was something about him that touched her, now that she knew him better. That was why they had made a deal, and she was determined to keep it. Not only would she protect him, but she would do anything to make sure that he didn't go down with her if this crazy endeavor turned into a disaster. If someone had told her one week ago that she would get involved with the "little creep" in a conspiracy, she would have laughed and told the person to get mental help.

Now all she needed to do was wait until tomorrow. Then she would receive the gift of privacy. It would only be for short periods, and she had to be extremely careful, but soon she would be able to decide herself when she wanted to slip off the grid and needn't rely on random glitches to do it for her.

She knew that it was crazy. Finwick was right, they would kill her if they found out. Metatron would probably take it personally, and kill her, himself. She couldn't even blame him. He was offering her something every other Angel dreamed of. And she thanked him by going rogue.

"If you want to keep a secret, you must also hide it from yourself."

That was what she needed to do. If she wanted to start escaping the grid during the night, she had to hide any trace of it during the day, when her eyes were open. She needed to hide anything suspicious from herself when she was online. And she had to start right now.

Nephilim took off her clothes, went to the bathroom where she spent a good while inspecting herself in the mirror, showered, and went to bed. She required a drug to fall asleep; otherwise, she would have been too excited to even close her eyes.

Usually, Angels didn't dream. The implants in their brains prevented it.

But Nephilim dreamed that night.

She dreamed of mountains.

Behind Blue Eyes

They aren't very high, yet beautiful, covered with lush green woods, clear creeks running through gorges and ravines. And there's a river; fresh, cool water falling down a steep slope. She goes into the water with her feet and notices how tiny they are. So are her hands. She isn't herself, she's a child, a little girl. Turning her head, she sees a village close-by, wooden houses spread over a clearing, hidden by the vast forest all around.

Everything gets blurry for a second, then she sits inside a house, at a table, her feet dangling from the chair, too short to reach the floor. Vegetables on the plate. She wrinkles her nose.

"Eat your veggies," a woman says, her voice echoing, far away and close at the same time. And familiar, so sweet. "Or you'll go bald like your Dad."

She giggles. The woman comes closer and kisses her on the cheek. The scent of her hair, so wonderful and unique.

The woman smiles, she's so pretty. Black hair framing a delicate face with almond-shaped eyes. Happiness. Warmth.

Lightning. Outside the window, in the darkness. She's sitting in her bed, crying. But she's not alone. Big hands are holding her. She's cuddling against someone's chest, wetting his shirt with her tears.

"It's just a storm," a soft male voice says, "There's no need to be afraid. I'm here."

"But there are monsters out there," she cries, "Evil monsters with glowing blue eyes. They want to kill us."

The hands stop stroking her. "Who told you that?"

"The other kids...they say-"

"Shhh, now listen to me. Don't pay attention to what the others say. There *are no monsters. Monsters do not exist. No one is coming for us, OK?"*

She stops crying. "OK."

He kisses her forehead, and she looks up at him. He has no hair and many scars around his head. There are empty sockets where his eyes should be. But she doesn't care; to her, he's the most amazing man in the world.

"I will never let anything happen to you and your Mom," he says, "Now go to sleep before we wake her, OK? You know she hates that."

She giggles then hugs him close. "I love you, Daddy."

Everything gets blurry again, and she stands in front of a mirror.

The face of her five-year-old self is looking back at her. She feels an itch on her skull and scratches. A huge tuft of her hair comes out in her hand. Puzzled, she carefully tries pulling her hair at another spot. And plucks another clump out, leaving a big bald spot on her head. Becoming scared, she inspects the spot on her skull and notices that there's metal below her skin. Then she freezes as the skin of her hand and arm starts peeling off, revealing a metal skeleton. Her hair is falling out by itself, quickly now, and there's metal on her skull everywhere. The skin on her other arm is peeling off as well while her whole body is changing and turning more and more into a machine.

Her eyes start burning with horrible pain, and suddenly they are gone. She has empty eye sockets for a moment. Then from the depths of her skull, something blue is shining through, forming up and finally filling the hollow cavities until she is staring into cold, artificial, neon-blue eyes.

"You are the monster," a chilling voice says.

She screams.

Nephilim woke up. Her whole body was shaking, and it took her a

BEHIND BLUE EYES

moment to realize where she was. In her own bed, one hour before sunrise. She took a deep breath and tried to calm herself. For the first time in her life, she experienced an emotion previously unknown to her: fear.

Chapter Eight

Going Rogue

Nephilim was summoned to Metatron's office first thing in the morning, right after arriving at HQ.

Walking down the gloomy corridor to the double doors, she could not help but feel uneasy. Could it be that he had already noticed her betrayal even before it really started? No, it could not be; she tried to calm herself. If she didn't make a careless mistake and reveal herself, he would have no possible way of noticing anything.

She was perfectly cool and self-controlled when she entered his office.

The High-Archangel stood by the window and was gazing at the pyramid, a cup of coffee in his hand.

Angels did not need caffeine in the morning to battle sleepiness. Their neural implants brought their brains online from sleep mode to the highest performance within seconds. They could easily stay awake for forty-eight hours if they wanted or be content with only a few hours of sleep per night for weeks without showing any drop in efficiency. Therefore, Metatron's fondness for coffee was purely out of pleasure. Actually, a very human habit.

He turned his head and watched her approach before he spoke, "Nephilim. I hope you're doing better."

He did not tell her to sit down, so she stopped a few feet before him and stood there. "I am. Thank you for your concern. I appreciate it very much."

He nodded, studying her attentively. Nephilim doubted that he knew anything about her plans, or he wouldn't have started a friendly conversation. But if he suspected anything, this could be a test.

"I also wanted to express my gratitude," she said.

"For what?"

"For sparing me at the algae plant."

He tilted his head, and his characteristic smile appeared on his lips. "I enjoy your gratitude. But don't you think sparing you and sacrificing Kushiel instead was a matter of course in this situation?"

Nephilim remembered how the rookie looked at her before he ran off with the bomb. He died so she could live. And he had only been seventeen years old.

She nodded. "It was."

"And why is that, Nephilim?"

"Because he was expendable."

Metatron took a sip of his coffee. "Exactly. He was only a rookie, nothing special; we have many like him. Maybe he would've become a great asset in time, maybe not. The only regrettable matter is that we couldn't salvage any parts from him, there was nothing left. You, on the other hand...well, I don't need to repeat why you're irreplaceable, do I?"

"No, you don't. I am still grateful."

He waved his hand. "It's why I had a serious talk with Dumah yesterday. She made some terribly inferior choices during the mission and was outright eager to sacrifice you. I'm perfectly aware that she's jealous of you, and she has every reason to be. You'll outperform her within weeks once you're one of us, perhaps within days. Nevertheless, if she pulls a stunt like that again, I'll instantly send her into early retirement. And she knows it."

"Your performance, however, was outstanding," he continued, "That's why I've summoned you today. To congratulate you on your great job."

Nephilim smiled. Not only because of the compliment but because she was relieved. He had no idea and wasn't suspicious at all. "Thank you."

"No, it's me who has to thank you. You're the reason this mission didn't end up a total disaster."

"Were we able to retrieve any intel from the fallen Wasp officer?" she asked.

He grimaced. "Unfortunately, they are now using a new self-destruction tech on their fallen soldiers. Once the brain stops all activity, a capsule with highly effective acid opens, destroying all data stored on the neural implants—and the implants itself. Very sophisticated, I have to admit."

"So, we have nothing?"

His eyes narrowed as he grinned. "I didn't say that. Thanks to you, my dear Nephilim, we have salvaged a full brain of intact implants."

She raised her eyebrows in surprise. "How so?"

"The Wasp you killed in the water. Apparently, the saltwater prevented the acid capsule from opening. Our experts are decoding the data stored in the brain as we speak."

"I'm glad."

"We desperately need the data," he said, "You have witnessed the Wasps in battle yourself, how advanced they are. How superior to us. We lost six Angels that night; eight were wounded, two of them so gravely that we'll most likely have to euthanize them. That's a devastating balance. And we almost lost you, as well..." he paused a moment before continuing, "This cloaking system they are using gives them a huge advantage, and the EMP weapon is more than concerning, but I believe I don't need to convince you of that. If we don't upgrade quickly, next time, they'll crush us."

Nephilim kept silent. This was bad news, indeed. On the other hand, she realized that he shared his thoughts with her, which was flattering in a way. Only one week ago, she had been a nobody, just one Guardian Angel of many. And all of a sudden, she found herself in the center of power.

"But," Metatron said, suddenly appearing highly pleased, "A crisis is always something profitable if you play it right. I've talked to the Board, and they are very concerned. I've convinced them that countermeasures are crucial for Olympias' survival. They'll raise our funds by thirty percent, effective immediately."

He crossed his arms and took another sip of his coffee, watching her closely. It almost seemed as if this crisis was exactly what he had been waiting for. As if the circumstances had played right into his hands. He watched her to see if she understood that. Apparently, he was pleased with what he saw.

"You're a very smart girl," he said, "I need to be careful you don't outsmart me one day."

She smiled, showing him that she understood he was joking, yet he just kept watching her.

"And that's not all the good news, by far," he said after letting a moment pass, "The Board has finally given us permission to set up our own genetic engineering facility with state-of-the-art equipment and high-class personnel. Surely, you're aware of what this means for us, aren't you? It won't be necessary to search for suitable candidates anymore, which always has proven to be time-consuming and difficult. We don't need to take traumatized children and turn them into elite soldiers anymore; we can create our own people, design them from scratch, using the best genetic materials available. Can you possibly imagine how the next generation of Angels will be? They'll be perfect, unstoppable."

His face took on an almost dreamy expression, which made him look more human than Nephilim had seen him ever before. These changes were exciting news for the Angel corps and himself. Yet, somehow, it made her feel uneasy, and she couldn't clearly say why.

"How did you convince the Board to give you permission?" she asked.

Of course, she hadn't known that he had previously been attempting to accomplish this. Up until recently, she hadn't had any insight aside from protecting and killing. But how he stated the concept, it seemed to be something that he had been trying to achieve for a long time.

His lips curled into a smug smile. "Simple. I told them it was what TogbuaXiang had been doing for years and that we would lose in the long run if we didn't upgrade eventually. This latest attack has made them nervous, and they are having some internal power struggles at the moment. They have that from time to time, trying to backstab each other or dethrone the CEO to replace them with someone else. They're like a pack of hyenas, feeding on their own whenever it suits them. So, it was the perfect time to scare the shit out of them and play them against one another."

He took a sip of his coffee and kept studying her, the smile still on his face. Nephilim could not help but feel fascinated. She still couldn't tell even a bit what this man was really thinking or what his intentions were, but he played the system masterfully for his needs. It was probably the reason why he had stayed alive for so long.

"How are your glitches?" he asked, changing the subject.

"Better," she answered, "I believe Dr. Emrich was right. The episodes are getting shorter and less frequent. I hope it will be over soon."

"How does it feel to be cut off the grid?"

She frowned. "Odd. Very unfamiliar. As if I couldn't use one of my senses anymore. I feel relieved every time I get back online."

He kept silent for a moment, then nodded. "I can relate to that. However, I wish that you take it slow as long as you suffer from this condition. You won't participate in any deployments which go beyond simple routine, and you can start your recovery by taking the rest of the day off."

"As you command."

"Additionally," he said, "And this is something I dislike saying, you can trust me on that—we need to postpone your promotion until you're back on track one-hundred percent."

"I understand." For some reason, she felt relieved hearing that.

He placed his cup on the desk, then slowly moved closer to her.

"Don't get me wrong on this, Nephilim. I made my decision, I want you to be an Archangel. And you will be. But not like this."

She nodded. She wasn't fully functional as long as she kept slipping off the grid. And he couldn't control her anytime he wished, which probably highly annoyed him, although he did not show it on his cool, perfectly controlled face.

He stood directly in front of her. "Now, tell me. Since when do you spend so much time looking at your naked body in the mirror?"

She tilted her head and looked him in the eye. "Since I believe you might enjoy it."

"Teasing me, aren't you?"

"Just trying to show my devotion."

"You know," Metatron said, "For some reason, I've never done it in my office before. I always thought it inappropriate. Perhaps it's time to change that..."

He took her face between his hands, pulled it toward him, and pressed his lips on hers. His lips were cool, so was his tongue as he forced it inside her mouth. There was no passion in his kiss, only cold lust, and expression of power. It was almost like kissing a machine.

He released her after a few seconds yet rested his hands on her cheeks. "Not today, however. I am expected in the pyramid. Endless meetings and discussions with executives, such a waste of time. One day it will be we who reside there, and they will come to see us, but until then..." Metatron stroked her face, then walked back to his desk. "You can go now. Get some rest. The sooner you are fully functioning, the better."

"I will do as you say," she said, taking her leave.

"And, Nephilim," the High-Archangel said as a smirk appeared his face, "Friendly advice. It's not that I don't enjoy it, but you better stop teasing me. Don't try to play games you can't win."

BEHIND BLUE EYES

"I will remember that."

His smile turned cold. "You can never win against me."

We will see about that, she thought after leaving his office and walking down the hall.

***

The day turned out to feel like an eternity. Nephilim wasn't used to having so much time to herself. Normally, Angels didn't get any kind of vacation or days off. Neither did they know a free weekend. Their duty was seven days a week, three-hundred sixty-five days a year. From since before they could remember, until death.

So, even under normal circumstances, it would have been very unfamiliar for Nephilim to remain idle a whole day, but in this situation, it was outright torture. She could hardly sit still and wait until it finally became evening or until her next glitch episode occurred. She was excited like never before in her life.

But she did not dare to work out or go for a ride. Metatron had commanded her to stay put for the rest of the day, and she would obey.

Nephilim was convinced that he was oblivious to her secret activity and her plans, but she still needed to be extremely careful.

It was around 7:00 PM when she finally arrived at Finwick's apartment. Her partner in crime lived on the twenty-fourth floor of a middle-class high-rise, and his door was the last down the long hall. This time he had been expecting her and opened quickly right after the first knock.

"Hi Nephilim," he greeted her, "You look gorgeous tonight."

Actually, she didn't. She looked as she always did. Black clothes, knee-high boots, a dark leather jacket concealing her weapons. And of course, sunglasses. Finwick, on the other hand, had dressed up for the occasion and gave a very different impression than the night before when she had caught him in his PJs with ruffled hair. Today, he was dressed in fashionable clothes, his red hair was neatly combed, and he was even wearing cologne.

"Hi Fin," she said, entering, "You look good, too."

It wouldn't do any harm if she played nice. At least a bit. Too much, and he would develop hopes she wasn't willing to fulfill.

He beamed. "Thank you! Would you like something to drink?"

She shook her head. "I'm afraid there's no time for that. My current glitch will most likely last for only two hours, maybe less. I want to be out of here when I go back online; otherwise, you might get in trouble, and that's the last thing I want."

"I understand," the disappointment in his voice was unmistakable.

"Do you have what I need?"

"I do! I started working on it right away when you left yesterday, and it took me almost all night, but I wanted it to be perfect. And it is!"

She smiled at him, and he blushed. "I'm glad. Can you implement it now?"

"Of course! I've already prepared everything. I...I know this might sound weird, but can you lie down on the bed, please?"

Nephilim noticed how different the place looked compared to last night. When she was here yesterday, Finwick's apartment was one chaotic mess, making her wonder how it was possible for a human being to live here and if he ever found anything once it got swallowed by the chaos. Today the place was tidy and clean and would have even looked nice if it wasn't for all the geeky stuff spread around as decoration.

The bed was thoroughly made and covered with a plastic tarp, a small, bright lamp was shining right on it, several instruments were prepared on the nightstand.

"Don't worry, I know how to take care of myself," Nephilim said, laying down and placing her head under the lamp.

Finwick laughed. "Oh, yes, you do."

He grabbed a chair that belonged to a small desk, pulled it next to the bed, and sat down on it. Then he put on a headband with an attached lamp.

"I'm sorry, I know, this isn't really a sterile environment, but it's the best I can do," he said, putting on rubber gloves.

"It'll do just fine, relax. I know I'm in good hands."

She just hoped his hands wouldn't shake too much. But he seemed focused and calm today, almost self-confident. Nephilim had never seen him like this before.

He smiled then tenderly removed her hair, revealing her neural ports.

"Now, please, turn your head to the left. I will attach the device to the implant on your right." Nephilim did as he asked, and he continued, "You might have noticed that most of the time, we use the ports on the left side for examinations and analysis. The ones on the right side are mostly left untouched unless it's time for maintenance, or there's a malfunction of some sort. The reason for that is trivial, really. When you sit down in any examination chair, the console and instruments are always on your left." He chuckled. "So, no one should find our little stowaway.

Besides, I'll bury it as deeply as possible. Now, please, hold completely still."

He reached out for the instruments he had ready and started working on Nephilim's implant, reaching deep inside. Nephilim knew that she was taking a grave risk here. Not only because she was doing something that would get her killed for treason, but because one mistake from Finwick could ruin her implants. This could lead to malfunctions, brain damage, or—in the worst instance—death. But she was certain that her confidence in him was justified. After all, he worked with Angel implants on a daily basis, and he knew his job well. Mistakes weren't tolerated when working in the Guardian Angels HQ. Besides, he would never do anything to harm her.

Finwick's hands were perfectly steady as he worked on her, and Nephilim's sensors showed that all his vital functions were steady. Something had changed him. Maybe living a real adventure for once in his life instead of playing pretend in the VR was good for him?

After a few minutes, he showed her a tiny piece of semitransparent hardware, which he held in precision tweezers. "This is it. Your last chance to bail out before I put it in."

"I'm ready."

He moved the tweezers with the device into her implant and started installing it.

"By the way," he said, "When I adjusted it for your needs, I also checked it for any kind of virus or malware. There was nothing there, but I cleaned it up anyway, as thoroughly as it can be done. You are one-hundred percent safe...but please don't say thank you now! It would move your head too much."

Nephilim didn't. It touched her how much he cared. He was a strange, little man, but she was genuinely starting to like him. And she would never let anything happen to him.

"OK," he said a few minutes later, "It's all done, and looks good to me. I'm closing the port now."

This was a simple, routine procedure, and only took him a moment. Then he carefully pulled her hair back in place, and if it hadn't been for her eyes, she would have appeared perfectly human again. His eyes were gleaming when he looked down at her. Obviously, he was very pleased with his own work. But there was also pure and honest affection in his gaze.

"You should be able to access the device over your night activity protocols. There you can activate and deactivate it, but I strongly advise you to test it when you're home and pretending to go to sleep."

Nephilim focused on the artificial part of her brain and accessed the mentioned protocols. "I see it. Everything seems to have integrated flawlessly with my system. Wow, the system didn't even notice that there have been any changes made. That's brilliant."

He looked to the side, flattered. "It was nothing, really."

She sat up. "Thanks for your help. You can't possibly know how much this means to me."

Suddenly, he looked miserable. "I only hope that I didn't sign your death sentence by doing this. I tried to hide it as well as possible, but I can't guarantee they won't find it, eventually."

Nephilim smiled. "Don't be concerned about me. And whatever happens, it wasn't your fault. It was my choice."

"I can remove it anytime you want, if you change your mind."

"Thank you." She got up. "I need to go now."

"Already? Don't you want to stay for just a bit longer?"

She shook her head. "Another time, maybe. For now, it'll be safer for you this way."

Nephilim walked to the door, and he followed her, visibly crestfallen. She opened the door, but then turned back to him.

"Fin, you did me a great favor tonight, and I will always be grateful. You're a genius. And if anyone ever claims anything else, they will have to take it up with me, OK?"

He smiled, and her sensors clearly noticed his heart pounding heavily. "OK."

She leaned down and kissed him on the cheek. "Thank you."

The skin on his cheek turned hot the instant her lips touched it.

Nephilim turned around and left the apartment. When she walked down the hall, her sensors indicated that he was standing in the door, watching her go.

She turned her head one more time. "Remember. I got your back. Always."

***

Nephilim would have never believed how good this felt. Something *so* simple.

Freedom.

Being able to make her own decisions. Being able to do whatever she

BEHIND BLUE EYES

desired. No restraints, no rules, no control, no one watching her. A sweet peace in her head. Just being alone, spending time with herself.

It had been a desire she wasn't even aware she'd had until she experienced it through her glitches. Now she knew, deep inside, it had probably always been there. The escape from control through the glitches had been a pleasant experience but no comparison to what she felt now.

She felt truly alive.

She had managed to reach home before the latest glitch episode ended, which was fortunate. That way, it would seem as if she had never left her apartment. Shortly after she was back online, she prepared herself for bed, although it wasn't even 10:00 PM and therefore extremely early for her habits. But since she was on sick leave and commanded to take it slow, it seemed only fitting. She went to bed and into night mode.

And then activated Finwick's device.

It worked perfectly, exactly as he had predicted. The device simulated sleep mode, and the grid shut off. As far as the main system in the HQ was concerned, she was sleeping in her bed, until she switched the device off. It was, indeed, brilliant.

She got up from her bed, dressed, and went out into the night.

At first, she was a little overwhelmed. She had the entire night to herself, not just a few hours. She just needed to be home and in bed before sunrise and her usual waking time, which gave her almost seven hours. What should she do? The possibilities were endless.

She decided to let herself drift through the nightlife of Olympias and see where the journey would take her. There was no rush, there was no destination. The sole journey was the reward. And it was exciting.

She started walking alongside the nightly streets, watching vehicles and people rushing by, always in haste during their search for the perfect life. For something even better than they had yesterday. The countless, huge holo and 3D advertisements shining from the high-rise buildings were constantly promising them exactly that.

One ad she passed was particularly impressive and shiny. It belonged to Olympias GenEn and said: "Conquer evolution, beat chance. Natural selection is the past, GenEn is the future. Free consulting now!" It was showing a baby of unearthly perfection with a DNA double-helix circling above its outstretched hand.

Olympias GenEn was one of the three big players in the human genetic engineering market. As the ad truthfully said, natural selection was the past. Only a few people had their children the traditional way nowadays. It wasn't really forbidden, but highly discouraged, since it only could mean massive disadvantages for the offspring and what parent in their right mind wanted that?

The citizens of tomorrow were genetically engineered, which not only allowed to eliminate any kind of genetic diseases, it also gave parents the possibility to create the child of their choice. There were few young people below twenty who hadn't been created like that, and the results were more than promising. The future belonged to beautiful, healthy, talented people who would bring society's prosperity even further.

Of course, the quality of the genetic engineering varied from institute to institute, and depended on the amount of money future parents wanted to spend. Pregnancy, too, had become obsolete. Though not forbidden, hardly any woman was willing to go through the bothersome process, which only slowed them down and prevented them from enjoying life and pursuing career options. Babies were born in vitro.

Finding the right partner for reproduction naturally wasn't left to chance either. Olympias provided a genetic database where every citizen could find their perfect genetic match. Of course, these weren't necessarily men and women. Genetic engineering made it easy to convert a female egg cell into a male sperm cell and vice versa. The perfect genetic match could just as likely be two people of the same sex. Since reproduction did not mean the creation of a family unit, as in pre-corporation times, there was no necessity that the partners even liked each other. A legally binding contract was made which committed both partners to provide for the offspring—which was educated in dedicated facilities after birth. After all, no one wanted to be restrained in pursuing their way of life. Parents were, of course, allowed to visit anytime, and were even encouraged to celebrate birthdays or public holidays—such as the Founding of the New Era—together.

It was a perfect system. One which provided benefits to everyone.

Usually, Nephilim would have ignored the screaming ad, since reproduction wasn't an option for Angels anyway, but tonight it had woken her attention after what Metatron had said. Soon the Angel HQ would have its own facility like this, and the High-Archangel was right; the possibilities were endless. Considering the spectacular abilities the Angels showed today—because of their training and augmentations—what would they be capable of if they had been specifically designed for the job from the beginning?

Her train of thought then, for some reason, made her think of the previous night's dream. Was it really a dream? Angels weren't supposed to dream, and she couldn't remember ever having dreamed before in her entire life. Could it be true that the EMP shock had caused greater damage to her brain than it seemed? Or had it been a memory? Of her childhood? Her parents?

This was even more impossible. Like every other Angel, her memories had been completely erased when she was recruited for as a child. This was necessary, so the Angels did not feel any other attachments other than to the corps. Their lives practically started the day their training and education began. Nephilim couldn't remember anything before the age of six. Yet, the dream had felt so real...so true...so horrifying.

It was plausible that she was the natural child of some outcasts. That was a common way a child ended up in the corps. Another possibility was that parents didn't like the outcome of their reproduction for some reason or weren't able to provide for them anymore. They were then entitled to "sell" their offspring to the corporation.

Whatever the truth behind her origin was, it was probably better to forget the unsettling dream and stop thinking about it. There was nothing she could do or change about it. And all she wanted now was to enjoy her newly found freedom, for it could end quicker than she hoped if she wasn't careful.

Walking on, she ignored another huge ad close to the GenEn one, which didn't pertain to her either. It was for Olympias' biggest abortion clinics chain. The evolution of contraception had gone a long way, and it was crucial in a society where promiscuity was encouraged, yet even the most bulletproof system sometimes had its flaws. Flaws, which were easily eradicated, with seasonal discounts and coupon awards for harvested stem cells.

Nephilim continued her journey through the night by doing something she had never done before. She walked up to the public transport level and took the monorail in a random direction. Inside the train, she watched the seemingly endless metropolis flying by, a jungle of concrete, metal, and glass. Myriads of lights coming from the countless high-rises reaching up to a sky that never fully darkened, and never showed stars, due to the heavy illumination on the ground. Nephilim only knew a sky full of stars from missions outside the city, and she did not have much time to admire them when in combat.

She wished she could just sit somewhere now and gaze up at the sky, exploring the wonders up there with her eyes.

This would be considered suspicious behavior, equal to what she was doing right now. Angels weren't supposed to dream, not even daydreams.

Behind Blue Eyes

The other passengers didn't pay attention to anything around them. They were busy with themselves, staring into the holo-glasses that projected everything they needed, right in front of their faces. It provided access to the grid, they could update their statuses, take calls, or message other people. Nephilim wondered if anyone would notice if she took off her glasses.

The train stopped, and she exited without looking where she was. To her surprise, she had taken one of the two stops the monorail had that went to the Oldtown district. She smiled to herself. Somehow, she always ended up here, recently.

She walked down to the ground level and started strolling through the nightlife of Oldtown. The area around the monorail station was one of the busiest Oldtown had to offer. The Underground was not far away but, mostly, the streets were crammed with places offering entertainment of various kinds. Bars, restaurants, clubs, funtels of every imaginable fantasy and décor—some cheap and shabby, some almost as exclusive as the ones in the richer districts, others focusing on customers with special tastes. Loud music was played everywhere, and the high numbers of patrons in the establishments and on the streets were not only the residents of Oldtown, but also well-dressed people with costly implants, seeking adventures. This area was Oldtown's infamous red-light district. Nephilim passed brothels for every imaginable taste, fetish or perversion. When it came to sex, hardly anything was illegal in Olympias.

An AI police patrol passed her once, but this did not concern her at all. Of course, the police would know who she was, but the AI was programmed to leave Angels alone whenever they encountered them, so their cover wasn't blown. They only took action if commanded by the cyborg to do so. The patrol most likely wouldn't file that she was there. People like her could be—and were supposed to be—everywhere.

When she crossed a narrow side street in between a buzzing discotheque and a table-dance place, which offered human and robo dancers, something caught her attention. Cold, neon-blue light was shining from the alley.

She decided to take a look, and when she walked closer, she saw that the light came from the entrance to a club, which was located in a basement area. A sizeable queue of people was lining up in front of two broad bouncers. Considering how many different entertainment locations were vying for customers in the district, this indicated that the place had to be something extraordinary.

When she stood in front of the entrance and processed what the place actually was offering, she was completely stunned for a second. It was a brothel. But none like anything she had ever seen before. She couldn't help but stare at the holograms and pictures displayed on the building.

The employees of the establishment were styled up as Guardian Angels. Well, a cheap, fetish version of them. The club was a BDSM place, and the female and male whores were dressed up in very revealing, black leather, and latex clothes—and had shiny, neon-blue eyes. Of course, their eyes weren't real, even on the pictures Nephilim could recognize that they weren't artificial prosthetics but well-made contact lenses. Still, she could hardly believe what she was seeing.

"Interested?" a voice asked. A young man dressed in a black suit approached her. A neon-blue emblem was printed on the suit's collar. It looked similar to the Guardian Angel wings emblem but consisted of two whips instead. "If you line up now, your waiting time will be only about two hours before you enter Purgatory."

"I see," Nephilim said, "How much is a session?"

The host had a charming smile. "Four-hundred for a female, two-fifty for a male. They're yours until you beg them to stop."

That was incredibly expensive. A regular brothel charged less than half that, only the upscale ones in the upper-class districts were so expensive. Did people really pay so much to get humiliated by whores wearing blue contact lenses?

Obviously yes. And in a way, Nephilim could understand that. Like any other Angel, she had encountered many men and women who wanted to have sex with them in a submissive way. It was the thrill of having sex with a killer.

Some Angels enjoyed that kind of game of dominance and submission, Nephilim was rather bored by it.

This club gave its customers the opportunity to live their fantasies without taking the risk of encountering an actual sociopath.

"Why are the females so much more expensive than the males?" she asked with a smirk, "Isn't that sexist?"

The host shrugged. "Market rules. Popularity makes the price."

He eyed her up and down. "You don't seem to be much of the submissive type though. We also offer the possibility to torture them and make them pay for their sins, if you prefer that. No limits. Apart from mutilation and death, of course."

"Of course," she said, "Sounds intriguing. But, aren't you concerned a real Guardian Angel might show up and not take this very kindly?"

Actually, she found this whole thing hilarious. She wished Adriel was here. It was exactly his kind of humor. He probably would pay the entrance fee, and once inside, scare them to death. Others, however, wouldn't take this very kindly indeed. If Metatron found out this place existed, he would burn it to the ground—with everyone inside, employees and patrons alike.

The host grinned widely and waved his hand. "Don't worry about that! They never come here. They're busy with other stuff, like killing and torturing innocents."

"Good to know."

He lowered his voice and winked, "Honestly, I'm personally not sure if they even exist. If you ask me, they're an urban legend, some boogeyman authorities have invented to scare people. But whoever invented them had a taste for a pretty sexy boogeyman."

Nephilim smiled. "You're probably right."

"Anyway, are you interested or not?"

"Maybe another time."

He shrugged. "Whatever."

Nephilim turned around and was about to leave, but then decided otherwise. She went back to the host and poked him on the shoulder.

He turned around and smiled. "I knew you'd change your mind."

She grabbed his arm and pulled him with her, a few feet away from the crowd, into a dark corner. "Come with me."

He snickered. "Hey, you got that wrong, I'm not for sale. But my shift ends-"

Nephilim took his chin in her hand and held it, so he couldn't turn from her, but from further away, it would look as if she wanted to kiss him. Then she lifted her glasses.

He sucked in air like a drowning man and turned pale like a sheet, his skin almost glowing in the dark.

"Now, listen to me, dumbass," she said in a low voice, "The boogeyman is very real, and when they come for you, you'll wish you were never born."

He started shaking. "Please...I-"

BEHIND BLUE EYES

She cut him off. "It's your lucky day, though. I'm off duty from killing and torturing innocents, and I won't tell anyone what I saw here. But I promise if my brothers-in-arms stumble across you—and sooner or later this will happen—they will rip out your eyes, replace them with your balls, then kill everyone while you slowly bleed to death. You might want to reconsider your business model. Do you understand?"

He tried to nod, but she was still holding him by the chin. "Yes, yes!"

"Good," Nephilim put her glasses back on. "Now behave normally, we don't want to scare the people, do we?"

She let go of him, and he just kept staring at her and shaking as she turned around and left the alley. Most likely, they wouldn't listen, they'd keep their business running, and get a lot of people killed. But at least she tried. She wondered why she cared. Why should she be bothered by a few dead morons? She had no answer to that.

Back on the main street, she resumed her walk, sunk deep in thought. She remembered having seen some bars not far from the Underground that looked interesting when she drove by with Finwick the previous night. Some drinks were exactly what she needed now.

On the way there, she passed another brothel. This one was monumental and had large windows on two floors, lit up brightly. It was like a department store; the difference being that the wares displayed in the windows weren't clothes or furniture, but people. Nephilim didn't pay it much attention, she wasn't interested, and as long as the whores didn't try to resemble Angels, she didn't care. When she passed by the door, though, a host jumped in her way.

"Hey! Are you looking for company?"

"No thanks," she said, shoving him to the side in a gentle yet assertive way and walked on.

For some reason, he was persistent and started walking next to her. He was shorter than her and stocky, definitely not a product of genetic engineering. It took him a great effort to hold pace with her.

"Why not? We have everything you could wish for. Men, women, trans, boys, girls, sexbots, beasts...I can give you a first-time customer discount!"

Nephilim turned her head and was about to tell him to leave her alone or else when her gaze fell on the window behind him. She froze and stared inside. First, she felt disbelief, then anger.

Several girls were displayed in the window, in between six and twelve years old, dressed up like dolls. And Nephilim was staring at a face she knew. The girl was about eight years old, with black hair and big brown eyes. Last time she had looked into those eyes, they had been scared and full of horror, now they were sad and empty.

It was one of the children Nephilim had saved from the fanatics, the outcasts living in the wild they had wiped out. She had told them she would bring them to safety, offer them a better life. And now this girl ended up here?

The host noticed what she was looking at and smiled. "Oh, little girls? We have more of them inside. Or is it this particular one who has woken your desire..."

She turned her head toward him, took her glasses off, and stuck them in her hair.

He gulped but tried his best to pretend he wasn't bothered at all. "Oh, Madam...Angel. We'd be delighted if you visited us...F-for you, I'll make an extra deal. How about buy one get one free?"

He grinned while big beads of sweat appeared on his forehead.

Nephilim grabbed him by his collar with one hand, and he gasped.

BEHIND BLUE EYES

"Bring me the manager. Now."

She let go of him, and he stumbled back. "Yes...as you wish. Yes, of course!"

Then he disappeared inside.

Some people passing by saw what was going on and who she was and quickly hurried along. Most, however, did not notice a thing. Nephilim turned back and stared at the girl. The window was actually a one-way mirror, and from the other side, the girl didn't see what was going on there. The expression on her face hadn't changed at all.

A warning voice somewhere in Nephilim's head asked her what the hell she was doing here and if she had completely lost her mind, but she shut it down. All she could feel was cold rage. Mostly at herself. She had believed what she was saying when she promised this girl a better life, away from poverty and a fanatic lifestyle beyond any reason, oriented on times long gone. Yet, her words had been proven to be wrong.

What life did you expect to give her then, Nephilim? A cynical voice in her head asked, which sounded like a mixture of her own and Metatron's. *The life of a monster, a blue-eyed killer, a sociopath like you? Would that have really been any better?*

She did not know. But one thing she did know was that she did not save this child's life so she could spend it in a brothel.

Her sensors indicated that someone was approaching, and she turned her head. An overweight, middle-aged man wobbled toward her. He was wearing an expensive suit, and a broad, fake smile on his face. In his tow came two bulky, young men, and the sweating host. The manager did not seem to feel intimidated by her presence, and Nephilim didn't notice any bodily reactions that could indicate stress or fear. Perhaps he felt well protected by his thugs, who were equipped with costly augmentations. Nephilim's scan showed both had their arms replaced by prosthetics designed for combat. It didn't impress her much. She could break these arms easily out of their sockets if she wanted.

"Good evening," the manager said faking friendliness, "Is there a problem?"

She stepped closer to him with a sharp move indicating violence. People were scared of the Guardian Angels. All of them. This one was no exception, even though he did a good job not showing it. She would play that to her advantage.

"This girl," she said as she pointed at her, "How did she get here?"

Her threatening stance had its intended effect, at least a bit. He moved a step back and lifted his arms in front of his chest. "Everything is one-hundred percent legal here. I have a license, I can show you. And I have papers."

"That's not what I asked," she said, lowering her voice.

Of course, it was legal in Olympias, and Nephilim knew this very well. She didn't like it, but it wasn't her job to make the rules of a society most people claimed to be perfect. She couldn't offer all these kids a better life, but she would at least keep her promise to this one girl.

"There was an auction a few days ago," the manager explained, "Olympias authorities were giving away wards of no further use to them. There's nothing to it, really. You must have confused our honorable house with some other shady place. There's one down the road that-"

Nephilim lifted her hand, and he fell silent. It was exactly what she had suspected. Of the children they had saved during the raid, the suitable ones had been sorted out for the Angel corps or other duties, while the rest...Well, the corporation was in no need of outcast offspring who were of no use. FUBAR, as Adriel had called them, fucked up beyond any repair.

BEHIND BLUE EYES

This little girl was probably so traumatized that even memory erasure wouldn't have helped. She was traumatized because a blue-eyed monster had destroyed everything she knew.

Nephilim was aware that what she was going to do next was an insane risk, but she had already begun putting her life in jeopardy by going rogue, so why stop now?

"Here's what you're going to do," she told the manager in a voice with no patience for objections, "You're taking all these girls out of the window for tonight. Tomorrow first thing in the morning, you take the girl I pointed out and bring her to the orphanage close to Illumination Plaza in the third district."

Few orphanages existed in Olympias. They were for children too FUBAR to be of use for anything else, yet not sick or disabled enough to be euthanized. Orphanages were mostly financed by private people who donated money to brag about how altruistic they were.

The manager stared at her in utterly puzzled disbelief. "You're joking, right?"

"Do I look like I'm joking?" she asked with a sharp voice, "I'll tell you even more: you'll also donate a generous amount of money for her education when you bring her there."

He gasped for air, his face turning red in anger. "This is ridiculous! I've done nothing wrong. You don't have the authority to demand that!"

"Of course, I have. Willing to bet your life on it?"

Actually, he was right. She had no authority to do that. It wasn't an Angel's job to harass law-abiding citizens. She was playing a dangerous game.

"I will file a complaint!"

In the blink of an eye, she jumped onto him, and grabbed his neck, squeezing it to scare him yet without causing damage. The two thugs moved forward, but she pointed a finger at them and gave them a look so chilling that they stopped short.

"One more step and someone will have to collect your little brains from the pavement. It takes me less than a second to draw my gun and shoot you in the face. And I have *every* authority to do so."

To show them she was serious, she lifted her jacket, showing them her gun hidden beneath. They held their hands in front of their chest, indicating that they wouldn't try anything. Obviously, they weren't as dumb as they looked. The manager had been smart enough not to arm them with firearms, which he probably had—guys like him always did. If they were armed, Nephilim would have had the authority to shoot them on the spot if she wanted. The manager most likely knew that.

Her stunt began to draw attention. People realized what was going on and quickly went another way. Others stood at a safe distance, watching the show. Nephilim had to wrap this up quickly before someone had the glorious idea to call the police. If the AI saw her involved in a conflict, it would probably offer assistance, and that kind of attention could cost her life. Since, technically, she wasn't here, but sleeping in her bed.

"And you, you miserable fuck, will listen carefully now." She turned her piercing eyes back to the manager and squeezed a little harder. "You will do exactly as I say. And go ahead, file a complaint if you like. What do you think will happen? I'll be back with a few friends tomorrow, and we'll burn this place to the ground. Then we'll spike you, toss you inside, and watch the barbecue."

The brutal threat started to show an effect on him. His eyes got wide, and the cockiness turned into fear.

"If you mess with one of us, you mess with all of us, do you understand?" she continued, "You can't win against us. Ever. We will always get you. We *are* the authority."

She squeezed a little harder until he started gasping for air, then let go of him.

"So, do we have a deal?"

He coughed and visibly had difficulties standing upright. One of his bodyguards jumped to his side and held him up.

"Yes...we have a deal," he finally said after the cough stopped, "First thing in the morning, I'll bring her to the orphanage. No complaints to anyone, no hard feelings."

She smiled, patting his cheek. "See? Wasn't so difficult, was it?"

She moved a few steps away, indicating that she was about to leave, then said, "Oh, and, don't even dare to try and fool me. I'll check the orphanage tomorrow. If the girl isn't there, I'll come back and break every bone in your body before I squeeze your neck a little further. And there's nothing you can do to stop me. Are we clear?"

Now she had him as horrified as everyone else. He had seen the blue-eyed monster.

"Clear," he said weakly.

Nephilim nodded to him, then quickly went off. She had drawn a lot of attention now. People were staring at her and hastily cleared the way as far as they could as she approached. She noticed a young man standing close by, who had witnessed the whole situation. He caught her attention because he did not seem scared at all. Their eyes met for a second as she passed by, then Nephilim put her glasses back on and disappeared into the nightlife of Oldtown as quickly as possible.

***

A short time later, Nephilim had escaped the hustle and bustle of Oldtown's entertainment district and was by herself again, brooding. She stood on the roof of the abandoned building she and Adriel had been attacked from after they chased down that hacker. Compared to modern standards, this old building was laughably low, covering not more than thirty floors, but it was enough to give her some distance from what was going on downstairs.

She crouched on the rim, only inches from the abyss, yet knowing that she would always keep the balance. Below, she could hear the music coming from the countless clubs, saw flashing lights, people roaming the streets.

After what had just happened, she came to the conclusion that something had to be seriously wrong with her. She must have suffered brain damage, or perhaps she had simply gone insane. All these strange feelings and thoughts which had been bothering her lately, which shouldn't even exist in a fully functioning cyborg's mind. Now she also was having dreams...or memories that shouldn't be there.

She had started to doubt. And to care for individuals that meant nothing to her. Why should she care if anyone lived or died? The life of an individual was worth nothing. There wasn't much difference between a human and any other biological form; it was all cells, DNA. Shapeable, transformable, optimizable—and recyclable. In a way, they all were machines, some biological, some technologically augmented. Superior, as Metatron loved to point out.

The only thing that mattered was the system, which was unique in its perfection. Or was it not?

Nephilim was confused.

BEHIND BLUE EYES

First, she had believed that it had been the EMP incident that had changed her, damaged her. It would have been only logical. But then she remembered that it had happened before. Something happened to her the day she encountered this little girl and the other kids. When she saw herself through her eyes and realized what she was for the first time. The EMP had only woken her desire to temporarily break free from the grid and experience the world on her own, without restraints.

And what did she do with this new freedom? She jeopardized it carelessly. For someone she didn't even know. She couldn't wrap her mind around her own actions.

To achieve what she wanted, Nephilim had intimidated people into obedience, had bullied them most hideously. That wasn't something Angels usually did, after all, they were the righteous protectors of Olympias. Or were they not?

She had played the terror card on them. Shown them the monster she was, the monster everyone expected her to be, as soon as she lifted her glasses. It had been easy. Really easy.

In a way, Metatron probably would have enjoyed seeing her like that. Provided this would have been an assignment ordered by him and not her going rogue without any reason. Embracing her ruthlessness would surely be something he would encourage her to do, once she became an Archangel. If it ever happened.

Metatron had faith in her, so much so that he didn't let anyone touch her. But maybe the High-Archangel was wrong and Dr. Mendez was right. Maybe Nephilim was a flawed unit?

FUBAR.

Dangerous.

Today, Nephilim had learned how dangerous she and her kind could indeed become, when out of control. She alone could cause so much damage, create mayhem and terror. What about all of them? It was the reason why everything they did was strictly controlled. Every step they took, every thought they had. It could never be allowed for any of them to go rogue.

Suddenly, she heard steps. Someone approached her on the roof. A man, unarmed, as her scan showed. He walked slowly, relaxed.

"It's a long way down," he said, "Even for someone like you."

Chapter Nine

Jake

Nephilim turned her head and saw a young man. She realized he was no total stranger; she had seen him before. He had been there when she intimidated the brothel manager into obeying her will. She could not say how much of the scene he had witnessed, but whatever he saw hadn't scared him—which was unusual, to say the least. What did he want up here?

"I'm not planning to jump," she answered his comment with a smirk.

"I'm glad."

He stood there, his figure partly hidden in the semidarkness of an old rusted billboard frame, which, for some reason, still remained on the roof of this building. Nothing about his bodily functions indicated that he was excited in any way. He appeared relaxed and self-controlled. Nephilim wasn't sure what to make of him.

"You seem to know what I am; if you're planning to attack me, you might want to consider jumping instead. It'd be a quicker and friendlier death," she remarked.

He smiled. She could clearly see it, although his face was hidden in the shadows. "I would never dream of doing that."

Nephilim rose from her crouching position and turned around toward him. "Yet, you have followed me."

"I have," he confessed calmly, "I wasn't sure if you noticed me before."

She slowly moved closer, studying him. His clothes indicated that he was a resident of Oldtown, since they were neither fashionable nor expensive. They weren't worn out or scruffy either. He was dressed in dark colors, boots, and a jacket with a high collar.

"Do you want sex?" she asked bluntly after a moment had passed.

What else could it be? He played cool, and she had to admit that he did it quite well. But in the end, he was just another guy seeking the adventure of his life by letting a true Guardian Angel have her way with him. Normally, she would have verbally told him to go straight to hell, but he had awoken her interest. Besides, she liked what she saw. He was tall and well-built, and as far as she could tell, he was in his mid to late twenties. Her sensors showed that his body was in exceptional condition. Basically, he was hot.

He smiled. "I would rather buy you a drink first."

She was stunned for a moment. "Seriously?"

"Seriously. Why not?"

BEHIND BLUE EYES

She had no answer to that question. This situation got weirder by the minute.

"There's a nice bar right around the corner, they make decent drinks," he continued, his smile disarming, "I'd like to get to know you better. Or is this something you're not supposed to do?"

"No," she said, "I mean, of course we're allowed to have a drink."

Actually, she was free to do whatever she desired. So, why not do something she had never done before?

"Let's go then."

***

The bar was called "Dali" and looked very different from the places Nephilim usually frequented. It was a basement location accommodated in an old building. The walls were brick-lined and decorated with old posters, which displayed a style of art unfamiliar to Nephilim. Most likely, the pictures and the art were from the pre-corporation era. Soft music was playing in the background, which Nephilim didn't recognize either. The light was dim, and the whole place had an antiquated and exotic atmosphere. It was clear at first glance that the only district it could exist in was Oldtown.

The bar was full when Nephilim and her strange companion entered. From the look of the patrons, they were all locals. Fortunately, several people had just vacated a small table in the corner. After sitting down, Nephilim was surprised that an actual human waitress came to take their order instead of a common robotic one. Nephilim ordered a whiskey, while he asked for a beer.

"My name is Jake," he said after their drinks came.

He waited for a moment to give her time to introduce herself as well, but she nipped on her whiskey instead and studied him from beyond her dark glasses.

"What about you?" he asked, "What angel name did they give you?"

The noise around them, overflowing with music and muffled voices was adequate enough that no one would hear what they were talking about. Unless the place was under surveillance, of course. Nephilim doubted that, and her scans showed nothing to that effect. She wasn't used to mentioning her name to others, however. Inside the corps, everyone knew each other, while the human employees had a device that helped them identify the Angels. And outside the corps, no one ever had asked her about her name. She had never been to a bar with a human either. She frequented such places alone or with other Angels, lately mostly with Adriel. The whole situation was very unusual for her—and somehow exciting.

"Nephilim," she said.

"Oh, a fallen one."

"What are you talking about?"

"Nothing," he said quickly, "Forget about it."

They looked at each other for a moment. Nephilim felt attracted to him. Up close, she could study his face better. His eyes were of an uncommon grey-blue, and his blonde hair partially covered them when he let it. His smile was charming, and he clearly appeared like someone who knew exactly what he wanted. He did not seem to be intimidated by her presence, even the slightest.

Tension built up between them. Something unfamiliar to Nephilim, yet not unpleasant in any way.

BEHIND BLUE EYES

"You aren't scared of me," she finally said.

"Why should I be? You don't mean me any harm, do you?"

She smiled. "That always depends on the situation."

He smiled back. "I enjoy the situation as it is right now."

Only now did Nephilim notice something about him that was so unusual it should have struck her right away. She had been too distracted by his demeanor and the whole encounter.

He had no implants or augmentations. No body enhancements of any sort, no neural ports, not even hidden ones. Nothing. Her scan didn't show anything on him but biological tissue. He was one-hundred percent human. This was incredibly rare. And strange.

"It was stunning what you did there before," he finally said after a moment of silence, "I've never seen anything like it."

"I have no idea what you're talking about," she said quickly.

His glance turned warm. "You know what I'm talking about. I witnessed it, and you know I did. It's the reason I followed you, wanted to talk to you. You saved that child, although I'm pretty sure it wasn't out of any duty, but your own will. It was courageous, it was noble...and so humane. Much more humane than humans are to each other nowadays. I never thought something like that possible. And...," he smirked before continuing, "Those pricks had it coming."

Nephilim couldn't do anything but stare at him for a moment. She wasn't sure how to react. Her first impulse had been to stand up and leave. But then she noticed the way he looked at her and knew that every word he had just said was true. This wasn't a set-up of some sort or anything malicious. He simply felt the same way she did about the situation. Somehow it felt comforting. Maybe she wasn't crazy after all.

"Thank you," she finally said, at a loss for words.

"May I ask, why this particular girl?"

"That's none of your business," she replied much harsher than intended.

"Because I murdered her family, destroyed her home, and everything she knew, which left her a traumatized, FUBAR wreck," would have been the honest answer to that question.

He lifted his hands, palms-up. "OK, OK. I'm sure you had good reasons. All I wanted to say is that I admire what you did."

She took a deep sip of her drink instead of saying anything. For a moment he had almost made her forget what she was.

"I'm sorry if I made you feel uncomfortable," he said, "I would never judge you in any way."

"You can't make me feel uncomfortable," she replied, in perfect control of herself again, "I'm not human."

He smiled. "Yes, you are."

"Want to bet on that?" she asked, "I'll take off my glasses, and we'll see how fast all these people run when they see my eyes."

"I would like you to take off these glasses," he said, "I'd like to look into your eyes. I want to see what is hiding behind those blue eyes."

His words stood between them for a moment. She felt this attraction again. The strange tension.

Nephilim was sure that he did not want to see what was hiding behind her eyes.

A monster. Who had killed more people than she could remember.

BEHIND BLUE EYES

It was something different he wanted. And she wanted it, too.

"If you don't want to create mayhem here, I believe we should go somewhere more private," she said with a smile.

"I believe so, too."

***

They went to his apartment, which was a very unusual thing to do. No one ever did that with a stranger, many even didn't invite their casuals into their homes. It was an intimacy they weren't willing to share, and funtels came in all price ranges.

But for Nephilim, everything that had happened this night was unusual, so she decided not to question it. And Jake was the strangest of all.

He lived not far from the bar, and they easily reached his place on foot. His apartment was located in an old-fashioned building which, was in urgent need of renovations both outside and inside. Jake's home was small, not much more than a bed, a closet, a TV, a tiny bathroom and, surprisingly, a little kitchen which was no doubt a relic from the old days. The windows were small, too, and instead of showing a panoramic view, they faced the bleak concrete wall of the opposite building.

Jake didn't switch on the lights, as there was enough illumination coming through the windows from the never-dark city around them. Faded reflections of neon-lights fell through the dulled glass and hushed around them as they faced each other, standing a few steps apart.

Nephilim took off her shades and put them in the pocket of her coat, then looked him in the eye, the tension between them almost tangible again. The place was instantly filled with a slight blueish light radiating from her face.

"Here are my eyes," she said, "What do you see?"

"A spirit set free," he answered, "And beauty."

His words hit her hard. How could he possibly know that? How could he know that she indeed had broken free, at least temporarily? It was impossible.

"And now what?" she asked, trying to hide her sudden insecurity. She was used to handling these kinds of situations differently. But this time, everything was beyond typical circumstances.

"You tell me."

"Now," Nephilim said, attempting to get back in control, "You take off your clothes and lay down on the bed."

He laughed. "That was probably the most romantic thing I've ever heard in my life."

She wrinkled her forehead. "What's that supposed to mean? Isn't that what you expected, bringing me here? Isn't that what you want?"

He slowly shook his head, the disarming smile back on his face. "Not really, no."

She was done guessing. "What the hell do you want, then?"

Jake did not answer. Instead, he slowly approached her, his eyes locked on hers. When he was close enough, he kissed her. His lips were warm and smooth, and the kiss was tender. Nephilim closed her eyes and let him pull her closer toward him, feeling the warmth he radiated. She embraced him while he stroked her hair and her face, their kiss growing in intensity. She perceived that his heartbeat was quickening now, his blood rushing through his veins, his breath going faster—all bodily functions indicating arousal. She quickly forgot about that. The passion he showed was new to her. And it was intoxicating, contagious.

Then, all of a sudden, everything happened fast. Without thinking any further or hesitating any longer, she started pushing him toward the bed in a non-violent, yet assertive way. Still kissing her, he went along; he couldn't have done anything anyway since she was so much stronger than him. She pushed him on the bed and was on him with unhuman agility. Now it was her pressing her lips on his with a stormy kiss, which he returned eagerly.

She tore at his clothing hastily, moving her hands at a speed no human could, and then got rid of her own as much as necessary. Before he knew what was happening, she was sitting on him and he did not have much choice but to give in to whatever she wanted, which he did lustfully.

Jake was about to experience something which countless men like Finwick would gladly have sold their souls for—a Guardian Angel was having her way with him. What they were both famous and infamous for.

"Wow," he said when she was done with him, hardly able to speak, "That was..."

He broke off, catching his breath, trying to think of the right word to express the experience.

With most of his clothes now gone, it was clear that he was more than just in good shape, especially for a totally natural human. However, his body was covered in sweat, and his heart raced like he'd just sprinted a long distance.

Nephilim was lying next to him on the bed, resting her head on her arm, and studying him with her cold, blue eyes. She did not appear exhausted at all.

"Are you OK?" she asked.

Suddenly she wasn't sure if she had been too rough with him. It had felt to her like being swept away by a wave. She could not remember ever having felt like that before. But maybe she had lost herself and accidentally hurt him?

"Yes!" he said and reached out to her, tenderly stroking her cheek and neck, his fingers slightly shaking, "It's just...I've never experienced anything like this before. And I'm not sure yet if I'll be able to walk more than two steps tomorrow."

He laughed. Her sensors showed a high amount of endorphins in his system. She smiled.

"Was it what you hoped for when you approached me?" she asked.

He still was breathing heavily but slowly got better. "Will you believe me if I say otherwise?"

She chuckled. "No."

"Please do. I didn't walk up to you in hopes of getting laid."

He moved closer to her, resting his face right next to hers and continued caressing her cheeks, hair, and neck, his hand steady now.

"But it was amazing," he said, "*You're* amazing."

They kept laying in this position for a while, looking into each other's eyes. Nephilim experienced an intimacy formerly unknown to her. It was pleasant, but also confusing.

When his breath and heart rate went back to normal, he kissed her again. His kiss was softer now, less lustful than before, and she answered it in the same way. Somewhere inside her head emerged the absurd idea that she could do this all night long. Finally, she broke free from him and was about to get up, but he held her back.

"Wait. Please."

She stared at him with raised eyebrows. What else was there to say or to do? They both had their fun and their climax, his energy was depleted, and she would have a unique experience to remember.

"Don't you think it's my turn now?" he asked with a convincing smile, "It would only be fair..."

She struggled with herself for a second then let him pull her back toward him. He quickly got rid of the rest of his clothes before he helped her remove hers.

When she was completely naked and stretched herself comfortably on the bed, her head on the pillow, he looked down on her and said, "My God, you're so beautiful."

She smiled. "And you're hot. For a human."

He leaned down and kissed her, and that brought back her lust. So she wrapped her arms around him and pulled him down. If he thought he could handle a second round, he should have it.

He broke free from her embrace, saying, "Please, just lean back and close your eyes. Relax."

She looked at him with surprise then did as he asked. "OK."

He leaned down to her and gently kissed her forehead, then her lips, then her cheek, before he whispered in her ear, "Let me please you."

Jake continued kissing her neck while his hands started caressing her breasts and upper body. He moved downwards, and his lips covered every part of her biological body with kisses, his hands stroking her tenderly. Nephilim had never experienced such passion before, and his touch created previously unknown sensations in her.

He took time pleasing her, enjoying the reactions of her body and her growing lust. When he finally entered her again, it wasn't fucking, it was making love.

Afterward, they stayed in a tight embrace for a long while. The awkward feeling she'd had before when experiencing intimacy was gone now. She enjoyed being close to him, feeling the warmth of his body, how his chest moved up and down against hers and his hands resting on her hips. Among the countless sexual encounters she'd had in her life, there had never been anything even close to what she experienced with this man. Jake was truly exceptional in many ways.

Finally, she realized that she only had less than two hours left until her usual waking time. She had to hurry to make it back in time to keep the illusion up that she was sleeping in bed.

Nephilim kissed him one more time, then got up and quickly started dressing. This time he did not try to stop her but watched her in silence instead.

When she was done and about to move to the door he said, "Nephilim."

She turned around, looking at him. Never before had she heard her name being said in such a tender way.

He gazed into her eyes. "I want to see you again."

It took her a second before she could answer.

"That's not going to happen, Jake."

She left his apartment without saying another word.

BEHIND BLUE EYES

***

Nephilim was lucky to catch a Skytrain going in her direction, and she arrived at her apartment just in time. Once there, she quickly undressed, went to bed, and deactivated the device. Her internal system assumed she had gone back into wake mode from sleeping and connected her to the grid. She opened her eyes and stretched herself out in bed.

It was incredible. Finwick's device had apparently worked flawlessly. Of course, she would only know for sure once she arrived at HQ. If any suspicious readings had shown up, they would ask her for an examination—or arrest her right away.

Even though she hadn't slept all night, thanks to her augmentations, she did not feel tired at all. But she had difficulties acting naturally as if nothing had happened. She knew she had to behave unsuspiciously if she wanted to stay alive, but after last night she could not blame herself for feeling thrilled.

Last night had been the craziest and most exciting of her entire life. The freedom to be master of her own will and to do whatever she wanted, had simply been amazing, and she had done so many things that she had never experienced before. She knew she wanted more, she couldn't get enough of it. It was addictive, better than any drug she had ever tried. It almost felt as if she had seen the world in mono colors until now, and her vision had evolved into the full spectrum of colors during the last several hours. How could she ever go back to seeing the world in black and white again?

And then there had been the encounter with that strange man. Jake.

He had confused and astonished her. He had completely blown her mind.

Never before she had met anyone like him, and never before had anyone treated her as he did. Like a human, an actual person. A woman. Not something abnormal, repelling, frightening. It was almost as if he understood how she thought. And the sex with him had been like nothing she ever had experienced before.

Nephilim knew that he did not deserve the harshness she had treated him with, in the end. She had never seen anyone more than once because it would not have been worth it. In his case, however, it was absolutely out of the question. It was too risky to visit the same place more than once as she continued her nightly adventures. Besides, getting attached to anyone was the last thing she needed now. She had to stay focused. Seeing him again would be dangerous for her and ultimately for him. So, it might have been harsh, but it was the right thing to do, telling him there would be no next time. She would file him in pleasant memories, though.

Nephilim forced herself to stop thinking about last night and to behave as if nothing particular had happened. In fact, she had spent all day and night at home, trying to regain her performance.

"If you want to keep a secret, you must also hide it from yourself."

When she left her apartment a short while later, she appeared completely normal.

***

At the Guardian Angel HQ, no one asked her to undergo an examination, and no fellow Angels waited at the gates to arrest her. It seemed that the device worked just fine, and no one had noticed anything suspicious.

However, everyone at HQ was agitated when Nephilim arrived. A mandatory general assembly for all Angels had been ordered in the gathering hall. This rarely happened, and it meant that Metatron had something to announce that was of the highest importance. Nephilim was curious about what it could be.

Adriel waited at the entrance to the assembly hall and intercepted her when she was about to enter.

"Neph!" he said with a smile, "It's good to see you up and running again."

She smiled back. "Bad weeds grow tall, you said so yourself."

He looked her in the eye. "Actually, you look better than ever. You almost seem to glow from the inside. Whatever they've done to you in the lab, I want that, too!"

"A day off works wonders," she said, grinning, "And you don't need anything extra. Everyone knows that you're the pretty one out of the two of us. And I'm the badass."

He rolled his eyes. "Yeah, I missed you, too."

They went into the hall. It was already more than two-thirds full, while more Angels were still pouring in. An excited murmur filled the air. Everyone was curious.

"I wonder what this is about," Adriel whispered as they stood in the crowd, "I bet it has something to do with the latest Wasp attack."

"Possibly."

Less then five minutes later, the assembly started. The murmur instantly stopped when Metatron entered, followed by his Archangels. He went to the podium, directly under the huge, neon-blue angel wings symbol, and stood there for a moment in silence, looking into the crowd, his face unmoved.

The Archangels took position around him. Zephaniel close-by, the other three left and right of him. Dumah, taller than everyone else, her posture full of pride. Uriel, brown skin and impressive stature, his long, black, straight hair cut in layers, partially hiding his face. He always appeared a bit grumpy and yet was known to be the friendliest among the Archangels. And finally, Leliel; with her feminine curves, long, curly, bright-blonde hair and beautiful face, she indeed seemed like an angel come to life; the only thing missing was a pair of shiny wings. This was pure irony, and an appearance she chose on purpose, since her cruelty and cold-blooded nature made even Zephaniel look humanistic in comparison.

Looking at them, Nephilim once again wondered why Metatron thought she would fit in there. After last night she was more than ever convinced that she wasn't anything like them at all.

It was silent now as everyone focused on Metatron, waiting for him to speak. Nephilim realized that he was so much more than just their commander. They admired him, adored him, worshiped him. He was the ultimate authority. One word from him and anyone in this hall would kill the person next to them without hesitation—or slit their own throat. Anyone but her.

"Angels," he began, "You performed outstandingly at the algae plant, and I want to acknowledge that today. We lost some good people there. The loss of every single one hurts me deeply, but their sacrifice was not for nothing. We prevented the Wasps from committing a cowardly terror attack on our beloved city, which might have had catastrophic consequences. We did our duty, what we have been created for. Custodio et mortifico!"

"Custodio et mortifico!" they all repeated as one.

"However, this is not why we came here today. I don't need to remind you of your purpose," he paused for a second before he continued,

BEHIND BLUE EYES

"Thanks to the extraordinary performance of one of our people, a soon-to-be Archangel, we were able to recover a full hostile brain, with intact implants. The data we found there is the reason I have gathered you today. Olympias is under attack as it has never been before, and I need every one of you at full performance capacity from now on. I want you to understand how serious this is."

He paused again and looked into the crowd with his piercing eyes. Everyone held their breath. Even Nephilim was fully captured by his speech and charismatic presence.

"For the first time in history, TogbuaXiang and Rosprom have joined forces against us," Metatron said, "They aim to destroy us once and for all."

Suddenly there was unrest in the big hall. No matter how disciplined as the Angels were, this news took everyone off guard. Gasps could be heard, movement, and whispers. Many just stared in disbelief. The Archangels stayed completely cool. Surely this information wasn't news to them.

Nephilim and Adriel exchanged a puzzled glance. She hardly believed what she had just heard, herself. As long as anyone could remember, the three mega-corporations had been at constant war with each other. TogbuaXiang always slightly stronger at an advantage over the other two, while Olympias and Rosprom were more or less equal in both strength and influence.

Rosprom was the third big player in the world. It controlled what was left of Europe, which was mostly Eastern and Southeastern Europe, what was once Russia, Caucasus, and Central Asia. Its HQ was in Moscow, with Satellites in Warsaw, Athens, and Ulan Bator. Their system resembled the pre-corporation world, and was, therefore, most despised by Olympias. Rosprom's cyborg army was less advanced than the Angels but much larger in number, more heavily armed, and fierce in battle. The Angels called these hostiles Proms for short. Their main strength was their excellent intelligence service, which had been built on the principles of old Russia. They had outsmarted Olympias more than once. And now they had apparently forged an alliance with TogbuaXiang.

Metatron lifted his hand, and the huge hall was instantly silent again.

"I know what you're thinking," he said, "That's impossible! It has never happened before! Yet, it is happening now. I assure you, the data we got is one-hundred percent reliable. And it's very unsettling, to say the least. Their operation has the code name 'Operation Golden Sunrise.'"

A contemptuous smile flashed over his face for a second. "That so has TogbuaXiang written all over it. They like it poetic. However, it's obviously been prepared for years. The plan is to distract us with smaller attacks like the one at the algae plant and then strike from within when we are most vulnerable and expect it least. Which has Rosprom written all over it."

Metatron paused again for a moment then raised his voice to support the importance of his next words. "This means they're *HERE*! In our city. Hiding somewhere in plain sight, waiting to strike. We've been outsmarted, blinded. Most likely, it was possible with the cloaking system the Wasps developed. They're sitting somewhere, sneering, preparing the final blow. But we won't let them! We'll crush them! Because we're better than them! We are the Guardian Angels of Olympias! Custodio et mortifico!"

"Custodio et mortifico!" They all were excited now.

"I want all of you to perform better than ever. You'll be assigned into four groups, each led by an Archangel. Each group will have different tasks on a different approach to flush them out. It won't be easy, and many of us will die, but we will succeed. Tonight, however, we will enjoy the slaughter."

He smiled. "We have the target and time for the next Wasp attack.

223

BEHIND BLUE EYES

We will wait for them when they strike, and take them out without any casualties on our side. After that, they'll know that we know their plans, but it doesn't matter. We'll eliminate them all, Wasps and Proms. Operation Golden Sunrise will become the biggest failure in their history. Custodio et mortifico!"

"Custodio et mortifico!"

"Await your orders. Dismissed."

The gathering was over. After Metatron and his Archangels left, the common Angels started to move to the door. Everyone seemed utterly stunned by the incredible news and Metatron's speech.

"Wow," Adriel said when he and Nephilim reached the door, "That's the craziest thing I've ever heard. Wasps and Proms in bed with each other? What the fuck?"

"Yeah," Nephilim agreed, "Sneaky bastards. But I'm confident we'll defeat them."

"Of course we will. I think..."

He couldn't finish his sentence. Zephaniel was waiting in the hall and stopped them.

"His office. Now," he commanded Nephilim.

She shrugged at Adriel. "See you later, I guess."

***

Nephilim followed the First Archangel, who rushed to the elevators at a fast pace.

"That was...exciting," she said once they were inside and away from the other Angels.

Zephaniel smiled. "I love it when he speaks like that. After all these years, it still gives me goosebumps."

For a second, Nephilim was stunned. There was no irony or mocking in Zephaniel's voice or face. Only honest admiration. He meant exactly what he said. She understood why Metatron kept this one so close; Zephaniel admired him from the depths of his heart. He could trust him blindly.

"Yes, he's impressive," she said.

Zephaniel looked at her. "Do you realize how lucky you are, Nephilim? He cares for you, in particular. I don't know why, but he does."

"I'm flattered."

Out of nowhere, his eyes narrowed, and his tone changed. "Listen to me closely. I really like you. I'm looking forward to you becoming one of us and getting to know you better. But if you do anything, anything at all, that upsets him, I will ask him for permission to torture you before he kills you. Do you understand? And that's something I'm extremely talented at, you can trust me on that."

"Why would I do anything like that?" she asked calmly, "I adore him. It's my deepest wish to become one of you."

The smile returned to his face. "Good. That's what I thought. I just wanted things to be clear between us."

The elevator doors opened, and they walked to Metatron's office.

"He has high hopes for you, and so do I," Zephaniel added before they went in.

Metatron was busy at his desk when they entered. He looked up and studied her for a moment, then continued with reading through data files on a holo-screen while talking to her.

"Nephilim. Unfortunately, I don't have much time for you today. You look good, though. Do you feel better?"

"I do," she answered, "You were right, the day rest was exactly what I needed."

He smiled his thin smile. "Of course, I was. Anyway, I need to take back what I said yesterday. You can't take any more time off. We need you in the current crisis. But you won't be on duty more than twelve hours, and no night shift for you. You're still recovering, after all."

"Thank you."

"Don't thank me, it's only logical. Plus, you won't participate in the mission tonight. No combat missions for you, for now, that order stands."

"I understand," she said. Then she added, "This is horrible news."

He glanced up from his work and smiled at her. "It's not that bad, actually. I made it sound more dramatic than it is. You see, that's how you control people. You'll learn the mechanics of leadership in time. Even though Angels are indoctrinated from childhood, sometimes they need extra motivation if we want to push them to their limit—and beyond."

"So, it's not true?"

"It sure is. And it's a dangerous situation I take very seriously. We're simply not as helpless as the enemy believes. I'm good at playing games, remember?"

"They will regret coming here," Zephaniel added. He had moved closer to Metatron.

"They will," the High-Archangel said, "And they've brought us an invaluable gift. The Board has increased our funds by seventy-five percent instead of the promised thirty. Just last night, right after we acquired the data. They're horrified like never before, outright shitting their pants. Pathetic creatures. Of course, I made the news sound even more dramatic than at the assembly."

He exchanged a look with Zephaniel and they both seemed extremely pleased.

"That's brilliant," Nephilim said.

"It is," he agreed, "You can go now, Nephilim. Report to Dr. Emrich. He wants to run some tests on you. I told him he has fifteen minutes, then he has to declare you fit for duty. I don't want neither yours nor his time wasted, we have more important matters to attend. Zephaniel, you stay. I need your assistance here."

***

Dr. Emrich was already expecting her in his lab. He greeted her with professional coolness and asked her to take a seat in the examination chair. But someone else was happy to see her. Finwick was assisting him.

"Good morning, Nephilim!"

He smiled, but she did not return it. "Morning Finwick, Dr. Emrich."

Nephilim hoped he would understand that it was better to pretend that she was still looking down on him. She watched him closely as he prepared everything for the examination. If he was nervous, he did not show it. In fact, he seemed much more self-confident than ever before. Nephilim had to admit that she was a bit nervous. So far, no one suspected anything, even Metatron, who observed her so closely. She was pretty sure that this examination had nothing to do with her nightly prowl, and that the lead scientist was just still trying to figure out what was wrong with her after the EMP attack. But it was a dangerous situation. What if he stumbled over the device by accident? Or got some strange readings?

She was glad that Finwick was there. He would do everything he could to make sure the device stayed unnoticed. Who would have thought that the odd little man would give her a feeling of security one day? Of all people, Nephilim certainly had not expected he would put her mind at ease. She wondered if him being there was a coincidence.

"How are the glitches, Nephilim?" Dr. Emrich asked in a friendly tone while Finwick pulled back her hair and opened her port—on the left side.

It was exactly as he had said, they always used the left side. While he turned his back to Dr. Emrich working on her, he winked at Nephilim. She smiled at him.

"Much better, Doctor," she replied, "The last one was less than two hours. I'm confident it will all be over soon."

"Let's hope so," the scientist said dryly while studying the console, which was now connected to her implant, "I'll perform a scan of your brain and neural implants. Have you experienced anything else out of the ordinary? Memory loss, dizziness, confusing thoughts...dreams?"

"No, Doctor," she said calmly, "Nothing of that sort. I couldn't even tell you what a dream is."

"Hmm," Dr. Emrich was focused on the data rushing over his screen, frowning.

"Is there a problem, Doctor?" Nephilim asked innocently, "Because, you see, the High-Archangel told me you are ordered to declare me fit for duty. I'm afraid he might be very upset if you claim any doubts about my performance without concrete proof. Especially in the current situation. I also remember him saying you had fifteen minutes for your pointless examination; every minute more would be a waste of time, and therefore, a waste of resources. And I'm sure you know, he hates that more than anything else."

Nephilim had decided to play her cards. She had witnessed how Metatron had chewed out the scientists the other day, and how intimidated they were, especially Dr. Emrich. She was now using that fear to her advantage. For some reason, Emrich was suspicious about her and was about to start digging. He also didn't seem to want to stick to Metatron's time limit for the examination. She needed to stop him right now.

Dr. Emrich turned his head and stared at her in disbelief, his little pointy ears turning fire red. "I am the lead scientist of this facility-"

"And I'm following the High-Archangel's commands to the letter," she interrupted him with a smile that resembled Metatron's in an almost eerie way, "If you want some friendly advice, you should, too. He doesn't take it kindly if someone chooses to ignore his instructions, and you'll surely understand that it's my duty to inform him about any irregularities. My internal chronograph is telling me that I've been here for eleven minutes and twenty-five seconds. You better hurry up. Doctor."

Her smile was friendly, yet her tone had turned cold. Metatron would be proud; she was learning quickly.

Dr. Emrich gasped for air like a fish, his whole face red now.

"Fine," he said, "Examination is over. You're fit for duty. Finwick, unplug her."

"Thank you, Dr. Emrich," she said when Finwick was done unplugging her, and then she stood up. "We're at fourteen minutes and thirty-five seconds. That's perfect timing. The High-Archangel will be pleased. Have a nice day. See you around, Finwick."

She left the room without saying another word or waiting for an answer.

***

"What a bitch," Dr. Emrich said once Nephilim was gone, and he had pressed some keys on the device mounted on his wrist implant.

Finwick, who was delighted about how Nephilim had handled the situation and was now staring at the door dreamingly, flinched. "Um...what?"

Emrich turned around toward him, his face red and his small eyes glowing with anger. Once again, Finwick realized what an ugly man the chief scientist was. Ugly Elf appeared still a too flattering nickname for him, he reminded Finwick more of a nasty goblin.

"Didn't you notice how she played us?" The Doctor was outraged. "She's exactly like her boss. Arrogant, malicious, and she thinks she's better than us! In truth, she and her monstrous kind wouldn't exist if it wasn't for us. Maybe it would be better that way...We opened Pandora's Box, and now there's no closing it. They'll be our end one day, I'm telling you."

"If you dislike them so much, may I ask why you decided to work with them?" Finwick asked carefully. Obviously, the goblin was crazy. He had no idea what he was talking about.

Emrich slowly calmed down. He sighed. "Because we need them. Without them, the other two corporations would crush us. Sometimes you need to fight fire with fire."

"I understand," Finwick said. He wasn't sure why Emrich was telling him all this. Maybe he was so outraged that he needed to talk to someone, and he was the only one available.

"But if you play with fire, it's crucial to keep it under control constantly. And this unit is flawed, therefore uncontrollable. You can't possibly know how quickly this can become dangerous," Dr. Emrich continued, "I can't exactly tell what it is, it would require a deep analysis of her brain. But we clearly got some unusual readings today. Of course, it's not enough to approach Metatron and ask for further examinations, especially in her case. Damn bitch knew very well that something was wrong, that's why she forced me to end the session. Dr. Mendez was right, euthanasia would have been the best option for her from the beginning. She contains many valuable parts we could use in other ways. By vivisecting her brain and taking her implants apart, we would surely have all answers we need."

Finwick's heart almost stopped for a moment when he heard the words coming out of the ugly goblin's mouth. Euthanasia? Vivisection? On Nephilim? He had to hold himself back not to jump Emrich and strangle his thin neck. How did he even dare talk like that?

The scientist had returned to his console and was oblivious of the feelings raging in his assistant.

"What stopped you?" Finwick asked with clenched teeth after a few seconds.

Emrich shrugged. "Metatron, of course. You should've seen how he jumped us for only mentioning the idea. I almost thought he would send *us* to the euthanasia chamber instead. He is completely obsessed with that unit. Always was."

Finwick was relieved hearing that. If Metatron protected Nephilim, no one would ever dare touch her. But his curiosity had woken. "Why?"

Dr. Emrich shrugged again. He was calm now. "How the hell should I know? It's not that we're close friends, and he's not human. Maybe he's horny. Or he's simply getting old."

"How old is he exactly?"

The lead scientist turned around and faced him. "Honestly, I have no idea. I've been working in this facility for fifteen years, he was here when I started. My predecessor told me that Metatron was already here when *he* started. And he worked here for twenty years. In all this time, he hasn't changed even a bit. He must have an engineering team working exclusively on him—and they're better than us, with more advanced tech. However, if you ask me, he's too old. No one should get that old. There's a reason we put old people to sleep, right?"

All of this was interesting information, but on the other hand, Finwick suddenly realized that it was nothing he actually wanted to know about. All he wanted to know was that Nephilim was safe. The other stuff Emrich had just told him could easily get him killed. The goblin really had to be out of his mind. Why would he talk like that about Metatron?

"There were two of them once, did you know? Of course, you didn't, how would you," the lead scientist said, interrupting his thoughts.

"Two of what?"

"Two High-Archangels. But that was a long time ago. I only know stories about it, myself."

Finwick did not bother to hide his surprise. "There was another one like Metatron? What happened to him?"

"As far as I know, he was killed in action. Good, if you ask me. One of them is more than enough to deal with."

"Aren't you concerned someone might not like what you're saying?" Finwick asked carefully. It was high time to stop this conversation now. If the goblin was suicidal, it wasn't his business. But he did not plan to go down with that lunatic. "I mean, you surely know that all rooms are surveilled."

A broad grin appeared on Emrich's ugly face. "My dear boy, do you think I would still be alive if I didn't know how to shut down the surveillance? No one can see or hear us now. All they see is an empty room. I can upgrade your wrist multi-tool, so you can do that, too, if you like."

Finwick was utterly surprised for a moment. The goblin *was* crazy, there was no doubt about it. To mess with surveillance was dangerous, but who knew if it might come in handy one day or not?

"I would appreciate that very much," he said.

"No problem. After all, we humans need to stick together against the monsters we've created, right?"

***

It wasn't even 9:00 PM when Nephilim arrived home. She was ordered to end her duty after twelve hours, and it was what she had done. Adriel and all others of her group had to stay and keep on working. She wished she could spend some time with Adriel and talk to him privately, maybe carefully explain the situation she was in.

There had been no time for this since the incident at the algae plant, and she missed being around him. At least she wanted to tell him about her being constantly watched and that he should be careful what he said around her. She could *not* tell him about the device and her nightly adventures. As much as she liked Adriel, Nephilim was almost sure that he wouldn't understand her. He did not share her doubts and confusing thoughts, he was content with what he was and what he did. Sometimes she envied him for that. He worked under the exact parameters every Guardian Angel should, he was a perfect member of the corps. While she...she was FUBAR. She saw it clearly it in Dr. Emrich's face that he thought so, as well. Only her special favorite status with Metatron and the scientist's fear of him had saved her from being taken apart.

After her exam, she and Adriel had been assigned to the group led by Zephaniel, which would mostly analyze data and identify possible targets for upcoming attacks. Other teams would roam the city, following clues, busting facilities, and organizations, which had given reason for suspicion lately. Hundreds, if not thousands of citizens would be arrested in the next days and brought in for questioning, many of them never to be seen again. The Guardian Angels had been given full authority to use any means necessary to stop the menace threatening the very existence of Olympias.

Meanwhile, all units of law enforcement had been deployed to support the cyborg troops. All drones Olympias had were in the air, scanning every inch of the city for foreign and unauthorized technology.

In less than an hour, three heavily armed squads would be sent to the coordinates found in the data of the dead Wasp. They would prevent a terror attack on an important energy supply junction.

It felt a bit strange for Nephilim to sit at home instead of the briefing room for the mission. Usually, she would have been one of the Angels going out there tonight. It was the most serious threat Olympias had to face in decades, and she could not perform her duty as she should. She still could hardly wrap her mind around the fact that Wasps and Proms were working together to destroy them. It was something she would never have thought possible. For some reason, Metatron wasn't that concerned; it almost seemed as if he had been anticipating such an incident. And it was playing in his hands. Nephilim trusted his judgment on the situation and hoped she could contribute to a quick victory against the invaders as much as possible.

She stood at the window for a while, watching the city go into night mode as the sky turned half-dark, and myriads of lights illuminated it instead. The millions of people out there were oblivious that a deadly enemy was hiding among them, determined to destroy everything they had been given. Of course, the government kept the current crisis a secret. A perfect society in a perfect world could not be threatened by such grave danger, ever. Then it would no longer be perfect.

The people out there would never learn that it was monsters like Nephilim and her kind, who stood on the line to protect them. Sometimes you needed monsters to destroy bigger monsters.

Staring into the darkness, she realized something else. It was almost funny. By commanding her to take it slow and keeping her away from combat missions as long as the glitches occurred, Metatron involuntarily gave her the key to her nightly freedom. She wondered how he would feel if he knew he was helping her become rogue. That she was beating him in his own game.

Nephilim was aware that it was more madness than ever to go out there tonight, prowl the nightly metropolis by her own will. Guardian Angels were everywhere, AI police were on their highest alert. The risk of being exposed was high. The smart move would be to wait until everything was over, Olympias was safe again and back to normal.

But she could not do that. It was like a vortex, a magnetism she couldn't resist. No matter how much she tried to stay reasonable, it was stronger than her. She wanted to activate the device and go out there. She needed it. It was like a drug, more addictive than anything she had ever experienced. A drug that would ultimately destroy her, that was almost certain. And yet, she could not resist.

Besides, she had to visit the orphanage and check if the girl had arrived there. Otherwise, she would have to go and kill the brothel owner, who thought he could take her for a fool. Most likely he would be waiting with an army of thugs. It wouldn't stop her.

Nephilim took a shower and prepared herself for bed. When she left the building fifteen minutes later, she had convinced herself that she would only check for the girl. Nothing more.

***

She took her motorcycle this time and arrived at Illumination Plaza less than half an hour later. The orphanage was on a smaller side street only five-hundred feet away. It was located on the third and fourth floor of an older high-rise, which was mostly residential.

Nephilim took the stairs. She had chosen to dress in a black, hooded coat today, which partly hid her face. Together with the large glasses, her facial features would hardly be recognizable by any common software. Naturally, an outfit like this should have arisen suspicion, but no one in Olympias was interested in anything but themselves, people didn't pay attention to her.

The lobby of the orphanage was on the third floor and deserted when Nephilim entered. As with almost everything in Olympias, the place's open hours were 24/7, but this did not mean that anyone was coming here at 10:00 PM. Most likely, hardly anyone ever came here. For what purpose would they in the first place? People donating money didn't need to show up in person to make themselves feel generous and righteous. No one else cared for the children living here.

The foundation running the facility had rented two floors in a cheap building and transformed them into a place where children no one wanted, grew up into adults no one wanted. It wasn't exactly a great place to live, but better than a brothel—or the Guardian Angel recruitment center.

The bleak, gray walls were decorated with pictures painted by children. It did not really cheer the place up, especially since the pictures were everything but cheery.

Nephilim crossed the lobby toward a reception desk, which was served by an outdated hostess-model robot.

"Welcome," the robot said with the slightly tinny voice typical for the old models, "How may I help you?"

"I want to speak with someone in charge," Nephilim said, "Bring me the night-shift manager."

"I'm afraid that's not possible," the robot replied, "Please return during our regular business hours, which are Monday to Friday..."

Nephilim sighed. "I don't have time for this shit."

It took her less than three seconds to hack the robot and override its protocols. It was a very outdated model, indeed.

"Welcome," the robot repeated, "How may I help you?"

"Bring me the manager," Nephilim said.

"Certainly," the robot said and quickly disappeared through a door with a sign that read, "STAFF ONLY," its joints squeaking.

"There we go," Nephilim murmured to herself. She was curious if the brothel owner had stuck to his words or if she would soon find herself in the center of a blood bath. To let him get away with it was absolutely out of the question.

BEHIND BLUE EYES

Shortly after, a woman in her early thirties appeared in the door. She had a friendly, honest face and seemed overworked. This was a person who worked here because she wanted to help. The pay was probably lousy. Nephilim decided to be polite.

"I'm sorry," the woman said, "We're not open to the public now. We run on minimum capacity for the night, and..."

She stopped and stared at the visitor. Although Nephilim had her glasses on, the woman seemed to sense something disturbing and intimidating.

Nephilim gave the woman a friendly smile. "I don't need much of your time, I promise. Just some quick information, and I'm gone."

"Fine." The woman sighed. "How can I help you?"

"Did a girl arrive at your house this morning? Around eight years old, dark hair?"

"Yes, we had a new arrival today. Sarah. She fits your description," the woman answered and started browsing through files on an outdated holo-screen.

"Sarah," Nephilim said, "Is that her name?"

"It's what she said it was." The woman had found the file and showed a picture to her.

Dark hair, big, sad, brown eyes that had seen too much. It was definitely her.

Nephilim smiled. She was relieved. She hadn't been scared to take on the brothel owner and his thugs, even armed they were no match for her. But she had been horrified that someone might have hurt the girl. Sarah.

"The man who brought her also left a generous donation," the woman said, raising her eyebrows as she studied the file, "Very generous even."

Nephilim could hardly hide a grin. Obviously, she had scared the shit out of the man.

"Here's another donation," she said, putting a C-Card on the counter, "I want it to be spent on Sarah. Give her a medical examination, psychotherapy if necessary. Send her to school."

The woman took the card and scanned it into her system, then stared on the screen in disbelief. "Do you mean to donate everything on that card?"

Nephilim nodded. "Everything. Is there a problem?"

"No, not at all! It's just...a lot."

It was, indeed. More than an average person earned in a year. But Nephilim had enough; she did not spend everything she earned like the other Angels since most hedonistic activities had started to bore her over time. And once she was an Archangel she would have even more.

"I want it spent exclusively on Sarah," she said, "Can you guarantee that?"

"Yes, of course. Who should I note as the beneficiary?"

"Anonymous donor."

The woman looked up and into Nephilim's face. "You have a good heart."

She couldn't be more wrong. Nephilim knew that she had no heart at all. She did not show any reaction to that comment.

"Is there any message you want me to take to Sarah?" the woman said after a moment.

"Just tell her, she's not alone. Someone is watching out for her."

The woman smiled. "I will gladly do that."

"That's it," Nephilim said, "You're rid of me now. As promised, it didn't take long."

She walked to the exit.

Just before she reached the door, the woman called after her, "I will tell Sarah an angel is watching over her."

Nephilim stopped for a moment, then quickly left the lobby and the building.

Outside, she jumped on her motorcycle and drove off into the nocturnal city without choosing a particular direction.

Had the orphanage woman recognized who she was, or did she refer to something else? It did not matter. She was glad that the girl, Sarah, had been delivered, and was safe. Maybe the money she had donated would help to make a difference in the child's life. Nephilim decided that she would drop by on a regular basis and see how Sarah was doing. She would easily donate more money in time. It was the least she could do. Assuming she stayed alive, of course.

Nephilim felt happy. Excited, alive as never before.

She knew it was time to go home now. It was the reasonable thing to do. She had accomplished what she planned when she decided to leave the house earlier, right?

She drove up the Deathway and accelerated to full speed, feeling the cold wind stroking her face as if it was the first time, the lights rushing by so fast, resembling long, illuminated ribbons. She closed her eyes for a second and smiled.

Death was omnipresent. It was time to be alive.

***

Lights flickered in the hall; they needed to be replaced. Voices and music could be heard from behind the doors, which Nephilim passed at a quick, resolute pace. She turned around the corner and reached the apartment she was looking for. Without hesitation, she knocked at the door.

It did not take long until he opened. Jake smiled, seeing her. They looked at each other for a moment without saying a word. Then he moved in closer and kissed her. She returned his kiss, opening her lips and embracing him stormily. They moved inside, and he barely closed the door behind them before they started ripping off each other's clothes. Moments later, they were on his bed, touching each other everywhere, their kisses growing more lustful every second.

Suddenly, he stopped. He took her face in his hands and stroked it tenderly, looking into her eyes, his arousal showing all over his body and vital functions.

Nephilim smiled at him, then laid down on her back, letting go completely of her usual behavior. She pulled him down toward her, and again their lips met into a feverish kiss. He seemed to reflect her own desire now. and she closed her eyes and let him have his way with her this time. As she had never done before with anyone.

They both became one, a perfect symbiosis of human and machine.

Chapter Ten

Dreams

"I knew you'd come back," he said.

They were tangled in a tight embrace, their naked bodies pressed together, his exhausted, hers relaxed—both satisfied.

Nephilim chuckled. "A bit full of yourself, aren't you?"

He slowly shook his head. "That's not what I mean. I knew you felt the same as I did."

"What was it you felt?"

"That there was something special. I could hardly think of anything else, besides you, all day."

He caressed her cheeks and kissed her softly before he added, "And I was right. You came back, even though you said it wasn't going to happen."

Nephilim closed her eyes for a moment. Now that she was lying in his arms again, feeling the warmth of his body, she knew that he was right. She had suppressed it all day, had tried to think of anything else but him. Had convinced herself that she wasn't going to see him again. She had been lying to herself. In truth, she had known she would come back to see him all along. There was something special between them indeed. He was special. Like no one she had ever met before.

She gazed into his bright, grey-blue eyes. "Jake, I'm sorry if I was harsh. I did want to see you again. But...it's dangerous to do so. For me, and ultimately for you. And the last thing I want is to endanger you."

"If that's true, don't you think it should be my decision whether or not I'm willing to take the risk?" His smile made her body feel warm from the inside in an unknown, but pleasant way. "Because I am."

"I knew who you were when I approached you," he continued, "But why is it dangerous to get involved with you? Aren't Angels allowed to have casuals?"

"Technically, we are," she explained, "I mean, there's no rule against it. It's just not common, especially not with humans. And I'm...well, let's say I'm not just any Guardian Angel."

"I know that," he said, "I knew you were unique the moment I saw you dealing with those guys. You think for yourself, you doubt, you feel...you care. You're a free spirit who broke the chains. I have no idea how you did it, and you don't need to tell me if you don't want to. But you were able to break free."

She was totally perplexed for a moment. "How do you know that?"

He started stroking her hair and leaned back, looking at her dreamingly. "Because I'm a free spirit as well."

"Is that the reason you wear this?" she let her fingers slide up his chest until they reached his neck and a thin leather strap with a little cross on it.

"This," he said as he took her hand, holding the cross in his, "Was once my mother's. She gave it to me when I was a child. I've been wearing it ever since, in her memory."

"You weren't wearing it yesterday."

"I was. I just took it off before I walked up to you on the roof, knowing you would scan me. But today, there was no time for that." The disarming smile appeared on his face again. "So, are you going to report me now?"

She smiled back. "That would be stupid of me, don't you think? They would arrest you, and who's going to please me the way you do then? I'd rather keep you as my personal prisoner..."

Nephilim pressed her lips to his and kissed him, moving on top of him.

"I have nothing against being your prisoner," he said with a grin as she started caressing him and rubbing her body against his, "You can throw away the cell key if you like."

"Jesus," he said afterward, short of breath, "You're killing me..."

He was lying on his back, and she cuddled against him.

Nephilim grinned. "I can do that all night long. And the next day."

Jake sighed. "I see. I need to work out more if I want to be with you."

She let her fingers wander over his sweaty body playfully. "Actually, you're in extraordinarily good shape for a one-hundred percent biological human. And no worries, I monitor your vital functions at all times. You won't get a heart attack on my watch."

He laughed. "I'm delighted to hear that."

"Why don't you have any augmentations, Jake?" Nephilim asked after a moment, "Not that it bothers me. I'm just wondering. Everyone is augmented, in one way or the other."

"I don't need them." He shrugged, then smiled. "Or do you think otherwise?"

Nephilim stroked his hair and explored the scar on his temple with her fingertips. Usually, he hid it well with his hair, which was longer on this side, and fell in his face, which gave him an even more charming look. However, studying him closer, she had discovered it, of course. It clearly was a scar left by a removed neural implant.

"And what about this?" she asked.

Jake turned his head and kissed her hand, then looked at her. It was only now that she realized that he treated her artificial body parts with the same tenderness as her biological ones. He treated her as a whole person.

"Nothing escapes your attention, does it?"

"You knew what you signed up for, you said so yourself."

"I used to have a neural implant," he said, "But I developed a silver allergy a few years back, and needed to have it removed."

That was a plausible explanation. Many people had complications with their implants for various reasons, especially with the cheaper models.

BEHIND BLUE EYES

Allergies and bodily rejections happened frequently. Tens of thousands died from implant caused strokes every year, but of course, the numbers never were made official.

"Why didn't you get a new one with gold or nickel contacts?"

He sat up and leaned against the wall, facing her. "Because I learned that I didn't need it. It needed me."

"What do you mean?"

"The augmentations give us possibilities we'd never had before, they make life easier, faster, better. Until we realize we can't live without them anymore. And this is where freedom stops and control starts. The augmentation technology is nothing bad per se, but it's not right how it's used. It's being exploited."

Nephilim lifted her head up and rested it on her arm, listening to him. The passion in his voice was intriguing.

"The implants make us traceable, controllable," he continued, "They make us property of the corporation. That's not how it should be, don't you think? The corporation has ultimate power over everything in our lives. They say it's perfect, but what if it's not? What if I want to decide for myself how I want to live my life? And what if it's a different way than anyone else? What if I don't believe what I'm told?"

What he said was highly dangerous. Open doubts in the system weren't tolerated. Nephilim was in bed with one of the people she would usually hunt down and kill. Did he know that? Did he know that he was trusting her with his life?

Would she kill him if she had to? Never.

In truth, she was one of these people as well. She was a doubter, a traitor—who should be hunted down and destroyed.

"What you're saying is very dangerous," she said, "It can get you killed if the wrong person hears it."

He looked her in the eye. "It's the truth. You know it in your heart. Sometimes the truth is not what everyone says. And I know in *my* heart that I can trust you."

She returned his gaze. "You *can* trust me."

Jake leaned down and kissed her, then stroked the glued wound at her side.

"What happened to you? I noticed it yesterday, of course, but I thought you might not appreciate me asking," he changed the subject.

"It's a souvenir from a close-combat encounter with a hostile cyborg," she replied.

"It must have been very painful," his voice was full of compassion, "Did it happen recently?"

"A few days ago," she said, then smiled, "It's just a scratch."

"No, it isn't," he disagreed, "You could've been killed."

Again, she felt this unfamiliar, warmth inside her body. And it was spreading.

"That's true, and I almost was. But that's why I'm here, Jake. It's my purpose."

He shook his head. "To fight and die in a pointless war with no end? No, it isn't. Your purpose is to be free to live a self-determined life. As it should be for everyone."

"It's a beautiful dream, but not for the ones like me," she said.

Jake smiled. "Who knows?"

BEHIND BLUE EYES

They both kept silent for a moment. Then he let his finger slide over the red line Metatron's blade had left on the skin of her chest and upper body. It was almost healed but still visible.

"And what about this?" he asked softly, "What happened to you here?"

"That," she struggled a second to find the right words, "Is a souvenir from a close encounter with my boss."

His eyes turned wide. "Why would he do something like this to you?"

Nephilim sighed. "It's complicated, Jake. Things at the Angel corps are different than among humans in many ways. I guess it's his way to express affection and establish dominance at the same time. Besides, it's a part of his initiation for me to become an Archangel."

He was surprised. "You're an Archangel?"

"To be. The High-Archangel hasn't made his decision official, yet. Which I'm glad about because then I never would've met you."

"Why?"

"It's not something I'd like to talk about now."

"I understand," he moved closer and took her face between his hands, stroking it gently, "What I don't understand is, how sick Metatron has to be to show his affection by hurting you."

"It's nothing, really. Don't worry about me."

Jake was very close to her again. And again, she felt the almost tangible tension between them, like a magnetism. He began kissing her body, caressing her skin with his lips, tenderly.

"This is my way to show affection," she heard him saying.

He kissed the red line where Metatron had cut her from her neck all the way down where it ended, slowly touching every inch with his lips. Nephilim closed her eyes and smiled.

"I wish you could stay," he said later when she was getting dressed.

It was only one hour until her waking time, but she knew she would make the trip quickly on her motorcycle. The Deathway was almost empty at this time.

"That would get us both killed," she answered.

He nodded, then asked, "Will I see you later? I can't take no for an answer this time." The smile showed on his face, the one that she found so disarming.

"You will. I promise."

She left his apartment and hurried home.

***

The next day proved to be a real challenge for Nephilim. It was difficult for her to focus on anything, and none of her state-of-art implants, enhancements, or augmentations were able to help her with that. No matter how hard she tried, her thoughts kept drifting from her duties, and back to the night before.

What she experienced with Jake went far beyond sex—which, too, was amazing, the best she ever had.

It was the way he looked at her, the way he treated her that was unique.

Jake wasn't afraid of her at all, he never had been, from the very first moment. It almost was as if he could see behind her blue eyes into her soul and understand what was hiding there. Feelings, fears, doubts. And more than that. He seemed to almost share her thoughts.

Nephilim never believed it possible to meet anyone like him, she didn't even think it possible someone like this existed in this world. And yet, here he was.

She knew it would become more dangerous every time she went out in the night and met him, but she also knew she would not be able to resist. He had made it clear that he was willing to take the risk as well—although she wasn't certain if he fully comprehended the gravity of it. For there were worse things than death.

Apart from the memories of how he touched her, Nephilim also brooded over what he had said about the world they were living in. The blunt criticism, his clear vision of how it should be. It was intriguing to listen to him, but his beliefs were more than dangerous. They would get him killed sooner or later, and the thought alone made her sick to her stomach, a feeling she had never previously experienced. How could she possibly protect him? She couldn't. This, too, seemed to be something they had in common. They both drifted toward their doom, knowing it, yet unable or unwilling to change the course.

But there was something more about this man that fascinated her. She could not really put her finger on what it was, but she had a feeling that below his handsome face, his charming smile, and his agile, independent mind, something else was hiding. That he was something of an enigma made him even more desirable to her.

Her day at Angel HQ was busy. Everyone was excited about the previous night's mission, which had been a huge success. As anticipated, Wasps had been oblivious about their enemy obtaining their plans and had run straight into an ambush. It had been more of a slaughter than a battle, with forty destroyed hostile cyborgs, and only two lightly wounded on the Angels' side. Metatron was highly pleased, as he announced at the mandatory debriefing. This was a great victory, and a painful blow for the enemy—yet, it was only the beginning. For sure, this wasn't all the TogbuaXiang forces deployed, and there was so far no trace of any Prom activity. They were plotting in the shadows, waiting to strike, as was typical for them. Or maybe they simply let Wasps do the dirty work for them.

While forensics tried to recover some intel from the dead cyborgs, which would probably prove futile this time, Nephilim's team spent the day plowing through myriads of data fragments caught in the grid, searching for anomalies and suspicious activity. Of course, they had AI doing the same thing, but hostile cyborgs knew perfectly well how to outsmart AI search patterns. A human mind with the processing power of a computer was necessary to have any chance of tracking them down—and it was still like searching for a needle in a haystack.

The interrogation rooms were full of suspects, of which many would never experience life again outside the black walls of Angel HQ. To run a huge operation like "Golden Sunrise," the hostiles needed help from Olympias residents. Most of them never learned what they had been involved in. One such instance was the hacker Bhanu, who thought he was doing a simple job like many before. Others were professional criminals who did anything for money, no questions asked. Sometimes ordinary people got involved. Hiding among the civilians was a Prom specialty, which was the reason they were much more difficult to spot than Wasps.

Dozens of raids had been scheduled for the coming night, spread all around Olympias in several districts. Nephilim wasn't to participate in any of them; Metatron's order still stood. She wasn't scheduled for another exam today, which she was more than grateful for, and the High-Archangel didn't have time to summon her either. The crisis required his full attention.

BEHIND BLUE EYES

Nephilim wondered if he had time to watch her or not. Maybe he was so busy that he had forgotten about her for once? But as she had discovered firsthand, he was an expert in multi-tasking. She forced herself to focus and perform her duties as well as possible, so no one noticed anything was off about her.

During the short break they were permitted, she finally had the opportunity to warn Adriel. When no one was watching she took his hand in hers for a second and placed a tiny piece of paper in it. It read, *"Being constantly watched. Be careful what you say."*

She had written it during her latest glitch, which had occurred only a few minutes after she got out of bed. It had lasted less than ninety minutes and was over shortly after she had reached the HQ. To write the message, she had used an eyeliner and a piece of tissue. No one used paper and pencil anymore, and she did not have any at home.

Later on, he said: "I'm grateful we've been prewarned about the hostile plans." He nodded briefly as he spoke.

Nephilim smiled. "Me too."

She knew he had read the note and that this was an inconspicuous way of telling her.

Although she was relieved that Adriel would not get into trouble accidentally now, Nephilim felt sad. It would probably mean the end of their friendship, or at least spending less time together. But wouldn't this happen anyway once she became an Archangel? After all, they weren't supposed to mingle with common Angels.

"I hope this will be over soon, and everything goes back to normal," Adriel added and discretely squeezed her hand for a second before he turned back to the holo-screen he was working at.

"Yes," she agreed.

It was all she could say without lying to him. The truth was that nothing would be as it had been before. There were only two options of how things could go down from here. Either she continued her insane nightly endeavors and eventually got caught and executed, or she got a grip on herself, became an Archangel, and Metatron's pet.

In any case, it was better if Adriel stayed away from her. At the moment, this was made easy for him since the Angels were kept busy, almost 24/7, with only short breaks for three or four hours of sleep. Nephilim was the only one who had her nights off.

They weren't able to extract any valuable data, and no other teams managed to make any progress, either, when Nephilim had gone home after ten hours. Hopefully, the raids would bring more promising results.

However, for her, it was good to know that no raid was planned anywhere near where she was going. That way, she needn't be overly concerned of running into her comrades that night.

***

Finwick was excited. He did not know what to expect. He wasn't sure if the place really existed, or it was an urban legend. So far, he had only heard rumors, and wanted to check it out, but never had the courage.

Until now. Now his life was changed. *She* changed it, turned it completely upside down. He realized that he did not want to spend it simply doing his job or wasting time in VR.

One week ago, he would not even have dared to come to Oldtown after dark; he had been a pathetic, weak loser. And now, here he was.

Finwick was proud of himself. Well, he wasn't proud of *where* he was going. Admittedly, he could have picked a classier place to test his newly found courage, but he wanted to see for himself if the place he had heard so much about really existed—and he wanted to brag to his online friends that he had been there.

It took him a while to find the location. He only had a vague description of where to look for it and did not dare to ask anyone for directions. After an hour of searching the maze of side streets and backstreets of Oldtown's entertainment district, just when he was about to give up, he saw blue neon light coming from a narrow alley.

He went to take a closer look and could hardly believe what he saw. The Purgatory truly existed!

Of course, he had come there to find it, but actually standing right in front of it was another story. The rumors were true. Was it bold to run a place like this? Or ignorant madness?

Now that he had found it, Finwick wasn't sure if he wanted to go in, or if he had ever actually wanted to. It somehow felt odd and not right.

Looking at the pictures and holograms displayed on the building, he had to admit that they turned him on. When the host approached him and invited him inside, he was unable to say no, despite the unreasonably high prices.

He was lucky; at this early hour, the waiting time was only twenty minutes before he could enter the building. Inside, steep stairs led into a spacious basement area. The light was dimmed and mostly consisted of blueish and neon shades. Loud, aggressive Industrial-Techno music was playing, and strobe lights flashed on the walls giving the place a somehow dangerous and violent atmosphere, which was no doubt intentional.

Finwick was led to a corner with comfortable white leather sofas where he was offered a drink. A beautiful girl appeared, all dressed in white latex that was so tight that it revealed more than it covered. She asked him a myriad of explicit questions about his preferences, taking note of his answers thoroughly, a sweet smile on her face. Finally, they established a safe word he could say any time to end the session. After that, he had to wait for another fifteen minutes until the girl came back.

"Your Angel is ready for you," she said, "Please follow me."

She led him past alcoves with white sofas where other patrons were waiting, and then through a maze of halls and corridors, all black and blue with dimmed light. It became clear to Finwick how huge this place was, and how many customers it served simultaneously, even though it did a pretty good job giving them an exclusive feeling.

They arrived at an iron door, and the girl signaled to him that he may enter. But all of a sudden, his courage was gone as if it had never been there, and he hesitated. She smiled and opened the door for him.

Not knowing what to expect, he slowly went inside.

The chamber had black walls and blueish illumination as everything else in the establishment did. A big bed dominated the room. It was covered with black latex linen and equipped with restraints and shackles of various kinds. Beside the bed was a variety of other equipment which could be used to bind and torture people. Some of it Finwick had seen before—at least on pictures and videos—the function of others he could only guess.

In the middle of the room stood a woman. She was dressed in tight, black leather and latex vaguely resembling a combat suit. The outfit was so over the top sexy and revealing—the wet dream version of an Angel outfit—that it was almost laughable. To make it perfect, she was wearing knee-high boots with such exorbitant high heels that it seemed miraculous to Finwick how she was even able to walk one step in them.

Her hair was long and black. Shiny neon-blue contact lenses covered her eyes.

BEHIND BLUE EYES

She placed her hands on her hips and gave him a stern look. "Who do we have here? A puny human? What should I do with you?"

He did not answer, just kept staring at her.

"Let's see," she continued with a faked threatening tone, "I could kill you right now, but that would be boring. I'd rather restrain you and fuck you first." She moved closer. "I can do whatever I want with you, little human, and there's nothing you can do about it. I'm a Guardian Angel of Olympias and you're nothing but dirt under my heels."

Looking at her and hearing her talk, Finwick knew that coming here had been a really bad idea. What had he been thinking? That something like this could replace Nephilim? Nephilim was perfect in every possible way. Nothing in the universe could replace her, ever.

While this...this was a travesty, a cheap joke. An offense to her and all other Guardian Angels putting their lives on the line every day.

Suddenly he felt very shabby, standing here in this place with this woman.

"I'm sorry," he mumbled, "I can't do this."

He turned around, back to the door. It had been closed behind him, and he didn't even know when.

"Hey," she snapped, "Did I give you permission to leave?"

"I'm sorry," he repeated, "This isn't the right thing for me."

"Wait!" she said, her tone changing.

He turned his head around and looked at her.

The stern expression was gone from her face. "If you've changed your mind and prefer to dominate, I can switch. No problem. You can torture your Guardian Angel if you like..."

Finwick shook his head. "No, thank you. Listen, it's not you, it's me. I just can't do it."

He wanted to open the door, but she put her hand on his arm. "Please. I don't get paid if you leave now. And my boss will be upset with me. Is there really nothing I can do for you? A blowjob, maybe?"

He sighed. "No. Really, I-"

"How about a drink then? We can sit down and talk if you prefer that. Believe me, you wouldn't be the first man to do that here."

Finwick studied her face, which was now simply that of a pretty young woman with blue contact lenses who was scared to get in trouble with her boss. He related to that quite well since his boss loved to give him a hard time, too. Although his job and hers couldn't be more different.

"OK," he finally said, "I guess we can do that."

She smiled happily.

They sat down on the bed, and she mixed him a drink from a small bar, which was located in a wall niche next to a second iron door leading to a small bathroom. At first, Finwick felt awkward sitting there with this woman he had intentionally paid for fetish sex. But then they started talking, and it turned out that she was a person like everyone else, and this was just a job to her.

Her name was Melina, she was twenty-four years old, and the more she talked about herself and daily life things, the more relaxed Finwick became. After a while, she asked if it was OK for him if she took off her wig and the contact lenses, since he obviously wasn't interested in the "Angel Experience," anyway. Finwick was more than content about the idea. Without wig and lenses, Melina turned out to be a sweet girl with short, blond, dyed hair and dark brown eyes. She was also witty, and made him laugh more than once.

Finwick started to feel so comfortable around her, he almost forgot that she was a prostitute. When she asked him questions about himself, he told her he was an IT specialist working on implant development. It was what he always said if someone bothered to ask, which didn't happen too often. None of the Angel HQ employees were allowed to talk about their jobs, and where they worked to anyone, ever. It was part of the contract they signed and breaking it would lead to instant termination. It wasn't specified if the exact wording meant the termination of the contract or something else, and Finwick wasn't keen on finding out.

Melina appeared to be interested in his work, or at least pretended to be so, and asked about the implant on his wrist, which was of a kind she had never seen before. Finwick evaded the question, saying it was something experimental from his job.

He had so much fun with her that he hadn't even realized an hour had passed, and she said, "You know what? We can stay here longer if you like, but since you're my last customer for tonight, I can wrap up, and we could go somewhere else. What do you think?"

He was surprised. "Um...what kind of place were you thinking about?"

She shrugged. "Dunno. Whatever you like. There's a cool club close by. I know the bouncer. We can dance, have some drinks...have some fun."

"I'm afraid I'm not much of a dancer." His cheeks turned hot as he blushed.

Melina chuckled. "That's OK, I'll teach you."

She looked at him with big eyes full of anticipation. He was unsure what to do, this kind of situation was new to him and had caught him completely off-guard.

"Are you even allowed to go out with a...client?"

She moved closer, whispering, "If you keep it to yourself, I certainly am. So, what do you think?"

Finwick struggled for a moment, then gave himself a push. Where had his courage gone? Where was his newly found taste for adventure? Sure, this girl wasn't Nephilim, but she was cute, so why not go out with her? And for some reason, she seemed to be interested in him.

He smiled. "Alright."

She giggled happily. "Great! I'll change into something more comfortable, and you pick me up at the back door, OK? It's right around the corner to the right. Please don't forget to tell the hostess what a fantastic time you had with me when she asks you on the way out." She winked.

Finwick did as she asked. On his way out, the girl in the white latex dress asked him if his experience had been satisfying and how he would rate it on a scale from one to ten. Finwick gave it a ten and left a generous tip. Although his experience had been nothing like he expected, he indeed had a very good time.

He found the back door without a problem, and less than ten minutes later, it opened, and Melina came out. Without her ridiculous boots, she was just about his height. And dressed in normal clothes, she looked just like any sweet, young woman. Finwick was charmed.

Melina smiled, moving closer to him, then kissed him on the cheek. "Thank you. You're a good guy, and cute. There're not many like you around."

He felt his cheeks blushing and hated himself for it.

BEHIND BLUE EYES

"I need to make a quick stop at home to fetch something, then we can be off to the club," she said, "I live close by and it'll only take a few minutes. OK?"

"Sure," he said.

"Awesome," she took his hand and pulled him away with her.

***

"I missed you," Jake said.

Nephilim had just walked through the door, and he was holding her tight, kissing her softly.

"I missed you, too," she answered, hardly believing what she was saying. Only a few days ago, she would have thought something like this impossible. There still was a warning voice somewhere deep in her head, which said getting attached like this was a bad idea. But she wouldn't listen.

Feeling his soft lips on hers, smelling the scent of his skin and embracing his firm body against hers felt so good. She wanted this man. More than anything ever before in her life. She slid her hands under his shirt with the intention to pull it off and him to the bed, but he grabbed her hands with an astonishingly quick yet soft grip.

"Wait," he said with a smile, "As much as I love having sex with you, I thought we could start a bit differently today. I want you to know sex is only one of many reasons for me being with you."

"Too bad," she said, returning his smile, "Because sex is the only reason I'm interested in you."

He moved closer and playfully bit her lip. "You're a bad liar."

"Only if I want to be."

Jake turned around to a tiny table which he had prepared for two.

"Please take a seat," he said, "I would have loved to take you out somewhere, but after everything you've told me, I figured it might not be the best idea, so I had to improvise." He disappeared into the small kitchen. "Would you like a beer?"

"Sure," she said, sitting down. This guy was the strangest man on earth. And he never failed to surprise and fascinate her.

Jake brought two bottles of beer and put them on the table then went back into the kitchen. A moment later he was back with two plates of food.

"I hope you like pasta," he said, putting them down.

"Don't tell me you cooked that yourself," she said, raising her eyebrows.

His typical smile appeared. "Of course I did. I'm the perfect man."

Nephilim chuckled. "No, you didn't."

He sighed. "You caught me, I didn't. It's take-out."

"If you did, you probably would be the only person in Olympias capable of doing so."

"It's my intention to charm you, not to poison you."

They clinked their bottles and started eating. Nephilim realized how happy she was. In fact, she realized that, until now, she'd had no idea what true happiness felt like. Happiness was to share a special moment with someone she cared about. And wishing the moment could last forever.

But the moment did not last, and their meal was abruptly interrupted.

A strange, beeping, alarm-like noise rose from Nephilim's coat pocket. Jake gave her a curious look as she reached down and pulled out a small device, frowning.

"Is something wrong?" he asked.

"I'm afraid so," she said looking, at the device.

It was about the size of a credit card, but heavier.

"What's that?" Jake wanted to know.

"A tracking device," she replied, deep in thought, "An illegal one."

It was the one Finwick had given her after acquiring it at the Black Market together with the upgrade for her implant. After they had made the deal that she would be there if he needed her, it had been clear that he would need a way to contact her outside the grid. Finwick had the counterpart of the device Nephilim held, and if he pushed the emergency button, she would get an alarm and see his position. It was a simple device, in fact, but since it could be operated outside the grid, it was naturally illegal to obtain in Olympias, and usually only used by shady individuals. The downside of it was that Nephilim could not tell at all what exactly was going on. It could be a grave situation, or merely a trifle.

In the end, it did not matter. She owed Finwick not only her life but all the amazing experiences her freedom from the grid had given her.

"I'm sorry, Jake, I need to go," she said getting up from the table.

His face showed more concern than disappointment. "Will you at least tell me why?"

She looked at him. "A friend needs me. He might be in trouble."

He got up and kissed her. "Please, be careful. Will I see you later?"

Nephilim smiled. "Nothing can stop me from that."

Then she inspected the windows. "Is it possible to open them?"

"Yes," he said, "But-"

She kissed him one more time before she moved to the window and opened it. Then she stepped onto the ledge, and leaped out into the night without saying another word, her coat flapping behind her like huge, black wings.

Jake rushed to the window and stared outside. His apartment was on the fourteenth floor, which was high, even for her. He saw her grabbing a drone in mid-air, which was flying by at high speed, then she disappeared in the shadows of the night.

***

Nephilim let herself drop from a height of sixty-five feet, and navigated her drone into a hiding position on a nearby roof. The place she landed was at an intersection of two back alleys; remains from a bygone era, and no longer in use, hidden among the high-rises of Oldtown. Not far away, the ruins of a white dome shone through in between the other buildings.

Once, the main administration building of old Atlanta in the pre-corporation times, it used to serve as Oldtowns biggest night club before it had burned down a couple of years back. For some reason city planners did not see a necessity in tearing it down and building something new instead, so far, which was why that the half-collapsed building was used by Black Market dealers and other criminals. AI police cast them out regularly, and from time to time, Angels were dispatched to "clean up," but all of this did not stop said people from coming back after a short respite.

The Dome, as it was called, provided the whole area around it with a bad reputation, which was why most people avoided it. The district's buzzing nightlife was barely noticeable here, and the abandoned intersection gave off a grim atmosphere.

Nephilim looked around and wondered what in the world someone like Finwick might have been doing in a place like this. This was the last position she had gotten from him before the signal went dark, shortly after she left Jake's apartment. Now he was nowhere to be seen, and her scans indicated no traces. One thing was certain, however, if he had been here and pressed the alarm, he probably was stuck in some deep shit.

It did not take long, and her scanner showed a smashed electrical device lying next to an old, corroded dumpster. It was Finwick's. Someone had noticed him having it, took it away, and destroyed it.

Nephilim frowned. Whatever had happened here, clearly wasn't a simple robbery; it was an abduction. She had seen cases like these before and did not like the look of this at all. If she was correct with her assumption, her odd little friend was in grave danger. She needed to act fast, or it would be too late.

There was only one reason to kidnap people like him.

She crouched and inspected the place around the dumpster thoroughly, using her various sensors and vision settings. There were footprints in the dust. Five different people had been here recently, all gathered in one place. Nephilim clearly recognized four sets of male footprints and one that belonged to a woman. One man with relatively small feet, and the female, had come together from one direction and met with the others. The woman had left the group alone, going back to wherever she had come from. The men went in another direction—dragging someone.

It was now clear to Nephilim what had happened here. And since the device had been destroyed recently, and they had dragged him, it was logical that they went somewhere close-by. The question was, where? It would take too much time to scan the surrounding buildings, and following footprints was difficult, even for a cyborg. As soon as they met more frequented paths, it was likely to lose track. She needed something more reliable to follow, such as DNA.

Nephilim focused her scanner on biological tissue and searched around once more. She smiled.

There was a tiny drop of fluid on the floor, and it was fresh, only a few minutes old. One of the kidnappers had a cold and wasn't a big fan of using tissues. Not covering his mouth when he sneezed would cost this man his life.

Nephilim leaned down and dipped her index finger into the fluid. Unique sensors located on her fingertip analyzed the chemical structure of it in less than a second, the software in her brain processed and memorized the genetic code.

When Nephilim looked up, her visual HUD showed her a trail on the ground, indicating the way the person with the particular code had taken, more fluid drops marked in red on the way. People always wondered how Angels were able to track them down, no matter what. This was their secret. They were designed for hunting humans.

Nephilim's smile turned cold as she rushed in the direction which the trail led. Time to play.

***

BEHIND BLUE EYES

Finwick was shaking. He knew it was pathetic, but he could not help himself. He was going to die and was scared, completely terrified. Fear paralyzed him, made it difficult to breathe. It was as if something heavy was sitting on his chest, choking him. He would have screamed in panic, but he was too horrified to even do that. He had been a loser all his life, a weakling, a freak, a no one. And now he would go out like this. Somehow it was only fitting. He deserved it.

They had stripped him naked, except for his underwear, and pinned him to an old-fashioned examination table in a half-sitting position, restraining his arms, legs, and chest with heavy leather cuffs and belts. His head had been fixed between iron bars, which made it impossible for him to move.

It was ironic. How often had he fantasized about being restrained, and now he would die like that.

"Just look at that whiny piece of shit. He's almost pissing himself." The Brute standing next to him laughed. He was tall and bulky, covered in ugly tattoos, with a mismatched synthetic arm. Obviously, he was having a good time.

"Yeah, but a valuable piece of shit," the woman examining Finwick said.

She was in her early thirties, had a green Mohawk haircut, and at least six different implants around her skull and face, one replacing her right eye. In her hands, she held a portable body scanner, which she used to check Finwick's body for hidden implants.

"You think?" the man asked, "Doesn't look that way."

The woman rolled her one eye. "Quality and quantity. How often do I have to explain to you the difference, moron?"

He did not seem to mind the insult, and she continued, "Our wimp here has only two implants, but any of them is worth more than your entire body."

"Hey, I'm awesome," the Brute said and sat down in a chair next to the wall.

The room they were in had no windows, only raw concrete walls, as it was in a basement. A big, bright lamp hung above Finwick, and a small table with surgical equipment stood close-by. A drain was built into the floor, and when he was brought into the room, Finwick noticed stains around it, which could have been blood.

"His neural implant is of high quality and combines state-of-the-art VR access and cognitive enhancements. It's worth a lot of money," the woman explained, "And this," she said, pointing at Finwick's wrist, "I honestly have no clue what this is. Seems like the lower part of a bigger device that can be plugged in and out. But it looks custom made and unique, or at least rare. And rare is always good."

The man grinned, pulled out a long knife, and started playing with it. "Seems Melina did a decent job for once."

Finwick closed his eyes and sighed inwardly. How could he have been so stupid? If he wasn't so frightened, he would be embarrassed. Was he back to being a pubescent kid, unable to use his brain as soon as his dick got involved?

He had followed Melina, a hooker he had just met, who pretended she wanted to spend her free time with him, blindly, into a shady looking area, under the pretext she needed to fetch something from her home. But instead of her home, she had led him into the arms of three thugs, who paid her off. Then, these men had subdued and dragged him away at gunpoint. They had brought him to a run-down building close-by, which was crawling with guys like them. Then into the basement, where this horrible woman they had referred to as "Doc" had been waiting. They seemingly had more rooms like the one he was in, he had seen them while being dragged along. This was a huge operation.

Finwick had heard horror stories like this but always believed them to be urban legends. After all, how could something like this exist in Olympias, the city of light?

Organized crime families where members abducted people to harvest their implants and augmentations to sell them on the Black Market? Yet, here he was. And he was going to die. There was no way he would survive the extraction of his neural augmentation, implanted so deeply in his skull and brain. Only a highly qualified surgeon could pull off such a complicated procedure—in a sterile environment, no less.

Meanwhile, this "Doc" examining him was more of a butcher. She did not even bother wearing rubber gloves.

Unless...

He almost did not dare to think about that. It was a foolish hope. Yes, he had pressed the emergency button on the device he shared with Nephilim when he realized what was happening, but the thugs had found and destroyed it. Most likely, the signal had been too short for her to see where he was. It led to an abandoned alley where the broken device was, how should she ever find him here? And even if she saw the signal, she was probably on the other end of the city and would never arrive in time.

In the most optimistic case, even if she managed to find him and reach him in time, this building was full of thugs, armed to the teeth. Even an Angel couldn't take on a whole army by herself. What if she tried and got killed because of his stupidity? That would be the worst thing that could happen. It would be better to let him die than for her to take the risk.

And what if—this thought hurt him all over his skinny chest—she saw the signal and just did not bother looking for him? Because she had more important stuff to do...

"I'm gonna extract the neural one first," the woman said, and brought him back to reality, "He should pass out quickly once I start, and kick the dirt soon after I crack his skull. Then we move to the wrist. There will be less screaming that way."

"You're the boss, Doc," the Brute said with a shrug, "I don't mind when they scream."

Finwick's body became ice-cold. This couldn't be happening. This had to be a nightmare.

"Call Mo and tell him that he can send someone over to fetch the organs. Wimpy here seems to be healthy, overall. I'll extract the valuable ones, and they might fetch a good price. Besides, there'll be plenty of brain tissue left."

"On it," the Brute made a call through the implant in his ear.

The Doc smiled at Finwick and patted his cheek. "Don't worry. It'll be over soon."

"Please," he tried once more. The first time they had only laughed at him. "Let me go. I have money...I earn a lot...I can pay you double whatever I'm worth. And I won't tell anyone, I swear!"

"Right," the butcher said, "You might be an idiot, but we're not."

"I...I have important friends!" he blurted out in desperation.

She raised an eyebrow. "And who might that be? Amelia? The Inner Circle? The Board?"

"The Guardian Angels."

She stared at him for a moment, then started laughing. "That's a good one! Never heard *that* before."

BEHIND BLUE EYES

The Brute had finished his phone call and was back in the conversation. "What did I miss?"

"Wimpy says the Guardian Angels are coming to save him," the woman said, still laughing.

"Wow. Who would have thought?"

"No, really! I work at the Guardian Angel Headquarters. The implant on my wrist you don't recognize? We all wear them there, it's part of the job. You've never seen one before because it's classified technology!"

Now it was the Brute who started laughing heartily. But the woman wrinkled her forehead and again studied Finwick's wrist.

"You don't believe the fucker, right?" the man said, "He's bullshitting us, that's all."

"It doesn't matter," the Doc replied after a moment, "Even if it's true it doesn't mean they would bother to rescue him. Let's get started."

She turned to her torture utensils and grabbed a laser scalpel.

"*They* won't, but one of them will," Finwick said, suddenly calm, his voice solemn.

"Time to shut up, piss-head," the butcher said, turning the scalpel toward his temple.

"She will come and kill every single one of you. And I will wait here and listen to your friends' screams before she enters through this door, grabs you by your necks, and snaps your spines with two fingers. The last thing you'll see before you go to hell will be her blue eyes."

He had no idea where these words had come from, but they had an impact. Both his torturers froze and stared at him, considering if anything he said could be true. It bought him a few seconds, but that was all

Finwick needed.

"Bullshit," the woman said angrily, "I'm done with you, you stupid fuck."

She placed the scalpel at his temple.

The Brute poked her arm.

"Lila..." he said in a completely changed voice.

She turned around and snapped at him, irritated, "What?"

His fleshy, round face had grown pale, and his eyes were wide. He pointed to his ear, where he heard the comm from the building over. "They're here."

"Who?" she yelled at him.

"Blue Death. They're killing everyone."

Finwick smiled.

***

The five men lingering around the entrance did not suspect that it was the grim reaper approaching them. All they saw was a pretty, young woman, dressed in black, her eyes covered by dark shades. Although this was an infamous part of the city, and she was alone, she did not seem to hesitate even one bit coming toward them. Two of the thugs exchanged a surprised glance, then took a pretentiously intimidating stance.

"Hey," one called out, "Where do you think you're going?"

BEHIND BLUE EYES

She did not answer, but stopped right in front of them, instead, her face unmoved.

The thugs exchanged another look, then the other one asked, "What the fuck do you want, bitch?"

Two more of them came closer now, surrounding her. Only one stayed behind, leaning at the door frame and watching, apparently high.

"I smell a gang-bang, guys," a thug, bulkier than the rest, said with an ugly grin.

He reached out to his potential victim but never got the chance to touch her.

Nephilim's hand rushed up faster than a snake and grabbed his wrist while she turned her head and looked into his face where the grin disappeared to make room for a stupid *"what the fuck"* expression.

"And I smell blood," she said.

Faster than an eye could blink, her wrist blades appeared, and she cut through the necks of all four men with sharp, simultaneous moves of her arms. They gargled, and before their twitching bodies had hit the ground, Nephilim had lunged at the fifth thug leaning at the door and stabbed his skull through his wide, terrified eye.

"Lots of it," Nephilim added, opening the door.

After she managed to catch the guards unaware, no one inside had raised the alarm yet, and she would try to keep it that way as long as possible. Anyone who dared to step in her way would die without mercy. This wasn't only about Finwick, whom she was determined to save no matter what. She knew exactly who these people were and what they were doing. By coincidence, she had stumbled across one of the prominent organized crime operations, which had been a pain in the ass for law enforcement lately.

There had been hundreds of cases of abducted people in the last months, who had turned up murdered and mutilated, their implants violently removed. But this wasn't all. Gangs like this dealt with illegal narcotics and were involved in human trafficking with the intention of forced prostitution, and the creation of snuff films—one of the very few fetishes banned in Olympias.

Any Angel who came across such criminals was not only authorized but obligated to terminate them on the spot. Although she was off duty and technically not even here, she would gladly oblige.

Nephilim took off her sunglasses and put them into her coat pocket.

Slowly, she moved forward down the main hall of the building. It was from the pre-corporation era, and in bad condition, even though it must have been an upscale residential structure in its heyday. The reason why law enforcement had such a hard time getting a grip on organized crime, was, that they changed their locations frequently, mostly around Oldtown, but not exclusively, by far. They also never ran all their operations from one spot.

Nephilim's sensors showed that someone was approaching. She pressed herself to the corner wall and waited. Seconds later, a woman with a cruel expression on her face appeared—and died at Nephilim's blade.

Her HUD was still showing the trail of the kidnapper with the cold. It led down a hall and up the staircase on the second floor. Quickly, she moved forward.

Voices and music came from behind an open door she had to pass. Her scan showed six people inside. Nephilim drew her guns, which she had equipped with silencers in advance of her assault.

She charged through the door and into the room. It was the former living room of a once spacious apartment. Four people inside moved toward her in surprise, and she put bullets in their heads before they could even flinch. Then she stormed through the side door to the adjoining room. There, a man and a woman were making out on a kitchen counter. They both tried to grab their guns, which they had placed on a cabinet shelf but never got the chance. Nephilim eliminated them and quickly left the apartment.

She climbed the stairs, knowing it was now only a matter of time until someone realized there was an intruder and sounded an alarm. It was pointless to try and be quiet now, she was better off making a hasty advance.

Upstairs two thugs were walking down the hall, and she shot them on the run. The noise of their bodies falling alarmed some of their friends close-by.

"What the fuck is going on here?" she heard from behind where two more men approached and instantly opened fire on her. She rolled across the floor, dodging the bullets and turned to the attackers at the same time, then shot both of them in the face.

In an instant, she was on her feet and running to a closed door where the trail led. Her hope was to find Finwick there and, if not, then at least one of the guys who had kidnapped him.

Nephilim kicked in the door and found herself in a semi-dark room with four people inside. None of them was her friend. Two thugs were sitting at a table, about to get high, when they heard the shots a few moments ago. They didn't even manage to raise their guns before Nephilim executed them with two successive shots from the gun in her right hand, while she rushed forward in the other direction with such speed that the third man in the room had no chance to aim at her with the assault rifle he was holding. He fired a salvo against the wall before she was on him, pressing her other pistol against his face without firing it.

The man gulped and lifted his hands, slightly shaking, his nose running heavily.

He was sitting on a mattress, leaned against a wall, his pants open. A young woman of maybe eighteen years old huddled next to him. She had been in the act of giving Snot-Nose a blow job. She stared up at Nephilim with big, brown eyes, as if she was the devil incarnate.

Nephilim classified her as a hooker, and therefore harmless.

"Go," she told the girl, who moved away, horrified.

Then Nephilim addressed the man, "Where is he?"

He sniffed back his snot noisily, shaking his head. "The boss isn't here. He-"

"I'm not here for your fucking boss," Nephilim interrupted him, "The guy you kidnapped earlier. Short, red-haired. Where is he?"

Snot-Nose's eyes widened in disbelief. "You're here for *him*?"

Nephilim pressed her gun hard against his cheek. "I won't ask you again."

"Basement!" he replied hastily, "Third room on the left! Please, have mercy..."

Nephilim backed up. "I wonder. How many have asked *you* for mercy and never got it? How many have you dragged into that basement?"

She had been so focused on Snot-Nose that it was almost too late when she perceived what was happening. The girl she had spared did not leave the room. Instead, she had produced a huge knife from somewhere, and was now about to stab Nephilim in the back.

Nephilim moved around, and instead of being rammed between her shoulder blades and into her heart, the knife just streaked over her shoulder before it bounced off her titanium arm bone, nevertheless, leaving a deep cut in her flesh.

BEHIND BLUE EYES

She grabbed the girl by the neck, whose hateful expression turned into fear. Obviously, her judgment had been wrong, and she had almost paid dearly for that. A mistake that shouldn't have happened to a Guardian Angel, since they were taught in their training that the enemy came in any shape and that mercy was a weakness.

"Bad move," Nephilim said coldly, breaking the girl's spine with her hand and shooting snot-nose at the same time, who was already trying to exploit her moment of carelessness and grabbing his gun again.

Nephilim reached back and inspected the wound on her shoulder with her fingers. It was painful, unfortunate, and bleeding badly. But as far as she could tell, no muscles or cords had been hurt, and the bleeding would subside eventually.

She jumped up, and sprung back to the door. It was bad luck that she had ended up on the wrong floor. Now that everyone was alarmed, she would have to shoot her way down to the basement. It did not matter, she had enough ammo.

***

"Fuck! Fuck! Fuck! I can't believe this is happening! What the fuck?"

The tall, muscular man with artificial legs and tattoos on his face was scared like a little girl. Despite all his fear and distress, Finwick could not help but feeling a bit of Schadenfreude, watching the man and the other two in the room. He was still strapped to the table and knew that it was far from over yet, but he also knew something incredible was happening. Nephilim was coming for him. And she was such a badass. She was unstoppable.

Tattoo-Face had joined them a few minutes ago once the shooting had started, and the first reports had come in that Guardian Angels had been sighted. He had barricaded the heavy door in the hope that this would be a safe place to hide out. Even though, in Finwick's opinion, the guy had to be stupid as he was ugly. After all, what idiot ran into the basement when a killer was coming for him? Everyone knew that running upstairs to hide from a killer or monster was pretty dumb enough...but the basement?

After the Doc had explained to him that he had chosen the worst place to hide out, in the whole building, he began freaking out.

The Brute had grown paler by the minute listening to the comm. "You still there? Can you hear me? What's going on...Jen? Jen..." He looked at the Doc and whispered, "She's gone...she was screaming like crazy. They're being wiped out..."

They heard shots being fired, close-by now, in the basement. Then screams.

"Fucking hell!" Tattoo-Face shrieked, pointing at Finwick, "Who is this son-of-a-bitch? Why is he so important? And why the *hell* did you bring him here?"

"We had no idea," the Brute tried to defend himself, "He seemed to be just another loser!"

"I told you to let me go," Finwick reminded them, "I warned you."

"Shut up!" the woman yelled at him.

"Let's kill the piece of shit!" the Brute suggested brandishing his knife.

"Are you insane?" the Doc snapped at him, "He's our life insurance! The only chance we got. If the bitch wants him so badly, we need to play that to our advantage."

"What are you talking about?" Tattoo-Face asked.

"Apparently, it's only one. One damn blue-eyed bitch."

"And she's taking out all of us? By herself?" Tattoo-Face was close to fainting.

All of a sudden Finwick realized why everyone was so keen on keeping the Angels under strict, one-hundred percent control at all times. How dangerous they really were. What an incredible weapon. If Nephilim alone took out a whole army of heavily armed thugs, what were they capable of when working together? What would happen if they *all* went rogue? Could anyone or anything stop them? Finwick doubted it.

"Because of *him*?" Tattoo-Face was almost hysterical now.

"Because of him," the woman repeated dryly.

Finwick smiled. Then he noticed that the Brute was studying him.

"I have no idea what you did," the big guy told him with a sudden acknowledgment in his voice, "But you must have done something right, man."

Yes, Finwick knew that, too. For once in his life, he had done something right. Back when they made their deal, if he had chosen option one and went to bed with Nephilim, he would be dead now.

"Idiot," the woman hissed, "Take position behind the door and ambush the bitch when she enters. I'll distract her by threatening to cut wimpy into shreds. And you-" She nodded to Tattoo-Face. "Try not to shit your pants, moron."

Finwick stiffened as she crouched behind him, grabbed him by the chin, and placed her laser scalpel against his carotid, which was pulsing nervously.

"Don't move, or I'll let you bleed out like a stuck pig. And not one sound from you."

The Brute did as commanded and took position behind the door, drawing his long knife and an old-fashioned pistol. Finwick worried. What if they succeeded to ambush Nephilim when she entered the room? Should he try to warn her? Would the butcher slice his neck if he tried?

Everyone in the room was very tense now. They could do nothing but listen to what was going on outside. The shots and screams had stopped and been replaced by a menacing silence. All that could be heard was the heavy mouth-breathing of Tattoo-Face. A few seconds passed, which felt like an eternity.

Suddenly the metal door was smashed open with such immense power that it hit the Brute forcefully in the face and made him stagger. For a moment, everything seemed like slow motion for Finwick. It was so intense and breathtaking.

Nephilim appeared in the door like an angel of death.

Her usually lovely face seemed like a cold, pale mask. Focused, not showing any emotion. The artificial neon-blue eyes gleaming. Her black clothes were slick with blood, as were her gun-wielding hands.

For the first time, Finwick realized why people were so horrified of the Guardian Angels, for Nephilim was a blood-curdling sight; in full combat mode, coming to kill her enemies, without mercy, like a machine.

And yet at the same time, for him, she was the most wonderful, beautiful sight in the world.

Then everything went so incredibly fast that it was over before it even started.

Nephilim wasn't up for any games. Not hesitating for a fraction of a second, she first shot Doc in the head and spread her brains all over the wall behind her.

Without turning around, Nephilim grabbed the Brute's artificial arm in which he held his gun and yanked it out of his shoulder with one sharp twist. Spinning at him, she hit his other hand—the one holding the knife—with her elbow, at an inhuman speed, forcing it toward himself, and ramming the Brute's own weapon through his chin, up into his skull. His eyes went blank as he collapsed.

Not even finishing her twist, Nephilim hit Tattoo-Face in the neck with her foot, breaking his spine so forcefully, that his head sank back in an impossible angle.

It was over. And it didn't last two seconds. The three thugs didn't stand a chance. They never did.

Finwick stared at her, open-mouthed, as she slowly turned around and looked at him. Her face changed, the cold mask of the killer cyborg disappeared, and she smiled at him. He knew how lucky he was, being on her good side.

"Nephilim..." was all he could say.

He was speechless. What he had just witnessed was incredible. So many contradictory feelings stormed around inside him, simultaneously, that he almost became overwhelmed.

He was relieved. Euphoric, even. Because he knew he was going to live. In a way, he was horrified by what he had just seen. But he also was fascinated. And thrilled. And—he could not help himself—aroused.

Watching her approaching him, frightening and wonderful at the same time, he knew he loved her, always had and always would.

"Are you alright?" she asked, inspecting him from head to toe, scanning him.

He tried to nod, but the iron bars holding his head prevented it. "Yes. I'm so glad you came!"

She smiled while her blade appeared at her right wrist. "Did you ever doubt it?"

"No, I didn't," he said as she cut through his restrains and opened the iron bars simply with the strength of her hands.

"I told you, I have your back."

He noticed big drops of blood running down on the table as she leaned down.

"You're hurt!" he cried out.

"It's nothing," she said, helping him up, "We need to get you out of here quickly. I believe I got all of them, but more could be on their way. Besides, AI police could have noticed something is going on here, and I want to be gone when they arrive."

Finwick did not share the opinion that this was "nothing," but he didn't want to argue with her now. She probably knew what she was doing.

Nephilim grinned. "You better put some clothes on."

He nodded, then hugged her.

"Thank you, Nephilim," he said, fighting not to let his voice break, "You saved my life. It was close."

"Always," she said, hugging him back. He felt the blood running down her shoulder, and it hurt his heart. She let go of him and added, "It was no big deal, really. It's what I do for a living, as you know. Now, hurry."

BEHIND BLUE EYES

Luckily his clothes were still there. At least his shoes, pants, and jacket. His shirt, they had cut off him after he was restrained. He got dressed quickly.

Nephilim signaled for him to follow her out the door, and he did. In the basement, they encountered several dead thugs that Nephilim had eliminated on her way to him, but that wasn't all. The door next to the room Finwick had been kept in was open. He peeked inside when passing by, and what he saw made his flesh crawl. Another person was restrained to a table similar to the one he had been on. And this person hadn't been as lucky as he was. All he could tell was that it had probably been a woman, but he even wasn't entirely sure about it. The body was shockingly mutilated; the skull cracked, the chest open, with intestines hanging out, one hand, and a leg missing. It was so horrible that Finwick almost threw up, even though he only glanced at the massacre for a second.

"I know," Nephilim said, grabbed his hand, and pulled him with her at a faster pace, "Bastards. They won't perform vivisections like this again anytime soon."

There had been two corpses lying in the room, executed with headshots. The Angel had paid them a visit on her way to him, as well.

When they reached the ground floor, they encountered more dead gang members. Finwick's hair stood up, seeing so much death around him. Until now, he had never seen a body, even once...

"How many did you kill to get to me?" he asked, panting.

She shrugged. "A few. They had it coming."

Her words and the ease which she said them with sent a cold shiver up his spine. They reminded him, again, of what she truly was at her core: a killer.

But although she played it down in front of him, he knew that she had risked her life to save him.

Nephilim led him into a former apartment with more dead people inside where she smashed a glass door leading outside.

"We better not take the front door," she said.

She jumped out, then helped him down, and they ran off the premises and into the night together.

Nephilim accompanied him to the transport level where he could get a robo-taxi that would drive him home. In the darkness, the blood on her black clothes was barely visible, and if anyone should look out of the window of a cab driving by, they probably wouldn't care—if anyone looked out of the window at all.

"How did you even end up there?" she asked, "How did they get you?"

Finwick stared to the ground, deeply embarrassed. "I followed a hooker."

"Classic honey trap." Nephilim shrugged. "Nothing to be ashamed of. Where did you find the hooker?"

Finwick hesitated before he answered. Now it was getting really bad for him. "At a club called the Purgatory. But, I...I only went there to look! I was curious, and she was nice and..."

Nephilim chuckled. "It's OK, I'm not offended, even if you did more than just take a look."

Then her expression got stern. "But I warned them to close that place down. And now their personnel are selling out patrons?"

He glanced at her in disbelief. "You've been there?"

BEHIND BLUE EYES

"I stumbled on it by accident," she said before a cold smile flashed on her face, which reminded Finwick of someone, but he could not say who, "They won't exist much longer."

A cab stopped. "Again, thank you so much, Nephilim," he said, getting in, "I would be dead now if it wasn't for you."

He just wished he could stay with her.

She looked into his eyes. "You gave me freedom, Fin. Nothing could ever be big enough to repay you for that."

She closed the door. He felt a sob in his throat.

When he turned around to look at her one more time, she was gone.

***

When Jake heard the knocking, he at first thought it was at the door. It took him a moment to realize that it was actually at the window.

Nephilim stood behind the glass, balancing on the ledge. Jake quickly moved to the window and opened it to let her in.

"I was worried," he said, kissing her.

She smiled. "You shouldn't be."

He noticed her bloody clothes.

"It's not mine," she said before he could worry more, "But I thought it might be a good idea not to scare your neighbors, so I returned the same way I left."

Jake wanted to hug her but noticed the wound on her shoulder. The bleeding had almost stopped, but it was still clearly visible.

"This is yours, though," he said, his voice full of concern, "What happened?"

"Bad judgment and a moment of carelessness," Nephilim explained, slowly taking off her coat, which caused her visible pain, "I tried to spare someone's life, and that's how I got repaid. I'm afraid I need your help with that."

"Of course," he said, "Whatever you need."

Nephilim had brought a small First Aid Kit, which every Angel had stored inside their drone. After she had removed all the clothes from her upper body, they sat down, and she asked Jake to tend to her injury. The First Aid Kit contained everything he needed, special disinfectant cloths to clean the wound and a small portion of glue to seal it.

"So, what happened?" he asked while carefully cleaning the wound. The cut was deep, and started bleeding again as he worked on it.

"My friend got kidnapped by implant harvesters, and I had to break him free."

She then told him the whole story in a few short sentences, as if it was nothing special.

"Wow," Jake said, "That's incredible. But you could have been killed..."

"I wasn't."

He was done cleaning the injury and grabbed the glue. "Who is this friend? Why is he so important to you that you risked your own life to save him?"

Nephilim sighed. "It's hard to explain. He gave me freedom. To make my own choices. To see you. I would go through hell for him, I owe him that."

"What exactly did he do?"

Jake was done gluing the wound. It was fire red, but the bleeding had stopped, and the glue would hold it together no matter how she moved until it healed.

"All done," he said, kissing her on the neck.

She turned around. "Thank you."

"Nephilim," he said and took her hands in his, "You can trust me. With anything. You know that, don't you?"

"I know," she replied before going quiet for a moment, searching for the right words. Then she told him everything. About the device Finwick had implemented, how it worked, and why she was so grateful.

Jake listened, then asked, "So, you're completely cut off the grid? They can neither listen to you nor track you?"

"Yes."

"That guy's a genius."

"He is," Nephilim agreed, "Now you understand why I had to cut our dinner short for him."

Jake smiled. "I do. We can continue now if you like. I can warm it up, it should still taste acceptable."

"I'd rather use your shower, if I may," Nephilim said, "I literally have blood on my hands."

"No, you may not," he answered and waited for her surprised look before he continued with a grin, "Unless I can join."

Jake's shower was small but had enough room for both of them if they stood close together, which they did not mind. He helped her wash the blood off her body, and Nephilim relaxed under the warm water and his touch. His hands grew more passionate and eager, and the two of them embraced with a sensual kiss.

After having sex in the shower, they finally sat down and finished dinner, which had turned into a late-night snack. Both were wearing only towels.

"Now it's your turn, Jake," Nephilim said after a while.

He looked up from his food. "For what?"

"To tell me more about you. You're not like any other person I've ever met."

He smiled. "I'll take that as a compliment."

"You should. You're an enigma. How you behave, what you say, what you know...what you think and believe. You're different, and I want to know why."

He fell silent and just looked at her for a moment.

"You, too, can trust me," she added, "You know that."

"OK." He laughed nervously. She had never seen him like this before. "If anyone would have told me a week ago that I'd be talking about this with a Guardian Angel, of all people, I would have thought they were completely crazy." He laughed again, then got serious. "Nephilim, I might be stupid and crazy for sharing with you what I'm about to, but I trust you with all my heart. I believe you're extraordinary. And I believe we think alike."

BEHIND BLUE EYES

"Tell me," she said.

"I'm part of a group of people, a movement, which is determined to end the corporate dictatorship and establish freedom for everyone."

Nephilim stared at him, utterly perplexed. For a moment, she wasn't sure if he was joking. She did not know what she had expected him to say, but not...this. This was insane. Looking into his eyes, however, she knew that he was serious, very serious.

"Such a movement does not exist, Jake," she finally said, "It can't. We eliminate anything that could even lead to forming such a group. Any wrong speech, any thought which could pose a danger to the system. That's why we are here. To protect Olympias from dangers from the outside and the inside. From-"

"People like me," he finished her sentence with a smile, "Yet we do exist, Nephilim. And we are stronger and bigger than you could ever imagine."

They looked at each other in silence for a moment before he continued with his typical, disarming smile, "Did you really believe I was some loser who couldn't do better than live in such a shoebox?"

"To be honest, I wondered about that. But I didn't care. Besides..." She looked around. "It definitely has its charms."

"No, Nephilim. I used to be a corporate associate like everyone else. I lived in a fancy apartment, pursued a hedonistic lifestyle, and had everything I thought I desired to have. Yet, inside, I felt empty, and it got worse every day. Everything seemed shallow and unreal to me. Until I met others who felt the same. After that, I gave up everything I had and dedicated my life to the cause. So, here I am."

"That's the true reason you had your implants removed," Nephilim said, "To make yourself difficult to track down, even for us."

"That's right. And I'm sorry I lied to you about that. I feel bad about it."

"You had to. The alternative would have been to tell me the full true story. I understand your hesitation, considering what I am."

He looked her in the eyes. "So, are you going to report me now?"

"It would be my duty, of course," she said, "But, do you see me doing my duty now? By going rogue from the grid, I commit treason which will cost me my life if it's discovered. And even if it wasn't so..." she paused for a moment before continuing, "I would never do anything to harm you. Yes, you can trust me completely."

He took her hand in his and kissed it. "I know."

"But why, Jake?" she asked, "Why does this group of yours exist? Is our society really so bad that it needs to be destroyed and changed forcefully? Aren't humans living better now than ever before in human history? After all, we eradicated almost everything that made humans miserable in earlier centuries, everything that led to violence, war, and suffering. Everyone is equal now, everyone can be anything they want, no matter who they are. Is that really so bad?"

"That's just what they're telling you, Nephilim," Jake said, "It's what they tell all of us from early childhood, indoctrinating us. What they are teaching at schools, what they call history, is mostly wrong; they twisted it to fit their narrative. They make us believe everything was bad in the past, and that there's no alternative to happiness than the system now, which is perfect. It's simply not true. Of course, the world wasn't perfect in the pre-corporation era—we shouldn't forget it led to the Great War—but what they will never tell you is what role the mega-corporations played in that war, and who profited from it. And they will never tell you about the beauty of the old world, how rich its various cultures were, full of art, philosophy, ancient traditions preserved from generation to generation. It's why they banned old books. Because they contain facts that Olympias doesn't want people to know anymore. You can change digital information and twist it to your liking, but old books, they stay the same as they were on the day they have been printed. That's why they're dangerous and need to be destroyed."

"*Who controls the past controls the future. Who controls the present controls the past,*" Nephilim quoted.

"Yes, yes!" Jake smiled happily, then jumped up, moved to her side of the table to kiss her, excited. "That's exactly what I mean! How do you know that quote? That book has been banned for *decades*; it's one of the most forbidden to have."

"I know someone who owns a copy," she said.

"Really? I'd love to meet them!"

"I don't think so. Trust me on that."

He crouched in front of her, holding her hands. "See inside yourself, Nephilim. You know everything I've said is true. You think the same. I know you do."

"Maybe," she said slowly.

"I'd like to know something you weren't willing to tell me after we met. Why is this girl you saved from the brothel so important to you? Would you share it with me now?"

She hesitated with her answer, "My squad killed her family and destroyed her life. I was the one who brought her to Olympias with the promise of a better life. I wanted to fulfill that promise at all costs."

He smiled. "You're amazing."

She shook her head. "No, I'm not, Jake. Look at me, what I really am. I'm half machine; a cold-blooded killer."

"That's not what you are, it's what they *made* you to be. And I don't care. I see something else in you."

Nephilim had to look away. His words touched her to the core. She knew, if her artificial eyes were able to produce tears, she would be crying now.

"Do you know why they make you do this?" Jake asked after a moment, "Raid these villages and kill everyone inside, leaving nothing behind but ashes?"

"Because these people are terrorists. Enemies of Olympias and its citizens, dangerous subjects..."

Jake slowly shook his head and she fell silent. "No, Nephilim. It's what they tell you. The true reason why you kill these people is another. They have escaped the system, they prove life away from it is possible. They made a choice to live a different life, to pursue values that are frowned upon in Olympias, if not outright forbidden. They want to live their lives as they see fit, not as the system tells them to see it fit. They want to have a partner to share it with, a family, a community built on solidarity and cooperativeness. They don't want to live only for themselves and the system, which in fact, is nothing else than the corporation dictating everything. And because they chose this lifestyle and manage to succeed with it, they have to die, they have to be destroyed. Because they are proof, the system is not perfect. There are alternatives."

Listening to what he was saying, she knew that he was right. And she realized that deep inside, she had known it for a long time.

"This is what the movement I belong to is fighting for," he continued, "For freedom. For everyone's freedom to decide how they want to live their lives. With whom, where. For the freedom to die of old age surrounded by family. For the freedom of speech. For the freedom of thought." He lifted his hand and stroked her face tenderly. "For the freedom of me being with you."

BEHIND BLUE EYES

She leaned down and kissed him, softly caressing his hair and face. He opened her towel and let his hands slide over her naked body. Then he started kissing her all over.

After sleeping together, they cuddled close in bed. The lack of sleep and exhausting rescue mission caused something Nephilim didn't expect; she fell asleep.

And she dreamed.

***

She's the little girl again. Walking through tall grass full of scented wildflowers, her little feet are bare, feeling the warm soil under her toes. It's a hot day, the sun is shining on her long, black hair, heating it up. She can hear the river behind her and the waterfall, which is not far away, as she knows. The woods surround everything with a scent of bark, leaves, and fresh mushrooms. And even higher than the tallest trees are the mountains. Like gigantic walls, they shield the village from anything on the outside that would cause them harm.

She sees some other kids playing close-by; her friends. But she doesn't want to join them now. She's picking the colorful flowers from the high grass, making a bouquet for her mom. Mom will be happy about it, and the girl loves to see her mother happy and smiling.

One blink later, the flowers are in a vase. But her mom is not smiling. Her face is pale and tense, her eyes wide. She has never seen her mom like this, it scares her.

It's night, it storms. It's a night for monsters to come.

Her mother peeks outside through the front window of the small house, a long rifle in her hands, two pistols stuck in her belt. "They're almost here! Hurry!"

She can hear screams, terrible screams, and shots being fired.

Her father takes her by the hand and leads her to a small window at the back of the house, finding his way easily even though he's blind. He, too, is armed with a huge knife and a shotgun.

He opens the window then crouches next to her.

"Listen to me carefully," he says, his voice calm, yet assertive, "Once you are out of that window, I want you to run as fast as you can. No matter what you see or hear, don't stop. Never stop. Run until you reach the waterfall. Hide in the cave behind it and don't come out until the next day. No matter what. Do you understand me?"

She nods, her eyes welling. "I'm scared, Daddy! I want to stay with you!"

"No," he says as he grabs her shoulders, "You're not scared. You're strong. You need to be strong now, Evelyn. Do you understand?"

She sobs. "Yes, Daddy."

He hugs her close. "I love you so much, sweetheart."

"I love you, too."

He lifts her up and through the window into the darkness.

"I'm sorry I failed you," are the last words she hears before he closes the window after her.

She does as he told her, and runs as fast as she can. She tries to ignore what is going on around her. Shots, people screaming, children crying, fire, smoke

BEHIND BLUE EYES

burning in her lungs. She leaves the village behind her and crosses the meadow with its flowers. It's dark, but the tree line is illuminated by reddish light coming from the fires. The grass moves with her, the stormy wind blows leaves through the air and into her face.

Suddenly there's lightning. Huge, blueish lightning in the black sky, followed by deafening thunder. She shrieks and stops running for a moment, her lungs aching, her side in stitches. But then she remembers her father's words and moves on. Toward the river, and from there, to the waterfall. She slips behind it into the cave and hides behind a rock, shivering, whimpering. Never in her life has she been so frightened, so alone, so lost.

She doesn't know how long she's been there until she notices someone is coming. Peeking out from behind her rock, she sees blue eyes glowing in the darkness. Many of them, moving closer inside the cave. Coming for her.

She shrieks weakly and tries to hide more behind the rock, shaking. It's pointless, and she knows it.

Blue eyes approach her. A slim man dressed all in black crouches in front of her.

"There's no need to be afraid, little one," he says with a soft, friendly voice and a smile on his face, "We're here to save you. We are the good guys."

She looks up to him, tears running down her cheeks. Sees that he means no harm to her. Sees how friendly his smile is. Something about him reminds her of her father.

He carefully reaches out his black-gloved hand toward her, his blue eyes gleaming in the dark.

"Come with me, Evelyn. I'm going to show you a new world. I will give *you a better life."*

Slowly her little fingers reach out toward his hand. She hesitates.

"Where are my parents?"

"They're gone, Evelyn. They went away and left you behind."

"No!" she cries out.

"But don't worry," he says softly, "I will take care of you now. I will always protect you, always watch over you."

Her fingers touch his, and he takes her by the hand.

It's only now that she recognizes his face. It's Metatron.

***

Nephilim woke up, gasping for air. She sat up in bed, shaking. Jake, who had fallen asleep next to her, opened his eyes.

"Nephilim. Is something wrong?"

She did not answer; instead, her body was shaken by something she had never done before. She cried without tears.

Jake sat up as well and put his arm around her. "Oh my god, Nephilim...please tell me what happened. What's wrong?"

She could hardly speak. "I know what happened to me. I've seen it."

He kissed her temple and her forehead, hugging her close. "You dreamed. It was just a dream."

She shook her head. "It wasn't a dream, Jake. Cyborgs don't dream. It was a memory. From before I became what I am now."

"From before they *made* you what you are now," he said soothingly.

"Before *he* made me what I am now. And he's not done with me yet," she said, frowning.

"Who?"

"It doesn't matter. I need to leave."

She realized that she had only one hour left until her waking time, and she needed to hurry. Freeing herself from his embrace, she kissed him, and got up to get dressed. Jake moved to the edge of the bed, his face concerned.

"OK," he said, "I'm sorry this has upset you so much."

"I'm fine," she answered, back in control of herself.

"Will I see you tonight?"

"Oh, you will. And I want you to introduce me to your friends in the resistance."

"You...what?" Jake almost fell off the bed in surprise.

Nephilim stepped toward him half-dressed, sat down, and took his hands in hers.

"Please, Jake. Bring me to your people. I want to become part of your movement. I want to help to end this once and for all."

Chapter Eleven

Behind Blue Eyes

Nephilim was more than grateful that she hadn't encountered Metatron the following day. She wasn't sure if she would have been able to hide her emotions in front of him. Last night's dream, or more precisely, her long-buried memories that had surfaced in the form of a dream, had disturbed her and shaken her to the core.

Of course, she had been aware that she wasn't born a Guardian Angel and that she had to have been a normal child once before she was recruited and augmented, but remembering how exactly it had happened had changed everything for her. All these years, she had been struggling with herself, asking herself over and over again who she really was. Now she understood. In the first place, she was a victim. The victim of a brutal system. A system, beautiful on the outside, and rotten on the inside. A system so "perfect" that it needed killer cyborgs to search out and destroy anyone who disagreed with it.

And it was no wonder now, how Metatron knew her so well—he could read hidden emotions on her face. He had known her since childhood, since before she could even remember. It was him who had made her what she was today. After his people had murdered her parents.

The irony was that she was doing the exact same thing. It was what she had done to Sarah's family, and the community she had lived in. This cycle would go on forever until somebody broke it.

She had realized that everything that Jake had told her was the truth. He was right, the corporation rule had to end. Knowing all of this, how could she possibly go back to her old life and continue as if nothing had occurred? How could she become an Archangel? No, if there was any possibility for her to support the movement Jake was part of, she would do it. She owed it to all the little Sarahs out there who deserved a happy life among their families and friends.

Jake had changed her life, and there was no turning back. She smiled when thinking about him.

For the first time, she did not pay much attention to what was happening around her at HQ. The Angels had raided multiple locations last night, and now the cells and interrogation rooms were full of suspects, but there hadn't been a new Wasp attack so far. Everything indicated that their last encounter with the Angels had been a hard blow to the TogbuaXiang troops and that they were lying low, for now, coordinating something big with their allies.

Nephilim did not really care. Her thoughts were elsewhere. She didn't miss the opportunity to take care of one matter, though. Plowing through endless amounts of data, she fabricated a report claiming out-of-the-norm activity around a certain address in Oldtown. It was added to the list of scheduled raids for that night.

It wasn't important if there was truly suspicious activity at this address or not, once the Angels had been led to the Purgatory, the place for sure wouldn't survive past the end of the night. Nephilim had warned them. And after what had happened to Finwick, Purgatory deserved to burn in hellfire.

She left HQ with no further incidents and hurried home. Slowly the lack of sleep started to show its effects on her. She felt tired, and her energy dwindled greatly. Even a cyborg needed to rest after a few days, and she hadn't slept in a while now, not counting the two hours catnap last night. The fresh wound on her back did not help either. The pain had subsided and turned into a slight burning sensation, Jake had done a good job gluing the injury, but the blood loss had been heavier than she had thought. Lying down and having some rest for a few hours was out of the question, though. She was way too excited. Jake had promised that he would consult with his people about her wish to join them. Though, he *had* warned her about having high hopes on the matter. Just because he trusted her blindly did not mean the others would. She couldn't blame them. After all, she was their natural enemy.

***

"OK, so as promised, I talked to them," Jake said, once she had arrived and freed herself from his stormy embrace and kisses.

"And?"

"And I had to throw all my eloquence and charm into the ring, but they agreed to see you."

She beamed. "That's great news! Thank you, Jake."

BEHIND BLUE EYES

He looked into her eyes. "No, it's me who has to thank you. You joining our cause will surely give us opportunities we never imagined. I just hope the risk you're taking isn't too high. The last thing I want is something happening to you."

Nephilim caressed his cheeks. His words created a warm sensation inside her belly. "You should stop worrying so much about me. Don't forget what I am."

Jake wanted to say something but then seemed to bite his tongue and remained silent.

"So, how did you convince them to bring me in?" Nephilim asked after a moment.

"I told them that I trust you with my life. It eventually convinced them to give you a chance. But they said they would give you a trial run to see if you're really serious about your decision."

"What kind of trial?"

"They didn't tell me, but you'll find out soon enough. I suppose it'll be a small assignment, a task you'll surely be able to complete without much effort."

"OK, I'm ready. Let's go."

Jake kept holding her in his arms. "Nephilim. Are you absolutely sure you want to do this?"

She gave him a questioning look. "Why do I get the feeling you're trying to talk me out of it, Jake?"

"No, not at all," he said quickly, "I just want to ensure I didn't talk you into something you're uncomfortable with. Joining our movement will change everything for you forever."

She smiled. "Meeting you changed my life forever. Can we go now?"

***

They left his apartment on foot, and when Nephilim questioned if they should take her motorcycle, Jake smirked. "It's very close, just a ten-minute walk. Why do you think I chose to live here?"

They walked away from Oldtown's nightlife hub and into a residential area, which was quieter at this time. Some buildings had been replaced by modern ones, although of the simpler type, while others still remained from the old days, which gave the district a unique charm. The public transport viaducts wound through the high-rises here, and when they made their way beyond them, Jake asked, "Do you know why the majority of people use public transport in Olympias? Why only so few own personal vehicles?"

"Because they don't need them," Nephilim replied, "Public transport is so well organized, it will bring them anywhere."

Jake looked at her with an elfish grin on his face. "Of course it will."

"What are you trying to say?"

"You'll understand in a second. Tell me, would you ever want to give up your motorcycle?"

"That's different. I'm an Angel. I need to be mobile at any time."

"Sure, but you also use it for private needs. It gives you the mobility to go anywhere—really *anywhere* you want—any time. Would you abstain from that?"

BEHIND BLUE EYES

"No...why would I?"

He chuckled. "Exactly. Why would anyone? Why would anyone give up private mobility, which is nothing less than the freedom to go anytime anywhere they like, in exchange for a form of mobility that's limited by capacity, schedules, and most of all, destinations?"

Nephilim stared at him. "Wow. I never thought about that."

"The limitation of public mobility is a very efficient tool of control," Jake explained, "People can only go where you want them to go. They can't leave certain areas if you don't want them to, at least without great difficulties. The vast majority will never leave Olympias City their entire lives; many won't even leave the district they live and work in. They don't know how the world looks outside their own districts, much less the gigantic city they live in. In all honesty, most don't care, but if they did, they would never go far. The limit will always be the end of the line."

"And they're made to believe it's for their own good, it's a progressive life; why should they need individual transport?" Nephilim added.

"Exactly. Unless you're a resident of the Inner Circle, of course. Such rules never apply to the elites."

Luckily, the street they were walking down was mainly deserted, and nobody would hear their conversation. Residents of the district were either enjoying the nightlife of Oldtown, earning their money here, or sleeping in their homes.

"*All animals are equal, but some animals are more equal than others,*" Nephilim quoted.

The smile she loved so much brightened Jake's face, and he kissed her before he explained further. "Exactly. And it's always the more 'equal' animals who push the seemingly progressive ideas on the 'less equal' ones without living with the consequences themselves. It's not a new concept;

it was practiced in the pre-corporation era in a similar manner."

They had left the massive viaducts behind them, and Jake continued, "The concept of limited transportation isn't new either, you know. It had been tried in the old days, in the 20th and early 21st centuries, but our beloved leadership established it much more discretely. OK, we're here."

He stopped in front of an old, run-down building. Nephilim inspected it in surprise. "Here?"

Jake grinned. "What did you expect? That we reside in one of the fancy glass towers?"

"No, but..."

He turned to her and held her by the shoulders, looking into her face. "This is the rabbit hole, and it leads deep. You'll see how much I trust you showing you this. Come."

Jake took her hand, then opened an ordinary-looking door at the side of the building. Behind it was a steep set of stairs leading down into the darkness. He pulled a flashlight out of his pocket and switched it on.

"I know your extraordinary eyes don't need the light, but some of us are outdated models," he said, grinning and started descending the stairs.

Nephilim followed him, her curiosity and excitement rising with every step.

At the end of the stairs was a dark corridor that led straight to an iron door with no handles. Using his flashlight for orientation, Jake placed the index finger of his right hand on a small plate hidden at the side of the door. It opened with a soft click.

They entered a massive hall which, too, was laid in complete darkness. Jake's beam of light fell on faded white stripes on the floor and gray pillars and it became clear that this was an underground parking garage.

"The upper floors of this garage have been flattened and filled up, and now a new building is standing above us," Jake said as they crossed the seemingly endless parking deck. His voice echoed in the darkness.

"That's where your people meet?" Nephilim asked.

It was a pretty good hiding place. Most likely, people had been forgotten that the place existed, and common scans wouldn't reach down there.

Jake chuckled. "No."

At the end of the hall was another iron door, this one massive and impossible to crack, even for a cyborg—at least without the use of heavy explosives. Nephilim's sensors detected a tiny camera positioned above the door. Jake stood beneath it and looked up. A few seconds later, the door opened.

They went through some rooms that appeared to have once served as maintenance rooms, long ago, then up a staircase into an area which might have been used by visitors of some sort, but was in bad shape now. A musty smell hung in the air, and it reminded Nephilim of the odors from the algae plantation, which of course, was absurd.

From there, they entered a place that made Nephilim wrinkle her forehead and look around in surprise. She had never seen anything like it.

"What is this place?"

Jake's flashlight only showed a small area around them. They were in a long tunnel composed entirely of plexiglass. The glass was astonishingly intact and had to be of immense thickness. Seemingly endless darkness lurked on the other side and walking through it almost felt like walking through space, or a dark abyss. It was an eerie atmosphere.

But Nephilim could see the whole picture. The darkness behind the glass wasn't endless, after all. The tunnel led through an enormous dome.

"Impressive, isn't it?" Jake asked.

"Who built such a place? And why?"

"Believe it or not, this used to be an aquarium, in the old days," Jake said, "This tunnel we're walking through was under water, and the dome is a gigantic fish tank. When the aquarium was still operational, huge fish swam beyond this glass, like whales and sharks."

"I thought those only existed in fairy tales."

Jake smirked. "Trust me, they were very real. Actually, they still are. They aren't as extinct as everybody presumes."

Nephilim looked at him. "How do you know all of this?"

"Let's just say, we have our sources."

"How comes nobody knows this place exists?" Nephilim asked as they continued walking through the tunnel. She tried to imagine all the water and the fish swimming around in it and decided it must have been beautiful.

"The higher structures have been demolished, and the entrances to the lower ones, filled in. Then they built a park above it. This dome has been covered with earth, and serves as a nice hill people can walk on."

Nephilim stopped for a moment. "Merit Park? I can't believe it!" She laughed.

Jake nodded. "That one, exactly."

"And over the decades, this place was forgotten, and nobody is interested much in Oldtown anyway," Nephilim shook her head.

BEHIND BLUE EYES

"You wouldn't believe how many places like this exist all over Olympias," Jake explained, "After all, many things have been built over the old cities."

They had reached the end of the tunnel.

"We're almost there," Jake said, "They will want to take your weapons, but don't worry, that's OK. You'll get them back later, I promise."

"OK, although I'm telling you that I won't like it."

He sighed. "I know, but these are the rules."

After leaving the tunnel, they went through another area that had seen better days, and climbed a flight of stairs to a higher level before they reached another door. This one was guarded by two people, a young man and woman. They were heavily armed with automatic rifles and pistols. Nephilim's scan showed that, like Jake, they had no implants or augmentations whatsoever. A small lamp installed above the door created a tiny island of light in the seemingly endless darkness of the abandoned facility. Jake switched off his flashlight.

"Hey Jake," the guy said while the girl frowned at Nephilim.

Jake gave them a friendly greeting and opened the door. Behind it was a small, dim room with two more heavily armed guys- who had no implants either. One of them was sitting at a table with several small holo-monitors, which displayed the door Jake and Nephilim had passed through at the parking deck, as well as other places.

Both guards looked more curious than scared or upset upon seeing Nephilim. They looked her up and down before the older one said, "I need your weapons."

She lifted her coat and withdrew her pistols, then placed them on the table.

"Don't try to fire them. They'll just explode in your hands," she said.

The guard nodded. Neither he nor his companion seemed very surprised by this information. He then stepped closer to search her for any hidden weapons.

"That won't be necessary," Jake intervened.

The young man stopped short. "If you say so."

Jake smiled at Nephilim. "Ready?"

She smiled back. "You bet."

"Welcome to our humble abode," he said, opening the next door.

***

This "humble abode" was nothing like Nephilim expected. Behind the door, they stepped onto an iron catwalk that led over a huge hall. It connected to several rooms with glass windows on the other side, located close to the ceiling. More catwalks branched out in other directions, leading into the darkness.

The catwalk was located about thirty-five feet above something that only could be described as a vast, artificial, underwater grotto. The walls were in the shape of rock formations and covered with fake coral. On the other side was a gigantic plexiglass wall. This, too, must have been an oversized fish tank in its heyday. Unlike the tunnel, the glass front hadn't remained intact. Someone had cut a hole into it, resembling a door.

Jake glanced at Nephilim as they crossed the catwalk towards the dim-lit rooms on the other side and shrugged. "I know all of this seems a bit odd, but it's the safest place we could find."

"Not at all," she replied, "it's a perfect choice. You're facing an enemy who would have found and destroyed you a long time ago if you'd chosen a more typical hideaway."

They kept on walking. Around thirty people were present in the grotto area, maybe more. Nephilim could have scanned the place and the people, but she decided not to. After all, she was a guest here, and it would have felt somehow impolite to do that.

The people were mostly young or middle-aged, and without scanning them, Nephilim could tell that none had any augmentations, since nobody showed any visible implants or prosthetics. However, all of them were armed.

This place was a makeshift shelter, as well as a training grounds, and storage. Camp beds were set up in a remote corner behind piles of crates and boxes, which probably contained things like equipment, guns, ammunition, and provisions. The central area was dominated by tables, chairs, and benches. It was used as a meeting, briefing, and hang out space. A group of people had gathered there, engaged in a vivid discussion, some of them eating or having a drink. There had to be some kind of kitchen somewhere, which could not be seen from up there.

The group fell silent when they saw Nephilim walking down the catwalk and stared at her for a moment before going back to their business as if nothing unusual had happened. Nephilim did not care. Accustomed to open hostility in her daily life, she could handle a few nervous looks.

They arrived at the other end of the catwalk and walked on a concrete path at the edge of the cavern to the rooms. A ladder led down to the bottom from there, hidden by fake rocks. Besides this one, Nephilim had spotted two other rope ladders leading from the walkways down into the cave, so the people residing here could move up and down quickly.

When this facility had still been an aquarium, the platforms were clearly above the water, and used for maintenance, invisible to the public, standing behind the glass. The rooms had been used by maintenance personnel to clean and monitor the giant fish tank.

The first and biggest one was now a command center. The blinds in the windows had been closed, but they were old and didn't shut properly. Passing by, Nephilim spotted an impressive amount of tech inside. Screens, computers, and communication devices. A holographic map was displayed on the opposite wall, showing Olympias. Some parts of it were pointed out, arrows linking them. Plenty of comments were written beside those arrows.

Of course, Nephilim was more than curious to find out what these people were planning, but she curbed her curiosity and didn't look any further. They distrusted her kind for good reasons. She needed to earn their trust, then they would surely fill her in on their plans.

The next room was smaller and appeared to be used for meetings. It was equipped with a table and chairs. A holo-monitor stood on the table, but it was currently switched off. The walls were still decorated with faded posters from the aquarium, showing fish Nephilim had never seen before. Some appeared more like monsters from fantasy VR-games than anything that could actually exist in real life.

Three people were waiting in the room when Jake and Nephilim entered.

A woman in her early forties was sitting at the table. She had brown, curly hair, a nondescript face, and, of course, no visible implants. She wasn't ugly, neither was she attractive; she was one of those people whose face bystanders forgot within seconds. The perfect face to stay unnoticed. Most interesting thing about her was her narrow, greenish eyes, which revealed a high intelligence and maybe even ruthlessness, to anyone closely observing.

Next to, and behind her, stood a man and woman, both heavily armed, and more than capable of using their weapons efficiently, judging from their looks.

"Nephilim, this is Lena. She's the leader of this cell, and a high-ranking member of our movement," Jake gave introductions as they entered.

"Welcome, Nephilim," Lena said, "Please, take a seat."

She pointed to the chair opposite herself, and Nephilim did as asked. Jake stayed standing behind her.

"Would you like some tea?" Lena's voice was deep and smooth, yet she spoke with the tone of a person who has been in command for a long time.

"I would appreciate it," Nephilim said.

Lena opened a thermos flask standing on the table, poured some hot tea into a cup, and placed it in front of Nephilim, then she took a sip from her own drink.

"Thank you," Nephilim tried the beverage. It was new to her. Only a few people drank tea, because most preferred coffee, so it was a rarity in Olympias. It was an unfamiliar taste, but good.

"So, Nephilim," the resistance leader began, "Jake tells us you'd like to join our movement."

"I would," Nephilim replied.

"I'm sure you're aware of what a great risk we're taking by letting you come here." Lena's sharp eyes studied Nephilim closely with every word she said, "And, frankly, I never would have thought it possible to sit here with a Guardian Angel—and live. There are quite a few among us who say it's madness to trust you. But Jake convinced us to give you a chance, since everybody deserves one, and he believes in you. I'd like to hear it from you, however. Why have you come here? What are you trying to accomplish?"

Nephilim kept silent for a moment before she spoke. She wanted to find the right words. "I was abducted as a child and made into what I am today. All my life I have been led to believe the system was just, and what we were doing was righteous. Until one day, I started doubting, but didn't know what to make out of these doubts. Then I met Jake, and he opened a whole new universe of thoughts to me. I realized that I can't sit by and let everything be as it is any longer. I want to contribute to change. So that no child will be made a monster ever again."

"You don't want others to become like you?"

"Not against their will, no."

"Are you aware that by helping us, you would stand against your people?"

"Yes, but in the end, I'm helping to set them free. Once the corporation system is gone, my people will be able to live a self-determined life like everyone else. Right now, we're slaves, property of the Olympias Conglomerate, and technically, so is everyone else in the three cities."

Lena raised an eyebrow while Nephilim was speaking, and smiled. "You're damn right. It's about time to end corporate slavery and set everybody free. Seems to me, Jake was right about you."

He stepped closer, his arms crossed, and shrugged. "Told you so."

If he had any doubts about the outcome of this conversation, he wasn't showing them.

"We all came from somewhere, and left our old lives behind at some point or another, so why not a Guardian Angel?" Lena said, "It gives us hope for the future. And with an ally like you, Nephilim, we might accomplish things otherwise unreachable for us. You can help us shave

BEHIND BLUE EYES

years off of our plan."

"Years?"

Lena laughed, and her two guards joined her. "Did you think such a strong, malicious system can be beaten in a few weeks or months? This is the most important and difficult fight humanity has ever had. Yes, it will take years, maybe decades. Maybe none of us will live to see the outcome. But we *will* succeed." She took a long sip of her tea, then added, "Don't worry. The people you see here aren't all we have. This is just one cell of many. We're everywhere, and we're strong. If any of these people here get caught and tortured, they will only be able to sell out this one cell, not the entire movement."

Nephilim nodded. "A smart tactic."

"What we need to ask of you is that you be our eyes and ears at the Guardian Angels HQ, Nephilim," Lena decided, "You can bring us invaluable intel about their plans and what they know about us."

"Sounds easy enough," Nephilim said.

"It is," the resistance leader agreed, "Which is why we need proof of your loyalty first. We want to know you're serious about helping our cause."

"What do you want me to do?"

Lena placed a small, metallic tube on the table. A standard portable data transfer stick, tiny, yet capable of storing enormous amounts of data. "Take this. Plug it into the internal system at Angel HQ, and download information about all upcoming raids against autonomous communities living outside of Olympias." She paused for a moment, looking Nephilim in the eye before she continued, "I believe this won't be much of a challenge for you. It won't hurt your fellow Angels in any way. But we'll be able to warn these poor people, and evacuate their settlements in time."

Nephilim grabbed the data stick. "Consider it done."

Lena smiled. "Very good. Bring me the stick with the data, and we'll welcome you officially. I'm sure you're already curious to learn more about our plans and the organization, aren't you?"

"I am. To be honest, I have many questions."

"And they'll all be answered, I promise you that," Lena said, her smile broadening.

She stood up and extended her hand to Nephilim, who followed her example, and took it. The leader had the firm, strong handshake of a person who knew exactly what she wanted.

"If you would excuse us now," Lena said, ending the handshake, "Jake and I have another important matter to discuss. Lou and Marc will accompany you outside."

Nephilim nodded. The two guards moved to the door and waited to escort her.

Jake stopped her on the way out, holding her by the arm. "I'll be right there with you, OK? This will only take a few minutes."

"Take your time," Nephilim said, "I'll wait."

He smiled at her warmly.

"We hope to see you again soon, Nephilim," Lena said, then Nephilim was out of the door, and Jake closed it behind her.

**

BEHIND BLUE EYES

"I'm impressed, Jake," Lena said after Nephilim was gone, "You've accomplished something everyone thought impossible, including me. Congratulations, the High Command will be more than pleased with you."

Jake stood at the window, watching how Nephilim crossed the catwalk escorted by the two guards, then disappeared through the exit. "I was just lucky. She was going rogue anyway."

"Nonsense," Lena disagreed. She walked towards him and placed her hand on his shoulder. "Stop downplaying your merit, it doesn't suit you very well."

"If you say so," he smiled, yet this was a cool, calculating smile as far away as it could be from the disarming smile Nephilim got to see and love.

Lena's green eyes filled with contempt. "It was hard for me to stand how that thing was sitting here, staring at me with its eerie eyes, pretending to be human. Sickening. I can't possibly imagine how it must have been to fuck it. Guess you took one for the team, huh?"

"Guess so."

She squeezed his shoulder, then clapped it before walking back to the table and her tea.

"Who would've ever thought a machine could fall for the 'prince charming' trick?" her voice was full of scornful amusement now.

Jake turned away from the window, facing her. "*She* is not a machine, she's a person."

Lena stopped short in the middle of drinking. A broad grin appeared on her thin lips. "Hear, hear. Don't tell me you got emotionally involved here, Jake. That would be not only stupid but highly inappropriate and unprofessional."

He went stiff, irritated. "No, of course not."

"Good. You see, I would hate to put that in my report."

Jake did not answer. The words stood between them for a moment. Lena continued, "Besides, you know very well where this romance of yours is going, right? You knew from the beginning."

"Of course, I do."

"Let me remind you anyway, just in case." Lena approached him with a resolute pace and poked his chest with her index finger, right where his heart was. "It —'*she*'— needs to be destroyed. All of them need to be destroyed. There's no way for us to succeed with the Guardian Angels around. You know that as well as anyone else here. She's the best chance we've had in years, if not ever! The virus on that data stick is one of the most potent ever created. She can't detect it by scanning the device, nor will any of their counter measures be able to spot it before it's too late. Once it enters their internal system, there's no way to stop it. It'll spread through their network and infect every single one of the fuckers, corrupting their neural implants and ultimately destroying them, which will also kill the biological parts of their brains. This will be incredibly painful, it will make them go insane, they'll go berserk before they die. And within less than twelve hours the Guardian Angels of Olympias will be history."

She looked him in the eye and a crooked smile appeared on her face. "No matter what we've tried so far, their network always proved to be impenetrable. The only way to get to them was an inside job. You, Jake, brought us this new operative on a silver platter. I wonder what *she* would think of you if she knew what you really are behind *your* pretty blue eyes. It would break her innocent, little, metal heart, to be sure. You might consider it an act of mercy, killing her off without letting her know."

Jake listened to her without showing any emotion, finally, he asked coldly, "Is there anything else I need to be briefed on, or are we done here?"

She waved her hand. "We're done. Go and finish your 'prince charming' scam. Make sure she goes through with it."

He nodded and took his leave, but she held him back one more time. "Oh, and don't you dare fail."

***

Nephilim waited for him outside the resistance base, in the shadows, not far from the door protected by the two young guards. Only her bright neon-blue eyes gave away her position, her black clothes almost made her seem invisible. She smiled when Jake approached her.

"Did you get your guns back?" he asked.

She patted the sides of her jacket. "As promised."

"Let's go then."

They walked in silence for a while until they reached the glass corridor again.

"Is everything alright?" Nephilim asked, "You seem...tense."

He stopped and smiled at her, yet somehow, he looked tired. "I'm fine. There was an issue, but it has nothing to do with you, and it's just been on my mind. But I'm all yours now."

She tilted her head. "Something serious?"

"It's nothing you should worry about, really." He kissed her. "Sorry if I seemed brooding. Let's go home quickly, OK? I want to be with you."

However, when they reached Jake's apartment, it became clear that they had different ideas about how to spend the rest of the night together.

"Thank you for taking me along tonight, Jake," Nephilim said, "You can't possibly imagine how much your trust means to me."

He did not answer, just stood there in the semi-darkness of his place, looking at her. The faded lights from the street reflected in his eyes and made them almost gleam. He was calm on the outside, yet his heart was beating heavily as she could tell.

It was nothing new to her. She had learned quickly that he was one of the few people who controlled their appearance very well, he even could control many of his body functions astonishingly well. Many things that gave others away for being suspicious in any way never happened to him. She understood why, now. Most likely, the resistance trained their members in special techniques which gave them a better chance of survival if they ever happened to encounter their arch-enemies: her people.

Today, his calm façade and agitated internal self did not sync. Nephilim could clearly tell that something was troubling him, even if he tried to hide it from her.

She smiled at him. "I wonder how I can ever repay you?"

She let her jacket drop to the ground, followed by her weapons, then slowly got rid of her top. He came closer, and their lips met. For a moment, Nephilim felt the fire that always burned between them whenever they were close, as he embraced her and let his hands slide over her body. She pressed herself against him, her own hands wandering under his shirt, pulling it off of him. Then she went on to unbuckle his pants.

But he took her hand, preventing it from going any further, pulling away from her.

Nephilim blinked at him, confused. "What's wrong?"

He shook his head, avoiding her eyes. "I...Nephilim, I'm sorry, but I can't."

"What? Why?"

Jake seemed to want to say something but instead bit his lip, turned around and stepped to the window instead. His vital functions were in a frenzy now; heart racing, pulse much higher than it should be. He was under high stress... and upset.

Nephilim watched for a moment as he struggled with himself, then slowly approached him. Placing her hand on his shoulder softly, she said, "If I did or said something that hurt you, please forgive me. I'm not good with interpersonal relationships. This is new to me...I'm not human..."

"What?" he asked, and it seemed like waking up from some kind of trance, "Oh my God, no."

He turned around towards her and took her hands in his. "Stop saying that! You did nothing wrong. You're more human than any human I've ever met."

He stroked her face. "You're perfect."

Usually, Nephilim would have replied something witty in a situation like this, but she could sense how important it was for him. And it felt good. It felt like he was caressing her soul, saying things like that.

She just kept silent and smiled at him, noticing how his body began to calm down again.

"Run away with me," he said.

She laughed. "What?"

"Run away with me," he repeated with determination, his eyes focused on hers, "I mean it."

At first, she had been sure he was joking. Even thinking such a thing was absurd. It made no sense. But in his eyes, she saw that he was dead serious. His body functions were steady now. Whatever had been tormenting him was gone. He knew exactly what he wanted.

"What are you talking about, Jake?" she asked slowly, "Run where?"

"Anywhere. I don't really care. As far away from here as possible. Far away from everything. Somewhere where you and I can be together, always. Let's go right now and never look back."

"But...what about the resistance? The cause?"

"Fuck it!" he said with sudden sharpness.

He let go of her hands and started pacing up and down his tiny apartment like a caged animal. "To hell with it, I don't care! Why does it have to be us who fight? Who sacrifice everything?"

"Because we care. Because somebody has to do something if things are supposed to change," Nephilim answered, watching him, "Because you care the most."

Jake stopped. "Wrong! I don't fucking care." He moved back towards her and took her face in his hands. "All I care about is you."

Nephilim smiled. "Jake-"

"No, listen to me," he interrupted her, "I love you, Nephilim. It took me a bit to realize it, but now I know. I've loved you from the moment we met. I never believed something like this possible, and yet here I am. Every scar on your body feels like torture to my soul. I can't sit by and wait until you get killed, I just can't. If not in the line of your own duty, which could happen any day, then because I convinced you to work for the resistance. The risk is too high, Nephilim. I can't take it. Please, run away with me. Be with me."

BEHIND BLUE EYES

She looked into his eyes, which were wide, bright, and full of emotion. He meant every word he said, and it touched her in a way that she had never known before.

His idea to run away was wonderful, so fantastic that she did not even dare to think of it. It was absolutely impossible, and she knew it.

How many people had thought they could get away? Start a new life, far from the system? Her own parents had believed they could escape. But there was no escape. There was no place to hide. *They* would always find them, hunt them down. Without mercy. Her fellow Angels.

"Jake," she said softly, "I want to be with you, more than anything else. Every minute of the day. But there's no place for us to run. They will find us anywhere that we go."

"No." He shook his head. "There must be a way! If we go far enough-"

"No, Jake, there isn't. You have to trust me on that. I'm one of them. Do you want to end up like the settlers we hunt down and kill like animals?"

"I'm willing to take the risk," he said, stubbornly.

"It's futile, Jake."

He sighed. "Nephilim, I-"

"Now, you need to listen to me, Jake," she said with a soft voice, "There's only one way for us. One way for everybody. We need to end the corporate rule, once and for all. We need to set everyone free. Only then will there be a place for us, a place for anyone to live their lives as they wish. After a life of brainwashing and deceit, I've finally found purpose, a path to redemption for everything I've done. And I have only you to thank for that." She smiled at him and started caressing his face with her fingers, tenderly, as she continued, "Remember, after we met, you told me that it's your decision to make if you want to take the risk of getting involved with me? Now it's my decision to make if I want to take the risk to get involved with the organization you belong to. And I do want to take it. It might cost me my life, but you need to understand that I was made to fight. Angels don't die of old age. I'd rather die knowing that my life meant something, something good. That I helped to achieve something. I'm not like anyone else you know, Jake."

"No," he whispered, his voice full of sadness, "You're better."

He moved his head to the side and stared out of the window for a moment. She could see that his eyes were moist.

"You gave me so much more than I could have ever wished for," she said, "Now, let me give something back."

He turned back and pressed his lips to hers in a passionate kiss. Instantly, the fire between them was back on, burning stronger than ever. Jake maneuvered her to the bed, and she let him push her down gently. Still kissing her, he pulled off the rest of her clothes.

The world around them disappeared for Nephilim as he loved her in a way he had never done before, tender yet fierce, so full of eagerness and passion that it almost left her out of breath for the very first time. When he came, he grabbed her and held her close, so close and tight as if she otherwise could disappear any second. So close that he would have hurt her if she were human.

"You won't lose me," she whispered in his ear as he clung to her, breathing heavily, "I'll always come back to you."

"I love you," he said.

When it was time for her to go, she kissed him once more, then got up and started dressing. He watched her doing so as he always did, his face not showing any particular emotion.

Nephilim smiled at him when she was done and ready to go. "I'll see you later tonight," she said, anticipating his usual question.

"Yes," he answered, deep in thought.

When she moved to the door, he jumped up from the bed and held her back. "Nephilim, wait!"

"Jake, I really need to hurry now."

"It will only take a moment," he promised, searching for something in the pockets of his clothes, which were spread around the room.

Finally, he found what he was looking for and stepped towards her, something small in his hand. It was a data stick of exactly the same model Nephilim had been given by the resistance leader.

"Here," he said, "Take this one and give me the one you got."

Nephilim wrinkled her forehead. "Why?"

"I don't know how often you work with these things, but we do it all the time. Unfortunately, they tend to be unreliable," he explained, "Not sure how long Lena had hers, or if she'd even used it before, but this one is brand new, I bought it just yesterday. If you take such a risk for us, I would hate it to be for nothing because the data device was flawed. And you want your first assignment to be a success, don't you?" He smiled that disarming smile she liked so much.

"Fine," she said, reaching into her pocket, "If you insist."

"I do," he said as they exchanged the data devices.

"You're like an overly protective mother hen, you know that?" Nephilim said with a grin.

He shrugged. "I can live with that."

Nephilim let the new data stick disappear in her pocket before she pulled him closer for one last kiss. "That was amazing earlier," she said, giving his lip a tender bite and squeezing his naked butt. Then she quickly let go of him and left the apartment at a steadfast pace.

Jake moved to the door and watched her walk down the hall until she was out of sight, not bothering to cover up. His fist was firmly clenched around the original data stick.

***

Driving towards Angel HQ, Nephilim was full of determination. Never before in her life had she felt happier, more content with her existence, and who she was. For the first time, she knew she was doing the right thing, and it was something she had chosen to do herself. She was about to make a difference. Of course, she couldn't make up for all the things she had done in her life, for all the innocent blood she had shed, the fear and terror she had caused. But she could help prevent it from continuing to happen, over and over again.

Sure, the task she had been assigned with was small, but it could make a huge difference in many peoples' lives. If the resistance could warn the settlers about upcoming raids against them, it would save many souls. And this was just the beginning. Once this task was accomplished, and Jake's people trusted her, she would be able to do much more. Maybe Lena was wrong. Maybe it would be possible to change things much quicker than everyone thought. Maybe she and Jake could have a future after all.

Her heart was beating faster, just thinking about him. Love was something she never had believed in; it had been eliminated in this perfect society she lived in. Ridiculed, claimed to be something unreal, oppressive, exclusionary, and unnecessary for a modern human being. Nobody was supposed to have a close relationship—especially not a Guardian Angel. And yet, against all the odds, this love between her and Jake had happened. Not only was she able to love, but she was also loveable—no matter who or what she was.

Nephilim felt as if she was lighter than usual when she left her motorcycle in the garage and entered HQ. Her happiness filled her whole body and gave her a feeling like floating above the ground. But she needed to focus now. Not only so no one would read how good she felt by looking at her face, she also had to complete the task assigned to her by the resistance leader. It should be easy enough. Once she reached the console she had been working on for the last several days, she would look for the required information, plug in the data device, and copy it. If she was quick, nobody would notice what was going on.

She did not reach the main area of HQ.

The corridor leading to the locker rooms was suspiciously empty when she entered. Halfway down, she noticed two Archangels, Leliel and Uriel, come around the corner and move towards her, like black shadows. Their faces, unreadable.

Nephilim flinched. This was unusual, suspicious even. It immediately gave her the feeling that something was wrong. But what? How?

She forced herself to keep moving, not showing any reaction as they closed in on her at a fast, marching pace. She heard footsteps behind her and knew two more Angels were near.

This was bad, very bad. They knew. They were after her.

The two Archangels stopped a few feet away, blocking her way. Silent, unmoved, their hands ready at their weapons in the holsters strapped to their thighs. It was one thing to have a shoot out with humans and another with fellow angels. The message was clear. One false move and they would attack. Even if she took a stand against the two in front of her, there were two more at her back, and her sensors indicated who.

Nephilim froze. It was over.

The cold muzzle of a gun was pressed against her neck from behind.

"One move and I'll blow your brains out, Nephilim," she heard Zephaniel's familiar voice, in a cold, hateful hiss, "And trust me, it will be my pleasure to do that."

Another black-clad figure came around the corner and walked down the dimly lit corridor.

The two Archangels made room respectfully and let Metatron pass. He stopped in front of Nephilim, his neon-blue eyes slightly glowing. His head tilted a little as he studied her for a moment in silence, almost like a parent to a disobedient child.

Then he slowly extended his palm towards her.

"Give it to me," he said.

Chapter Twelve

Revelations

Nephilim was unable to move an inch. She was secured to a chair in a half-lying position, her arms and legs spread. Although there were no visible restraints, there was no hope for her to escape from that chair. The special recesses her limbs were positioned in were equipped with a particular kind of magnetism which secured Nephilim's titanium limbs, immobilized them, and rendered them useless, while at the same time not causing any damage to her implants. She was paralyzed, which wasn't painful, but extremely unpleasant.

The small room she was in had dark walls and an unsettling atmosphere. Among the Angels, it was known simply as the Pit. It was a torture chamber, but not just any basic sort. It wasn't for prisoners or suspects, but exclusively for Angels. Sometimes even cyborgs had to be disciplined, if they performed badly, were insubordinate, experienced an incorrect way of thinking, or were just fucked up. This rarely happened, but it still occurred from time to time. Then they ended up in the Pit. Some never came back. And if they did, they were never the same again.

There were Angels who specialized in the art of torture. Zephaniel was one of them, if not the best. His duties as Archangel did not leave him much room for side activities, though. Nephilim wondered if he would make an exception to volunteer his skills for her. So far, he was nowhere to be seen.

Two rookie Angels stood in the room, watching her. They were both relatively young, and Nephilim did not know them well. Obviously, they had been instructed not to talk to her, which she appreciated since she wasn't in the mood for chit-chat anyway. She could see the curiosity in the youngest one's face, though. He was asking himself what she had done to end up in the Pit.

Nephilim was asking herself the same question. Well, not *what*, of course. She knew exactly what she had done, and from the corps' perspective, she more than deserved to be there. What she was asking herself and could not understand was, *how* in the world they could have known about her plans. Somewhere along the way, she must have made a grave mistake, and she didn't know when. They had caught her in the act. It was almost like Metatron had known all along as if she had run into a trap. But how?

In the end, it wouldn't matter. She would die. Nothing would save her now. And she could not hope for an easy, clean death in the euthanasia chamber. It would happen in this very room. Most likely, Metatron would grant Zephaniel the pleasure to torture her to death—if he didn't do it himself. Tearing her limbs off would only be the start.

Nephilim wasn't scared. If she was honest with herself, she had known all along that the adventure would end like this sooner or later. Everything else was just a dream that could have never come true for somebody like her. A sweet dream, nothing more.

Yet she had enjoyed every second of her freedom, she regretted nothing, and she would do it again if given the opportunity. What she had experienced in the last several days was worth everything. She just wished she would have had more time. She wished she could have accomplished more. And spend more time with Jake.

No, Nephilim wasn't afraid of torture nor death. She also knew that there was nothing in the world they could do to her that would make her sell Jake out. They would never learn anything from her about him, or his people. Zephaniel could cut her into pieces if it pleased him, he would get nothing.

There was only one thing that horrified her so much that she could hardly catch her breath when thinking about it.

Jake. What if they already captured him? What if he was already here? She could endure anything they did to her, but imagining what they would do to him made her feel sick, desperate. When she remembered how he had loved her this morning, how passionate he had been, how they had kissed...she never would've thought it would be the last time. Thinking back now, there had been something in his eyes. Sorrow, grief. Almost as if he had known it was the last time. But that was, of course, impossible.

After what felt like an eternity to her, the door opened, and Metatron entered.

He was alone; Zephaniel had not accompanied him. Maybe he was supposed to join in later. Nephilim forced herself to push all feelings aside and focused. Whatever he was up to, he wouldn't get it.

"You can leave us now," the High-Archangel told the two guards with a wave of his hand, "Report to the main briefing area."

The two Angels did as commanded. Once they were alone, Metatron did not move for a moment, just kept standing close to the door where he had stopped. He studied her, his ageless, androgynous face impossible to read, as per usual.

Finally, he smirked, saying, "Nephilim, Nephilim. So beautiful, so many talents. Sadly, paying attention isn't one of them."

Slowly, he approached her, his artificial eyes glimpsing upon her. Like a smooth, deadly predator who had trapped his prey.

"I gave you friendly advice, remember? I told you not to play games you can't win," he said, stopping right in front of her, "And you can't win against me. Ever."

"When did you find out?" she asked.

There was no point in denying anything or playing dumb. He knew. The only question was, how much.

"Oh, you need to be more specific with that question, my dear Nephilim," he said sneering, and she clearly sensed how much he enjoyed every second of this conversation. It was as if a spider was talking to a fly trapped in its net, before devouring it. "When did I find out what exactly? You trying to destroy us? Just recently. You going rogue? From the beginning."

Nephilim stared at him in disbelief. He had to be bluffing.

"How?" was all she could ask.

Metatron chuckled. "I wish you could see your face. You believed that you were so clever. You thought that you could take me for a fool."

Suddenly his face turned ice-cold, and his voice became a hiss: "Anyone else would be dead by now for even considering that. You should consider yourself fortunate."

"What makes me so special?"

BEHIND BLUE EYES

"Does it really matter now?" He turned away and towards a display that contained torture utensils of various kinds. Some sophisticated, others more old-fashioned or classical.

A bone saw and pincers for pulling teeth could be found there, as well as laser scalpels, electro-diodes, equipment for violent implant removal, and different kinds of drugs.

"But to answer your first question. When I told you I was watching you, what made you think I did this only through your eyes? There are other, more conventional methods as well, as you might remember. It all depends on how much somebody cares. And I-" He turned his head and looked her in the eye. "Care a great deal about you, as you should have noticed by now."

Metatron moved back to the display and started inspecting the various utensils as he continued, "Drones, Nephilim. Good old drones. I use them to check on you from time to time. Particularly when you sleep. I like looking at you when you sleep, you truly look like an angel then. Until one night, when I wanted to check on my sleeping beauty, and she wasn't there. Which made me wonder because the internal system was showing that she was in sleep mode. Recovering from her injuries suffered in battle. So, how could that be?"

He made his choice and turned back to her, a small laser burner in his hand. Although not much bigger than a lighter, it would burn several inches deep, round holes into flesh within seconds when put into action.

"Clever," he said, smiling that thin smile, "I have to give you credit for that. You used your glitches to sneak away and get a little upgrade. Who helped you install the device in your implant?"

He started caressing her face with the instrument without switching its horrible functionality on.

"No one," Nephilim said, "I did it myself."

Metatron would kill her anyway. She would be dead when this session was over, she was convinced about that. It did not matter if he burned her face before or not. At least he didn't know about Finwick. And she would be damned if he learned anything from her.

"But of course, you did," the High-Archangel said with amusement. He slowly moved the burner from her face down her neck to her chest, where he circled her breasts. "You opened your neural implants and imbedded a tiny piece of very complicated hardware. Somebody highly skilled helped you, probably from under this very roof. Who?"

"No idea," Nephilim said, "Must have slipped my mind."

"Has it? Well, I'm sure it will come back eventually."

He moved the torture device further down her biological body, over her belly, and between her legs.

"You're enjoying this little game very much, aren't you?" Nephilim asked with the courage of the doomed.

"As a matter of fact, I am," he agreed, "I believe I'm entitled to. After all, you've been enjoying yourself a lot lately as well."

He tapped her between her legs with the switched-off device while looking into her face.

Nephilim returned his gaze without flinching. He knew about her and Jake. She needed to play it cool as much as she could if Jake had any chance of surviving this. If only she could warn him somehow...

"I wasn't aware fucking was forbidden in Olympias," she said.

Metatron grinned, circling the device down her torso. "Oh, it always depends on the circumstances, Nephilim. Usually, it wouldn't be a problem. You and Jake, however, is a different story."

BEHIND BLUE EYES

He watched her face closely to see how she would react to the name. She forced herself to show no reaction. Metatron knew his name, but this did not mean anything yet.

"How you fucked, how you spent time together, how he treated you...and most importantly, what you talked about."

He slowly started moving the burner up her body again while talking. Nephilim stiffened. He knew. He knew everything.

"You watched everything..." she whispered.

"I did. The second night you went out while pretending to sleep, I sent a surveillance drone after you. It flies so high in the sky that even an Angel won't spot it when followed by one. I was curious where you were going, what was so important to you that you took such a risk. Once you entered the building, I set one of the tiny ones on you, hiding in the opposite building with an impressive zoom lens."

He chuckled. "And guess what? You were so busy that you didn't notice that one either. I must say, at first, I was highly disappointed in you that it was nothing but a petty booty call that you had sneaked away for—although I have to admit that you found yourself a nice piece of ass. I was wondering if I should pay the little prick a visit and slit his throat, so you'd find him like that the next night before I arrested you. But then I looked into the transcripts the lip-reading software gave me of what was being said."

His torture device had reached her neck again. He stroked her with it one more time then suddenly pulled back without using it on her. "Then, things started to get truly interesting. So interesting, in fact, that I decided to let you continue your little charade. I even helped you by giving you the nights off—for recovery." He smiled.

Nephilim could hardly restrain herself from panicking. He knew what they were talking about. He knew about the resistance. That would be the end of them. It was she who had brought that end upon them. And Jake...

Never in her life had Nephilim felt so helpless. Restrained, unable to even move a bit, she couldn't do anything to stop terrible things from happening.

"Of course, I wasn't able to witness everything, which I deeply regret," Metatron said, "For example, who did you save from the implant harvesters and why? It wasn't your gigolo, as he was sitting safely in his apartment, waiting for you. So, who did you rescue?"

Nephilim pressed her lips together. "I have no idea what you're talking about."

"Too bad. Since you impressed me so much that night. According to the report of local law enforcement who found the mess later, you single-handedly killed forty-three thugs to get to that person, suffering merely a scratch yourself. An outstanding accomplishment, even for one of us. The useless human police have been trying to get rid of that particular gang for months, and you just walked in and took everyone out. It doesn't matter who you wish to be, Nephilim, who you pretend to be. I know who you really are, and stunts like this prove it. You're a cold-blooded killer. The best."

He glanced into her eyes, for a moment displaying a glint of honest admiration on his face, then shrugged. "However, I'm sure we'll find out who you came for eventually, once all data has been reviewed. It's only a matter of time."

Metatron switched on the torture utensil, and a short beam of reddish light appeared on its end. He studied the deadly device, weighing it in his hand, seemingly deep in thought. "A beautiful piece of equipment," he said, "You know, for what you've done, I should use it to riddle your body with holes until you beg me to kill you to make the pain stop."

"Then just do it, if it pleases you," Nephilim said defiantly, "Get on with it."

He looked down on her, and for a moment, it seemed as if he would use the burner on her indeed, then he switched it off and put it away.

"You can relax, Nephilim. I'm not here to hurt you."

Nephilim couldn't help but feel relieved that the horrible device was gone. But this did not mean she was off the hook. In truth, he was simply enjoying his game a little longer. He would punish her, that was sure, in the worst way his sick mind could come up with.

"On the contrary to what you might believe, I'm not your enemy," Metatron said, sitting down on a stool standing next to her chair, "He is."

"What are you talking about?"

He made himself comfortable, crossing his legs and resting his chin on his hand. "I'm talking about your *lover*, Jake," he said the word "lover" with explicit contempt, "Every word that came out of his mouth was a lie."

Nephilim did not give an answer to that and forced herself not to visibly react. She didn't know for sure if he had Jake or not. In any case, it was better not to provoke him into anything. But it was clear to Nephilim now that, below all the indignation because of her treason, a much more trivial emotion raged inside Metatron: jealousy.

His voice was soft now, his face full of fake compassion as he continued, "I know what I'm going to say will be hard for you to swallow, but I believe you're a big girl and deserve to know the truth—even if it hurts. Everything your beloved Jake has told you about himself, his ideals, the resistance...it was all a lie. He played you, Nephilim. He told you so many beautiful things you wanted to hear; how valuable you were, how unique, that he loved you for who you were. And that's not all, by far. He appealed to your doubts, which have been tormenting you for some reason, he magnified your remorse for who you are and what you do, and he told you many beautiful stories about how the world used to be before the corporate rule and about freedom which should be everyone's right. He made your head spin, and I must admit his approach was brilliant, considering he fucked your reason away in between brainwashing you."

He winked at her, and a smug expression spread across his face. Nephilim felt anger rising up within her.

"All of this just to convince you to join a resistance, turn against your own people. Your family. Us," he continued, "A resistance that doesn't exist, and never did. It's a travesty, a scam. These people aren't interested in liberating anyone here in Olympias. They couldn't care less about anybody in this city. They are here to destroy. Not only the Guardian Angels but all of Olympias. They're our sworn enemies."

Metatron paused for a moment and looked into her face, knowing that he had her full attention now.

What he was about to say next would be like ramming a glowing dagger into her heart, and he would savor every word and the expression on her face.

"Congratulations, my dear, sweet Nephilim. You've literally been screwed by an agent of Rosprom."

***

It took Nephilim a moment to process what he just had said. Memories flashed through her consciousness, moments she had spent with Jake. Things he had done and said. Could it be true? Could any of what Metatron just had said be true? The man she had fallen in love with, a hostile agent? Exploiting her feelings? Or was this just one of Metatron's games? A different kind of torture? Maybe even a way to give him the information she had?

She stared at the High-Archangel, how he sat there, relaxed, self-confident, watching her. Suddenly she wished nothing more but to break free from her restraints, jump up, and wipe the smug grin from his face. Once and for all.

"Liar," she finally said, pressing her lips together.

His eyes sparkled with malicious joy. "Now, now. Just because one man in your life has proven to be lying scum, that doesn't appeal to all of us. Quite unfair to generalize, don't you think?"

Metatron reached into his pocket and produced a device the size of a credit card. He shook it out sharply, and it instantly unfolded into a black, flat pad, ten times its size. It was a portable data screen that could be directly connected to a neural implant to share visual information with somebody else.

The black screen sprang to life, showing a picture. Metatron turned it towards Nephilim, so she could see. It showed Jake, the smile she liked so much on his face. It made her heart ache.

"Tell me if I'm wrong, but I believe this is him, Jake. Right? Although I highly doubt this is his real name."

Nephilim did not answer.

The screen changed to a picture of Jake and Nephilim in his apartment, naked, in a tight embrace.

"Yes, there can be no doubt about it, it's him," Metatron confirmed.

The screen showed a sequence of photos, all featuring Jake and Nephilim in the act, in various moments and positions.

"He screwed you pretty well," Metatron said, "I have to give him credit for that."

Nephilim looked away. If he wanted to humiliate her, she wouldn't play that game.

"What? You don't like looking at yourself?" Metatron asked sardonically, "In that case, I have other pics more of interest to you. Do you know this woman?"

Nephilim turned her head back and saw a completely different picture displayed. It showed Jake and Lena walking down a street somewhere in Oldtown, deep in conversation.

"I bet you do, Nephilim. He probably introduced her to you as part of the resistance when you visited their hideout. I've done some research, even put our own intelligence on them, and guess what? She, too, is a Rosprom agent. Actually, a high-ranking officer. And he's no rookie, but one of their specialists. So, to give you some solace, you fell for an ice-cold pro."

"That proves nothing," Nephilim said, "You're bluffing."

Yet somewhere deep inside her, a sickening feeling started crawling up like an ugly, horrifying insect. Fear; he could be right.

"You're right, it doesn't," he agreed, "But this does."

The screen changed to another image. Seeing it, Nephilim felt as if all of her blood suddenly froze at once and as if a trap-door had opened right in front of her feet, pulling her into an abyss.

It was a still taken from a security camera from a vendor inside the Underground. It was a location Nephilim knew well, the door to Bhanu's shop. The timeframe on the side showed exactly twenty-five minutes before Nephilim and Adriel had entered the store to inspect it, which had led to the hacker's escape attempt. Two women were leaving the store, their faces clearly visible. One of them was Lena. The other one was wearing big, black sun-glasses, but Nephilim recognized her anyway. It was the Wasp officer who had shot her with the EMP bullet at the algae plant.

The screen changed again, showing a photograph from high above, obviously taken by a surveillance drone. Nephilim recognized the roof above the Underground as well as three small figures standing on it, herself, Adriel, and the hacker. It must have been seconds before Bhanu's execution. The perspective of the picture changed as the high-resolution photograph was zoomed in at the building opposite, closer and closer towards one particular window. A shooter stood there, the sniper rifle, partially covering his face. But Nephilim was able to recognize him anyway. Jake.

Now she fell through the trap-door into the abyss. Darkness closing around her, suffocating her. She felt as if she was dying.

She wanted to believe that all of this wasn't true, that it was fake, or one of Metatron's games to punish her. But she knew it wasn't. It was true. He was right: she had wandered right into a trap.

"Nephilim," his voice was soft and friendly again, almost fatherly, "Did it never occur strange to you that none of them had any implants? Jake and his "resistance" friends? Do you know why? Because if they had any, we would spot their foreign tech. You see, while TogbuaXiang chooses a straightforward approach, Rosprom wields a different kind of warfare. Their cyborg units are no match for us, and whenever we've clashed with each other in the last few decades, they've always suffered heavy losses. You know that, yourself. However, they are superior to us in other fields. Rosprom has a long tradition of intelligence agencies' warfare that reaches way before the corporate era, more than one-hundred years ago, to the Cold War. As you see, they had enough time to master this field. They're like rats, hiding in the shadows and trying to destroy the fundamentals of our society from within. We knew special agents from their intelligence have been hiding in Olympias for a long time, watching, infiltrating, but we never managed to reveal them. Until now."

Nephilim could not answer. Everything inside her felt numb. Dead.

"Now, they've grown bold—or maybe desperate—and recruited you. I believe that uncovering their secret alliance with TogbuaXiang, our aggressive approach against Wasp operations, and the push for intel gathering might have driven them into executing this maneuver. Plus, having their best man on it made them careless. It'll be their downfall. *You* will be their downfall, Nephilim. Do you know who is possibly the most dangerous agent? A double-agent. And the best double-agent doesn't even know she is one."

He leaned forward and stroked her face in a tender gesture. Then he seemed to remember something.

"There's one thing I don't understand, and I was hoping you could help me out," he pulled something out of his pocket and put it on the table where he had placed the burner. It was the data stick Jake had given her.

"What was this about? I was certain it would contain some nasty virus to wipe all of us out; it would have been typical Rosprom style. Besides, our intelligence has been warning for months that they've been working on something they referred to as "Angel Dust". But when we checked it—carefully on a secure system, of course—it turned out it was completely blank. There's absolutely nothing on it. So, why did they give it to you? What were you supposed to do with it?"

Nephilim did not answer. Her head was spinning. Angel Dust; a virus to kill them all. It had been on the data device Lena had given her, she was sure about that. Yet Jake had insisted to exchange it for this one, which was blank. Something wasn't right about this story. Something didn't add up. But she was too tired to think it through now. Everything inside her felt sore. She felt so stupid, humiliated. She wished Metatron would just have burned dozens of holes into her instead of telling her all this.

"I see you have nothing to tell me," he said, "You'll change your mind in time. For now, you'll have to excuse me. As we speak, a massive assault is being prepared against your friends of the 'resistance.' Thanks to you, we now know where they are, and they have no idea what's coming for them. With a bit of luck, not only will we find the core Rosprom agents there, but the remaining Wasp units. We'll strike today, and we'll strike with our full force. There won't be much left when we're done." Metatron got up and smiled his thin smile. "Don't worry. Our troops have orders to take pretty boy alive. I can't wait to get to know him better." He patted her cheek then walked to the door.

"You know," he said, stopping one more time, "It's really such a shame, Nephilim. It hurts my heart. I was willing to give you everything. You were about to enjoy a life most can't even dream of. And you throw it away for some cock."

He shook his head and proceeded to open the door and leave her.

"You son-of-a-bitch, you murdered my parents," Nephilim hissed in sudden, cold rage, "You murdered them and abducted me from the village in the mountains to make me like you."

Metatron stopped short.

"Who told you that?" he asked without turning back.

"Nobody. I remembered."

Slowly, he turned around and gazed at her, his face a cool, unmoved mask. The amusement he had experienced was gone completely.

"That's impossible."

"Is it? And yet, I *do* remember. I remember the village, my parents, the attack of blue-eyed monsters. How I hid in the cave. How you found me there. You were looking for me, you knew my name."

Her words stood between them as they looked at each other in silence for several seconds.

"You're exceptional, Nephilim," Metatron finally said, his voice calm and almost loving now, "You never fail to amaze me."

She snorted disdainfully. "Yeah, right. I'm exceptional. So exceptional that you murdered my parents and abducted me. Why? So you could fuck me?"

A look appeared on his face she had never seen before. First, she thought it was anger, but when he spoke, she realized it was offense, hurt.

"I never touched you," he said, "Do you really think I'm one of these degenerates? None of them would be left breathing if I had the final say in this city. Besides, my personal tastes are no secret to anyone."

He paused a moment before he continued, "I did what I promised when I took you from that cave. I took care of you, I protected you, I gave you a better life. And I never did anything against your will."

She laughed bitterly. "Besides turning me into this! A monster."

He had walked up to her again and stood now close. "I turned you into something better, into perfection, into the next step of evolution. Nephilim, don't you see what you are? You are so much better than any human. Superior. You're even superior to any other Angel."

She stared at him. "What are you talking about?"

He smiled. "Didn't you ever wonder why you perform so much better than your fellow Angels? Why you're the best in everything? It's because I made you the best. You got better education and training than anyone else. Inside you are parts of the highest quality, your hardware and software is more advanced than any other Angel's. It's only exceeded by my own."

"All animals are equal..." she said slowly in a disbelieving tone.

"And some are very special and dear," Metatron continued, "Didn't you notice that I always have looked out for you, always have protected you? I made sure you never went out into a battle that couldn't be won. I always gave you the best partners, who would have given their lives for yours without hesitation. It was you who chose to be on the front-line, not me, I would've preferred to give you less risky tasks. But I let you your will because I knew it would make you better and stronger, and it did. My eyes were always on you, however, always controlling the situation, all for you. If I had to choose between the survival of a full squad and yours, it would've always been you."

Nephilim remembered the battle at the algae plant where he had intervened at the last moment to save her, even though it had jeopardized everything. Looking back, she now realized there had been many such incidents. Her promotion to Archangel was no coincidence either. How could she had been so blind? All her life there had been a puppet-master behind her back, watching out for her—and controlling her every move.

"The truth is, I groomed you. I'm a patient man, time does not quickly fly by for me as it does for humans. I waited and watched your development. Waited until you were ready to stand by my side for the things to come."

"Well, I guess that won't happen now," she commented dryly.

Metatron shrugged, and the smirk appeared on his face that she had come to know so well. "We'll see about that."

He wanted to turn away and leave her for good, but she suddenly yelled at him, "Why me? Tell me fucking *why*! What makes me so special?"

He studied her for a moment, his face unreadable. Then he said, "Fine."

Nephilim watched as he leaned back against the chair where she was restrained, casually crossed his arms and turned his head to look at her. "Tell me, what exactly do you remember of your parents?"

She tried a defiant shrug but didn't move much since her arms were paralyzed. "Isn't it enough that you murdered them?"

"Maybe some more details than that? Let me ask you more precisely; what do you know about your father? Who he was before he decided to become a blind farmer—which already sounds like a bad joke. Who he *really* was?"

"My father was a good, loving man."

Metatron sneered. "My dear Nephilim, did you ever ask yourself why your father had no hair, and empty sockets instead of eyes? Looking back, did this never seem strange to you?"

Nephilim thought about her father's face. His bald, scarred head, and the empty sockets. How much she had loved that face. A terrible thought started forming in her head. She tried to suppress it, but Metatron did not give her a chance.

"Your father used to be one of us," he said, enjoying every word, "He was a Guardian Angel."

"No..." Nephilim whispered, yet she knew it was true. It was only fitting.

"Oh, yes. And it gets even better. He wasn't just any Angel. He was a High-Archangel. *The* High-Archangel. He founded the Angel corps. He was our creator."

BEHIND BLUE EYES

***

Nephilim was unable to speak. Her head felt like it would burst at any second, yet she also felt hollow. She was lying there, captive, unable to move, and Metatron, slowly, piece by piece, destroyed everything she believed she had known, her entire reality. It was a special form of torture, and she was convinced that he enjoyed every second of it.

"What's wrong, Nephilim?" he asked after a minute had passed, "Cat got your tongue? I was waiting for the right moment to tell you all this, tell you about your legacy, but you had to rush it, so, here we are now. And before you insult me and call me a liar again..."

Once more, he unfolded the portable screen and switched in on. This time it displayed a picture of himself. Although the photo must have been taken at least twenty-five years ago, he had only slightly changed since then. On the screen, he must have been a young man in his mid-twenties, whereas his ageless face now looked as if it had been frozen in his late thirties forever. The photograph showed him, all in black, his neon-blue eyes glowing, talking to a man he obviously deeply admired. The other man was a tall and impressive figure with handsome features, dark hair, and the cyborg-blue eyes, also dressed in black. He had the posture and body language of a self-confident leader who did not tolerate any position but his own.

Her father.

Nephilim stared at the image, hardly believing what she saw. This was her father, yes, but also a completely different person than the quiet, patient, blind, loving man she remembered. There was so much hubris in this man's posture, he radiated dominance and power. The smile on his face was ruthless, and his hand rested on Metatron's shoulder. There was an undeniable intimacy between the two men that went far beyond professional admiration.

Yet, one man had murdered the other.

"This picture was taken almost forty years ago," Metatron explained with a hint of nostalgia in his voice, "Your father and I were...very close back then. He made me what I am today. I am his creation. The prototype for a new, higher evolved species. Everything I am is because of him." He stroked the picture tenderly and smiled.

"TogbuaXiang were the first who came up with super cyborgs which they sent into the field against the other two corporations. It was soon clear that Olympias had to gear up if we wanted to survive, and the Board assigned the task to their best tactical specialist and pre-corporation veteran of the great war—your father. What he created to stand against the hostile force was us, our corps. Your father was not only the most brilliant man I've ever known, but he was also the most cynical and ruthless. Black was *his* favorite color, and that's why we all dress like that, to this day. He gave us the blue eyes, to make us look intimidating, unhuman. He designed us to be living, killing machines, the most dangerous weapons ever created."

Listening to Metatron, Nephilim felt sicker in the stomach by the minute. The realization that her own father had created everything she had learned to despise almost made her shiver. Her father created the angels, and in the end what she was now.

Enjoying the bafflement and pain displayed in her face, Metatron continued, "The whole Angel thing, the ranks, the names, it was his idea. In a society which had gotten rid of religion and banned the bible, this was pure cynicism, and a cruel jest towards everyone who still remembered the true meaning of angels, which were still quite a few, back then. We were like a twisted, perverse reflection of what those spiritual beings were supposed to be, and he liked that. So did I. Do you want to know the name he gave himself? Lucifer!"

Metatron laughed. "This makes you, sweet Nephilim, Satan's daughter. I can see from the look on your face that you have no idea why this is hilarious, but how could you, when the book this is all from is banned? Let me explain: Lucifer was the highest, most powerful angel, yet he fell from grace. He was considered evil, a fallen angel. He was also known as the devil. This makes your father's choice cynical. It's one of the reasons I named you Nephilim, which are fallen angels, too. No matter what you try to be, no matter where you run or hide, you'll always be the devil's daughter. It's your legacy. Your destiny. You will change the world, finish what your father started."

He looked into her eyes in silence for a moment to let his words sink in. "Anyway, I helped your father to build up the corps and lead it as it was growing, and we were assigned the task to not only fight the other corporations but also protect Olympias from dangers coming from within. I was his second in command, his right hand, his companion, his lover. He shared everything with me. Until he did something unspeakable."

He paused for another moment to keep his thoughts from getting lost down memory lane. "TogbuaXiang sent envoys to us to discuss a possible truce. Of course, in reality, this was a false flag, and an attempt at industrial espionage, to steal our Angel tech in particular—a ploy which your father saw through instantly. We took the alleged envoys captive. One of them was a Japanese woman. And then something happened which I'll never be able to understand. Your father, this highly intelligent, cynical, ice-cold man, somehow lost his mind. The woman stayed our prisoner for several weeks, and he took a particular interest in her from the beginning. He interrogated her every day, transferred her from a cell into more comfortable quarters. Finally, instead of executing her, he set her free. If this wasn't treason enough, he committed an unspeakable atrocity to himself; he had his eyes and implants ripped out to make himself untraceable, and then he ran away with her. Him, of all people! He never had his arms and legs replaced like the rest of us since he didn't go into combat, but I wonder to this day if he would've eventually amputated them, too, crippling his body the same way he had crippled his mind."

Metatron stopped and took a deep breath. Suddenly his expression turned cold and his voice was filled with hate and bitterness, "He gave up everything. He betrayed everything! He betrayed ... me. And for what? To play house with a woman! A fucking Wasp whore!"

"So, you killed him," Nephilim said quietly, "You murdered them both."

He crushed the screen in his hand into pieces, the picture of him and Nephilim's father disappeared back into his mind. Then he slowly turned his head and looked at her, his eyes dull, his face a cold mask.

"Damn right, I did. And I enjoyed every second of it. They thought they could hide from me, but they were wrong. Your father taught me too well, his own creation proved to be smarter than him. It took me a while, but eventually, I tracked them down, being appointed the High-Archangel after his betrayal."

A malicious smile contorted his face. "You know what I did? I killed his beloved Wasp whore, slowly, and let him witness it. He had no eyes to watch, but I made sure he heard. Then I killed him...in a way which will remain between him and me."

Nephilim closed her eyes. "So, that's why you took me. To get back at my father."

"At first, I wanted to find and kill you. I was furious. You were their natural child. If anything, you should have been *mine* and his child! But then I saw you and knew I was wrong. You were a gift, a chance to start all over again. Whenever I look into your face, I see *his* face, just more beautiful."

He smiled at her, and it made her blood freeze.

"I will never submit to you," she said.

"As I've said, we'll see about that," he answered, "But that was enough ancient history for one day. I really am needed elsewhere now."

BEHIND BLUE EYES

He moved to the door then stopped halfway as if he had an idea. An ugly grin appeared on his face when he looked over his shoulder back at her.

"I'll bring a gift for you when I come back. I'll let you watch when I first rape your boyfriend Jake, and then skin him alive. Unfortunately for you, you still have your eyes."

"I thought Angels didn't rape."

Metatron shrugged. "*Quod licet Iovi non licet bovi.*[6] Double standards, my dear."

He left the room. Nephilim was shaking. The torture was finally over for now.

***

Nephilim was devastated. She felt like she had been torn apart. Inside, her everything felt frozen, yet emblazoned with hellfire at the same time.

She had suffered many wounds in her years of active duty, some more some less severe than others. Nothing ever had been so hurtful as the pain she was experiencing now. She felt broken. For the first time in her life she wished for death.

In just one hour, Metatron had shattered her world, destroyed everything she had believed to be true. He had lifted a veil of illusions she had been surrounding herself with. Metatron had enjoyed the psychological pain that he had inflicted, more than any pleasure using torture utensils could have given him. Nephilim was sure it was far from

---

[6] Latin proverb: What Jupiter is allowed to, the cattle is not.

over; he wasn't done yet. It wasn't only that she had gone rogue and committed treason of the worst sort possible, he also took everything that she had done personally.

After these revelations, she understood why. In his own twisted, sick way, Metatron cared for her.

Everything was so clear to her now. How could she had been so blind all her life? How could she not have realized the special interest he had shown her? She couldn't really blame herself for that, and she knew it. Until recently, since he openly favored her to become an Archangel, he had done it in a discreet way, from the shadows. Yet, thinking back, there had been countless little things she could have noticed. She had not.

She had been blinded by her own vanity, believing she was better than everyone else, the best at everything. Gifted, and working hardest to be at the top. In truth, she wasn't. She was exceptional because *he* made her so.

The thought brought back something else Metatron had just said.

"I am his creation. Everything I am is because of him."

It made her shiver. He had been referring to her father, and yet the same could be said about her and him.

Her father was the root of everything. He was her legacy, as Metatron had put it.

Nephilim could still hardly wrap her mind around all of this, and she wished dearly it were only a lie, but she knew it was true. There was no point in denying it.

Her father had created them, had made the Guardian Angels what they were—soulless killers. Remembering the picture Metatron had shown her, and seeing her father's face there, she was horrified. It was the face of a cruel man; cold, vain, narcissistic, unscrupulous. A monster. The devil himself. And she was his daughter.

Had Metatron been right, though? *Was* she her father's daughter? Was this her true nature, and was it time to set doubts and scruples aside and embrace it? Was she fooling herself, believing she could be something else? Something good?

On the other hand, she remembered her father in a different way. A friendly man who loved her and her mother more than anything. How was this possible? Could people change so much? Or were these two faces of the same person? One day he must have realized that he had been wrong. That he had created monsters. Had it been her mother who made him realize that? Was it love? Nephilim would never know.

One thing was certain, though; he had been wrong in thinking he could ever step away from his own creations, even by crippling himself. Deadly wrong.

Metatron had done exactly what he had been created for: he searched for and destroyed the traitor, an enemy of Olympias. And he had taken it very personally.

So much so that he still held a grudge against a dead man after all these years.

And now what she had done to him was almost like déjà vu. It must have hurt him badly. Nephilim felt some satisfaction about that.

But, it was only a small comfort. The revelation about Jake hurt her even more than her twisted family history. Somebody had torn her heart out and replaced it with a bloody chunk filled with thorns.

Considering all of the facts, she had to admit that Metatron was right; she had been taken for a fool. She couldn't believe she had been so naive. On the other hand, she could still hardly believe Jake was so malicious.

When she thought back about the time they had spent together, especially last night, how he said he loved her, how they parted ways...it was unbelievable to her that it all had all been a lie. Yet, the facts were clearly stacked against him.

Nephilim felt both sad and furious at the same time. She had trusted this man, and he had abused her trust, abused her love. Betrayed her.

He deserved to die. But not the way Metatron had planned for him. For some reason, she didn't want him to suffer. Especially not for Metatron's pleasure and vengeance.

If anything, she wanted to kill him herself. She wasn't just any woman. She wasn't even human. Jake had messed with the wrong monster. Executions were a part of her nature. And she wouldn't hesitate to kill him. This was personal.

It would be a clean shot in the head. Closing his blue eyes forever. Silencing his twisted tongue.

But beforehand, she would give him the chance to explain why he had exchanged the data device. It was the only puzzle piece that did not fit in. Now, if she could only get out of there...

"Psst!" she heard a voice whisper, "Nephilim!"

She turned her head. Being so busy with her own brooding, she did not notice that the door had opened. Nobody had entered or was standing there. Her scanners showed her that there was somebody outside, however, and she knew exactly who.

"If you still have it, turn on your device," Finwick whispered, "Now!"

She *did* still have the device in her implant. Thankfully, there hadn't been time to remove it yet, and Metatron didn't consider it a high priority, now that she was in captivity.

"Done," she said, switching her system in fake sleep-mode.

The IT specialist entered the room, quickly closed the door after himself, and rushed towards Nephilim, his cheeks blushed with excitement.

"Fin, what the fuck are you doing here?" she asked, perplexed.

He stopped in front of her and smiled. "Saving you."

She stared at him, barely believing he was really there. He was the last person she had expected to enter this room, and the idea alone of *him* saving *her* was so absurd that she would have laughed if she wasn't in such a desperate situation—and so happy to see him.

"Are you OK?" he added, staring at her, his voice worried, "I was horrified I might be too late when I found out they put you in the Pit. Did they...*do* something to you?"

"I'm fine," she answered, "How did you even know I was here?"

He waved his hand. "You know how it is. Gossip travels faster than light. I had a bad feeling when I heard people discussing that an Angel had been thrown into the Pit, but when rumors came up that it was for treason, I was almost certain they'd noticed your double-life. So, I checked some security footage to be sure, and came as soon as you were alone."

"That's sweet of you. But I didn't save your ass just for it to get cooked now. You of all people should know that disabling my eyes won't help much if the whole room is under constant surveillance. *You* need to get out of here, Fin. Now."

"I love it when you call me that. No one else does," he said dreamily, his green eyes sparkling, "Don't worry, I know how to manipulate the surveillance. Nobody can see or hear us."

He proudly pointed at the maintenance device mounted on the implant on his wrist, then stepped to the console controlling Nephilim's restraints. "But now, let me get you out of here. It will take a moment. I don't have the clearance to operate down here, so I'll have to override some system protocols."

Nephilim watched him, fascinated by what this little man was capable of, the coolness he showed when doing it—and by his courage. He had changed a lot since she had first met him.

"How do you know how to shut down the surveillance?" she asked, "I didn't know it was possible."

He grinned but didn't stop working for a moment. "Emrich taught me."

She raised an eyebrow. "The ugly elf? Really?"

Finwick nodded. "Seems the old lunatic was good for something after all."

They both chuckled. Somehow, it felt liberating. Nephilim was amazed that it was this guy of all people who was helping her out in her darkest hour, in so many ways.

All of a sudden, the magnetism was gone, as if it had never been there, and Nephilim could move her arms and legs again.

"There you go," Finwick said with apparent pride.

With one smooth move, Nephilim sat up, letting her legs dangle down and stretching her limbs. "Thank you."

He beamed. "The least I could do. I've disabled the surveillance down the whole floor towards the staircase. This should buy you some time."

Nephilim took his shoulders in her hands and looked him in the eye.

BEHIND BLUE EYES

Sitting like this, they were eye to eye for once. "Listen to me, Fin. You're not safe. Metatron knows someone from under this roof helped me with implanting the device, and he's very keen on finding out who I came for at the harvesters' lair. I didn't tell him anything, but it's only a matter of time until he finds out—a short matter. He'll kill you when he does. You need to get out of here now."

He turned pale, listening to her. "But...how? Where would I even go?"

"Go to your supervisor and tell them you feel sick and need to go home. You bio-humans get sick and do that all the time, right? Go home as quickly as you can and grab some valuable, non-traceable stuff, all the money you have, if possible. Then leave and go into hiding."

His eyes were wide now. "How?"

"Go to the Underground. Find some illegally operating surgeon to remove your implants, make yourself disappear, become non-existent. Cover your tracks. Your life depends on it."

Finwick just stared at her, trying not to show how scared he was.

Nephilim smiled at him. "You're the smartest person I know, you're brilliant. I'm sure you'll figure something out. This should help."

She produced a C-Coin card out of her pocket and placed it in his hand. They hadn't taken it from her since it wasn't important. It neither contained data, nor was it in any way dangerous; it was simply money. Originally, she had intended to give it to Jake in case something went wrong, but their last encounter had been so emotional that she had forgotten about it. Now she was more than glad she did. The card contained all money she had.

"It's a lot," she added, "It will help you survive for quite a while."

"Nephilim," his voice was sad now, "This sounds like a goodbye."

"Because it is."

"Where are *you* going? Take me with you. Please!"

She shook her head. "No, Fin. I can't. I want you to live."

"No, no, Nephilim, please-" he protested desperately but she cut him off in a way he did not expect.

She took his face between her hands and pressed her lips to his. His resistance melted instantly. Like a drowning man, he wrapped his arms around her and returned her kiss. Nephilim let it last only for a moment, however, and ended it before it could become too intense.

"Thank you for everything, Fin," she said, "Take care of yourself."

He just stared at her, and in his eyes was all the sadness of the world.

Nephilim jumped up from the chair that had been her temporary prison, and grabbed the data stick Metatron had left on the small table next to the torture utensils.

"You're an amazing person and a wonderful man, always remember that," she told Finwick, and winked, "And if anyone dares to claim otherwise, I'll come after them."

He smiled. More than anything, he wanted to tell her how he felt, but the words simply wouldn't leave his mouth.

She hurried to leave the room. But then she stopped and looked back at him once more.

"I need to ask you one more favor. There's a little girl in the orphanage at Illumination Plaza, who's dear to me. Her name is Sarah. Can you take care of her for me?"

"I promise," he answered with such a huge lump in his throat that he could hardly speak.

She smiled. "Thank you. Goodbye, Fin."

Then she was gone, and he couldn't restrain himself any longer. Tears started running down his cheeks.

"I love you," he whispered, now that she couldn't hear him anymore.

***

The High-Archangel stood at the huge windows of his office and looked at the gigantic, black pyramid outside, his chin resting on his hand, deep in thought. The door opened, and Zephaniel entered the room at a fast pace. There was no need for him to knock. If not explicitly instructed to stay out, he could enter and leave as he pleased.

"She's gone," he stated.

Metatron lifted an eyebrow. "Already? That was quick."

"Yes, I was surprised, myself," Zephaniel agreed.

"Who helped her escape? One of our Angels? Her partner?" Metatron asked without moving his attention from the view.

The Archangel grimaced. "We don't know."

Metatron turned towards him, sharply, his eyes narrowing. "What does that mean?"

Zephaniel knew him well enough not to be intimidated so easily. He stayed cool as he answered, "It means that somebody disabled the surveillance system. We couldn't see who helped her or how she escaped the Pit, and there's no record of it whatsoever; visual *or* data. Whoever did it, knew exactly what they were doing. We only spotted her again when she went for her motorcycle and attacked the guards we had positioned in the garage."

"Did she kill them?" Metatron asked, visibly intrigued.

Zephaniel shook his head. "Following your instructions, I positioned two rookies there. They were no match for her. She had them down and unconscious within seconds."

Metatron smiled. "Saving resources, or is it mercy, I wonder?"

The question clearly wasn't meant for his second-in-command, he was just thinking out loud. Zephaniel understood this, and kept silent.

"As for Nephilim's escape from the Pit, I have a clear idea who helped her," Metatron said, turning away from the window and towards his Archangel, "There's only one person under this roof capable of disarming the surveillance system: our most-valued Dr. Emrich."

Zephaniel was stunned. "You knew he could do that, and you let him be? Why?"

Metatron smirked. "It gave the ugly leech a feeling of false security, of power. It made him believe he was smarter than me. And as long as all he did was run his mouth and jerk off in his office from time to time, I let him be. He might be a moron, but he's still a brilliant scientist and a valuable asset. Besides, you know me, I would never liquidate anyone for having the wrong opinion. Who am I, a tyrant?"

There was a hint of self-irony in the last part of his statement. Of course, he had anyone removed for anything he wanted, at any time. Inside these walls and out. He never acted arbitrarily, however, which would have made him a simple despot. That would have been a waste of resources, and therefore stupid in his mind.

BEHIND BLUE EYES

Zephaniel grinned, moving closer. "No, you would never do that."

Suddenly the intimacy between the two men became apparent: they had obviously been close for many years. But the relationship was clearly unequal, with one dominating, and the other showing all the admiration and devotion.

"But I thought Emrich hated Nephilim," Zephaniel said after a moment of silence, "Didn't he want to have her dismantled?"

Metatron shrugged. "All part of the scheme. Textbook deflection. The only question now, is *why* did he do it? But we'll deal with that later. Have him detained. You can visit with the good Doctor, once all of this is over. I'm confident he'll sing for you in no time."

A pleased expression flashed over Zephaniel's face, similar to when a cat brings its master a living mouse. "I'll see that he's detained at once."

"So, I suppose Nephilim took the bait?" Metatron asked, returning to the topic.

"Exactly as you said she would. You know her very well."

The High-Archangel smiled, pleased with himself, yet there was also a hint of softness in this smile. "Of course I do. I knew she would fall for the bluff that we have the position of the hostiles' hideout. I want our assault to be from multiple sides; a precise, well-coordinated strike with as few casualties on our side as possible. Are you positive the tracking is working as planned?"

"It is," Zephaniel confirmed, "We easily can track the Zirconium-89 that we applied on the data device. It's almost like Ariadne's ball of red thread."

"Good," Metatron nodded.

Knowing that the enemy—or probably even Nephilim herself—would notice any conventional tracking device, the High-Archangel had instructed to infuse the data stick she had brought in with Zirconium-89 isotope. It was slightly radioactive, and easily traceable—if someone knew what they were looking for. Otherwise, it would stay undetected. Anticipating that she would attempt to escape and try to find out the truth, Metatron had left the device in the room with her on purpose, pretending he had forgotten it.

"She will lead our full force directly towards them," Zephaniel said, "It's a brilliant plan."

"Don't flatter me, Zephaniel," Metatron said with a sudden chill in his voice, "You know I don't like that. Are the squads ready to be deployed?"

"Awaiting your command."

"Excellent. We'll give her a bit time to stir them up once she's inside, then we strike. You'll lead the assault, personally; I don't want any mistakes."

"There won't be any. Be assured."

"Make sure everyone knows the faces of the Prom leaders I want captured alive—especially the man. His corpse is useless to me."

"He'll be our guest before midnight," Zephaniel promised.

The smile on Metatron's lips would have given anyone chills and nightmares, yet Zephaniel hardly even noticed the cruelty and sadism mixed in with it.

"And what about Nephilim?" he asked.

"She's not to be hurt in any way," Metatron said.

"Even if she resists?"

BEHIND BLUE EYES

"Even then."

Zephaniel clenched his fist without Metatron noticing his angry defiance. "But...why?"

The High-Archangel looked at him before he answered calmly, "Since when do I need to explain myself to you, Zephaniel?"

"You don't, but," he said, moving closer until they were almost touching, "After what she did to the corps...to you. Why protect her? I don't understand. She has strong abilities, yes, but so do others. We could easily pick another one for Archangel."

Metatron kept silent, letting him speak.

Zephaniel continued in a soft voice, slightly tilting his head, "Let me hunt her down for you. Let me hurt her, let me kill her. Let me take vengeance for what she did to you. For betraying you."

The two men looked each other in the eye for a moment. Metatron's face was unreadable.

Then the High-Archangel lifted his hand and stroked the other man's hair and cheek in a tender gesture.

"Zephaniel," he said softly, "You're so right..."

Zephaniel smiled.

Suddenly Metatron grabbed his neck with one hand and his shoulder with the other with such inhuman speed that even the Archangel had no chance to react in any way. Metatron lifted him up, just to smash him to the ground with so much force that it left the glass in his windows shaking for a moment. Quicker than the blink of an eye, and he was on him, pressing his knee against his chest, still holding him down with one hand and choking him with the other. An expression of panic bloomed in Zephaniel's face as he desperately gasped for air.

"You're right, you don't understand," Metatron said, his voice like frozen steel now, "You don't understand where your place is. And you've clearly forgotten who I am and what I'm capable of."

Zephaniel tried to speak, but few words made it out of his mouth while he gasped for air, "Forgive me...I didn't..."

"You didn't use your brain, huh?" Metatron said, sneering, "But that's not your job. Your job is to follow orders. *My* orders."

He fastened his grip around Zephaniel's neck, and the Archangel gargled instead of speaking, his face turning red.

"I'm telling you once again what your orders are: you assault the Rosprom hideout, destroy it, bring me the leaders alive and under no circumstances—I repeat, no circumstances—hurt Nephilim. Bring her here, unhurt. Is that clear?"

Metatron pressed his knee harder against Zephaniel's chest until the sound of several ribs cracking could be heard, and he squirmed in pain.

"It's now your personal responsibility to make sure nothing happens to her, do you understand? If she should have an 'accident' of any sort, I will smash all the remaining natural bones inside your body, starting with your spine, and ending with your skull. Expect no mercy." He let go of him and got up.

Zephaniel gasped for air, his eyes full of disbelief, pain, and fear. A thin ribbon of blood ran from his mouth as he was finally able to speak again.

"Yes, Metatron, I understand. I'm sorry...forgive me, I'm so sorry..."

Metatron crossed his arms and smiled down at him, as if nothing had happened. "Go and get yourself patched up. I want the troops deployed in ten minutes."

BEHIND BLUE EYES

***

Nephilim rushed down the Deathway towards Oldtown at top speed. She looked back from time to time and constantly scanned her surroundings. Nobody followed her. At least, by now, they must have realized that she was gone, no matter how busy everybody was preparing the assault on the enemy base. But for the moment, nobody had taken up the pursuit.

Somehow it felt like her escape had been way too easy. Metatron had proven to be always one step ahead of her—and everybody else. So, could it really be true that she had escaped him so easily unless he had wanted her to do so? Of course, he couldn't have been responsible for Finwick rescuing her, but maybe he had anticipated that she would escape the Pit. Once she had left it, the rest of her flight had been downright laughably easy.

She had snuck through the lower levels of the HQ, only encountering some maintenance and science personnel, whom she was avoided easily. The only Angels had been two rookies that she later came across in the garage. Knowing that it would be not possible to sneak past them without being noticed by their sensors, she had no other choice but to attack them. She knocked them down on the run, knowing exactly how to strike an Angel to make them unconscious without creating any major damage.

It was strange. As much as Metatron's revelations had hurt and disturbed her, some of the information proved to be helpful now. At first, she had been disappointed to learn why she had been outperforming everyone else. In her vanity, she had believed she was more gifted than others, while the truth was that Metatron had equipped her with way better parts than anyone else.

This fact gave her a whole new dimension of confidence now. She *knew* that she was good. She was gifted and had been working hard all her life. This, combined with state-of-the-art technology, made her superior. No other Angel could stand up against her, and this was not conceit; it was fact.

Driven by this new confidence, she hadn't hesitated even for a second to attack the two Angels at once—and they never stood a chance.

Her motorcycle had still been parked in the garage where she had left it, and luckily, her spare guns and ammo were in the box under the saddle. She'd strapped holsters to her thighs and secured her weapons. It didn't matter if anyone would see them or not, and that way, she could draw much quicker. Then she had left the HQ unhindered.

Yes, it had to have been a setup of some sort; there couldn't be any other logical explanation. But Nephilim did not care about Metatron's plans now. She knew only two things for sure: she wanted to hear the truth from Jake, even if she needed to force him to speak. And she wasn't going back, no matter what. Metatron would have to find a new pet. There were plenty of others who wanted nothing more than to take that position.

Nephilim dearly hoped Finwick would be able to escape in time and be safe. Something told her he would. He was not only smart, but had somehow become a real man during the short time she had really gotten to know him. He had shown great courage, and she would never forget what he had done for her. Nephilim was sad that she had to leave him so upset and broken-hearted; he sure as hell did not deserve that. She knew that he was in love with her, probably had been for a while. But even in a perfect world where she would be free to lead a self-determined life, she wouldn't have been able to offer him more than her friendship.

Instead, she had fallen in love with a man who had deceived her, who was the enemy. Life was full of irony.

BEHIND BLUE EYES

Nephilim reached Oldtown without any incidents and took the ramp closest to the destination. Bathed in the light of the late afternoon sun, she could see Merit Park from above, when driving down from the transport lane to the ground. She smirked. It was amazing that, below this neatly landscaped green, Olympias' most dangerous enemy was hiding in plain sight, for who knew how long. It was a bold yet smart trick to play. Metatron was right when he described the sneaky approach of Rosprom agents as highly sophisticated. She, of all people, could tell a story about that.

Now, however, the rats hiding below the lush green were oblivious of what was coming for them. Nephilim took satisfaction in this thought.

Imagining the retaliation against the Proms brought an expression on her face that resembled Metatron—and her father.

Following her intuition, she did not drive right in front of the building with the hidden door leading down the rabbit hole but parked her motorcycle in a small side street close to the ramp about a quarter-mile away. She walked from there, reached the entrance less than two minutes later, and rushed down the steep stairs into the darkness. The first security door, which Jake had opened with his fingerprint, was massive, and an unbreachable obstacle for humans without proper equipment—but not for her. She took a powerful swing and kicked the door open, ripping it out of its hinges. It wasn't so easy to stop a pissed off cyborg.

Nephilim quickly crossed the former garage floor and stopped in front of the next door. This one was harder to crack. She wouldn't be able to open it by herself using brute force, after all.

Sometimes a pissed off cyborg had to use deceit to reach her goals.

She looked up into the tiny camera above the door and flashed a friendly smile. Then she reached into her pocket and produced the data stick. She held it in front of the lens and pointed to it, her face showing a proud expression mixed with excitement. As if she wanted to tell them that she had successfully fulfilled her task.

A moment passed, and she patiently waited in front of the door, standing in the darkness, the device in her hand. She knew the guards could see her. They needed time to ask for instructions on if they should let her in or not. Surely the leadership did not expect her to be back so early since it wasn't even dark outside yet. She hoped they would regard this as proof of her eagerness to become part of the team as soon as possible, and not grow suspicious. And she hoped Jake would be there. She was quite certain he would, after all, he had no reason to sit in his apartment, which was certainly fake, and not his anyway.

Finally, the door opened with a soft click, and Nephilim went inside. Lowering her face, the friendly smile vanished, turning into a grin that would have delighted Metatron if he could see it.

She had no difficulties finding her way in the labyrinthine underground structures of the old aquarium. Her built-in navigation system automatically saved every route she once took, and she could reconstruct it without thinking. Of course, her glowing neon-blue eyes made the pitch darkness around her seem like bright daylight.

After a few minutes, she reached the glass tunnel and navigated it without slowing her pace. The strange, magical effect the place had on her when she visited it with Jake for the first time was completely gone. Now it was just a rotting, deserted structure from a bygone era—infested with rats. Human rats.

And she knew that she only had a brief window before pest control arrived with full force.

She reached the door that was guarded by the two young fighters. They were the same ones as yesterday, and she inspected their equipment and body structures more thoroughly this time. They were in good shape; well-trained soldiers who pretended to be way more greenhorn and lax than they actually were. This wouldn't help them much, however, they would be dead before even noticing what was happening. She did not feel any pity.

"Hi," she said with a smile.

The girl again just frowned at her while the guy said, "You can go in, they're expecting you."

"Thanks," she said, opening the door.

Inside the small monitoring room, the two guards were a bit friendlier.

"You know the drill, you need to leave your guns here," the man sitting at the holo-monitor said.

"Of course," she answered, pulled her guns from her holsters and put them on the table.

The other one stepped forward. "I need to check you for further weapons."

"Be my guest," she said with a smile, spreading her arms and legs.

While he frisked her thoroughly, she wondered if this was really necessary or if he was taking advantage of the opportunity to touch an Angel all over. Was he aware that she could simply grab the back of his neck and rip his spine out while he was leaning down to search her legs? She also could extend a blade in the blink of an eye and pierce his skull, entering through one ear and exiting through the other.

He straightened up and smiled at her. "All clear. You're good to go."

Most likely, he knew. He was no idiot or idealistic resistance guy, he was a highly trained agent, as all of them were. Still, it was easy to forget, looking at Nephilim, that she didn't need any weapons to kill him and his friend in less than two seconds. She *was* the weapon.

"Thank you," she said in a friendly tone.

"Follow me, please," he said opening, the door to the "rebellion's" inner sanctum.

She followed him over the catwalk to the opposite side near the former aquarium staff offices. Downstairs, the alleged resistance members were pretending to follow their daily business, and this time, barely gave her any notice. She wondered if they did this charade just for her and otherwise followed a different daily routine. This time she scanned the crates piled up in the back of the cave. Some consisted of weapons, which was nothing suspicious for a resistance group. Others, however, were impossible to penetrate by her sensors. They had to be shielded by very advanced technology and possibly contained weapons and other equipment which shouldn't normally be possessed by such a group. Foreign tech; Prom, to be precise.

Nephilim smiled down at a young man looking up at her as she passed by. He was a dead man walking. They all were. Even if they had highly advanced weapons hidden somewhere, they wouldn't stand a chance.

They arrived at the other side where Lena stood in the door of the conference room, waiting for her. Nephilim flashed a broad smile as she approached.

It was time to end everything, once and for all.

Chapter Thirteen

Against All the Odds

"Welcome back, Nephilim," Lena said with a friendly smile that was so well-trained it outwardly appeared to be one-hundred percent genuine, "We didn't expect you back so soon. Is everything all right?"

"Certainly," Nephilim answered with a wave of her hand, "My squad has been commanded to raid a location in the southern part of the city, and since I'm technically still on sick leave, I was free to go."

"Oh, right, the glitches. Jake told us about that. It was your way to break out of the grid, which ultimately brought you to us, correct?"

"Correct," Nephilim confirmed, then looked around, "Where *is* Jake?"

"I'm afraid he isn't here right now. You're stuck with me," Lena said with a smile, entering the conference room where her two bodyguards were already waiting, "Let's sit down and talk."

"Tea?" she added after they both had taken seats at the table in the same positions as last time.

"I would love that," Nephilim said, "My apologies for kicking in the first security door, by the way, but since there was no doorbell, I had no other possible way to get inside."

Lena shrugged, still playing it cool. After considering her options, Nephilim decided that it would be best to come forward with a fake apology. Most likely, they had sensors at that door and knew she had broken it down.

"Yeah, we figured that was the case," Lena said while pouring the tea, "Don't worry, we'll have that fixed in no time. In the future, we'll need to think about a more practical solution for you getting in and out, though."

She handed one cup to her guest, then casually leaned back in her chair, her own cup in hand. "So, Nephilim, we've seen on the security footage that you've brought us back the data device."

Nephilim reached into her pocket, pulled the device out, and placed in on the table in front of her. "Here it is."

Lena took a sip of her tea. "And, does it contain the data I asked for? Did you manage to pull it from the Angel HQ internal servers?"

"It does," Nephilim lied, "There are two raids on settlements scheduled for the next ten days. It will be a close call, but if you warn them now, they should be able to evacuate in time. You'll find their exact locations in the files."

"Excellent," Lena said, and a triumphant gleam flashed over her narrow, green eyes, "We'll see to that at once."

For a brief moment, she had lowered her mask, and Nephilim could clearly see that she couldn't care less about any of the settlers out there.

"So, you plugged the device into a computer inside the HQ to get that information?" Lena asked one more time.

"Of course," Nephilim replied, wrinkling her forehead, "How else could I have obtained the information?"

"Good," Lena said. A broad grin appeared on her face as she exchanged looks with the two people standing next to her.

"Is something wrong?" Nephilim asked, pretending to be confused.

If she had any doubts if Metatron told her the truth or not, they were gone now. It was exactly as he had stated. The thought alone of what would have happened if she had gone through with Lena's plan made her cringe inwardly and filled her with rage at the same time. How could she have been so stupid?

It was only thanks to Metatron that they weren't all dead by now. Or was it not? Had Jake really given her a blank device? If so, then he had purposely sabotaged his own mission, betrayed his own people.

"Oh nothing, at least for us," Lena said, her smile turning into a sardonic grin, "Tell me, Nephilim, how do you feel? Is everything alright?"

"Now that you mention it...I do feel a little strange," Nephilim pretended, then decided to go full-frontal. Now that she was convinced the Guardian Angels were done for, Lena was about to end the charade as well.

"There was something on the device," she said with mock horror in her voice.

Lena laughed. "What was your first clue? Your implants acting up? Software malfunctions, maybe? Or is it something biological such as a headache or dizziness?"

Nephilim made a move as if to get up from her chair, but the two guards instantly drew their guns and pointed them at her.

"Stay where you are, Angel." Lena's cool green eyes were full of spite. "Let us enjoy the show. If you inserted the device into the main system this morning, then it shouldn't take much longer. We'll stay here and watch your suffering till the end. It'd be better to restrain you, though, for the end might be very ugly."

"Did Jake know?" Nephilim asked.

This made Lena laugh again, and this time, the guards joined her. "Of course, you stupid machine. It was *his* plan."

Her words hurt Nephilim more than she would have believed anything ever could. She had known the truth, but somehow sitting here and hearing it again in this way was almost more than she could handle. She had to force herself to keep going.

"Why?"

"Because we're here to change Olympias in a different way than you think," Lena explained, triumphantly, "We're not resistance. There is no *resistance* in this godforsaken place; never was, and never will be. The people here are so brainwashed, so content with their slavery without even noticing that's what it is. I have to give your leaders credit for that. We tried to build up a true resistance for many years. A true movement that could crash the system, but it was pointless. Then we started approaching select individuals who could prove useful, pretending to be a member of the resistance, and bringing them to our cause. After a while, we had them everywhere. Then our leaders forged an alliance with TogbuaXiang, and a joint plan was developed; They would create a diversion and take out facilities crucial for Olympias to weaken the society while we set our agents and new recruits in action to destroy Olympias from within. But, for some reason, we haven't figured out yet how your people found out we were working with TogbuaXiang. Not only did the Angels counter our most crucial attacks, but they started raiding all over the city, which came dangerously close to us."

"You're Rosprom," Nephilim said.

Lena snickered. "Hear hear, this machine isn't that dumb after all! Yes, we are. And proud of it."

"We knew you were here, it was only a matter of time until we would have gotten to you and smashed you," Nephilim said as she continued to fake feeling unwell.

"Yes, indeed, very unfortunate," Lena acknowledged, slightly irritated, "We had to eliminate most of our contacts and recruits inside Olympias because of that."

"You executed them?"

Lena shrugged. "There was no other choice; they had become a liability. Under no circumstances were they allowed to fall into your hands and sing. We still have some left in secure positions, though, mostly in the Inner Circle. However, we needed a plan B, fast. It was clear that we'd never succeed as long as you and your fellow blue-eyed fuckers were around."

Nephilim grabbed her head, pretending she was suffering a sudden, intense headache. Seeing it brought a malicious smile on Lena's thin lips.

"Gladly, our IT engineers back home have developed their latest masterpiece just in time," she continued, "It's called Angel Dust, and, as I can see, you enjoy it."

"Our people back at HQ have surely discovered it by now," Nephilim groaned, "They'll develop a countermeasure. You *will* fail."

"I highly doubt that. Once Angel Dust is in your system, it merges with your source code and corrupts it. It spreads into the neural implants and destroys your brain from within—a horrible way to die, I can imagine. But don't worry, it takes less than twelve hours."

She watched Nephilim appear to struggle with her disdain for a moment, a mixture of complacent contempt on her face, then continued, "You know, at first we planned to try and catch one of you in combat or maybe set up a trap, and then implement the virus into your system. However, this would've proven difficult and dangerous. Besides, we know your internal firewall is unbreakable. The only way to bypass it is to get inside HQ and access the system there. But sometimes even the best operatives need some luck to succeed, and then Jake stumbled across you. A stupid machine who desperately wanted to be loved."

That was enough. Nephilim had heard everything she needed. It was time to end the game.

Slowly she lifted her head and looked Lena in the eye, no longer appearing ill.

"Seems you've run out of your own luck," she said with a chilling voice.

Lena was stunned for a moment but tried to keep her composure. "What are you talking about?"

"Oh, nothing in particular," Nephilim said with a grin that could have been Metatron's, now leaning back casually in her chair, "Only that you're going to die. All of you. Soon."

In a matter of seconds, Lena's expression changed from disbelief to horror to anger as she made the connection. "You fucking bitch. You never plugged the stick in. You set us up."

Nephilim shrugged. "The best agent is a double agent. As we speak, the Guardian Angels are closing in on this position. They'll hit you with full force."

Lena drew her pistol from the holster at her hip and pointed it at Nephilim while she commanded one of her guards. "Inform TogbuaXiang. We need backup here. *Now!*"

The woman nodded and left the room, running. Now, Nephilim realized why Metatron had let her go. He had known that she would go there and do exactly what she was doing now, scaring and stirring them up so that they were forced to call in Wasp support. Most likely, the Angels were already in close proximity, lying low and waiting for Metatron's signal to strike. It wouldn't matter for them if the Proms knew they were coming a few minutes in advance; being humans, they were mere cannon fodder. If Wasps showed up, however, the Angels would have the chance to take all of them out at once.

The Prom leader slowly rose from her seat, her face full of cold rage, her eyes two green slits.

"Maybe your people are coming, but they'll be too late to save you," she said, hatefully nodding to her guard, "Kill her."

The man grinned. Apparently, he had been hoping for exactly that. "With pleasure."

"Don't you dare touch her," a voice suddenly said from behind her.

Both Lena and the guard stopped short in surprise. Even Nephilim was shocked. She knew that voice very well. Her sensors showed her that he stood in the door, a pistol in his hand, pointing it at Lena.

Jake.

Lena's mouth twitched as she tried to suppress her bafflement and rising anger.

"What are you doing, Jake?" she hissed, "Have you completely lost your mind?"

He ignored her, and slowly moved around Nephilim towards the two.

"Lower your weapons," he said calmly, "Nobody needs to get hurt."

Lena snorted contemptuously. "You're insane. What exactly are you trying to accomplish here?"

"Lower your weapon, Lena," he repeated with a threatening undertone, his gray-blue eyes filled with cold determination, "I won't say it again."

She stared at him for another moment in disbelief, then lowered her gun. Her subordinate followed her example.

"The High Command will hear of this, Jake," she said, "I promise you, you will deeply regret it. This is treason."

He shrugged, smiling. "Court-martial me, Lena. Right after single-handedly fighting off an army of Guardian Angels. They're here, everywhere. I've seen them on the surveillance cams."

Lena's face paled. Obviously, she had hoped there was time left for preparation. At the same time, her other guard stormed back into the room. The woman stopped for a moment, confused at how much the situation had changed during her absence, then reported, "Major Nazarova,! The Angels have breached the second barrier. They're inside! A whole army!"

"*Suka, blyad*!" Lena swore uncontrolled, ramming her fist on the table. She rushed to the door.

"Good luck," Jake said dryly.

"Go to hell!" she snapped at him, running out the door. The two soldiers followed her.

"After you," he answered calmly, then turned to Nephilim, who had watched the stand-off with astonishment. His gaze softened with sorrow.

He lowered his gun, reached behind him and pulled Nephilim's weapons out of his belt, where he had been hiding them.

"I believe these are yours," he said putting, them on the table in front of her.

She jumped up, grabbed one of her pistols, and pressed it against his forehead. He didn't flinch or try to defend himself in any way, just kept looking at her.

"Tell me just one thing," she demanded, "Is it true? Is everything Lena has told me true? About what this is? About who you people are and what you do? About you?"

He closed his eyes for a moment and nodded slowly. "Yes, Nephilim, it's true. I wish from the depths of my heart it wasn't, but it is. I'm a spy. And my mission was to destroy your society from within. By any means necessary. I'm sorry."

Again, Nephilim felt like she was standing next to an abyss, its darkness threatening to swallow her. She bit her lip. Her finger moved towards the trigger.

"You deceived me," she whispered, "I trusted you."

He looked into her eyes. "I did. There's nothing I could do or say to make up for it. I know you're going to kill me, and I deserve it."

He was right. He deserved to die. It was the reason she had come here. All she needed to do was pull the trigger. A clean headshot, exactly as she had planned.

Yet, her hand was shaking. Which was something that had never happened to her before.

"So, it was all a lie," she said.

Jake smiled sadly. "No, it wasn't. And this makes what I did even more despicable. My identity was a lie, the resistance, the talks about how I wished to change the world. My feelings were real."

Nephilim frowned, pressing the muzzle of her gun harder against his head. "Yeah, right. So real that you tried to turn me and all my kind into Angel Dust."

"That was the plan, but I couldn't go through with it," he said quietly, "I'm not sure how your people have figured out what is going on here, but if they checked the data stick I gave you, they must have noticed that it was blank. I destroyed Angel Dust. Even though I knew that it would ultimately lead to our own doom."

Nephilim stared at him. Although he clearly knew he was going to die, there was no fear in his eyes, just sadness and remorse. He was telling the truth, there had been no virus on the data device he had given her. Her hand shook even more when she tried to pull the trigger. It almost seemed as if her artificial arm didn't belong to her anymore; as if another deeper part of herself was controlling it.

Looking at one another, they were almost unaware of those around them in the camp preparing for the imminent assault. Sounds of people and equipment moving about echoed throughout the cave. Officers shouted out commands in English and another foreign language.

"Nephilim," Jake continued, "Do you really believe I faked everything that happened between us? I'm an excellent spy, but I'm not *that* good."

He laughed, but it was humorless. Then he was serious again. "Last night was as real as it could be. I meant every word I said, and I truly wished that you would've agreed to leave with me; more than anything."

They heard shots being fired, and a detonation caused by a grenade or small explosives shook the room. The assault had begun but hadn't reached the cave yet. Somewhere desperate human Proms were trying to make a stand against an unstoppable enemy. The excitement down in the cave grew, with more commands being yelled.

"They're here," Jake said quietly, then smiled at her, "Please, forgive me, Nephilim. Eventually. That's all I ask. And I beg you to have mercy and kill me now. I'm a high-ranking officer, which makes me valuable. The interrogation rooms in your HQ are infamous. Please, don't let me end up there."

Nephilim looked at him, into his calm face, his eyes locked on hers. What he said was the truth. He had exchanged the data device. Even if Metatron wouldn't have seen through the ploy and stopped her, and she had plugged the device into the Angels' intranet system, nothing would've happened.

She remembered how he had desperately tried to convince her to leave with him. It had been no act, she was certain of that now. His job would've been to make sure she went along with the plan and brought Angel Dust to HQ. He had been trying to stop his operation without blowing his own cover.

And could she really blame him for what he had done? Following orders, fighting for the corporation, killing without hesitation was her duty, her daily life. So was his, just in a different way. Who was she to judge? He had lied to her, yes. But in the end, when it was all or nothing, he had protected her.

Metatron's last words before he had left the Pit came back to her; what he was planning to do to Jake once he had him. Nephilim knew the High-Archangel well enough to be certain that he meant to do exactly what he had said. She couldn't let that happen. She wouldn't let Jake fall into Metatron's hands. Ever.

Jake closed his eyes. "Do it, Nephilim. Please."

She holstered her weapon. Instead of shooting him, she pulled him to her and pressed her lips to his.

Jake was utterly surprised at first, but quickly got a hold of himself and returned her kiss feverishly, embracing her closely.

Around them, the sounds of fighting and dying grew louder. The Guardian Angels were closing in fast.

"Nephilim, I..." Jake said as she pulled away from him after a few moments.

She placed her index finger on his lips, interrupting him, "We need to get out of here. I won't let you fall into their hands."

He smiled. "I'm afraid it's too late for that."

Nephilim reached out for her second gun on the table and checked the ammunition in one skilled, incredibly fast move.

"Clearly, you have no idea what I'm capable of," she said with a grin.

She walked to the door and scanned the cave. The Angels hadn't stormed it yet, but it was only a matter of time now.

"Is there another exit out of this trap?"

"Yes," Jake said, following her, "Downstairs, there's a tunnel that leads to the old sewer system, but-"

"Excellent, let's go."

"Nephilim," he said as he held her back, "Wasps are approaching from there. We'll have to get past my own people, the Angels, and the

BEHIND BLUE EYES

Wasp reinforcements. Even you can't possibly face all of them."

Nephilim smiled at him. "Watch me."

She leaped down into the cave.

***

Jake skillfully slid down one of the ropes hanging down from the catwalk into the cave and joined Nephilim, who was crouching on the ground behind some stacks of boxes. The Proms had put up makeshift barricades alongside the huge, glass wall, as well as a couple of heavy auto-turrets. While many of them had taken cover there, equipped with rifles and EMP grenades, others were fighting the invaders on the other side of the wall. Muzzle flashes could be seen in the darkness. And blue eyes. Seemingly countless numbers of them. They approached like a menacing swarm of oddly colored lightning bugs.

A salvo of high-caliber ammunition was shot in Nephilim's and Jake's direction, almost instantly destroying their cover. Obviously, Lena had positioned a shooter somewhere to greet them when they decided to leave the upstairs room.

"Shit," Jake swore.

Nephilim reacted lightning fast. Her combat HUD sprang into action, showing her the attacker's position. He was crouching on the opposite side of the catwalk above them. Pressing Jake flat to the ground with one hand, Nephilim fired one precise shot with the other, hitting the shooter in the center of his forehead. She spun around and fired in the other direction even before ending her move. Two consecutive shots executed another couple of men aiming at them from the other side. Outside, the blue eyes were coming closer.

"Where to?" she asked Jake, helping him back up.

"You know, I'm not some damsel in distress you need to protect. I can take care of myself," he said with a grin, but a slightly offended undertone.

"You can," she agreed, "But I'm ten times faster than you, and much sturdier. If one of us has to take a bullet, it should be me."

He stared at her, speechless.

"So, where are we going?" she repeated, in fully focused combat mode, not realizing the impact of what she had just said.

"Follow me," he said.

Keeping his head down, he ran to the back area of the cave and in between some fake rocks. Nephilim followed him, scanning the surroundings for hostile attacks, ready to jump into action any second. They approached a round opening in the wall which probably once served as drainage for the gigantic fish tank. It was big enough, so a grown person could fit through when hunching down. Two men were standing in front of it, rifles in their hands.

"Stand down!" Jake commanded them, "That's an order!"

They flinched, but then aimed their rifles at him. Apparently, they had been instructed not to let him pass. And to shoot him.

Not hesitating for a second, Nephilim lunged past Jake and stabbed both guards with her wrist blades in their necks. They gargled and collapsed.

"Sorry for that," she said, turning back to Jake over the twitching bodies, "I hope they weren't friends of yours."

"No," he said, astonished, "Not at all."

BEHIND BLUE EYES

"Why are you looking at me like that?"

"I just realized I had no idea what you were actually capable of."

"That was nothing," she smiled.

Suddenly, everything was shaken by an explosion. Nephilim and Jake both turned and saw the glass wall shattering into pieces and collapsing. One second later, the slaughter began as the Angels engaged a full-frontal assault on the Prom position. A loud rattle could be heard as the auto-turrets started, but Nephilim knew that they would not keep the Angels away for more than a few seconds.

She frowned. "They'll come after us. We need to leave. *Now!*"

Jake leaned down to the corpses and picked up something one of the men had on his belt: night vision goggles.

"Hurry!" Nephilim urged him, standing in the opening.

Just when they disappeared inside the pitch-black tube, the first pair of glowing blue eyes entered the artificial cave.

***

Slightly crouched, they ran down the steep slope as fast as they could, into the gaping darkness. More precisely, Nephilim adjusted her speed to Jake's quickened pace. He wasn't nearly as fast as an Angel, but he still kept up astonishingly well for a human. The night vision goggles aided him in moving easier in the dark.

Behind them, the sounds of battle turned into screams of merciless slaughter. The horrific sounds echoed down the tunnels as the Angels gave their enemies swift deaths. Jake's people were certainly excellent spies, but when it came to combat, they were almost as helpless against an Angel assault as the settlers Nephilim and her brothers-in-arms have raided. Standing up to them was like standing up to a tsunami.

But there was no reason for gloating. Nephilim knew that, when scanning the cave before the attack, the Angels had identified her exact position, and it was only a matter of a few minutes until they initiated a pursuit. She was convinced that they had explicit orders to hunt her down and bring her back. Metatron wasn't done with her yet. And, for sure, Jake had been classified as a primary target, too. The thought of fighting and killing her own people was terrifying, but she would do it if no other choice was left. She glanced over her shoulder, but there were no blue eyes on the upper end of the tube yet.

A hundred feet further down, the narrow tunnel ended abruptly. Nephilim stopped and looked around. The ledge they were standing on was about seven feet high. Below was a much larger, wider tunnel. No doubt they had reached the city's old sewer system that Jake had been talking about. It was dried out; no water was running here anymore. Olympias' city planners had designed and built a new, more effective one decades ago.

Nephilim could hear squeaks and saw movement from the corner of her eye; rats, many of them.

"OK, what now?" she asked Jake, leaping down from the ledge.

He followed, managing the jump without much effort, then pointed his finger down the tunnel. "If we follow this tunnel and take the first right, we'll find the old subway system. From there, it'll be easy to reach the surface at an unattended spot."

"How do you know all this?" Nephilim asked, bewildered, "I had no idea this place even existed."

BEHIND BLUE EYES

He shrugged with a crooked grin. "We had to be able to navigate the city without raising suspicion, somehow. Especially when moving equipment. Come on!"

He led the way at a fast pace, and she followed. A minute later, they took a smaller tunnel branching to the right. Just then, Nephilim heard something that sent shivers down her spine. She stopped for a second, listening, her sensors focused.

Steps. Heavy bodied. Many of them. Running faster than any human possibly could.

The hunters were on their trail. She turned ice-cold inside as her brain did the math calculating how long it would take the pursuers to catch up with them. So, that was how it felt to be the prey. Chased down by merciless blue eyes.

"What is it?" Jake asked, frowning. He had started breathing faster. How long would he be able to hold that pace? And would it be long enough? At this rate, probably not.

"They're coming," she said, "Run!"

She gave him a gentle push, and he sprinted down the tunnel as fast as his human feet let him. Nephilim followed while listening to the hunters as they came closer. If she could hear them, they could hear her. There was only one way: she had to find a good spot to confront them, giving Jake time to flee.

Suddenly, he stopped, and right when she began to ask why, she saw it. An old iron ladder reached down from the ceiling on the side of the tunnel. Jake grabbed it and started climbing. She waited until he had disappeared through the opening about eight feet up, keeping the tunnel she just came from in her view, ready to stop anyone who might emerge from its end. Then she jumped onto the ladder herself and climbed up quickly. Just before she reached the top, she saw a slight blue glow in the distance. They were closing in.

Upstairs, she entered another tunnel. This one was different, though. It was square-shaped, and had rails on the ground leading into seemingly endless darkness in both directions. Jake was already on the run again, but stopped for a moment and looked back at her.

"Keep moving!" she called, "Don't stop! Never stop!"

He ran on, and she caught up with him within seconds. The tunnel led into a large hall, which used to serve as a subway station in the old days when this was still a running public transport system. Jake climbed onto the platform, and Nephilim leaped up, close behind him. The station was mostly built of gray concrete that had been painted red in several spots. The entrances had been filled in, and as it was everywhere else, something new now stood above in modern-day Olympias. Moisture had found its way down below, giving the location a musty smell. Somewhere, water was dripping. "*Five Points*" could be read on one of the red walls, which probably used to be the station's name.

A train still stood at the platform, the silver-metallic body slowly corroding to a rusty brown, the name "*MARTA*" written on the side, barely recognizable anymore. Some of its doors were open, as if it were waiting for passengers that would never to come. The whole place spoke of decay and transience—an eerie and disturbing atmosphere—yet neither Jake nor Nephilim noticed it. They were running from a very real, deadly enemy who was closing in quickly.

When they reached the train, Nephilim turned back and listened. She knew that the Angels had almost reached the ladder. They almost had them, there was no way out.

She grabbed Jake's shoulder and stopped him. "Take cover inside the train. Run through it until you reach the end, then leave as quickly as you can. Don't look back."

"And you?"

"I'll stall them. It's your only chance."

His eyes widened. "No way in hell, Nephilim! I won't leave you behind!"

"And I don't have time for this discussion!" she snapped at him, "We only have seconds left, and I'll be damned if I let you fall into their hands. Move! *Now*!"

"No," he said in a calm yet stubborn tone.

She sighed, irritated at him. "Sorry, but you leave me no choice."

Without letting him object any further, she grabbed Jake and pushed him inside the train through the open door as if he were a sack of feathers.

He stumbled back, hardly believing what was happening. "Nephilim..."

She did not answer, reached out for the doors instead, and forced them shut, the old metal creaking. There was no chance he would be able to open them again, and the rest of the doors to that particular car were closed anyway.

"Nephilim!" He rattled the door.

"Take cover and run! Please!"

She smiled into his face which was displaying despair now, before she turned away from the train and towards the tunnel, drawing her guns. Blue eyes approached from the darkness of the tunnel. At least a dozen of them.

"Nephilim," a familiar voice called out to her. It was Uriel who was leading the squad. "Drop your weapons! We're not here to hurt you."

She pointed her guns at the force approaching her, standing her ground, unmoved. "That's too bad. Because I'm going to hurt *you* if you come any closer."

"Don't make this any harder than it is. You're one of us. Why are you doing this?" he said, clearly uncomfortable with the situation.

"Not one step closer, Uriel," she said, coldly, "I'll blow your head off."

"Damn it!" Uriel lost his countenance. "He's a fucking *Prom*!"

Nephilim wanted to reply, but the words were stuck in her throat. All of a sudden, she felt a movement in the air directly behind her. Her intuition and lightning reflexes saved her life.

She ducked. Seemingly out of nowhere, a long sharp blade appeared and swooshed through the air where her head had been less than a second before. Nephilim threw herself to the ground and rolled away towards the train, but she was far from being out of danger.

The invisible attacker pursued her, slashing at her with his sword at a frightening speed. She kicked at him, focusing all her strength, aiming where she anticipated his legs would be. And she got lucky. The sound of crushing bones was followed by a muffled scream, signifying that she had hit the enemy's kneecap. She aimed her pistol directly at the position her sensors where showing the scream had come from, and fired. The stealth system failed as the body of the assassin collapsed to the floor next to her, sword still in his hand, yet half his head missing.

"Wasps!" Uriel yelled, "Take cover!"

Three Wasps appeared from stealth at the Angels' position and started slashing through them. One Angel instantly lost her head, while the others were able to counter the attack just in time. They opened fire, and when Nephilim turned to look, she saw that at least two dozen hostiles were closing in through the abandoned station from behind; it was impossible to say how many more were in stealth mode. It had to be the reinforcements Lena had requested.

She knew that the first thing Uriel would do now was call for back-up from the other squads who had surely cleared the Prom hideout out, completely, by now. A huge battle between the cyborg factions was about to take place in these old tunnels—and she and Jake had been caught right between the lines.

Nephilim rose up, quickly moved to the train door that she had just forced shut, and violently tore it open. Inside the seats had been eaten by rats over the years, and debris was scattered on the floor. Jake crouched in the aisle.

"Are you alright?" he asked.

"Why didn't you do as I asked you?" she questioned back. But in truth, she was glad that he was unharmed.

He just smiled at her.

She shook her head. "You might be an excellent spy, but right now, if you want to live, you should do exactly as I tell you. Seems your friends are buying us some time; I never would've thought to be grateful stumbling across Wasps. Where's the exit?"

He pointed down the length of the train. "We need to reach the next station."

Nephilim sighed. "That's just great. I bet it's where they're coming from."

She looked through the stained window outside where Wasps and Angels were fighting each other, then started moving down the aisle. "We use the train as cover as long as we can. Keep your head down. Come on!"

Hunched down, they ran through the train while only a few feet away, titans clashed into each other in a battle that would have been spectacular to watch. Once the Wasps had lost their stealth advantage, they used all their acrobatic and swordsman skills against the heavily armored well-equipped Angels. So far, the battle was balanced with the Wasps outnumbering their enemies, but it was only a matter of a few minutes until the full Angel force would arrive and crush the hostile cyborgs once and for all. Nephilim knew that she and Jake had to make it out of the underground system before that if they wanted to have a chance.

When they arrived in the back of the train, Nephilim stopped for a moment and scanned their surroundings. It seemed that no further Wasps were coming down the tunnel to the station and that they were all busy fighting the Angels and trapping them in the front part of the station where they couldn't advance.

It was now, or never.

She kicked the rear door open, and they both jumped out. But Nephilim's plan didn't work out quite as she had hoped.

They ran down the tunnel as fast and as far from the fight as they could when it was, again, Nephilim's intuition that saved both of their lives—or maybe her sensor hardware was so much more advanced than the standard implants. It was impossible to know for sure.

Suddenly, she felt a presence sneaking up from behind them, and when she turned to look, she saw a slight shimmer in the corner of her eye, directly behind Jake.

Nephilim reacted at a speed ten times that of a human's. She threw herself against Jake, simultaneously pushing him out of the way and extending her blades, crossing them above her head. Sparks flew as the titanium collided with the razor-sharp Wasp sword appearing out of the darkness to where Jake's head had been only a second before.

BEHIND BLUE EYES

Jake stumbled and fell, yet was able to roll away. Nephilim turned around to face the enemy who uncloaked as he moved into full-frontal attack, slashing at her with his sword with frightening speed, his agility hastened as the aggression grew, the yellow stripes on his black suit adding to that murderous wasp vibe.

Nephilim dodged a deadly strike aimed at her face by mere inches, and she spun to the side, ducking. She tried to rise her guns and shoot her opponent, but he was way too fast, so all she could do was parry his blows with her blades.

"Stay back!" Nephilim called out to Jake, making a short retreat a few feet back. This bastard was an exceptional fighter. He cost them the valuable seconds they desperately needed for their escape.

The Wasp remained motionless, and Nephilim could swear that he or she was grinning below their helmet. Then the hostile charged her at neck-breaking speed. Nephilim's body tensed, ready to counter his attack, but just before the Wasp could reach her, he suddenly vanished into thin air, cloaking himself.

For a short moment, she was confused about what he was planning, then she felt the air move close by, above her, and understood; he was jumping over her to strike her down from behind. She tried to turn around, but her heavy body with its titanium bones which was so much faster than a human one, was much slower in comparison to the smaller, lighter Wasp. Before she was half turned, she felt a thump on her shoulders and pain shot through her upper back as he landed right on top of her, ramming his heels into her body with full force, using his own momentum. It made her stagger and fall to the ground, face forward. Nephilim caught her fall with her arms but wasn't agile enough to quickly defend against her assailant. The sharp pain made her scream as he stomped on her spine with full force, which created a horrible noise like a brittle tree branch being crushed. It left her out of breath for a moment, unable to move.

She turned her head as he became visible again, his sword lifted, preparing the final blow, aiming for her neck. She bit her lip, trying to lift her arm, but moved too slowly.

Then, out of nowhere, the Wasp's head exploded into a spray of blood, shards of metal, and bones. His body collapsed right next to her, the deadly blade falling to the ground just inches from her face. Jake stood a few feet away, his gun in his hands, which was obviously equipped with high caliber, high-velocity bullets—cyborg killers.

He fell to his knees right next to her. "Oh my God. Are you hurt?"

She looked up at him, seeing more pain in his face than she was actually feeling. And she saw something else.

Nephilim lifted her hand, pointing her gun seemingly at his head. His expression shifted to surprise when she fired.

He flinched as the bullets passed his face by less than an inch and hit another Wasp who had been sneaking up behind him. The hostile collapsed in his own blood. Jake turned his head and stared at the dead menace less than two feet behind him for a moment, then focused back on Nephilim.

"I'm fine," she said, slowly rising. Her back cracked with any fraction of movement, but the pain was already subsiding. Internal sensors indicated that while the bone was damaged, the nerves were still intact and held together by the titanium reinforcement the Angels had built into their spines. She should be good for now, although her movement speed had clearly been compromised. "Thank you."

He grinned. "Guess I'm not that useless after all."

"Actually, that was an excellent shot...for a human," she acknowledged with a smile but then frowned.

Behind them, three more Wasps were approaching at top speed.

BEHIND BLUE EYES

These assailants were uncloaked, however. Either they had run out of the energy source supporting their stealth mods, or they simply didn't bother to activate them. Still, three of them at once were impossible odds to face. And she was currently handicapped.

Nephilim looked at Jake. "Run!"

But he wouldn't listen. His face was focused and full of determination as he opened fire on them. The Wasps broke their formation up instantly, running evasive maneuvers that expressed spectacular acrobatic skills, which made it nearly impossible to hit them, even for Nephilim. They jumped, rolled, pirouetted, one of them managed to run along the tunnel wall, seemingly defying gravity—all of it without slowing down.

It was clear that they wanted to reach close combat proximity. In a shoot-out, their chances were fifty-fifty against Nephilim. Though there were three of them, Angels were more precise, and faster shooters. However, in close-combat, Nephilim wouldn't stand a chance against three Wasps, and they knew it. Most likely, they didn't consider Jake a real threat since he was only a bio-human.

But it turned out they were wrong to underestimate him. Highly focused, he held his weapon with both hands, fired, and hit. The projectile struck the Wasp on the right in the chest and closest to him in the thigh. Letting out a high-pitched scream, the cyborg staggered but didn't collapse. Obviously, the shot was only a graze. Wasps didn't have artificial limbs with titanium bones, instead, their muscles were infused with synthetic fibers to make them more flexible and endurable; otherwise, a high-velocity bullet would've torn right through their leg. But the enemy had still been crippled and was writhing in pain. That left only two fully functioning Wasps.

All of them drew their swords, and the wounded one took aim for Jake while the others clashed with Nephilim.

"Watch out, Jake!" she called out while simultaneously evading a deadly attack from two sides.

From the corner of her eye, she could see how he took on the wounded Wasp and was surprised. Jake demonstrated a swiftness and agility in close combat she wouldn't have thought possible. No, he wasn't helpless, after all, and he was using a close combat technique she had never seen before—highly precise, aggressive, and effective.

But as much as she would've loved to, Nephilim didn't have time to watch him now. She had to get rid of her own two attackers, and quickly. This time she decided not to let them impose their fighting style on her.

She focused all her strength, and while dodging and parrying one attacker, she made a half-turn, and kicked the second Wasp in the chest. The noise of breaking bones, as well as a muffled scream, could be heard, and the attack was so forceful that it sent the fighter flying and crashing against the wall where he remained motionless.

Nephilim turned her attention fully to the other Wasp now, offensively parrying the attacks of his sword with her blades.

A shot was fired. She turned her head for a second. To her great relief, Jake was OK. And more than that, he had managed to outsmart his opponent in close-combat, and shot them in the head. Nephilim smiled. Only one left now, and she was determined to finish him off quickly.

The tide had turned, it was now she who advanced aggressively while the Wasp was backing away, trying to fend off her forceful slashes. She almost had him.

Suddenly she sensed movement and noticed Jake rushing towards her.

"Nephilim, behind you!"

Turning, she saw that the Wasp leaning against the wall hadn't lost consciousness, after all. A gun was in his outstretched hand, directed at her head.

BEHIND BLUE EYES

Before she could do anything, two shots were fired almost simultaneously. She heard the terrible sound of a bullet hitting a body, but it wasn't hers.

What she saw when she turned around almost made her heart stop. The Wasp at the wall was dead, struck down with a headshot. And behind her was Jake, in immense pain, his knees about to give in under him.

"No!" she cried out, an unknown panic rising up within her.

He had taken a bullet meant for her. Why the hell did he do that?

Without thinking about what she was doing, she made her blades disappear, and caught him before he could fall, setting him down on the ground carefully. "Jake..."

This moment of weakness was what the remaining Wasp had been waiting for. Nephilim saw a flash as he raised his sword to finish off both of them in one slice, Jake's head first. At lightning speed, with a scream of anger and despair, she lifted her bare arm to fend off the attack. The sword blade cut through her synthetic flesh like butter but was stopped by the titanium bone with a heavy *clonk*. Before the Wasp could retrieve the sword for another blow, Nephilim grabbed his wrist with her other hand, twisting it so sharply that the bones in the attacker's entire arm shattered. But the Wasp didn't get much time to suffer the agony. Nephilim took the sword from his useless hand and decapitated him with his own weapon.

She dropped the weapon on the collapsed body, then brought her full attention back to Jake.

"You stupid, stupid man," she said, taking him in her arms, "Why did you do that?"

She couldn't possibly express how relieved she was that he was still alive and conscious. The bullet had hit him in his chest, below the left shoulder. He was bleeding heavily.

"I thought you'd be pleased," he tried to smile but grimaced instead.

She put pressure on his wound while scanning him. No bullet or shards remaining in his body, a clean shot, straight through. No main artery or vein damage. The wound was only inches away from the heart, but it was undamaged and beating steadily. He had been lucky, so lucky. She almost sighed in relief.

"I'd gladly die for you," he whispered, wincing from the pain.

Nephilim placed her other hand on his cheek tenderly. "You won't die on my watch. Ever. I will *not* lose you."

They looked at each other for a moment. It only lasted a second, but time seemed to stand still for them.

Then Nephilim grabbed his shirt and ripped it apart, creating improvised bandages.

"Not how I imagined you ripping off my clothes again," he said, attempting a grin.

She smiled. "Hush, you stupid man, save your strength. We need to get you out of here quickly. And we need a safe place to go, and a First Aid Kit to patch you up, preferably containing glue."

Her left arm, which had been sliced open by the Wasp, felt stiff and slow when she moved it. Sensors indicated heavy damage. It took her more effort than it should have to bind the wound.

"One of our safe houses is close-by. We should be able to make it there," Jake suggested.

"Sounds good to me. As long as we don't run into your people there."

BEHIND BLUE EYES

"I don't think there's anyone left," he said, sadly.

"OK, I've stopped the bleeding for now. We need to hurry. This battle won't last much longer."

She looked down the tunnel towards the station they had come from. Shots, screams, and other sounds of battle could still be heard coming from there, but she knew it was only a brief matter of time now. For sure, Angel reinforcements had arrived and would finish the remaining Wasps off quickly. Then nothing could save them.

She wanted to pick him up, but Jake shook his head. "No way, Nephilim. I'm only a human in your eyes but I'm still a man. You are not carrying me. I can walk."

"Fine." Nephilim sighed, took his good arm, and lifted him up on his feet as if he weighed nothing. "Would you at least lean on me?"

That, he allowed, and they walked down the tunnel to the hidden exit as quickly as they could.

***

They were lucky, making it just in time to the next subway station. Jake showed Nephilim a hidden passage that led directly into the basement of a run-down building in Oldtown.

Outside, it had become night, and the shadows helped them stay unnoticed as they left the building. They sneaked through some small side streets of a less habited area of the district. Nephilim had wrapped Jake into her jacket to keep him warm and hide his injury and blood-stained clothes, but the few people they encountered on the streets didn't pay them much attention anyway. For them, it looked as if Nephilim were dragging a wasted friend along—a common sight in this part of Olympias City. Nephilim continuously scanned the surroundings and watched closely for anything suspicious, but it did not seem that anyone was following them. Not knowing the hidden passage, it would take the Angels some time to pick up their trail. However, Nephilim was certain that they would swarm Oldtown soon. Metatron wouldn't let them get away. She knew she needed a plan, but had other more pressing concerns at the moment.

Jake was getting weaker by the minute and he struggled to keep walking, even though Nephilim helped to keep him upright as much as she could. He needed medical attention quickly, and if his condition continued to worsen, she would have to carry him, whether he wanted her to or not.

But it did not come to that. They arrived at an ancient high-rise with a distinctive pyramid on its top. The building had been modernized at some point along the way, and was in relatively good shape. Jake led them to the back entrance, and from there, into a small elevator. Inside, he put his finger on a scanner and spoke into a discreetly installed comm.

"The strongest of all warriors are time and patience."

The doors closed, and the elevator rushed upwards.

"Sophisticated," Nephilim said, holding him tight, "Finger-print, voice recognition, and password. Although I don't quite agree with the content."

Jake smiled weakly. "It's a quote from Leo Tolstoy, a great Russian novelist. I'm sure he would have reconsidered the content if he'd met you."

The elevator stopped, and the doors opened. Lights sprang on in a dark corridor leading towards a reinforced steel door. Again, Jake put his finger on a scanner and repeated the password—this time in Russian.

BEHIND BLUE EYES

"Identification positive," an automated voice said, "Welcome Lieutenant Sobieski."

The heavy door opened with a click, and they entered into a spacious, loft-like apartment with huge windows offering a panoramic view over Oldtown. It was nothing like the shabby place Jake had been entertaining Nephilim at, which had been part of his cover. It was designed to accommodate multiple people, equipped with comfortable furniture, but also containing equipment, which showed that this was no regular living space. Crates containing highly advanced technology of various kinds were lined up against the walls, including surveillance gear, weapons, and explosives. Several high-performance computers with holo and 3D-screens stood on a large table in the center of the loft. As Jake had promised, the place was deserted.

Nephilim led Jake to a sofa facing the windows and helped him sit down.

"Do you have a First Aid Kit somewhere here?"

Jake pointed at a side wall separating the main area from the hall leading to more rooms. A First Aid Kit box hung there. Nephilim opened it and was relieved that it contained everything she needed to help Jake. Like every Angel, she had been trained in paramedic skills during her education and could tend to any kind of wound as long as it didn't need surgery. She grabbed all the required materials and hurried back to Jake.

He was very pale, and his face showed that he was suffering greatly, yet he still tried to hold himself upright. Nephilim felt a sting in her chest, seeing him like that. He groaned when she helped him take off his coat and the rest of his shirt. She put on rubber gloves and began the treatment giving him a shot containing a strong painkiller, directly in his chest close to the wound.

Knowing that it would hurt anyway, she started a conversation to distract him while tending to his injury.

"There's so much foreign tech here. How do you keep it hidden from us?"

The improvised bandages were soaked with blood when she removed them, but the bleeding had subsided. Carefully, she started cleaning the wound.

"We're cloaking the whole place. It looks like an empty apartment on your scanners," he explained, grimacing, "Even the windows show something completely different when you look at them from the outside. Your best drones won't see anything."

Nephilim raised an eyebrow. "Impressive. We don't have any tech comparable to that. So, I guess we're safe here for now."

"We definitely are."

That relieved her a bit. Although she knew that this place could only be a temporary solution, it gave them time and the possibility to heal and rebuild their energy.

"I assume this isn't the only safe house your people have around Olympias?"

"No," he confirmed, "We have several all around the city. It's a huge network that we've been building up for many years."

"And you? How many years have you been living in Olympias pretending to be one of us?" She was done cleaning the injury and started gluing it.

"Almost five years. Like you, I have been recruited as a child, Nephilim. I've been training and preparing all my life for this assignment, we all have. We learn the language, your culture, to behave and speak like you. Everyone gets a second personality with a unique background. Some of us who show higher skills are being groomed for higher ranks and important missions for many years."

BEHIND BLUE EYES

"The ones like you."

"Like me," he sighed. When he continued, his voice sounded tired and sad, "I know what you're thinking. You're asking yourself how many I've recruited the way I recruited you."

"By fucking them? This is Olympias, it's not important to me."

"But it is to me!" he said with sudden passion, "I never understood the promiscuous lifestyle of this place. Most of my people don't; we do things differently. I never planned to recruit you by seducing you, it just happened...and every second meant a lot to me. You can't possibly know how much. It was a coincidence I ran into you that night. I'm not a recruiter. I'm a tactic, analytics, and believe it or not, combat specialist."

"Oh, I believe it. It was quite impressive to watch you in action. You single-handedly took out a Wasp in close-combat." She let her fingers slide over his chest and upper body with a smile before continuing to tend to his injury. "And I thought all of this was natural."

She now understood the complexity of the skills he had shown in battle. From the beginning, she had been amazed at what excellent shape he was in for an entirely biological human, but now it was clear to her. His athletic body was combat trained.

He gave her that smile she had fallen in love with. Now that the wound was almost closed, and the painkillers had fully kicked in, he was starting to feel better.

Serious again, he added, "In our fake resistance, I was the operations officer who assigned the recruits to the tasks best suited for them, and monitored the results. And I helped brainwash them. We have agents specialized in recruitment, however, and yes, they are trained to use any means; their bodies included."

"Did you believe anything you told me at all? I mean, about how wrong the system is, and that it must be changed?" Nephilim wanted to know, "You were very ... convincing."

Jake sighed. "That's complicated. I would never dare admit it to anyone else, but yes, I truly believe the system is wrong. Not only the one here but throughout the corporate system, in general. No matter if it's Olympias, TogbuaXiang, or Rosprom; all of them thrive by oppressing their people, although in quite different ways. I've enjoyed a broad education in history, anthropology, and literature of the old world, and I think that with all its flaws, it still used to be a much better place than what we have been born into. But, I don't imagine there's anything we can do to change that. In the corporate era, we are just pawns, tools, numbers on a balance sheet. All we can do is try to survive and somehow keep our dignity. I would have lost mine if it hadn't been for you."

Nephilim kept quiet for a moment, thinking about what he had just said. He was right, and deep inside, she had known it all along. Yet, she wished it wasn't so. She had fallen for a dream which could never become a reality.

"What about Angel Dust? Was it your idea?" she asked after a while. It was something she had to know.

He stared at her. "God, no. Did Lena tell you that? Our High Command had it developed, and it was Lena who wanted you to be the carrier. I simply should've stopped everything much sooner. I'm so sorry."

She put a finger to his lips. "Jake, you asked me to forgive you, and that's what I did. We were supposed to hate each other, kill each other. Yet here we are, you and me against all the odds. We need to trust each other, and I do trust you. You took a bullet meant for me, you almost died. I would be crazy not to trust you now."

He leaned forward and kissed her. "And I trust *you*. With my life."

She finished bandaging his wound. That would keep the glue in place even better. He would be good for now, but she knew he needed to see a real doctor soon to check him out.

"I'll give you some antibiotics, and another painkiller, and then we're done here," she said.

"Thank you."

She went back to the First Aid Kit to get two more shots, then took a bottle of water from the fridge before returning to him. "Here, you need to drink as much as possible to replenish your fluids."

He emptied half the bottle eagerly while she gave him the shots. Then he carefully touched her arm where it had been ripped open by the Wasp. The synthetic skin was sliced and showed the torn artificial muscles and titanium bones below. A biological arm would have simply been chopped off like straw.

"How about you?" he asked, "Do you need anything?"

"I'm OK," Nephilim lied. The damage was so substantial that moving her arm became more and more of an effort. If she went into another fight and pushed it further, it might go beyond repair and need to be completely replaced. And who would do that now? Besides, her back hurt and felt stiff. There was more damage than what she had believed at first.

"Does it...hurt in any way?" Jake wanted to know.

Nephilim smiled. "Thankfully not, but it feels odd not being able to move it properly. The only parts which are equipped with sensors are my fingers, I can feel what I touch almost like a human, pleasant or unpleasant."

"This is what I look like on the inside, Jake," she added after a moment, "Do you still like what you see?"

He stroked her face with his good hand. "I do. Your tech components don't bother me and never did. They're part of you. The most beautiful parts about you lay beyond them, anyway."

"Like what?"

"Your heart, your soul. I've never met anyone like you. So courageous and strong, yet so...pure."

Nephilim chuckled. "I'm a killer cyborg. How in the world am I *pure?*"

"That's what they made you to be. Not what you *are*," Jake said, "You're willing to sacrifice everything for the ones dear to you, you forgive where others couldn't. In a world that's lost itself, you embody everything which was once good about humanity."

Nephilim reached out and took the little cross he was wearing around his neck in her hand. "So, this was real, after all? Not part of your cover?"

Jake smiled. "It's very real, and important to me. The story I told you is true; it did used to be my mother's. I never take it off."

"It's not banned in Rosprom?"

He chuckled. "Oh, no. You see, many things are quite different over there. The corporation knew that banning religion would be a grave mistake in this part of the world. Slavs are very stubborn people. Another huge empire, the Soviet Union, which went down a hundred years ago, failed because they tried to take away peoples' faith. Well, it wasn't the only reason; the main reason was that the ideology it was built on couldn't work, but this was only one of them. Rosprom learned from that, and gives us freedom of religion, as long as it doesn't interfere with the corporate ideology, of course, and as long as the corporate ideology stands above all. And like your leaders, they have their ways to keep people on track."

"That reminds me of another question I wanted to ask you," she said,

"Is Jake even your real name?"

He slowly shook his head. "No, it isn't. It's Jacek. I was born in Warsaw."

"Close enough."

"But you can continue calling me Jake. I've had this name for so long, it's part of me now."

"As you like," she said, removing the gloves, "And now we need a bed for you."

He grinned.

Nephilim chuckled. "I doubt you have enough blood left for that."

"Watch me."

"I'll watch you sleep. You need to rest."

***

Nephilim brought him into one of the bedrooms down the hall and helped him get comfortable. She took off her boots and most of her clothes, leaving just her shirt and her underwear. She sat down next to him, put his head on her lap and started stroking his face tenderly. He smiled up at her. Then almost instantly fell asleep.

When Jake woke up a few hours later, it was the middle of the night. Nephilim was sitting in an armchair at the window, her feet stretched up on the window ledge, her chin resting on her hand. Her delicate face framed by the straight black hair was focused on the nocturnal megapolis outside, with all its lights, concrete, and glass. She appeared to be deep in thought.

Jake watched her for a while, fascinated. Never before had she appeared more angelic to him than at this moment. The room they were in was dark, and the only illumination came from outside. Shining through the window around her, the lights shining around the city at night made her pale skin appear to shimmer, and it cast a shadow behind her that almost looked like large angel wings upon the wall. She seemed fragile and lost, yet radiated so much strength and energy that it took his breath away, just looking at her.

Nephilim noticed she was being watched and turned her head. Her glowing, neon-blue eyes, which so many found intimidating, were beautiful to him. She smiled.

"You're awake. Do you feel better?"

"I do," he answered, even though his whole left side felt numb, and the wound was throbbing, "You look concerned. Is everything alright?"

"This place is just a temporary hideout," she said, "It's only a matter of time until they reconstruct our path here and find us. We need to leave soon."

He sat up using his good arm. "I'm ready to go."

"The question is, where?" she asked thoughtfully.

"I'd go anywhere with you, you know that," he said, "I meant what I said last night. Let's leave this place and go as far away as we can. Now."

She looked into his eyes then slowly shook her head. Her voice was sad when she spoke; "Jake, there's no place we could go where we'd be safe, ever. They'll always find us. *He* will always find us."

"I can't accept that!" he responded, passionately, "There must be a place we can go. Maybe if we try to find a remote area-"

"No, Jake. It's impossible. Others have tried that and failed. No matter where we run, how far away, how careful we think we are—he'll always find me. He'll never let me go. And he *will* kill you."

"Who are you even talking about?"

"Metatron."

Jake was visibly confused. "The High-Archangel? Why?"

Nephilim sighed. "That's a long and complicated story you don't want to hear right now. Short version is that it's personal for him. Very personal."

"Bastard," Jake whispered furiously, then added, "I'm not willing to give up. And I sure as hell am not handing you over to him."

Nephilim smiled. "I'm not saying I'm giving up either. I'm just saying we need to go somewhere he can't get to us. Somewhere he can't possibly follow, ever. A place out of his reach, where he has no power at all."

Jake looked at her in silence for a moment as he understood what she meant.

"Would you really do that, Nephilim?" he asked quietly, "Would you be willing to come with me and come over to our side?"

"Would that even be possible?"

"Yes!" He was excited. "I mean, it's never happened before, but why not? If you cross over and are willing to work for us, you would be an incredibly valuable ally. I'm sure the High Command would be delighted."

She got up from her chair, walked to the bed, and sat next to him. He took her hands in his and kissed her enthusiastically. "I never would have even dared to suggest that idea, but now that you say it...it's wonderful. Nephilim, I'd gladly spend the rest of my life on the run in a makeshift shelter with you, but this is so much better. I'd love to bring you to Rosprom, show you my homeland."

"Can we be together there?"

"I don't see any reason why not."

"Then I guess it's the best chance we have. The only chance, to be precise," she said, "How will we get there?"

"I can request emergency evac into a secure area. They'll be able to pick us up in a few hours," he said, already getting up. It took him some effort and he grimaced but seemed to be very excited about the idea. "I'll call for it right away."

Jake left the bedroom and went down the hall into the main area where he sat down at one of computers. Nephilim followed him. While he worked on decrypting the coded software , she opened the First Aid Kit and once more reached for the painkillers, this time in pill form. She took one dose herself and brought one to Jake, as well as another bottle of water. "Here, take these."

He did as he was told, again, drinking half the bottle at once. But his eyes were focused on the holo-monitor as his brow furrowed.

"Is there a problem?" Nephilim asked.

"No. Not at all," he replied, "I was just wondering about something. Evac is inbound already; the approximate arrival time is in five hours. Most likely, Lena requested it right before your people attacked, hoping there would be enough time to evacuate. Which didn't work out so well, as we know."

Jake shut the software down then got up and took her in his arms. "That gives us a few more hours we can spend together in peace."

He kissed her softly, holding her tight as if she might disappear into thin air otherwise.

"This means you should go back to bed and get some rest," Nephilim suggested after they kissed for a while.

"Bed sounds perfect to me," he replied taking her hand and walking back to the hall and the bedrooms, "I'm not sure I can comply with the second part this time though."

She grinned, then asked, "Tell me, how is life in Rosprom?"

"Well, as I mentioned, many things are different. Others will be familiar to you. It's corporation rule, after all, and everything needs to be productive and efficient at all times. It's an authoritarian system. One thing is very different from Olympias, though..."

They were back in the bedroom, which was only slightly illuminated by the lights coming from outside. Jake turned to her and gently pulled her close with his good arm.

"We're allowed to have relationships with whoever we want for however long we wish. Share our lives together. This simple thing is so precious, that people here are willing to take the risk and leave Olympias to live as outcasts. I want to share my life with you, Nephilim. I want to wake up next to you every day for as long as you'll have me."

"I want that, too," she said quietly, almost unable to speak, feeling as if something very heavy was sitting on her chest.

"I love you, Nephilim."

She did not answer, she just looked at him, overwhelmed by the contradicting feelings she was experiencing.

"Say it," he asked after a moment had passed, "Please."

Nephilim smiled. "Why? Why do I need to say something you already know?"

"Because I want to hear it from you."

"I love you, Jake," she said, "More than my own life."

He took her face in his hands, stroking it softly while looking into her eyes, then slowly moved his lips towards hers. Kissing each other, they approached the bed and got rid of the rest of their clothes. Both injured, they were only able to have sex in a slow and gentle manner, with Nephilim particularly careful not to hurt him. However, forced to do so made everything even more intense for them as all their passion and lust turned into complete devotion to one another. They loved each other as if it was the first time—or the last.

Afterward, they remained entwined with each other for a long time, while the world around them stopped existing, and nothing else mattered.

Later, when she rested snuggled against his chest while he nestled his cheek in her hair and wrapped his good arm around her, Jake said, "Thank you, Nephilim. For saving my life, for believing in me, for giving me a second chance. For loving me against all the odds."

"No, Jake," she answered, "I should be thanking you. Because it's you who saved me."

"From what?"

"From what I was about to become."

He kissed her head, and she cuddled closer against him, wrapping her leg around his naked body. Listening to his strong heart beat, she watched how he started breathing slower until he fell asleep.

Nephilim closed her eyes, her whole body slightly trembling. She didn't make any noise or shed any tears, yet she was crying.

Chapter Fourteen

Redemption

It was early in the morning when they left the elevator and walked back out onto the streets of Oldtown. There was one hour left until the evacuation transportation picked them up. Jake was wearing some fresh clothes that had been stored in the safe-house, and a watch-like instrument on his wrist, showing him the exact arrival time and location. The aircraft inbound was already in Olympias territory and cloaked in stealth mode, so any communication with the pilots would be impossible until they reached the rendezvous point. Nephilim had been quite impressed that Rosprom possessed such advanced stealth technology, but Jake just grinned and explained that their agents had to get in and out unnoticed, somehow.

Using small side streets, they snuck back in the direction of the former Prom base, trying to behave as inconspicuously as possible. Soon, rush hour would start, and that would help them blend in with the countless residents hurrying to work. Jake wanted to take one of the vehicles stored in the garage below the safe-house to reach their destination, but Nephilim had insisted they go back and take her motorcycle, which she had left at the ramp near the old aquarium.

Of course, she knew that they would be waiting for them there. She expected at least one or two pairs of Angels laying low somewhere and keeping an eye on her motorbike, which they definitely had found by now. Metatron would have posted them there just in case she was stupid enough to try and reclaim it. And she wouldn't disappoint him. Not because she was stupid, but because she was certain that this was the best chance they had to reach their destination.

The rendezvous point was about thirty miles north from Oldtown, in an abandoned area just outside the populated perimeters of Olympias. It would not only be difficult to get there with a regular vehicle, but it would also be much slower. And if they were spotted along the way, which was very likely, their chances to get to the evacuation zone would be almost zero. Her motorcycle was a high-speed, state-of-the-art machine, designed for pursuit. They were designed to be the fastest vehicles in Olympias, for Angels only. Besides, she could link her neural implants into the machine directly, which made it easier for her to steer it even under difficult conditions. It was their best chance to bring them safely to the extraction point. Even if this meant she had to go make a full-frontal assault from the start, they had to retrieve her bike. Her body wouldn't like that, but soon enough, it wouldn't matter, anyway.

Nephilim had checked on Jake's wound before they left, and given him another dose of painkillers. He had not noticed that she also took a high dose. She did not tell him about her worsening spine condition so that he wasn't unnecessarily concerned. They both needed to focus now—and stay positive.

BEHIND BLUE EYES

Despite his grave injury, Jake did his best to hold pace with her, holding himself upright. However, the sweat which soon started showing on his forehead indicated that every step was a great effort for him. Nephilim hoped he would hold out just a little longer.

"Remember," she said when they closed in towards the Deathway ramp and her motorcycle, "Always stay behind me, and do as I tell you, OK? I know you're an extraordinary fighter, and there's no need to prove anything. It's Guardian Angels we'll be facing here, and they wiped out all your people within minutes. There's nothing you can do against them, so leave them to me."

He smirked. "OK, OK. I won't get in your way, I promise."

She gave him a punitive look. "It's not that, and you know it. Our advantage is that they have orders not to kill us. I'm convinced, Metatron wants us alive, and nobody will dare to disrespect his commands. This doesn't mean they won't hurt us—you in particular."

He stopped her and gazed into her eyes. "Everything will be fine, Nephilim. In an hour, all of this be over, and nothing will separate us ever again. We'll make it, I know we will." He kissed her.

She smiled at him. "We will make it. Nothing in the world will stop me from bringing us there. Now come, we have a plane to catch."

A few minutes later, when they had almost reached the bike's location, Nephilim stopped and pointed at a narrow alley between two high-rises. "Hide here. This will only take a minute."

He did as asked. "Be careful."

Nephilim nodded and moved on, highly focused. Being careful wasn't her strong suit, but she did not want to make him nervous by saying things like that. They had discussed the plan in advance, and of course, he didn't like it at all, but he would go along with it since there weren't many alternatives.

She detected them on her scanner long before she saw them. Certainly, they had noticed her, too, especially because she hadn't bothered to try sneaking up on them. It would've been pointless anyway. They were waiting directly at the small side street where she had left her motorbike, two figures in black with dark sunglasses. They were wearing plain clothes, which Nephilim was grateful for. Angel combat armor would most likely have made this fight impossible to win for her.

Coming closer, Nephilim started faking a limp. Their sensors would show severe damage to several parts, but they probably wouldn't bother to make a deeper scan and check which ones. Showing clear signs of damage would hopefully make them underestimate her.

They left the alley and faced her with weapons drawn. Several pedestrians walking nearby shrieked and quickly scattered to safety. Others walking behind Nephilim froze in horror before trying to find cover. Nephilim kept moving forward, dragging her allegedly damaged leg behind.

"Freeze Nephilim!" Jequn, one of the Angels, called out.

"I yield," she said calmly, stopping.

Of course, she knew both of them well. Jequn was still young, but his partner Rikbiel was a seasoned soldier. They definitely played in a different league than the two rookies Nephilim had taken out in the Angel HQ garage. Back then, Metatron wanted her to get away; she was certain of that now. This time he wanted her back. Her scanner indicated that there were two more Angels in close proximity, closing in quickly. She did not have much time.

Jequn and Rikbiel exchanged a look, unsure what to think of the situation, then slowly inched closer. They surely were communicating with each other over their internal comms.

BEHIND BLUE EYES

"Drop your weapons!" Rikbiel commanded, "Get down on your knees and cross your arms behind your head."

She got down on her knees, pretending as if it took her joints great effort, then placed her guns on the ground in front of her and crossed her arms behind her back. The two Angels grinned as they closed in. No doubt they already imagined how pleased the High-Archangel would be with them. What they couldn't see was that she was extending her blades behind her back.

"Where's the Prom?" Rikbiel asked, now almost in front of her.

"Gone," she answered, "Son-of-a-bitch made a run for it, no idea where he is."

"So, you're thinking clearly again?" Jequn asked, "Malware influence gone from your system?"

Nephilim had to bite her lip not to grin. Was that what Metatron had told the troops? That she had been compromised by malware which made her behave as she did? Was it too embarrassing to admit that she had committed treason of her own free will?

"I'm myself," she replied, "But I'm severely damaged and need help."

They were both very close now, guns still in their hands.

Rikbiel smiled. "The High-Archangel wants me to tell you he's delighted you're coming back."

Nephilim looked up and into Rikbiel's eyes, knowing that Metatron was watching.

She smiled back. "My pleasure. Please let Metatron know I say thank you for the unique upgrades he has given me."

Her hands snapped forward with such speed that a human eye hardly wouldn't have been able to see more than a blur. The razor-sharp blades hit both cyborgs in front of her simultaneously, precisely cutting through the artificial cords at their wrists. Losing their connection to their brains, the hands instantly went limp. Unable to hold their weapons anymore, they dropped them while surprise and disbelief displayed across their faces.

But Nephilim didn't give them time to think. Before completing the arc of her blades, she swung her allegedly injured leg, striking out with powerful momentum against the knees of both men with such force that they staggered and tumbled.

Nephilim grabbed her guns while still on the move, rising up, pointing them in her opponents' direction. All of this lasted less than two seconds. Nephilim was not only able to move incredibly fast, much faster than an average Angel, she knew exactly where their weak points were.

And she wasn't done yet. Stomping on the men's artificial joints with extreme force, she shattered one kneecap of each, while precisely shooting both guns at their elbows, rendering their arms useless. Before Rikbiel and Jequn fully realized what was happening to them, they were incapacitated.

"But...what..." Rikbiel groaned, perplexed, as Nephilim leaned over them, taking their weapons and tossing them away. What she had done to them did not hurt in any way but felt highly unpleasant—and no doubt was humiliating as hell.

"Quiet," she said, "I don't want to kill you guys, but I will if I have to, so do yourselves a favor and don't try anything, OK?"

She quickly searched the men's pockets for spare ammo, and turned to the alley where she'd parked her motorcycle. The other pair of Angels was almost here, and she wouldn't catch them by surprise, which would make the fight much harder to win. And her scan showed that those two were wearing Angel combat armor.

"Nephilim!" Rikbiel called after her, his voice steady now.

BEHIND BLUE EYES

Without stopping, she turned her head.

"Metatron says he's impressed. But you won't beat him in the end."

"Tell him to go fuck himself," she replied.

Before she reached her machine, she started the engine and deployed her drone. Then she jumped on it and rode out of the alley on the street. Rikbiel and his partner were still lying on the pavement, unable to move, but she saw two more Angels sprinting towards her from the right. They had their motorcycles parked directly on the street and would reach them any second.

Nephilim accelerated and sped to where she had left Jake. He had watched everything and was already on his way towards her. His eyes were wide with fascination and disbelief.

"Incredible," he said, out of breath from the short run.

"Get on," Nephilim told him while checking his vital functions. They were steady.

She turned her head as he sat on the back of her motorcycle and saw that the two Angels were in pursuit of them on their own bikes.

"You better hold on to me with all you've got now," she said, "This will be one hell of a ride."

"With pleasure," he answered, yet soon realized that she had meant that quite literally, as she accelerated up the ramp to the Deathway—going the wrong direction.

***

Nephilim didn't head into the oncoming traffic out of recklessness. The Angels were coming from the direction of the on-ramp, therefore cutting off any other possibility of getting on that way. And taking the Deathway was the only chance they had to show up at the rendezvous point in time. Besides, now that he knew where they were, Metatron would no doubt send more Angels after them. They had to be quick if they wanted to make it.

Jake held his breath as Nephilim accelerated up the off-ramp, and they jumped the small crest at its end, performing a long arc through the air—and landed in the middle of the fast, oncoming traffic around them.

Nephilim did not slow down, but instead, sped up as she navigated between the vehicles coming at them. With her unhuman lightning reflexes, she dodged a car at the very last moment, then slipped between two others, and performed a spectacular zig-zag course a few seconds later. She was so fast that the drivers of the cars coming from the opposite direction didn't even notice her bike approaching until they were almost colliding, but Nephilim evaded each of them at the last split-second.

Jake clung to her back, doing his best to hold his balance, fascinated and horrified at the same time. Again, he realized that he had no idea what Nephilim was really capable of. It seemed that not only were her bones made of titanium, but her nerves were, too.

While continuing her neck-breaking maneuvers with one hand, she nudged his leg. Getting his attention, she pointed to their right at the lanes heading in the opposite direction, then reached down to her thigh holster for one of her guns. Jake turned his head and saw two Guardian Angels on motorcycles matching their speed in the other lanes. It was much easier for them since they were riding with traffic and not against it.

They, too, drew their guns—and opened fire. Nephilim evaded with raging speed, riding between the oncoming vehicles and bringing them between the attackers. The bullets hit a civilian car, making it lose control as it crashed into the vehicles next to it, creating a massive, multiple collision pileup. Nephilim navigated around the danger zone without difficulty and simultaneously returned fire.

Suddenly, Jake saw a drone coming at them from above. He was about to warn Nephilim when he recognized that it was her drone. It took him a second to process the fact that she was capable of riding a motorcycle at one-hundred eighty miles per hour—in the wrong direction—with one hand, shoot a gun with the other, and navigate a flying machine at the same speed with her mind, all at the same time.

Fascinated, he watched as the drone accelerated as it approached one of the hostile Angels. The cyborg noticed he was being chased, and turned around to shoot it from the sky, but it was too late for him. Nephilim's drone fired an electric charge hitting the vehicle and instantly disabling its electronics. The bike stopped short, its rider staggered and fell, skillfully rolling off as he hit the ground. Even though they had been traveling at top-speed, it would take more than that to kill or even seriously injure an Angel who was wearing the high-tech combat armor. But his pursuit was over for now.

That left only one, and Nephilim was determined to make short work of him. With a sudden move, she swerved passed the oncoming vehicles and rushed to the middle lane at a steep angle, then fired her gun. The other Angel tried an evasive maneuver but was too slow. Nephilim's bullets hit his front tire, shredding it into pieces. The front part of the motorcycle collapsed, making him fly above it and crash on the ground at least thirty-five feet away. He, too, surely would survive. Although they were hunting her, Nephilim did everything possible not to kill any of her people. Jake loved her even more for that.

She put her gun back in the holster and continued her neck-breaking maneuvers between the vehicles coming from the opposite direction. For a moment, she turned to Jake and said, "Hold on!"

Seeing what lay before them, he knew why. About one thousand feet in front of them, was construction on the lane closest to the middle. A heavy excavation machine stood there, its straight shovel resting on the ground at a forty-five-degree angle. Nephilim accelerated again, riding right towards the machine.

Again, Jake held his breath. Everything inside him screamed that this was utter madness and that he was going to die in a few seconds. But he trusted Nephilim. She knew what she was doing. Inside her exceptional brain, she had surely done the math. It would work out; it had to. And he had no other choice but to hold onto her and pray, anyway.

At top-speed, Nephilim rode up the flat shovel, using it as a ramp. Like a missile, the motorcycle rose up in the air and shot over the concrete barricade, the iron mesh fence, and the thirty or so feet separating the two opposite roadways.

The impact was heavy, yet left both them and the machine undamaged. While Jake tried catching his breath after the spectacular stunt, she rode on as if nothing had happened.

"You OK?" she asked, turning to him while the needle of the speedometer continued to rise towards two-hundred miles per hour.

"I'm good," he shouted, trying to be louder than the wind as it swallowed his words.

"It's not over yet. We've got more company," Nephilim answered turning back and pointing to the sky.

Jake lifted his head. Combat drones; this time, hostile ones.

Up at the front flew a smaller one, mostly used by police forces for pursuit and surveillance. Behind it was a slower, heavily armored military-style combat drone of immense size, with machine guns and rocket launchers mounted on its sides.

The smaller drone came closer, and a voice could be heard shouting at them through its speakers, "Nephilim, playtime's over! Turn around and come back! *Now!*"

It was an artificial voice, but the content clearly wasn't, and it made Nephilim flinch for a moment. Jake realized that she hadn't exaggerated when she had said that Metatron would do anything to get her back. But looking at the menacing contraption behind them, he wondered if he maybe had changed his mind about bringing her back alive. Or maybe the machine would simply kill his human ass, and Metatron thought that Nephilim would survive such an attack? Whatever his intentions, Jake felt like their odds were looking grim.

Nephilim, however, did not seem to feel intimidated. She lifted her hand towards the smaller drone and flipped it off. Then she did something spectacular.

She moved so quickly that it was almost over before Jake realized what was happening, yet so smoothly that the motorcycle didn't shake even the slightest bit. She pushed herself up into a sideways kneel, resting one foot next to the knee of her other leg on the saddle right in front of him. Holding the handlebar with one hand, she stretched her upper body and right arm up, holding her gun, which she had drawn during the movement. She fired three consecutive shots at the drone.

The thing staggered in mid-air, then crashed to the ground like a dead, metal bird. Nephilim maneuvered around the burning wreck while sitting back into her normal position.

"We're almost there," Jake heard her say with the cool voice of a machine, "I need to take care of the big one before we arrive, though. Its armor is too thick to shoot it down."

Jake decided it was better not to ask how she was planning to do that.

Nephilim decelerated to take the ramp leading down. The further north they traveled down the Deathway, the less traffic they had encountered. Here, at its most northern part, where it took a turn in to the Southeast and the city center, it was almost empty. The bigger drone followed them, quickly closing in now.

Once they left the Deathway, there was only one road they could take, the one on the ground. There weren't several layers of transportation in this part of the city, which had no residential areas, but consisted mostly of fully automated commercial buildings, warehouses, and production facilities of various kinds. The buildings were basic; only a few stories high. And this place varied greatly from the rest of the city with its shiny skyscrapers.

Nephilim continued on a straight road in a northerly direction, slowing down, yet still at a remarkable speed, then turned back to Jake. "Can you take over for a bit?"

"Yes, of course," he answered, surprised. He knew how to ride a motorcycle, but...

She gave him a quick kiss while letting go of the handlebar, pulling him closer and placing his hands on it. "I'll be right back. Watch out for the drone, it might attack you."

"Neph..."

He was still in the process of saying her name when she stood up on the saddle and jumped up in the air, using the motorcycle's momentum to boost the height and distance of her jump. Completely stunned, Jake watched how she reached out for the handles of her drone, which she had navigated towards them while he hadn't been aware. He quickly grabbed the handlebars firmly to steer the motorcycle.

It was only now that he realized that the other drone was almost above him. He did not need Nephilim's sensors to know that it had locked its target system on him. It was an instinct that saved his life. He slammed on the brakes. The motorbike staggered when it came to a full stop from such a high speed, its tires squeaking shrilly. Less than a second later, a rocket detonated in the middle of the road, only fifty feet away from him and exactly where he would've been had he not braked. He could feel the heat against his face, and the blast was so strong that he was pushed off the bike. A sharp pain went through his whole body as he hit the ground. Even though he had rolled off, his injury still hurt like hell under the impact. But otherwise, he was OK and alive. For now. The large, black, airborne killing-machine had stopped and was turning towards him. Obviously, taking him captive was no longer a desirable option. There was no way for him to evade the next strike.

Then he saw Nephilim. She approached the combat drone from the side at high speed, hanging below her own drone. The huge contraption noticed her, too. It quickly moved one of its machine guns in her direction and fired. The bullets hit Nephilim's drone, which exploded in mid-air, but it was too late.

Nephilim had let go of the handles at the very last second and leaped at the combat drone. Her fingers barely reached the hostile, yet it was enough. She grabbed the lower part of the thing's wing, where its weapon arsenal was stored, and hung there for a second while the aircraft tried to keep its balance, struggling with the extra weight on one side. Nephilim quickly moved closer to the center and extended her blade in one hand while she kept hold of the drone with the other. Knowing exactly where the combat vehicle's weak spots were, she rammed her blade into its lower part, just between the wing and the body. From there, she opened a hatch. Once open, she did not hesitate one second before slamming her blade into the vulnerable inside of the machine. Sparks flew. The machine began shaking and staggered in mid-air.

Then it started to fall, with Nephilim still hanging on below. Jake watched the drone approach the ground at a steep curve, gaining more momentum with every second. At the last moment, Nephilim leaped away and landed on the roof of a warehouse, while the drone crashed to the ground and exploded in a massive fireball.

Jake sighed in relief, seeing Nephilim unharmed on the roof. Yet when she jumped down to the ground, she flinched as a sharp pain shot through her lower back. She grimaced slightly while walking up to him.

"Are you hurt?" he asked, getting up.

"Never felt better," she lied, "You OK?"

He nodded. "Yes. That was...spectacular."

She grinned, picking up her motorcycle and switching it back on. "What can I say? You guys have sexy spies, we have better cyborgs."

She got serious again. "We need to hurry. They'll be here soon."

He climbed back on the bike behind her, and they quickly rode off.

***

As they closed in on their destination, the modern facilities were scarcer by the minute, and the road conditions became increasingly worse. They had reached the outer rim of Olympias City I. No humans would come here, ever. There was no reason why they should. Slowly, the last buildings of the new era vanished behind them, and all that remained were the ruins of an old city, which had been deserted since the great war, and the founding of Olympias. The buildings were in bad shape and falling apart, while many had already collapsed.

Nature was creeping over the decrepit structures with lush vegetation, reclaiming the surrounding area where the old structures stood. Grass and shrubs grew on the streets. Tall trees reached out of windows and shattered rooftops where people had once lived, worked, and went about their daily business. Birds sang, and armies of crickets filled the air with their distinctive sounds. The atmosphere was almost idyllic in a morbid way, and the abundance of nature stood in extreme contrast to the gigantic maze of concrete and glass only a few miles south.

Despite the beauty of nature reclaiming the environment around them, Nephilim and Jake barely noticed the scenery. They were racing against time, which was more difficult with every passing moment since the road was becoming nearly inaccessible.

"How do your people travel in and out from here to Olympias?" Nephilim complained, "This road is a nightmare."

"Usually we land directly inside the premises of Olympias in specified less occupied areas," Jake explained, "But in a case like this it would be too risky. Our command assumed half of Olympias to be on alert, that's why the evac had been sent to a remote area."

"How much time do we have left?"

"A bit more than ten minutes," Jake said, looking at his device, "The transport has already landed. It's waiting on us, now."

"How far away is its precise location?"

"We're almost there." He pointed to the right. "Less than half a mile."

They stopped under an old, corroded sign with the barely readable writing; *"Welcome to Peachtree Airport."*

"Good," Nephilim said, "Because I'm afraid we need to walk from here. This motorcycle is designed for highspeed pursuit in urban areas, not for off-road tracks. It's no use to us anymore."

They moved to a rusty mesh fence that was still astonishingly stable after such a long time but didn't withstand a single kick from a cyborg. Then, they entered the deserted and completely overgrown premises of what once had been a small city airport.

The runways were mostly hidden under shrubbery, but the main terminal and a few hangars were relatively intact, reminiscent of a time long gone in which people once traveled around the world. In the center of the airport, the tower still stood erect, rising above the abundant greenery. With its windows broken, only shadows remained inside overlooking the desolate land below.

Nephilim continuously checked the sky around them as they hurried to the hangar area as quickly as Jake could. She knew *they* were inbound. She could feel it almost as clearly as if she were still part of the grid.

And she was right.

Everything was perfectly quiet around them as they moved through the deserted place, the only noise being birds, insects, the high grass swishing against their legs, and Jake's loud breathing as the running started to take its toll on his tormented body. It almost seemed like they were the last remaining humans on earth.

Just when they were about to reach the hangar area, Nephilim heard a familiar sound. It was more of a slight hissing and buzzing than the noise that normal engines made. Lifting her head, she saw a black aircraft approaching swiftly. It stopped in the air above the main terminal, turned into a VTOL, and quickly began its descent towards the premises.

They had arrived. At least one squad of Angels. Probably the best, lead by one of the Archangels. There was nothing she could do against them. Their last chance was to reach the evacuation site before they reached them.

"Run!" she urged Jake, who, like her, had stopped to stare at the dark menace in the sky.

She grabbed his good arm and dragged him with her. Whether he liked it or not, this wasn't the time to prove his manliness. It was about survival. His survival.

They reached the hangar wall—which at least gave them cover from one side—and followed it. Multiple wrecks of smaller planes still stood on its end, badly corroded and partially swallowed by the spreading copses.

"There," Jake said, breathing heavily after looking at the device on his arm, "Behind this seems to be a runway which has remained mostly intact. The rendezvous point is right there."

"OK," she said, "Hang on just a little bit longer. We're almost there."

But only a few feet further, they both stopped short. A tall figure wearing a Guardian Angel combat suit crossed their path around the hangar corner, weapons drawn. Without hesitation, Nephilim pulled her guns, too, and brought herself between Jake and the potential threat. She did not attack, though. Neither did the other Angel.

It was Adriel.

They looked at each other in silence for a moment. Nephilim felt anger rising up in her—and despair. Of all possible people, Metatron had sent Adriel to stop her, knowing precisely that she wouldn't be capable of hurting him. After everything else had failed, he was playing this one final card.

"Nephilim," Adriel said with a calm yet firm voice, "Lay down your weapons. It's over."

"No," she replied in the same calm tone, looking him in the eye.

Slowly, she started moving closer.

"Nephilim," her partner continued, "I'm not here to hurt you. *We* are not here to hurt you. We're your family. Please, be reasonable. Where would you run, anyway? There's nothing here, there's no escape. Drop your weapons and come home."

"No," she repeated and kept walking toward him.

"For fuck's sake, Neph!" he suddenly burst out, "What the hell do you think you're doing? Have you completely lost your mind? Do you really think you would still be running and breathing if Metatron wanted you dead? He wants you to come back...and I want that, too."

Nephilim smiled. "I'm not coming back, Adriel."

"Why not?" he asked desperately, "Because of *him*? Fuck that Prom!"

"I'm not coming back," she repeated, very close now, "And I'm not giving him up, either." Before Adriel could respond, she continued, "If you want him, you'll need to kill me first. As long as I'm breathing, you won't get him, ever."

Adriel stared at her in disbelief.

"Nephilim!" Jake called out behind her with concern in his voice. She stopped him from intervening with a gesture of her hand.

Then she lowered her weapons and positioned herself in a way, so Adriel's guns pointed directly at her heart.

"Your choice, Adriel. You either let me go or kill me right now. There's nothing in between. What will it be?"

Again, they stared at each other in silence for a moment. Her partner slowly shook his head. "Why are you doing this to me?"

"I'm sorry."

He visibly struggled with himself and with whatever Metatron was whispering in his head.

Finally, he lowered his weapons. "You know what? Fuck you, Neph! I know I'll regret this, but what the hell...take your stupid Prom and run. I hope he's worth it."

Nephilim smiled, wrapping her arms around him in a fierce hug.

"Thank you, Adriel," she whispered, "Thank you so much."

"They're coming from the east, behind the hangar," he said, visibly touched, "You better run fast."

"Thank you."

"It's OK. Now move your ass out of here!"

She nodded, took Jake by his good arm, and quickly ran off with him to the bushes. Her mind was racing. On the one hand, she was more than relieved and happy that they had gotten away; on the other, she felt bad that she ever had doubted Adriel's loyalty and friendship. He had always felt the same towards her as she did towards him. He was a true friend she could rely on. No doubt, Metatron did not anticipate this outcome; otherwise, he never would've played this card.

They reached the thick bushes surrounding the desolate aircraft strewn about without any further hindrances.

"How much time?" Nephilim asked.

"Less than three minutes," answered Jake, "Look, there's a path here."

He was right. A narrow trail led through the copse in the direction they were heading. It seemed that someone had passed through here recently. They followed it for a short while until they reached a small clearance beyond the wing of a corroded jet. Somebody was waiting for them there who they didn't expect at all.

Jake, who had taken the lead on the trail, stopped short as he arrived at the clearing. A second later, Nephilim knew why.

Lena stood there, a rifle in her hands, an ugly grin on her face.

Obviously, she had escaped the aquarium on the same route as Jake and Nephilim, just a few minutes earlier, before the attack. It must have been her who had called for an evacuation before Jake did.

"Look who's here," she said, her voice full of hateful contempt, "Romeo and Juliet in person."

"Lena-" he tried, exhausted.

"Are you trying to bring your machine whore to Rosprom?" she interrupted him shrilly, "Have you gone completely insane? You-"

She was stopped short by a bullet through her forehead. Her mouth still open from her hateful rant, she collapsed like a wet sack.

Jake turned around and stared at Nephilim in surprise. She was about to stick her gun back in her holster.

"We don't have time for this shit now, and I was tired of her talking anyway," she said with a shrug, "Besides, don't your people know you can't win a stand-off against a cyborg, ever?"

Jake smiled. "We're here. The runway is right behind the clearing. We made it."

She kept silent for a moment. What she was about to say was the hardest thing she'd do in her entire life.

Jake moved forward, then noticed she wasn't following and stopped, looking at her.

"Go," she said, "I'll hold them off."

He did not seem to understand; or didn't want to.

BEHIND BLUE EYES

"What are you talking about? We're *here*. We'll be in the air in a moment, safe."

She just looked at him in silence, feeling as if she was dying inside while his expression changed from disbelief to heartbreaking certainty.

"You're not coming," he said in a hollow voice.

"No."

"You never planned to."

"No."

"You lied to me," he realized, "About this whole plan, from the beginning. Why?"

"Because it was the only way to get you here. The only way to save you," she explained, "There is no place we could've gone to. Not in this entire messed up world. And I know you would never have agreed to leave without me. I'm sorry."

"You're right," he said stubbornly, "I'm not going anywhere without you."

"Jake," she said, "They're almost here. You can't possibly have any idea what Metatron will do to you if he gets his hands on you, but *I* know. He told me. I can't let it happen. Please forgive me for lying to you. Please save yourself, please leave."

He came forward and took her hands in his. "Come with me."

She shook her head sadly. "I can't."

"Why not? Don't you trust me?"

She smiled at him. "I trust you, unconditionally. But I don't trust your people. Didn't you see the hate in Lena's face towards me? All of you feel like this, and I can't blame them. I'm not just anyone trying to come over, I'm a Guardian Angel. I'm a weapon, Jake. The most evolved weapon mankind has ever seen, a living killing machine. What do you think they would do to me if I went to Rosprom? They would torture me for information and then dismantle me for reverse engineering. Tear my limbs off, crack my skull open to obtain my valuable implants, and the data stored on them."

Jake shook his head vehemently, horrified by her drastic description. "No! I'd never let that happen. I'll protect you."

"You couldn't. You don't have the authority, and you know it. Tell me, would you like to bring me to your homeland just to watch me suffer and die?"

"No," he whispered, beaten, "Never."

"Please go, Jake. Save yourself. That's what I wish more than anything."

He gazed into her eyes, his face a reflection of infinite sadness and despair. His blue eyes, moist. "Nephilim..."

"I love you, Jake," she said, smiling at him. Then she pressed her lips to his for a kiss, which she knew would be their last. It felt like something inside her was breaking, shattering into a thousand pieces, never to be whole again.

"I love you, too," he replied, reluctantly stepping back, "I always will."

"Now go," she urged him while studying his face one more time, memorizing every single detail, "Please. Hurry!"

Jake nodded, wiping away tears, then moved to the end of the clearing.

He stopped one more time and looked at her with determination. "I'll come back for you."

"Don't," she said, "There won't be anything to find."

"I will anyway," he said, "This isn't a farewell."

He disappeared behind the thick bushes.

Nephilim had to hold onto herself not to tumble over. She felt as if it suddenly had become the darkest of nights around her. The feeling of loss hurt more than anything she had experienced in all her life. She had used all her willpower to stay strong when explaining things to Jake because she knew it had been the only way to convince him.

Now that he was gone, and she knew she would never see him again, she hardly had the strength to hold herself upright anymore.

But she needed to make sure that he had enough time to board the aircraft, and that it could take off unhindered. Once in the air, the Angels would have no possibility of tracing it, or be able to shoot it down, thanks to the advanced Rosprom stealth technology.

Nephilim turned around and went back to the end of the copse, and her sensors picked up where the Angels had taken position. They were waiting for her. She had another battle to fight and one thing she knew for sure: she wasn't going back.

***

They surrounded the entrance to the overgrown aircraft graveyard. Twenty of them. Nephilim's sensors indicated there were two on the roof of the nearby hangar. She quickly made her way through the thick shrubs, taking cover behind the wreckage of a small plane, which looked so antique compared to modern aircraft, that it was hardly believable people took off in such a contraption once upon a time.

Nephilim felt a sharp pain in her spine as she crouched and reloaded her guns. She had pushed her body far beyond its limits—biological and artificial alike. But, soon, it wouldn't matter anyway.

"Nephilim," she heard a familiar voice calling for her. It was cold and full of disdain.

Zephaniel. The fact that he was leading the mission in person indicated how important the outcome was for Metatron. He would be disappointed, Nephilim would see to that. And Zephaniel's blatant anger would prove useful in the end.

"It's time to stop this pathetic charade of yours! Come out of there, unarmed, hands where I can see them."

"Never!" she answered his request by leaning forward and firing her guns at the Angels, hitting two of them in the knees.

All of them instantly took cover. Nephilim used this short time to leap and roll forward. She cowered behind an ancient airport vehicle that had four wheels, yet was much flatter than a regular car or truck of the old times. She was very close to them now, only about seventy feet separated them, and nothing stood between the Angels and her cover aside from a few bushes and grass growing on the cracked concrete.

Zephaniel could hardly hide how enraged he was. "You leave us no choice but to use force!"

"Come and get me, Zephaniel!" she called out to him, "Or are you scared?"

A bit more pushing, and she would provoke him into taking action. He and his people had orders to take her alive, she was certain about that. But she wouldn't let them take her alive. She wasn't going back.

BEHIND BLUE EYES

"As we speak, another team is circling this area. They will track down your human, no matter where you've hidden him. And you know what? I'm sure you'll change your mind once you hear him scream," Zephaniel answered sadistically.

Nephilim wasn't concerned about that. By now, Jake had reached his people and was sitting securely in their aircraft. It would only be a matter of minutes until they launched, maybe less. All she needed to do was keep the Angels busy just a little longer.

Instead of answering, she leaned forward and opened fire on the Angels again. However, this time she wasn't able to hit anyone.

"Damn it, Nephilim!" Zephaniel was on edge now and about to lose his countenance. "You-"

He stopped short in the middle of what he was about to say. Nephilim knew exactly what that meant; he was listening to instructions in his head. A smile appeared on his face.

Suddenly, she felt this familiar tingling on her skin, indicative that someone was approaching. The air moved slightly as she turned her head towards the phantom and lifted her arms into a defensive position.

But she was too slow.

The invisible attacker charged into her with incredible speed and force, throwing her off her feet and slamming her to the ground. She rolled to the side, simultaneously shooting where she suspected the hostile to be, but her bullets went into thin air. Whoever he was, he moved unbelievably fast. Much faster than she or any other cyborg could.

Nephilim leaped to her feet, wielding her guns with outstretched arms, turning in a circle, trying to determine the position of the phantom assaulting her. She noticed that Zephaniel and the other Angels stood down, watching what was happening in front of them without any intention of interfering.

The air shimmered, similar to how it does close to asphalt on a hot day, right next to her. Then she was hit with such strength and skillfulness against her injured arm, that she dropped one of her guns. It was kicked away to the lurking Angels, and out of her reach by a fighter who she could neither see, nor localize with any of her sensors. Again, she tried to shoot where she suspected the hostile to be, but missed.

Instead, she was grabbed from behind; he twisted her arms and kicked the back of her knees so she would fall to the ground. The attacker held her down for a second with such strength that she was unable to move even a bit. It was as if he were trying to demonstrate his superiority. But instead of finishing her off, he let go and backed away—with her other gun.

Rising back up again, she watched how her weapon was crushed by invisible hands, the air around it glimmering slightly. All she had left now were her blades, but what use could they be against an opponent so much faster and stronger, whom she couldn't even see?

The invisible man chuckled amused. It was a chuckle she knew well.

The air in front of her flickered more, and all of a sudden, the stealth was gone, revealing somebody she would have never expected to see here.

"What's wrong, my dear?" Metatron asked, sneering, "How does it feel to be beaten?"

He was wearing a black combat suit, but of a different design than everyone else. It was made of shiny material, similar to chitin but highly flexible; otherwise, he wouldn't be so quick and agile. Its tight cut revealed that his body was not only slim but also athletic and perfectly shaped. Almost too perfectly.

"If you need stealth to beat me, then I can live with that," she replied defiantly, "I wasn't aware we had such technology."

"A prototype. Reverse engineered Wasp technology," Metatron explained with a shrug, "I thought it would be the perfect occasion to test it. And no, I don't need stealth to beat you, Nephilim. I just wanted to disarm you and be sure you stop hurting our people. I won't tolerate it any longer."

"Then try me without your stealth," she said, extending her blades.

Around them, the Angels had left their cover and were now silently watching the spectacle unfolding in front of them. For sure, none of them ever would have expected to see anything like this. Nephilim noticed how Zephaniel clenched his fists yet didn't dare to move.

Metatron tilted his head, studying her like a king cobra would a mouse.

"Do you want to kill me so badly, Nephilim?" he asked, "Do you think it would change anything? For you? For your fellow Angels? For Olympias?"

"Yes, I want to kill you," she said, "And then die, myself."

He smirked, slowly coming closer. "That's a bit melodramatic, don't you think? And it would be unfortunate. You see, if you really do want to change things for the better for everyone, if you really wish to help to create a better future, your best chance for accomplishing that stands right in front of you."

She did not answer, but instead attacked him with her blades, aiming right at his heart and neck. He dodged with the swiftness of a cat, and before she could even blink, stood a few feet away, expanding his own blades.

"Not bad, but you need to be better than that," he said, his smile turning cold, "You want to kill me, Nephilim? Come and try."

And she did. She attacked him with all she had, slashing at him furiously, using all her strength, agility, and skills. He parried all of her attacks easily, his moves smooth, fast, and extremely precise. He almost seemed more like a dancer than somebody in a duel to the death. Whenever he had the opportunity to counterattack, he hit her with the side of his blade. It didn't hurt, yet it showed that every one of these attacks could have been lethal if he had desired. It made her even more furious.

"Yield, Nephilim," he said, "It was very impressive what you displayed today. But I told you before, you can't win against me."

Just then, they heard the muffled sound of powerful engines started up, and the ground slightly vibrated. When Nephilim looked in the direction the sound was coming from, all she could see was shimmering air similar to sunshine hitting water. The stealth aircraft moved upward, vertically, with astonishing speed, and soon the shimmering effect was no longer visible against the blue sky. Nephilim sighed inwardly. It had worked out. She had no idea what had taken them so long, but the Rosprom aircraft was up and away now, untraceable from any radar. Jake was safe.

She turned her head back and glanced at Metatron, who was visibly stunned, as he realized what had just happened. At least in one instance, she had beaten him.

"So, that's what all of this was about," he finally said, "You did all of this to save *him*? You were willing to sacrifice yourself for *him*?"

Nephilim smiled. "I know, it's something you could never understand."

Suddenly she lunged at him, attacking like a coiled-up snake, exploiting his temporary puzzlement and lack of focus. With all the force she had, she slashed his chest diagonally from his left shoulder down to the abdomen. It was a deadly strike. At least should've been.

BEHIND BLUE EYES

Metatron staggered, gave her a surprised look, then started laughing. Loud and heartily.

Nephilim stared at him, her eyes wide. Due to the immense force of her attack, her blade had cut open his armor. Beyond it, she could see perfectly natural-looking skin, sliced open, but no blood. Not a single drop. Under the fake human skin was another layer of skin, a metallic one. Obviously flexible yet hard enough to withstand her titanium blade, not like anything she had ever seen before.

Metatron kept laughing. "What? Does this come as a surprise to you? Did you really believe the sixty/forty rule was absolute? Oh, Nephilim, you still have so much to learn."

He stopped laughing and looked down at himself. When he moved his gaze back up to her, his expression was changed. The amusement was gone, replaced by cold determination. "And I believe it's time to teach you a lesson."

Now it was he who attacked her. She tried to dodge and parry his deadly strikes, backing off. But her odds were almost as dismal as when a human attempted to fend off an Angel.

"And you couldn't be more wrong about me, Nephilim," he said, stopping for a second, "I do understand that kind of sacrifice. Very well."

With one smooth move, he was standing behind her. Nephilim tried to turn and duck away, but she was too slow. With cold precision, he stabbed her in her back all the way through until his blade stuck out in the middle of her chest, impaling her.

Nephilim felt a horrible pain as the blade went through her vulnerable, biological body. She looked down and saw it sticking out of her, covered in blood and internal organ tissue. Blood started gushing out, and her body instantly began feeling numb. Gasping for air, she sank to her knees. More blood rushed down her chest as Metatron slowly removed his blade out of her body.

"Was it really worth it?" he asked behind her. His voice was neither triumphant nor angry. It was sad.

Nephilim couldn't answer as her mouth filled with blood before it ran down her chin and neck. She collapsed, but she didn't hit the ground. Somebody held her in his arms, close and firm.

Her sight started to fade, and she knew she was dying. It was OK. This was the price of her redemption. She was free at last.

Then everything turned black.

***

Bright light hit her eyes when she opened them.

Nephilim blinked, closed her eyes for a moment, then opened them up again.

She was confused and disoriented. Her whole body felt strange. But she was alive.

Her first instinct was to be happy and relieved. The last thing she remembered was a blade plunged through her body and horrible pain. Dying. Now she was here, alive, with no pain at all.

Did she really want to die as she had said and expected would happen? She wasn't sure anymore. Then everything else returned to her, the overwhelming feelings of loss, anger, and despair. The joy of being alive had turned into bitterness.

The light was less jarring as her sight adjusted, and she could see more clearly where she was. She was lying in a bed in one of the intensive care clinic rooms, which were part of the Angel's HQ. Everything was bright white and sterile. Multiple medical machines were aligned around her bed, beeping softly and displaying data she did not understand. An infusion needle was stuck in her neck, and cords were attached to her head.

"Ah, you're awake, good," a voice close to her said. Dr. Weinberg, the chief physician and surgeon of the facility, stepped into her line of view, "Somebody is already eager to speak to you."

He put on a shiny, "things-will-be-fine" smile, which was typical for people of his profession. "How do you feel?"

"Why am I not dead?" she asked slowly. Her throat felt horrible, completely dried out, and irritated from being recently intubated.

Dr. Weinberg's smile faded for a brief moment. "Now, that's a morbid question to ask. But if you really want to know, technically you *were* dead. For almost five minutes as far as I was told."

"And yet, here I am."

"The High-Archangel brought you back." Dr. Weinberg shrugged. "He performed CPR on you after the medics said you were a lost cause. He didn't give up on you, it's the only reason why you're here."

"Why?" Nephilim was confused. The last thing she remembered was Metatron killing her.

The surgeon shrugged again. "You need to ask him that yourself, really. I have no idea. When they brought you here, we were able to stabilize you, but we had to put you in a coma to keep you alive. Frankly, you were a clear case for quick euthanasia and parts recycling, but the High-Archangel didn't share my professional opinion, and after what happened to Dr. Emrich, who am I to disagree with him? So, he had us fix you; rebuild you."

It was only now that Nephilim realized that she couldn't move. She lifted her head a bit to look at her body. Her chest was completely covered in bandages. Then she looked further and froze in horror.

Her arms and legs were gone. It was like a vision in a nightmare. She was crippled.

"What have you done to me?" she asked, unable to hide her shock.

"Oh, *that*." The fake smile was back on Weinberg's face as if it never had been gone. "Don't worry about it. Your arm was damaged beyond repair, and Metatron decided to replace all your limbs while we're at it. You'll get new, custom-made parts, much more advanced than your old ones. You should consider yourself lucky."

He checked her pulse and other vital functions using the device on his wrist then nodded, pleased with himself. "I have to say we did an excellent job on you."

"Indeed, Doctor." The door opened, and Metatron entered the room, Zephaniel in tow. "I'm very satisfied."

Dr. Weinberg flinched due to the sudden appearance of his superior, but quickly found his cool and smiled. "Thank you."

"You can leave us now," Metatron said with a wave of his hand, his eyes already focused on Nephilim.

"Certainly. I'm right next door if you need me," Weinberg said with a submissive tone on his way out.

But Metatron wasn't paying him any attention anymore.

"How do you feel?" he asked, approaching Nephilim.

"Not bad. Considering you killed me," she answered snottily.

Metatron smirked. "That was only fair, considering you tried to kill me first. Don't you think?"

"So, why bring me back, then?"

"Nephilim," he said, reaching out to gently stroke her face, "You really should pay better attention to what I say. I told you I will not lose you."

"What have you done to me?"

"I brought you one step closer to perfection. You already heard that you'll get new advanced limbs. Did you even notice that your spine was crushed? We had to replace a part of it to fortify the rest. I also had them give you a new, improved ribcage. It's titanium and carbon now, state of the art. And of course, your heart had to be replaced with an artificial one, since it was literally broken."

He paused for a moment to let everything sink into her mind about what he just had said, his neon-blue eyes glowing down on her. "You're almost seventy percent machine now, Nephilim. You're the prototype, one step further in human evolution. The very top of the food chain."

"No..." she whispered.

"Yes. The sixty/forty rule applies only to freshly augmented cyborgs. Once your body and mind get used to the hybrid existence, there's practically no limit."

"You should just have let me die," she said bitterly, "Instead, you turned me into even more of a monster."

He fell silent for a moment, looking at her. "It truly upsets me that you think this way. Well, no matter. You'll change your mind in time."

"Do you really think I'll be what you expect me to be once I'm out of here?" she said, anger rising in her despair, "I will never submit to you!"

"First of all, I'm still more advanced than you, so you can try me anytime you wish," he said, that thin smile curling his lips, "And secondly, you got a sophisticated upgrade of your brain implants, too. Once we're done here, I'll initialize a partial memory wipe and personality polish. You *will* see things differently afterward."

She stared at him in disbelief, horror creeping up what remained of her spine. "You can't do that."

"Oh, I can. And I will. I'll set the parameters myself. You'll be *exactly* what I want you to be, Nephilim. You'll be perfect."

"Fuck you!"

Metatron smirked. "No, thank you. I rather suffice myself with you."

He turned away and to Zephaniel, who was obviously enjoying the conversation.

"So, what about her partner?" Zephaniel asked Metatron, "You know, Adriel, the one who let her run. You still didn't make your final decision."

"Ah yes," Metatron said with a wave of his hand, "I'm tired of insubordination. Put him in the Pit and see that his parts are recycled once you're done with him. I don't want to see his face ever again."

"With pleasure," a cold smile flashed over Zephaniel's face.

"No!" Nephilim screamed, "No, please!"

"You can proceed at once," Metatron said.

"It's not his fault!" Nephilim said desperately. The thought of Adriel being tortured and killed because of her was too much. "I made him do it!

BEHIND BLUE EYES

I'm to blame, not him!"

"He disobeyed my direct orders," Metatron said, "We will set an example."

"No!" Nephilim cried out again, "I'll do whatever you want! Let him live. I'll do what you want."

He turned back to her.

Nephilim made eye contact with him, calming down. "You win."

"Zephaniel," Metatron said, yet kept looking into Nephilim's eyes, "Now that I think about it. Killing him would be a waste of resources, and you know, I hate that. After all, he's one of our best people. A thorough mental reeducation should suffice."

"As you wish," Zephaniel replied, disappointment in his voice.

A warm smile appeared on Metatron's face as he leaned down to Nephilim and whispered in her ear, "You played an excellent game, Nephilim. But you picked the wrong enemy. You can't beat the system by yourself. Only together can we do that."

Metatron kissed her on the temple. "You and I. Together."

He remained close to her for a moment; finally, he rose and walked to the door, waving for Zephaniel to accompany him.

"We stick to the schedule for her partial memory wipe. Have Dr. Mendez prepare everything."

Then they were both gone.

Nephilim wasn't sure if she should cry or laugh. She had played the game, and she had lost. From the very first moment, she had been aware of what kind of game this was, and what had been at stake, but she had played it anyway. Given another chance, she would do it again; she regretted nothing. She did not lose completely. After all, she had managed to keep the ones dear to her safe.

She hoped Jake would forget about her and live a happy life in his homeland—as happy as was possible in an authoritarian system. Finwick was intelligent and gifted enough to vanish from radar, she was almost certain about that. With the money she had donated and his help, Sarah would hopefully be granted a future equal to any other girl in Olympias, away from abuse or becoming something she did not want to be. And Adriel was content being a Guardian Angel. He wouldn't want to be anything else. Hopefully, his next partner wouldn't bring him such immense trouble.

No matter what happened to her, Nephilim wasn't afraid.

BEHIND BLUE EYES

Epilogue

It was a warm and pleasant summer night. He liked nights like this. They reminded him of times long gone, when the world was still unshaken, and he had been a child, looking up at the stars. Back then he had believed that there was something good out there, watching over him and everyone he loved. He had been certain that there was more good in men than evil. He had believed that heroes would always succeed over villains in the end.

He had been wrong about everything.

In truth, it was the villains who won. Maybe the world hadn't always been like that, but it was now.

He had learned since then, the hard way. Survived, evolved. Until the rules of the game had become his own. Survival of the fittest. Always be a step ahead, or be destroyed.

A cool breeze blew through his hair, ruffling it slightly. There was always wind up here on the one-hundred eighty-fourth floor. He enjoyed sitting outside on his balcony that overlooked this gigantic city, which was so magnificent to look upon, yet so rotten to its very core. It soothed him and helped him clear his mind, which was otherwise tirelessly working on multiple matters at the same instant. His true plans, intentions, and feelings, always well hidden behind blue eyes.

In front of him rose the black pyramid, the corrupted heart of the rotten society, eating itself and slowly decaying from the inside. Yet it was the building he liked looking at the most. It was almost mesmerizing.

He closed the book he was reading and took a sip of the red wine standing beside him on the table-stand in an elegant chalice. The book was "De Bello Gallico" by Julius Caesar. An intriguing read, especially in the original Latin language.

"Gallia est omnis divisa in partes tres."[7]

Metatron smirked. It should be, *"Terra est omnis divisa in partes tres."*[8] At least, nowadays. And for the time being.

The balcony door opened, and Nephilim entered. He had been expecting her.

Efficient as she was, she instantly began her report. The raid had gone well, but he did not expect any less. The purge they were conducting had been a full success so far. Soon, all remaining cells, hideouts, and contact persons the Proms and Wasps had left in Olympias would be eliminated. And while they were at it, they let other people disappear, who never had been associated with the enemy, but were—or could become—a

---

[7] Latin: "All Gaul is divided in three parts", De bello Gallico by Julius Cesar

[8] Latin: "The world is divided in three parts"

problem, for one reason or another. After the outstanding success covering the Rosprom conspiracy he had foiled, the Board not only had given Metatron even more funding, but also a free hand in any operation concerning remaining agents. And he used that to his advantage.

Metatron watched Nephilim as she reported to him. Her metamorphosis since the neural procedure had been incredible. She leaned against the balcony railing with her back, facing him, her posture and body language full of self-confidence. She was the best Archangel he ever had, and she knew it. He never had expected anything else from her.

Everything that had tormented her, that kept her from greatness, was gone. The self-doubts, remorse, her wish for redemption—even the deeply rooted, self-destructive wish for death had vanished. She was truly free now. Free to follow her true nature.

She had always been courageous and determined far beyond the average. Now she was a ruthless, cold-blooded enforcer: intelligent, cunning, efficient in everything she did. She never failed. She was a true angel of death.

And unconditionally loyal and devoted to him.

Metatron adored her.

She had become even more beautiful and gracious since the physical changes. Her new legs were longer and slimmer, but much more powerful than the old ones. The same went for her arms, which ended in perfectly shaped, delicate fingers that could break apart an iron bar. Her clothing style had changed, as well. She still preferred to wear a black leather jacket, yet underdressed in a more revealing, extravagant manner. All scars from the numerous surgeries were gone, her skin—natural and artificial alike—was smooth like alabaster. She had chosen a new wig, her straight hair was still raven-black but longer, with blue highlights matching her almond-shaped, cyborg eyes. Only her face was still the same, with its almost unearthly beauty and that eternally young, innocent look—hiding the most dangerous predator of Olympias.

Nephilim was perfect in every way. A higher evolved being. His creation.

She finished her report and gave him a teasing look that made him smile.

"Excellent work," he complimented her, rising up from his chair.

He approached her and gently kissed her long, pale neck. She tilted her head.

"Let's go inside," he said.

She smiled. "I was waiting for you to suggest that."

She entered the door and let her jacket slide to the ground.

Yes, she was perfect in every way. But nothing is ever entirely perfect; there is always a flaw. Nephilim's flaw was so profoundly rooted that neither Metatron nor herself could possibly be aware it existed. It was like a seed, planted deep inside, waiting to bloom.

"If you want to keep a secret, you also need to hide it from yourself."

About the Author

Anna Mocikat was born in Warsaw, Poland, but spent most of her life in Germany where she attended film school, worked as a screenwriter and a game writer for several years.
Her "MUC" novels have been nominated for the most prestigious awards for Fantasy and Science-Fiction in Germany. In 2016 Anna Mocikat moved to the USA where she continued her writing career. *Shadow City* was her debut in English. She lives in Greenville, South Carolina.

www.annamocikat.com

Acknowledgments

This book wouldn't have been possible without the help of many wonderful people.
I would like to thank my parents, my brother, and my sister-in-law for all their love and endless support!

A big thank you to my beta readers Heidi Mills and Martin W. Francis, for their valuable input, which helped me to make this book what it is.

Thank you very much, my editor Jessica Merchant, for helping me make this book so much better!

My gratitude also goes to my amazing designer Ivano Lago, who gave this book a face by creating its exceptional cover; and to my friend and fellow author A.W. Merkel, who helped me with my trailer animations, gave me valuable input and is always supportive.

I also would like to thank all my friends and fellow authors in the #WritingCommunity for their incredible support.

BEHIND BLUE EYES

Last but not least I want to thank

YOU, DEAR READER!

Thank you so much for reading my book; it means the world to me!

I hope you enjoyed your trip into the year 2095 and a "utopia," which hopefully will never become a reality.

This is not the end. Nephilim's story has only just begun…

If you liked Behind Blue Eyes, please, write a short review on Amazon and/or Goodreads. It only takes a minute but will make my day and help me very much!

And if you like to give me feedback directly or simply stay informed about my work, don't hesitate to connect with me on social media!

www.Twitter.com/anna_mocikat
www.Facebook.com/amocikat
www.Instagram.com/annamocikat
www.Goodreads.com/author/show/8072081.Anna_Mocikat
www.annamocikat.com

THANK YOU SO MUCH!

MORE BOOKS BY ANNA MOCIKAT

Shadow City

Los Angeles is an apocalyptic wasteland.

Without orientation, Colton stumbles through the vast, deserted city. He doesn't remember who he is and where he came from. Scavengers save his life from mutants and bring him to the only remaining inhabited area and safe Zone in former Hollywood.

There he learns that after a devastating catastrophe called The Glitch, reality shifted, allowing nightmarish creatures from another dimension to enter our world. These co-called Dark Ones feed on suffering and violence, wanting nothing less than the complete annihilation of humanity.

Colton discovers that he has extraordinary abilities and joins a league of unusual defenders: ex-cop Eric, female cyborg Bombshell and Vincent, a mighty entity from another world, disguised as a human soldier.

But the Dark Ones are evil beyond imagination and with their ice-cold enforcer, the traitor Eurydice, they are a threat nearly impossible to overcome.

Behind Blue Eyes

Cunning and ruthless, Eurydice sets a ploy in action, which leads to the destruction of the Zone's defenses weakening the tiny community from within. It's up to Colton and his friends to take a desperate stand against the superior enemy and save what is left of humanity from extinction.

Fast-paced, action-driven, and cinematic – an eternal fight of good vs. evil told in a way as never before.

Available as print book, ebook and audiobook!

Printed in Great Britain
by Amazon